PRAISE FOR ELIZABETH VAUGHAN'S
CHRONICLES OF THE WARLANDS

"Over the course of the series, Vaughan has built a fantasy world that is believable, relatable and filled with well-loved characters."

—*Not a Book Snob*, on the Warlands Chronicles

"This is a wonderful series with engaging characters that grow and develop with each book."

—Sharynn Blood, *reviewer*

"*Warsong* is a thrilling, romantic, and epic read filled with beloved characters and daring deeds."

—Vicki Stiefel, *reviewer*

"Vaughan's brawny barbarian romance recreates the delicious feeling of adventure and the thrill of exploring mysterious cultures created by Robert E. Howard in his Conan books and makes for a satisfying escapist read with its enjoyable romance between a plucky, near-naked heroine and a truly heroic hero."

—*Booklist*, on *Warprize*

"Ms. Vaughan has written a wonderful fantasy…The story is well-written and fast paced. Run to the bookstore and pick up this novel. You won't be disappointed by the touching relationship that grows between the Warlord and his Warprize."

—*A Romance Review*, on *Warprize*

"A classic read for me right up there with Linda Howard's MacKenzie's series or Nora Roberts' The Donovan's Legacy series or Anne McCaffrey's Tower and Hive series. If those three are favorites…enjoy this one too!"

—Kindle Customer, on *Warprize*

FATE'S STAR

ELIZABETH VAUGHAN

Published by Birch Cove Press

ISBN-13: 978-0-9984501-4-8
Worldwide Rights
Created in the United States of America

Cover Art by Craig White
Cover Design by STK•Kreations

To my beloved dead,
gone before,
unseen and unknowing,
yet knowing and seeing,
who wait for me beyond the snows,
within the stars.

The events in this book occur about five years before the events in Warprize *and* Dagger-Star

CHAPTER ONE

L ord High Baron Verice leaned against the cool stone of the window sill and fought the cold inner rage that burned in his heart. He stared down into the gardens below as the men in the room behind him spoke of war.

"You're certain?" Captain Narthing asked in hushed tones.

"Yes," Pernard's voice quavered. "The Barony of Farentell has fallen." Verice heard the weariness in his friend's voice; he shared his pain and grief.

Someone in the garden below was humming a tune that Verice didn't recognize. A faella's voice, someone with a lighter heart than his at the moment. He wished them well of it, for it would not last long.

The breeze caught a strand of his silver hair, and pulled it out of the window. Verice tucked it back behind his pointed ear and took in the scent of flowers and green growing things. Hard to think on death and war when such beauty lay just outside these walls.

But that was his duty and the reason for his visit to Pernard's manor.

Verice turned his head back toward the room. "What of King Everard and his family? Any word?"

Pernard, Captain Narthing and the others stood around the map table. They all shook their heads in the negative.

"None," Pernard whispered.

"All these months," Verice sighed, looking back over the garden. "If they'd escaped, they'd have gotten word to me somehow." Deep within, pain welled. A short life, made even shorter by violent death. Verice took a slow breath and closed his eyes.

"Life is fleeting, life is pain,
What need then to dance in the rain?"

The verse floated up from the garden on the gentle breeze. Verice frowned, trying to spot the singer. Odd, such bitter words sung to such a joyous tune.

Rather like life itself.

He straightened, shoulders back, his hand on his sword hilt and turned to face his people. All of his men, including himself, were armored in black leather and chain with weapons ready to serve. Pernard and his people were garbed in everyday attire, robes over tunics and trous. Verice wondered how long they would have the luxury of regular clothing. "Review the situation for us, Captain."

"Lord High Baron Verice of Tassinic, Lord Mayor Pernard of Anera," Captain Narthing tended to use full titles in meetings such as this. He stood at the head of the map table as Pernard's elven and half-elven warriors crowded around. "It's been confirmed by sources within Edenrich, and by the reports of our scouts that have penetrated the border. The Barony of Farentell has fallen to the forces of the Usurper and the Baroness of the Black Hills."

Dark mutters followed that statement.

"They have laid waste to the land, burning towns and villages," Narthing said. "The people have been killed, taken as slaves, or—" Narthing paused, then continued. "There are rumors that the Baroness is creating odium."

"Ancestors," one of the warriors breathed. "Undead?"

"We've only rumors," Narthing said firmly.

"That would explain the small number of refugees," another mentioned.

"And what refugees crossed over our border are for the most part hardened scum, or very desperate humans. They are causing difficulties all over Tassinic, stretching our City Watches," Narthing said. "But the worst of that tide is probably past," he added.

"There are exceptions," Pernard protested.

Narthing's voice didn't hold much apology. "We will deal with the humans fairly, until they prove otherwise. Interestingly enough, some of those fleeing are speaking of a prophecy of a Chosen One, that will restore Palins."

Verice snorted. Ancestors spare him that.

Narthing continued, "But for right now, with so many maels in the regular army, the watches are spread thin. Lord Pernard, your lands share borders with Farentell and Summerford. Let's see to the placement of your forces to the best advantage, eh?"

Verice stayed silent. Narthing excelled at this; Verice's services weren't needed at the moment. He already knew the ugliness of the reports that he was sharing.

"The Kingdom of Palins seems intent on tearing itself to ribbons," Pernard spoke. "What do we know of the other baronies?"

"Lord Mayor," Narthing said. "Of the eight High Baronies of Palins, six remain intact. To the best of our knowledge, Athelbryght has also fallen. If I may," Narthing pulled out a large map of Tassinic, and spread it out over the table. "So far," he said. "There have been skirmishes along our border, but nothing more than that. And they've usually withdrawn as soon as we arrive to confront them." Narthing made no gesture toward Tassinic's other border, the one with the Elven Kingdom of Valltera. Verice approved. These people had enough worries for the moment.

"They are testing us," a warrior growled.

"We thought them bandits, at first." Pernard pulled forth a smaller map of his town and the surrounding farms. "So far, only two farmsteads have been attacked. The families there managed to flee, and they report seeing the banner of the Black Hills on the attackers."

"I am ordering that you pull everyone in your district within the walls," Verice said. He held up a hand to fend off protests. "We can replace buildings, breed new herds. It's the maels and faellas I value above all else."

"We've stout town walls, thanks to your foresight, m'lord." Pernard said. "It's the farmers you must convince."

"I'll speak to them." Verice gave the mael a wry look. "And use more than words if there's a need. Any so stubborn as to stay on his land is welcome to, but I will demand that the faellas and children be brought to safety."

Verice kept the meeting brief, making sure they understood the important points. Actual details would be worked out later. For now, it was enough that they knew his plans to defend Tassinic.

After enough time for questions, he called the meeting to a close and dismissed them. "We'll reconvene shortly," he commanded. "With the guild-masters and farmers and any others that wish to attend."

They bowed, and streamed out, talking in quiet undertones. He didn't need to hear what they said; there was a lighter note to their voices.

Satisfied, he turned back to the window for a moment. The singer was still in the garden, humming, again. The sound was sweet.

"Lord Verice, perhaps you'd like to take some refreshment with me before the next meeting?" Pernard came to stand beside him. "There's something I'd wish to discuss privately, if you don't mind. Some kav, perhaps?"

"My thanks, Pernard." Verice gestured out the window. "Perhaps we could stroll in your garden for a bit?"

"You would do me an honor," Pernard smiled. "The cuttings you provided have done very well. My roses are particularly lovely this year. And, may I ask, how do yours fare?"

Verice's heart froze. "I've no idea," he clipped out the words. "I haven't stepped foot in the gardens since—" he cut himself off, trying to control his anger.

"Forgive me, m'lord," Pernard apologized with a tilt of his head. "I'll have the kav brought to you."

Verice gave a swift nod and strode from the room. He stalked the corridors, his thoughts grim.

Damn the Regent. Damn Elanore. Everard had been a rare human, with a sense of honor as strong as his own. He'd sworn fealty to the man, gone down on his knees to do it, a thing unheard of. An elf swearing allegiance to a human king. But Verice had known that Everard had been worthy of his oaths.

Human lives were so short compared to his own. Even worse, it seemed that Everard had been cut down by treachery within his own castle, by his own kind.

Verice growled under his breath. Now here he was, an elven High Baron in a human kingdom, with civil war on one border, and the elven Court on another. Somewhere, his ancestors were mocking him.

He stepped out into the garden, into the bright sun, and caught his breath. The area was walled in, and not large, compared with his gardens back home. But Pernard was clever in his use of the space he had, and the effect was lovely.

An apple tree stood to one side, providing shade over a bench. Verice remembered when Pernard had planted the seedling. To the other side, a small path wound around a series of thick rose briars, made to look as if they'd overgrown the area, but in fact were carefully trimmed. Verice took a deep breath, and forced himself to tread slowly and enjoy the serenity that the colors and scents brought. He'd just steal a few moments before—

> *"Life is fleeting, life is pain.*
> *What need then to dance in the rain?*
> *What need then to sleep in the night,*
> *safe in the arms of my lover held tight?"*

Verice looked around, curious. The song was soft and low, clearly not intended for another's ears. He didn't know the words, but the tune was sweet, and the voice... he walked forward.

> *"What need to love or laugh or sing,*
> *or bind you with my wedding ring?"*

He spotted a small foot peeking from under a tattered skirt, sheltered by the roses. It was fair, although bare and dirty. A faella, he guessed, although he couldn't see her ears. She knelt, half-hidden under one of the bushes.

He continued, barely breathing, not wanting to startle her, but wanting to see her face.

> *"Close or far, low or high, I shall love you ere I—"*

There was a gasp, a flash of movement.

Verice paused in mid-step. "Forgive me, lady. I didn't mean to—"

The rose bush trembled and petals fell to the ground as the faella jumped up, and darted past him. He had a glimpse of tattered skirt, tunic and head scarf all of faded dull color as she fled. She was headed for the apple tree.

The warrior in him rose and gave chase, his long legs eating up the gap between them. She'd grabbed for the lowest limb and pulled herself up, rose petals falling from her skirt. He reached up, capturing her ankle.

She looked down, her brown eyes wide. Her scarf caught in the branches, and her blonde hair tumbled down around her.

Ancestors, this was no elven lass. His singer was *human*.

The very idea made Verice pause, slightly stunned. Humans were rare in Tassinic, despite it being a Barony of a human kingdom. She was pure human, from the looks of her ears. Her brown eyes were large and startled, with flecks of gold in their lovely depths.

"Who are you?" he demanded as she tried to kick her leg free. He held her easily, her skin warm against his hand.

She froze, her lips parted . . .and then her stomach growled loudly. She flushed and dropped her gaze, golden lashes against her cheek.

Verice felt the loss.

A clatter came from the garden entrance. Two servants were wheeling in a cart, Pernard right behind. Verice turned slightly to call to him.

The woman kicked out, slipped from his hand, and vanished up the tree and over the wall.

Verice barked out a laugh, more at himself than anything else.

"M'lord," Pernard called. "What do you think of my— is something wrong, m'lord?"

"There was a human here, under the rose bushes. A woman." Verice turned to frowned at his old friend. "So much for the security of your walls."

"Ah." Pernard relaxed, settling on a bench and pouring kav. The servants bowed themselves away. "All's well, m'lord. We have sheltered some of the humans that fled Farentell. There are not many, mostly women and children. It was to be a temporary measure, but with the news you bring, I fear we will have to make more permanent arrangements. I was hesitant to mention it, because—"

Verice frowned as he sat on the bench next to him. "My preferences are known, Pernard, but I've never permitted humans to be treated unfairly."

"I know, m'lord," Pernard offered a mug to Verice before pouring his own. "But with the recent attacks…" His voice trailed off. "I wasn't certain how to approach you with the problem."

"Well, give Narthing the details, and we'll make such provisions as we can," Verice said. "I'm not inclined to encourage more of them to come here, but I'll send no innocents back into that conflict." Verice sipped the kav. "What Narthing didn't tell your people is that there has been a buildup of troops along the border with Valltera."

Pernard sucked in a breath. "Why?"

"I don't know," Verice said. "I've let my contacts lapse within King Barathiel's Court, and my diplomatic inquires have been responded to with vague diplomatic answers."

Pernard shook his head. "We don't need this right now."

Verice snorted his agreement. "You said you had something else to discuss…"

Pernard nodded, staring down at the mug in his hands. "M'lord," he said slowly, not lifting his gaze. "It's been months since the attack. Some of your other advisors and staff have asked me to talk to you about the castle and the keep."

"No," Verice said.

Pernard lifted his head, and Verice had to look away from the pity he saw there. "Verice—"

"No," Verice said, and this time he let the venom show in his voice. "My orders stand."

"You cannot continue in this manner," Pernard argued.

"Do not think to presume upon our friendship," Verice warned.

Pernard went silent.

"As to this assembly," Verice said, trying to return to a reasonable tone. "How many of the farmers have you managed to gather, and who is likely to give me the most resistance?"

Pernard took the hint. "All of them have gathered, and I fear they are all resistant. They're a stubborn folk." He glanced at Verice. "Much like their Lord High Baron."

Pernard was correct. The gathering with the angry and terrified farmers was as tense and difficult as Verice anticipated. But halfway through the questions and arguments, Verice found himself thinking about her. About the woman in the garden.

Pure humans were rare in his lands, and not permitted within his castle. Did that growling sound mean she was hungry? He frowned at the thought, causing the onion farmer in front of him to sputter and lose track of his speech. Annoyed with himself, Verice used the moment to cut through their protests and order that they take shelter within the town walls.

While Narthing was summarizing the scouting reports in detail, Verice found himself thinking about her again. Pernard was surely generous with food; it was in his friend's nature. So, why was she hungry? She hadn't picked the flowers, just sheltered there, singing.

Annoyed with himself, he forced his attention back to Narthing's words and the damned maps.

Later, while inspecting the town walls and examining the defenses, the flapping of a flag caused to him to blink, and the sight of tumbling gold hair flashed before his eyes.

He growled under his breath, causing the warriors around him to glance around for the source of his irritation. Even more annoyed with himself, Verice walked on.

Finally, the day turning to evening, he stood next to his horse, ready to depart.

"Send reports regularly," Verice said to Pernard. "Let me know if those farmers give you trouble. If I have to, I will return with more men, and—"

"Not necessary, Lord High Baron," Pernard said. "On behalf of my district, I offer our thanks for your care and watchfulness."

"Just see to them all, Pernard," Verice said. "And have a care for yourself, old friend."

"I'd remind you that sauce for the goose works for the gander, m'lord," Pernard said softly. "Have a care yourself."

Verice nodded, and put his foot in the stirrup. His horse shifted, and he gripped the saddle to mount—

—and caught the scent of roses from the garden.

He settled back to the ground with a thump, startling both horse and the warriors around him.

"M'lord?" Pernard raised an eyebrow as Verice turned.

"Take me to those humans."

CHAPTER TWO

Warna slapped another swaddling cloth into the tub of hot soapy water. Whatever else, she'd not go back into that garden, no matter how lovely the flowers were. The fear of being discovered was a lesson well learned, she thought as she started scrubbing.

As a child, she'd dreamed of elves and the Kingdom of Valltera, listened to stories about them and their magic. The reality was colder and harsher than she cared to think on. Although Tassinic was filled with more half-elven than anything else, not that she could tell the difference.

Children's voices rose, reciting their numbers. They were gathered together with their mothers, laughing at silly rhymes. Warna's fears eased as she scrubbed another cloth. So nice to hear, instead of weeping and tears. So nice to be worrying about laundry, rather than hiding in the forests and listening for the tramp of soldiers.

Warna grimaced as she reached into the hot soapy water and pulled out yet another swaddling cloth. Caring for the children had its pleasant moments, but this was not one of them. Still, it had to be done.

She scrubbed the cloth as clean as she was able, then added it to the rinse water. Lord of Light be thanked, at least they had hot water and soap. Amazing how grateful one was for the basics when you'd lost everything.

Warna glanced around the cobblestoned yard. She'd already covered every available surface with clean laundry, and she still had more to dry. Thankfully, the sun was shining.

She'd fled her home with naught but the clothes she wore. She'd spent months alone, hiding in ditches and the woods. It had only been in the last few weeks that she'd met up with others fleeing the devastation. They hadn't been certain they'd be welcome in Tassinic, but the people of Anera had offered them such shelter as they had, cleaning out one of the barrack's barns. They'd bedded them down in the lofts with plenty of straw and blankets.

It was supposed to be a temporary solution, or so it had been explained. But the conflict had followed them, and now Anrea had to see to itself.

The barracks were still filled with warriors, but they were gone most of the day. They'd shelter, food, and the basics, thank the Lord of Light and Lady of Laughter. The children were warm and safe for now. They'd learn their numbers, eat their suppers, and sleep in safety. And dirty yet another load of nappies for her to scrub.

She'd been brought in to this group, all the refugees sheltered together, but she'd had no time to get to know anyone well. The desperate needs of the children and the drive to survive banded them together for a time. There'd been safety in numbers, for both her life and her virtue. Warna shuddered. Others had suffered far more than she.

She slapped another nappy into the water. Her efforts let their mothers see to their children in these precious few moments of peace. If the day ever came that she'd children of her own, she'd teach them their numbers, and see to their tears, and hire someone else to do the wash.

A pang to her heart reminded that the chances of that were gone. It was all gone: her family, her life, her future. Her brothers had all gone off to fight when the High Baron of Farentell had called upon them. Her mother dead of a fever months before that. Father, Grandfather…

Grief washed through her like a wave. Warna closed her eyes for a moment letting tears well, feeling the anguish deep in her bones until it subsided, leaving her empty, tired, and numb.

She wiped away her tears, and forced herself back to dirty cloths, hot water, and soap. Better to not think about that. Better to think about… her song.

Warna started humming as she swirled the cloths through the water. She was still trying to fit roses into the verse, but it wasn't working. She couldn't get the words quite right.

"Life is sour, life's unfair,
Death takes us all without a care.

What need then to enjoy the rose?
What need then to..."

She let the tune trail off, trying to puzzle out the next stanza. What would work? What rhymed with rose?

Well, toes, but honestly...

Her rhyming distracted her, made the chore go faster. She'd need to dump the water soon. The few men who had managed to escape with them were working at whatever odd tasks their benefactors needed done. She'd get a few to aid her when the time came.

There was a stir behind her as horsemen entered the yard. She spared a glance over her shoulder to see elven warriors ride in, lofty and stern. They all sat tall and proud in their matching silver armor upon majestic black horses. She turned back to her laundry. The warriors weren't cruel, but they weren't exactly friendly. Best to stay out of their way.

That elf in the garden, for example. Warna shivered at the memory. He'd been so big, and so feral, in black leather armor, his sword at his side. His silver-white hair and silver-blue eyes had made him seem like something from one of her children's books.

His grip on her ankle had been terrifying, and he'd looked so fierce.

Oh, no. She wasn't going to sneak back into the garden no matter how large and lovely the flowers were. It wasn't worth—

A loud, deep voice spoke in elven, directly behind her.

Startled, Warna twisted to find that very warrior glaring down at her. Her heart threatened to beat out of her chest.

The elven warrior loomed over her, all black leather, silver chain, and swords. "Pardon, I spoke without thought." His glare didn't diminish, but his words were stilted, as if he was trying to remember the common tongue. "I asked how you fared." His frown deepened, and he gestured to the tubs behind her. "Why are you doing that?"

"It needs to be done," Warna replied without thinking, trying to remember to breathe.

Those silver eyebrows furrowed together as he glanced behind him. More of the warriors were approaching, with human males. "Did you get something to eat?"

Warna cringed at the memory of her growling stomach. "Yes, of course. There's bread, cheese, eggs, and milk. I just hadn't eaten. I wanted to spend a few minutes with the—" She cut her words off.

"That is well," the warrior said. "I was concerned. The noises…" he gestured at her belly

Thoroughly mortified, she dropped her gaze. "Thank you."

"Did you finish it?" he asked abruptly.

"Finish what?" she was confused by the question. "Finish my breakfast?"

"Your song," he dropped his voice, asking quietly.

Warna lifted her gaze then, looking to see if she was being mocked. But his expression was open, his eyes seemed sincere. "No," she said slowly, reaching up to tuck a stray curl behind one ear. "I can hear it in my head, but I can't find the words. It's…"

"Frustrating," he said.

She nodded.

He glanced around, his frown returning. "Who sees to you?"

"What?" She frowned back at him.

"Where are your kin?" he demanded.

Warna froze. Her throat closed and the pain just swelled in her heart.

"Where are your protectors?" The elf demanded, as if repeating the question would make her understand.

Grief gave way to fury. Warna turned her back on him, picked up a soiled swaddling cloth, slapped it into the tub, and started to scrub. "My lord, might I ask what business is that of yours?"

"What?" The elf came around to stare at her, his voice as cold and hard as his eyes.

Behind her came the tramp of boots, the sounds of warriors and the human males gathering. "Lord High Baron Verice," one of them stammered, and they all started talking.

Warna sucked in a breath, and kept her head down, eyes on her task. Of course, the lord of the land, a High Baron. Warna dropped the cloth into the tub, and swallowed hard. She was so damned tired, the pain his words had caused still sat in her throat, and come to find out she'd insulted a high baron. All she'd meant to do was steal a few moments in the flowers.

Somewhere, the Lady of Laughter was surely mocking her.

She glanced around. The Lord High Baron stood there, arms crossed over his chest, looking forbidding and angry. Everyone around him seemed to be talking at once, in both elven and common tongue.

She shuddered. She'd made this mess. It would be up to her to bear the consequences and see it right. Quickly, before she lost what she had left of her nerve.

She dried her hands on her skirt, slipped through the crowd, and knelt before the elf. With any luck he'd just lop off her fool head and be done with it.

The men around her stepped away, leaving her in a space and on her own. The babble mounted, but the Lord High Baron's hard voice cut through it all. "Get off your knees, woman."

Warna wasn't that stupid. "I offered insult out of ignorance, Lord High Baron. I beg forgiveness."

"Insult?" one of the men's voices squeaked. "She insulted him?"

"Stand up," Verice ordered.

The babbling escalated.

Warna studied the boots of everyone who was standing around her. She stared at the shiny black leather boots of the elf she'd offended. She'd hate to die without finishing her song. Maybe flower would work instead of rose. Flower, bower, power, shower. Cherish every hour?

A long thin hand appeared in front of her face, open and demanding. "Off your knees," the High Baron commanded impatiently.

Warna lifted her head. He towered over her, glaring down. Harsh. Arrogant. Elven to the core.

Not much else she could do in the face of his anger. She obeyed.

"Silence," Lord Verice ordered as she rose to her feet. His command cut through the talk around them. "Who are her kin? Her family?"

An older human spoke up. "Warna? She's got none."

"Warna." The Lord High Baron's eyes flickered over her, and left Warna cold. She lowered her gaze respectfully, her hands clenched in her skirts. She'd drawn his attention, and she swallowed hard against her growing fear.

"Warna is under my protection now," Verice stated firmly.

Warna stopped breathing. The implications of that were frightening. The Lord High Baron's men were exchanging glances that seemed at once confused, and resigned.

"You are all under my protection," Verice continued. "Now, about your concerns…"

The storm of protest shifted to fears as everyone started talking at once.

All Warna could make out was the roar of her heart, cold in her chest.

It wasn't the first time someone had expressed such an interest in her, and she was capable of dealing with unwanted attentions easily. But this elf had power and authority over them all, and he was not to be denied. She darted a glance around the crowd and caught the eye of one of the older women.

She jerked her head to the edge of the crowd. Relief flooded through Warna. The men might see her as a bargaining chip, but the women would help her.

Warna eased a step back, letting a man squeeze into her spot. They were crowding around the Lord, all talking at once. She kept her eyes down, trying to become invisible. No one seemed to notice.

One of the women tucked a kerchief into her hand. Warna ducked her head, and donned it. She'd be less noticeable with her hair covered. She slipped around one man, and then another, working her way to the edge of the crowd. She kept moving, keeping her head down. If she could get to the barn, she could hide in the hay lofts, burrowed down into the straw. With any luck, the Lord High Baron would—

She thumped against someone, who stepped directly into her path. She looked up.

Lord High Baron Verice was standing there, a grim scowl on his face. He wrapped his arm around her and pulled her in tight.

She sucked in a breath, surprised at the feel of his body against hers. She brought her hands up on his chest, trying to push him away.

He leaned in, his face close to hers, his silver-blue eyes bright. "Sleep," he whispered, his voice seeming to echo in her mind and ears.

The exhaustion caught her in mid-breath, and pulled her into oblivion.

* * * * *

Captain Narthing watched in horror as Lord Verice kidnaped the human woman, using his magic to render her helpless. Verice swung the unconscious woman into his arms, and arrogantly faced the humans before him.

"Ancestors above us," Narthing breathed as he gripped his sword. For all that the humans were elder males and females, they could still attack Lord Verice if they had such a mind. "I've never seen him do anything like this."

Pernard stood next to him. "Have you ever known Lord Verice to act without honor?"

Narthing didn't take his gaze off the crowd. "No, Lord Pernard, but what is he thinking?"

Pernard shook his head. "I'm not sure he is," the older elf said softly.

"You are now under my direct authority and protection," Lord Verice radiated power as he addressed the crowd. "Farentell has fallen, its High Baron killed by the Usurper. You are welcome here, if you are willing to swear fealty to me as your High Baron. Or, if you wish, free to journey on with our aid and blessing. Discuss it amongst yourselves, and then apply to Pernard with your decision."

"Is there anyone who lays claim to this woman?" Lord Verice continued, his tone daring anyone to contradict him.

Narthing held his breath.

No one did.

"You will excuse me. I must be about the business of the land." With that, Lord Verice spun on his heel and headed toward the waiting horses, the woman still in his arms.

CHAPTER THREE

Warna awoke slowly as the mists of sleep left her mind.

Horseback. She was on horseback, cradled in someone's arms, her head on his shoulder. Her skin felt tingly, an uncomfortable sensation that was fading quickly. She stayed limp, her eyes closed.

Where was she?

The sounds around her were of warriors dismounting, muted voices combined with the ringing of horses's hooves on stone.

"Narthing," a voice rumbled in her ear. "assist me, if you would."

The High Baron, it had to be. Panic flooded through her. He'd used magic on her; what other ways did he have to enslave a soul? She jerked up, out of his arms, and half-fell, half-slid to the ground. Verice cursed above her as his horse shied.

One look showed her a courtyard, buildings of smooth white marble, and across the way, an open door. She didn't know where she was, didn't recognize a building or a face, but that doorway called to her. A place to hide, with any luck at all.

"Lord of Light, aid me," Warna prayed as she ran.

Shouts rose behind her as she darted through the door. It was dark and cool within. She could make out a long, carpeted hall, and stairs.

Up. She fled up, running for all she was worth. Fleeing soldiers and slavers in the past had given her strength she hadn't known she'd possessed, as well as an instinct for survival. She'd not lasted this long to be just to be taken so easily. It was better to die.

Her heart in her throat, she ran up the stairs and down a long hall. If she could find the barracks, the barn, or even that rose garden, she could get over the wall and disappear. She'd not risk the others; if she got out, she'd keep going, back into the forests, hiding and moving by night.

The hall kept going, but she found another set of stairs, and then another. She wasn't really thinking in her panic. She could hear cries of pursuit far behind, but the dark and dusty halls themselves were silent and still, the only light from distant windows.

Finally, she saw great doors, and a white marble balcony beyond, gleaming in the sun. The stone was cold beneath her bare feet. She ran out, catching herself on the balustrade, looking for the garden—

—only to see castle walls, and beyond them, an enormous city stretching out before her. This wasn't Anera. Where in the name of all the Gods was she?

Cries behind her. She spun, and ran back to the door. There was no other way off the balcony, she'd be caught if—

Warriors filled the doorway. Warna slid to a stop, her heart in her throat. Only one way to freedom. Better death than a slave.

"Lord of Light, forgive me." Warna drew in a huge gulping breath as she sprinted for the balustrade, reaching out for the cold marble, feeling it under her fingers. The blue sky waited just beyond. Over, up, and free. "Lady of Laughter, open your arms and welcome my spirit—"

"Warna!"

Her name, screamed, as if torn from a soul. Warna hesitated, looked back into silver-blue eyes—

And cursed herself as she embraced oblivion once again.

* * * * *

We seem to have a misunderstanding." That deep, reserved voice woke her again.

Warna blinked at the suddenness of her awareness. One moment on the edge of the balcony, now...

Facing Verice, she was seated in a wooden chair, surrounded by armed guards.

She swallowed hard, dizzy. Odd to be alive after she'd faced her death. She took a breath, and then another as her heart raced.

The white marble halls were gone; instead they were in a room with wooden walls and floors, and shuttered windows. Chests lined the walls, and there was a table covered in maps in the center of the room.

"—not my intent to—"

Lord High Baron Verice was standing before her, his arms crossed over his chest, talking, apparently to her. At least, he was looking at her and speaking. Warna gripped the seat of the chair, looked away and trembled within. There was no escape now, none that she could see. Two guards by the door, and another at the window of this small room.

"—want you to understand that I meant no—"

He was talking. Warna was fairly certain his words were supposed to mean something, but she couldn't seem to make them out. She frowned at him, puzzled. He was angry, this elven lord. He was gesturing, and talking and—

"—name?" Verice frowned at her, fierce and cold.

The silence let Warna understand he was asking for her name. She looked around at the guards again and wondered just exactly how many they thought it would take to kill her.

One was probably more than enough.

The Lord High Baron sighed, and the sound made Warna focus on him. "In the camp, they said your name was Warna. Warna of Farentell?" he said again, this time softly.

"Yes. Of Farentell," she gathered her courage and rose to her feet. "I will not be your slave."

The Lord High Baron bristled. "That was never my intent. Here in Tassinic, there is no slavery, despite whatever madness may have infested the rest of the Kingdom." He lifted his chin in a graceful, arrogant gesture. "You are alone, and clearly in need of protection. I extend my safeguards to you, as a ward within my household."

Confused, exhausted, Warna blurted out her first thought, "Why?"

* * * * *

What do you mean, why?" Verice demanded, irritated beyond words. "You are alone, with no male relatives to see to your safety."

"Lots of the women in camp are alone," Warna said. She looked tired, standing before him, pointing out the obvious. "They're not being singled out for—"

"They are also under my protection," Verice snapped. "You are a maiden, are you not?"

The fiery blush over her cheeks was a sign he'd offended. "Unwed, I mean," Verice said impatiently.

"I'm fairly certain there are other unwed women among those that fled," Warna argued.

"Not with your gift of music," Verice countered, certain of victory. "That gift should be cherished and protected, and I'll see to it."

She crossed her arms over her chest, her eyes down but her face filled with doubt. "My music?"

"Your songs," Verice took in a deep breath. Was the woman thick? "Your songs. They are—"

"That's just something I do for myself," Warna said. "I'm not that good."

"You are," Verice insisted. "You are too harsh on yourself. I will see you and your gifts protected, even over your protests."

"Why?" she asked again in that maddening, all-too-reasonable tone. Again, she seemed to be staring off to the side, not looking him in the eye.

"Is there some reason you won't look at me?" Verice growled.

"Yes," she snapped back. "I'll not be charmed or bedazzled by your tricks."

A sudden feeling of shame flooded through him, catching him off guard. "It was necessary," Verice said. He caught himself before he continued to justify his actions to this human.

She didn't look up.

"I'll pledge not to use magic upon you if you will pledge to remain under my protection. I do not know your sense of honor; humans rarely seem to have one. But I—"

She bristled, standing stiff and staring him in the eye. "My word is as good as yours," she retorted. "But I'll not give that promise."

"Then I shall take what steps are necessary," Verice stated. "You will remain here."

"Why?" she demanded again.

Verice stood, and drew himself up to tower over her. "Because I say so," he gritted through his teeth. "And as I am the Lord High Baron of this land, my word is law."

Those brown eyes studied him with skepticism.

"Narthing, see to her needs," Verice commanded, determined to end the conversation by leaving the room.

"I don't even know where I am," she complained as he strode past. "This isn't Anera, is it?"

"No," Verice paused. "This is Octara, my capital. You have the freedom of the castle and its grounds, but understand, lady, you are not to venture outside its walls. Is that clear?"

Her gaze dropped, her lashes dark against her skin. She executed a perfect curtsey, sinking to the floor with grace. "Yes, Lord Verice."

He didn't trust that for a moment.

* * * * *

Narthing stared at the human woman in dismay. His Lord had commanded, and it was his to obey, but what in the name of all his Ancestors was he to do with her?

She stood there staring at him, waiting. His men were all staring at him too.

She'd given them all heart attacks, fleeing into the castle that was supposed to be sealed, running for her life and what she thought was her honor. Narthing admired her; he'd been just behind Verice and seen her determination to face death over degradation. It had been a close thing.

It was the sight of her bare feet that did it. She'd been just like any new recruit showing up at the gate with naught but the clothes on his back, and a willingness to serve.

Well, from the look in her eye the willingness wasn't there, but all else was the same.

"Welcome to Octara, Lady Warna," Narthing started with assurance. "We'll need to get you settled, and then—"

"Where is Octara?" she demanded. "How far are we from Anera?"

"About four days ride," Narthing said.

"Four days? I've been unconscious for four days?" she asked, her voice climbing higher.

"Nay," Narthing said. "Lord Verice opened a portal."

Her eyes were wide at that. Narthing had heard that very few humans were gifted with powers.

"He's been inspecting his border towns and seeing to the defenses. But we're based here in Octara, the capital of Tassinic. Now then—" he almost called her recruit. "What say we get you a wash and a meal, and then some sleep. Tomorrow's soon enough to show you around and answer any questions."

"I'd rather—" She stopped suddenly. Narthing's ear twitched as he caught the faint sound of a grumbling in her stomach. The lady smiled wryly. "Food would be good."

"This way." Narthing gestured toward the door, signaling two men to bring up the rear. He'd noted that she hadn't promised to stay, and she was too fleet of foot for him.

He escorted her out of the High Baron's office, and down to the barracks dining hall. The cooks there were setting another dinner shift, and he gestured Warna to a corner table. As the serving lads seated her and served kav, he gave soft orders to the others to see to her housing.

He'd talk to Constable Ricard. They'd shift maels and rooms around a bit tonight, give her a private chamber. Tomorrow they'd make more permanent arrangements.

From the stares of the men, word had already gotten around. Curiosity, more than anything, about the human woman Lord Verice had brought within the castle walls. Tongues would be wagging, that was certain. There's no worse gossip than a bunch of hardened warriors.

She made an odd picture, that was true enough. A slim, lovely human woman, with golden hair, seated in a roomful of armed and armored elven warriors. Narthing shook his head as he settled himself across from her. What was his lord thinking?

She gave him a nod as he settled and poured a mug of kav for himself. She was lacing hers with cream and honey, he saw. He preferred his black.

"The fare is plain, lady, but good and plentiful." Narthing leaned back as the lads brought platters with baked spiced fish and turnip cakes. A basket of bread and a crock of soft white cheese also appeared, along with a clatter of plates and silverware.

He saw an unwilling smile on her face as the lads banged the plates down before them.

Not condescending either, not like he expected.

But she was puzzled. "Why aren't we in the castle, Captain?" She reached for the bread. "One of your rank would normally dine at the High Baron's seat, at least in Farentell."

"Here as well, lady," Narthing said. "But the castle's abandoned, by Lord Verice's command. Left to the Ancestors."

"Why?" she asked.

"I'll leave that for Lord Verice to say," Narthing said firmly. "Tuck in, lady. While it's hot and within reach."

Thankfully, she did just that. Narthing breathed a sigh of relief. If the Ancestors were kind, she'd not press the issue. He'd see her safe in a bunk and then be off to his own.

Tomorrow was Lord Verice's problem.

CHAPTER FOUR

Verice waited until after midnight to begin his casting.

He'd planned the spell the moment he found a long golden hair caught in his armor. A simple matter, really, but it was a casting he hadn't done in some time. It would involve the protections he'd built into the castle walls, but that was a minor complication.

He dug a silver bowl out from one of his chests, and set it on the table next to the pitcher of crisp, cold well water he'd drawn himself. Clearing off the maps and markers from the table, he set them carefully to the side.

He stripped off his chest armor, setting it on its rack, and hung his swords and daggers with care. Sometime soon he'd need a day to see to them. That wasn't a task he cared to have anyone else do, but he might not have a choice.

He stripped to the waist and pulled the ties from his braid, letting his hair flow free down his back. Kicking off his boots, he pulled off the thick socks he wore underneath. The rough wooden floor felt cool under his feet.

He took a moment to stretch, trying to loosen the muscles in his back. Tight and tense from a long day in the saddle, casting portals, dealing with his people and their fears. Just this one last little chore and then he'd sleep, if the nightmares would let him.

With the door and shutters closed and bolted, the room was dark, but his concentration was assured. With a wave of his hand he lit one small candle.

All was in readiness.

He stood listening for a moment more, for the silence of the warriors sleeping in the barracks, for the tramp of the night guard along the walls. He touched the web of protection that he'd set around his castle, even into the city itself. Those protections cost, in his time and energy, but it was well worth the price. This particular casting would add to the burden, but it must be done.

He started the chant, the words flowing soft and formal from his lips. The bowl began to glow as he poured in the water. Carefully he wrapped the hair around his fingers, and touched the water's surface. "Warna," he breathed.

The water shimmered, then grew still and obeyed.

She was sleeping, in one of the loft chambers it looked like. The small window was unshuttered, allowing the moonlight to spill within. Her bed was a simple bunk, filled with old camp blankets, and pillows.

Her hair was spread around her head, her lips parted slightly. She breathed evenly, and regularly, deep in some sweet dream, he hoped.

She shifted then and the blanket slipped down to reveal a bare shoulder. It was then he saw her clothing neatly folded over a chair, her slippers tucked beneath, and understood that she was naked underneath the bedding. He hesitated, wondering just for a moment what she'd look like, bare and sweet in the moonlight.

And chastised himself with his next thought. She was a vulnerable innocent, and a gifted one. Defenseless in a world full of treachery and deceit. Someone worthy and deserving of protection. His protection.

The grief rose, catching him unaware, like a bolt of pure pain through his heart. He'd failed to protect so many of his own.

She shifted then, rolling to her side, hugging a pillow. The blanket shifted further, and he could see the curve of her shoulder. Guilt flooded over him, adding to his pain. Honor demanded he finish his task, and be done. Not be some kind of disgusting voyeur.

If he really wished to protect her, he should send her away. He nodded in agreement to his thought. That would be best. Send her to safety somewhere else, or even into one of the other baronies.

He started to dismiss the spell, and paused as he looked down. A lovely woman, yes, but she was fairly fast on her feet. She'd slipped from his hands quickly enough, almost getting trampled by his horse. How had she slipped through the mage-warded doors, and how had that particular door come to be open? He thought about how she'd fled before him, terrified. She'd frightened the very breath from him as she'd run toward the balcony—

He paused as the image played out before his eyes.

It would take time to arrange a safe location. Perhaps, in the meantime,

ELIZABETH VAUGHAN

he should make sure…

Without giving himself a chance to think, he focused his will again. The bowl glowed, and now he took the fine strand of hair and let it fall to the surface of the water. As he chanted, the glow extended to Warna, outlining her against the blankets and pillows.

"This far," Verice whispered. "And no farther." He closed his eyes, seeing the castle and its walls. "Here, but not beyond. Within, but not without. As I will, so guarded and warded be."

The bowl flared bright, then the power faded, leaving only the empty bowl behind.

There. The geas was cast. He could release it temporarily, or dismiss it, at any time, whenever he made the arrangements for her safety. His work was done. Now he could seek his rest.

He threw the bowl back in the chest, replaced the maps and markers, and then opened the shutters. Moonlight poured in and over his bed. Verice stripped, and settled in. The casting had left him weary; with any luck he would sleep.

As he drifted off, a vision appeared in his mind's eye, of a sleeping Warna and the curve of her shoulder.

He slept deeply, untouched by nightmares.

CHAPTER FIVE

Captain Narthing looked down from a window to the courtyard below. Lord Verice was out there at sword-practice, attacking the pells like a man possessed. Which wasn't that unusual, but he seemed to have more energy than normal.

"He's been out there all morning?" He glanced at Constable Ricard.

"Aye sir, since before dawn." Ricard looked slightly smug.

Lord Verice's decision concerning the castle had placed a hardship on them. It required the Castle Watch, under the constable's command, and Narthing's men, the Army of Tassinic, to house together. For the most part, they'd managed to work through the inevitable tensions. But they each enjoyed a silent rivalry with the other, especially when it came to dealing with Lord Verice.

Narthing sighed, and stepped away from the window. "Looks like it's going to be one of those days, Constable." He finished buckling on his sword-belt.

"That it does, Captain."

"And the Lady Warna?" Narthing asked.

"At breakfast, sir."

They both went down to get their own meals, knowing full well they needed to eat before the Lord High Baron was done. Narthing was drinking the last of his kav when Lord Verice strode into the dining hall, slapping his gloves against his thigh with impatience. "Narthing, what's keeping you," he demanded as he stopped at the end of the table.

"Just finishing, m'lord," Narthing replied calmly. Ricard dabbed at his eggs with his last bit of bread. Thankfully, the Lord High Baron wasn't one of those that stood on ceremony at meals.

"We're due at Izteria," Verice growled.

"At mid-morning," Narthing said. He glanced at his Lord. "Of course, it's always a good plan to arrive before one is expected, m'lord. See what the real state of readiness is."

"Just so," Verice agreed. "And where's Warna? She wasn't in her chamber."

Down the long row of warriors, a golden head leaned forward. "Here, m'lord."

"What in the name of the Ancestors are you doing there?" Verice barked.

There was dead silence in the hall. Warna's brown eyes flashed for an instant, and then she lifted her chin. "Eating breakfast, m'lord."

The response was respectful enough, even if the tone was not. Narthing raised an eyebrow as the room held its collective breath.

"From this point forward, you take your meals with me when I am in residence," Verice commanded.

"As you say, m'lord," Warna leaned back, disappearing into the line of warriors.

"Constable, you have command," Verice said.

Ricard rose crisply. "Aye, m'lord."

Narthing stood, gesturing for the men to follow.

"We'll return tonight," Verice announced. "At sunset." He spun on his heel, then paused. "Oh, and, Constable, see to our guest. She needs outfitting."

"M'lord?" Ricard had a look of pure horror.

"Yes, Constable," Narthing said under his breath, unable to resist a satisfied smile. "It looks like it's going to be one of those days."

* * * * *

Warna sighed as the High Baron stepped out of the hall and gave the men around her a questioning look. "Is he always so grim in the mornings?"

She'd felt uncomfortable coming into a dining hall full of warriors, but by the time they'd seen her settled at a table and served, she felt more at ease. They reminded her of her brothers, rushing to introduce themselves, and talking too fast over their food.

"Grim most of the time, lady." Erenfet, the warrior on her left rolled his eyes. "Quite the temper, he has."

"He's a good lord to us all, though," Aeric, one of the castle guards on her right chimed in. "Treats all his people, elven, half-elven, and human with a fair hand. Even if he don't normally let your kind within his walls."

"Gwenwyth tea, lady?" Oines, the warrior across the table, held up a pot and poured. The tea had a scent, like flowers on a hot day.

"Eh, that's not for her," Aeric said, catching the cup before Warna could take it. "Your pardon, lady, but me mum was full human, and while she liked the taste, it gave her the flux something fierce."

"You've half-elven?" Warna asked, studying his features. She looked around at the others, not wanting to be rude, but curious.

"Sure enough," Aeric grinned. "So's all of us. Erenfet, pull back your hair, let her see."

Erenfet was in mid-bite, but he obliged, tucking his gray hair back behind his ear.

It wasn't just the ears. Both men had pointed ones, but there was a softness in Aeric's face, his jaw and cheekbones weren't quite as sharp. Erenfet's face was sharper, a lot like the Lord High Baron, but not quite as compelling as—

"Pure elves tend more toward silver-gray hair, straight as an arrow," Aeric said. "Half-elves, well, ya got a full range of colors."

"I saw elves pass through our town once or twice," Warna said, although as she thought about it, she wouldn't have known the difference.

"Tassinic as a whole is a mixture, lady," Erenfet said. "Halves, quarters, whatnot. Not that it matters."

"Even for pure humans?" Warna asked.

There was a hesitation, then Erenfet responded. "No, lady. Lord Verice's law is fair to all."

Something flashed in Aeric's eyes, but all he did was pick up the pitcher of kav, and offer to pour for Warna.

She nodded. "That's good to know, about the tea," Warna said. "Is there anything else I need be careful of?"

"Some of the elven healing herbs don't set well with human folk," Aeric said. "But the healers hereabout know what's what. Nothing that will flat out kill ya, lady. Just make ya want to die."

"Best to be aware, then. My thanks." Warna smiled.

A bell rang in the courtyard, and the warriors all stood, taking a last bite, or a last drink. "Time to serve," Aeric said as he rose, giving Warna a grin.

With that, they all filed out, leaving Warna in an empty room, nursing her mug of kav.

Well. It appeared that she was on her own. She rose from her bench, and went into the back. The serving lads and cooks were scrubbing dishes and pots. The looks of horror at her suggestion that she help them convinced her it would be better to move on.

Which left her free to explore. And maybe find a way to escape.

Not that she had a place to escape to, mind. But one thing at a time. She needed to know her way around.

She stepped outside slowly, waiting to see if there was any exclamation, or protest. But no one seemed to take more than a notice of her presence.

She stood in a large cobblestone courtyard, the barracks behind her. She hesitated, then settled on a bench beside the door to take a moment and stare.

The courtyard was huge, and it circled the keep, which rose in the center of the castle walls. The sight of it took her breath away, all smooth white marble, rising straight up. The lower part was solid stone, built to withstand a siege. Above soared tall, arched windows with colored glass panes. It seemed to her more like a cathedral than a castle.

The beauty did not stop there. The castle walls were white as well, fitted smooth stone, with hanging lanterns spaced along the walls. Various buildings were built into the walls as well, to serve the needs of the keep. The smaller buildings were also white marble with slate roofs. Even the stables, to her surprise.

There were warriors scattered about, some practicing their weapons, or drilling in the yard. Aeric seemed to be talking to a group carrying pole arms. Others stood guard on the walls. The barracks area felt very formal somehow. There was a farrier shoeing a horse, and sounds coming from the smithy, both buildings built up against the walls. But there was an odd feeling of order. A place for everything and everything in its place.

Which made her feel even more uncomfortable.

"Pardon me, miss." Constable Ricard strolled up, looking quite aggrieved.

"Constable," Warna said.

"Miss." The constable looked like he thought she was out-of-place as well. "Miss, I'm not—"

"Constable, I'm a merchant's daughter. I'm not expecting silks and lace,"

Warna reassured him. "Tunic and trous are fine, for now."

A relieved look passed over the man's face. "If you'd come with me, then."

He led her to a small door and ushered her inside.

The office they entered was crammed with shelves filled with scrolls, going as high as the ceiling with barely enough room to pass between. The constable had to shuffle around her to shut the door, so tight was the squeeze.

Two heads appeared, one younger, the other old and tired. After a quick glance the heads went back down over their work, even as the older one spoke. "Constable, what's the need?"

"A new recruit, Quartermaster." Ricard gave Warna a wink. "Need some gear."

"Name?" The question was barked out impatiently.

Ricard gestured to Warna.

"Warna of Farentell," Warna said, letting the constable have his fun. Sure enough, he grinned as the two heads popped back up, startled.

"Recruit?" sputtered the older man.

"Recruit?" Ricard laughed. "I said guest, sure enough. A guest of Lord Verice."

There was a rustle of papers, and a wizened old man came around a corner, slipping between the shelves easily. Behind him, a lanky elf craned for a sight of her.

"A lovely one at that," the older one said, and bowed. "Welcome, lady. I am Farnor, Quartermaster for the Army of Tassinic. How may I be of assistance?"

In no time, Warna had a small chest of the basics, and new shoes besides. The Quartermaster had trouble with standard gray tunics and trous, for all were meant for maels. They either threatened to split at the breast or the hip, or hung on her like sacks. But he'd a small sewing kit that he added to the pile with a shrug. "Seems to me this is only temporary," he said. "We've no real supplies for a lady like yourself."

"It's enough to get her started," Ricard said. "I'll help ya carry it, miss."

But Warna had other ideas as they left. "Where's the washhouse?"

* * * * *

Constable Ricard was standing guard when she emerged from the bathhouse, washed and changed. "Feel better then, miss?"

"Yes, thank you," Warna smiled.

"I've duties to be about, then." Ricard said. "The noon bell will ring for the meal, and the Lord said you'd dine with him this eve."

"Thank you, Constable." Warna settled on a bench in the sun to dry her hair. "I'll try not to be a trouble."

"Much appreciated, miss," Ricard gave her a nod, and walked off.

Aeric was still drilling his men. Apparently marching in formation with pole arms was more of a challenge than she imagined. But after a while they stopped and formed opposing lines.

"All right then," Aeric barked. "Front lines, take up sword and shield. Second line, halberds."

Warna watched while they practiced. She'd never really seen anyone use a halberd before. It did seem effective, as the men behind jabbed at the attackers over the shoulders of the front line. But it seemed to her that you'd really have to trust the man behind you to know what he was doing with that heavy pole.

Her attention wandered. As nice as it was in the sun, she felt the need to move, and explore.

She took the bundle of her clothing and her comb up to the small loft chamber she'd been assigned to, and left it there. Tunic and trous felt odd, but they'd do until she could get more suitable clothing. She figured that, to some extent, that was Lord Verice's problem, not hers.

She felt odd. Empty. As if there was something she should be doing.

Warna shook herself, and headed back outside. The least she could do was walk around and learn more about the castle.

The courtyard continued on, surrounding the keep at its center. Warna started to walk, thinking to circle the entire keep. She wanted to see the other buildings, designed to supply the keep with its needs. A laundry, an outside kitchen, storage of foodstuffs, perhaps a brewery.

But once she started around, there was an odd stillness. An emptiness.

Warna frowned, but kept going, curious. The sounds behind her faded as she walked the cobblestone yard as it curled around the white marble building in the center. Here the buildings stood silent and vacant.

She thought about the quartermaster, all crammed into those rooms with barely an inch to spare. Why not use the space available? As the daughter of an ambitious merchant, she'd been trained to marry a noble, and in the running of a noble holding. Not one as large as this place, but still. Narthing had said that the keep was not being used, which made no sense at all.

Unless its Lord had turned his back on all but war.

Warna frowned as she walked farther around. A castle's purpose was not just living quarters of its Lord. It was also a symbol of power, a key defensive position, a storehouse of supplies in case of siege. To empty it out? Abandon it? That made no sense.

There were guards on the outer walls, and one or two acknowledged her with a wave of their hand. They didn't seem to find it amiss that she was wandering this way.

She got dizzy, walking along, gazing up at the tall white marble towers and arched windows. She'd never seen anything like this in Farentell, not that she'd ever traveled far. She'd heard tales, of course, but to actually see it was quite another thing.

At the rear of the building, there was a large circular window. She shaded her eyes, and retreated a few paces, trying to make it out. It was dark, and she couldn't see any color. She narrowed her eyes. Was it broken out?

She continued on, filled with questions.

She was almost back around to the practice yard when she spotted the open doorway in the wall of the keep. The room beyond was dark and still. She stepped closer, peering in, seeing nothing but darkness.

Was it the same door? She thought maybe it was.

The guards were paying her no mind, and no one seemed worried as to where she was or what she was doing…

What had Lord Verice said? *'You have the freedom of the castle and its grounds—'*

Warna slipped inside the door and stood silent, letting her eyes adjust, listening for sounds of protest or pursuit.

The only sound was her own heartbeat in her ears.

She stepped farther in, looking around. This wasn't the door she'd bolted through. To the best of her memory, that had led to a hall. This one opened on to a huge kitchen, with two huge hearths and long tables for the work.

But what stopped her were the dishes set out, as if for supper, and the kettles hanging over cold hearths. Dust-covered spoons in bowls, and cloths tossed on the tables, as if just thrown by someone in haste. Something had happened here, something in mid-meal.

Fascinated, Warna stepped further in, but the sunlight only went so far. The deeper darkness beyond the next door pulled at her.

She checked the mantel, finding a small copper lamp, the kind used to keep a flame handy for lighting fires. She found flint and steel, and tinder besides, neat as a pin, as if waiting to be used.

She struck a spark, adjusted the wick, took up the tiny light and ventured further into the darkness.

The archway led to a long hall, stretching out to her left and right. Warna paused, hesitating for a moment. The idea of getting lost in a huge keep with a tiny lamp did not appeal to her at all.

But curiosity gnawed at her.

She noticed the dust, thick on the floor. The hallway was white marble, with a heavy carpet down the center. She took a few steps, leaving a clear trail. She could use that to guide her.

She lifted the lamp higher, trying to peer down the hall. There were doorways off to the sides, and there'd be stairs at some point. The lower levels would be dark, but a few floors up those glorious windows would let in the sun.

So, she'd treat it like a maze. Always follow the right wall, leave a trail in the dust, and head up at the first chance.

That odd feeling was back, a cold lump in her chest. She bit her lip for a moment and then it hit her, bringing a well of grief.

It had been so long since she'd done anything for pleasure.

Since losing her family, her home, all that she'd done was concentrate on survival. Doing what had to be done. This felt wrong, somehow.

"Sorrow comes of its own accord. Joy has to be invited," her grandfather's voice whispered in her ear.

Warna turned, lamp in her left hand, her right on the wall. She scuffed an arrow with her foot in the dust, and then started off, heart beating in anticipation.

* * * * *

We'll run the patrol along the river here," Verice pointed on the map. "I know you say that the water's high, but I don't trust to that alone. I know it thins our forces, but—"

His chest vibrated as his mage-wards broke. Someone was in the keep. Verice lifted his head, focusing on—

"True enough, Lord, but with message birds, the early warning will make all the difference," Narthing stepped in and continued talking, covering for Verice.

Verice blocked out the people around him, and concentrated. Was it an enemy, a member of his force? His anger built as he focused; his orders had been clear. No one was to enter the keep for any reason, and he'd see the offender punish—

It was Warna.

CHAPTER SIX

Warna wandered down the hall in amazement.

This was clearly a working area of the castle, with various rooms off the long hall. The first few doors she came to were ajar, and swung open at her touch. They all showed signs of a hasty departure, chairs overturned, scrolls left on desks, fireplaces unswept.

The dust was thick, as were the cobwebs. She stifled a cough, trying not to stir the air too much.

There was a rustling as well, and droppings. She didn't bother to investigate those areas too closely.

Some doors were locked, and she moved past those, careful to make scuff marks in the dust. Her little lamp burned bravely, its light steady and reassuring.

She started humming to herself, if only to hear another sound besides her breathing. Not that she was afraid, really. The empty rooms and hall didn't speak to her of menace. It felt like sorrow.

Although if her little brother had been with her, he'd have hidden in those wardrobes and jumped out at her just to hear her shriek.

Her heart clutched at the memory, and her eyes welled up. Grief swept over her, but then with a teary laugh, she could almost hear his joyful laughter.

Warna wiped away tears, took a shuddering breath and continued on.

But the next break in the hall, she had to make a choice. She could head up the small spiral staircase to her right, turn down a hall to her left, or continue straight on. She paused for a moment, and bit her lip.

Up. She wanted to see those windows.

There were arrow slits along the way, and she could see the walls, and down into the courtyard. There was a line of shadow as well, and she knew that soon enough she'd lose any sunlight. Besides, Lord Verice had said he'd be back at sunset. Best to be out and cleaned up before he arrived.

The stairs opened up into a dark hall, and again she chose to go to the right.

Here now, were the chambers of the keep. Each with an arched window that let so much light spill into the room.

This room had a large bed, covered with thick blankets and hung with heavy bed curtains. A woman had slept here, there were bright dresses in the wardrobe. Warna took a closer look, mindful of the flame of her lamp.

The dresses were lovely, vibrant and rich. But when Warna reached out to touch one, she pulled her hand back. It didn't feel right to disturb these things. Except for the layers of dust, it felt as if the lady would burst into her chamber at any moment, laughing, ready to change for a night of dancing and music.

Whatever had happened to her, she hadn't taken her things.

Warna sighed and moved on, peeking into rooms as she went. All bore the weight of their departed residents, even to perfume dried in bottles long unused. The hall went on, but she could not. Warna turned back, and returned to the spiral staircase she had ascended.

She paused there, holding the lamp, and considered. Up or down?

She went up.

Breathing hard, she emerged into a small chamber. There were linens here, some stacked on shelves, some bundled for the laundry. It had to be a servant's supply room. The door beyond was open just a crack, and there was a faint glow of sunlight beyond.

She pulled open the door, gasped in delight, and then sneezed.

Sunlight flooded through the huge arched windows and down the length of a long room, High and clear letting in a lovely light. Between them were four vivid colored-glass windows, staining the white marble below them with reds and golds and vibrant greens. This had to be the main hall of the keep, the Great Hall. Warna followed along the one wall, staring at the designs.

Only two on each side were of colored glass. The first depicted spring, with fresh green glass, and a lovely oak tree that arched over the scene: a meadow of flowers. The details were amazing, with animals of the forest at the base of the tree, and the birds building nests and courting in the high branches.

Warna hurried to the next. This one was summer, with the deeper greens, and the animals feeding and raising their young.

A glance showed her that the other side had to be fall and winter. She darted across the room, stirring the dust and coughing as she hurried to see the other designs. But the center of the room stopped her in her tracks.

Shattered chairs, tables and benches lay strewn about like broken toys.

There'd been a gathering of some kind. There were some tables still set with dishes, others overturned, with crockery broken on the floor. Something had happened here, something terrible.

The sunlight was diffused here, but she still had her lamp. There were wine-stains on the floor, and food dried in the bowls. The air was stiff and stale. Mice droppings on the tables and floor. Some of the debris was weapons, swords and daggers left where they'd fallen. There was a shield with a blade wedged deep within.

No bodies, thank the Lord and Lady.

Almost against her will, her gaze turned to the high table. It was overturned as well, the cups and plates smashed. The actual high seat was broken, splintered and cracked, as if it had been used in defense. And in the space before the high table?

Warna stopped just at the edge of the reddish-brown stain. It covered a huge area, with signs that someone had struggled within it. There were smeared hand-prints, and drag marks all around the deepest darkest part.

Warna could barely breathe.

She lifted her head as a breeze touched her cheek. In the wall behind the high seat there was a large circular window, its glass shattered and gone, open to the sky.

"Warna." The voice, low and deep, came from behind her. She wasn't even startled to see Verice standing in the opposite doors.

There was such pain in his face, and she knew instantly that she was the cause. She stood frozen, holding the tiny lamp before her like a shield. "M'lord, forgive me. I didn't think—"

"Come," Verice said, holding out his hand. "You should not be here."

Warna advanced to place her hand on his wrist. His skin was cool under her fingers, his eyes dark. Her mouth dry, Warna licked her lips, afraid, but unable to stay silent. "M'lord, what happened here?" Her voice was a whisper against the silence.

His eyes grew more shadowed, his mouth set in a line. "Death. Betrayal." He drew a slow breath, turning his back on the room.

"Come."

He led her slowly down the main staircase, to the wide double doors at the base. Out in the courtyard, his men waited, with Captain Narthing, their horses, and a very pale Constable of the Watch.

"Lord Verice," Ricard stammered

"At ease," Lord Verice said. "Lady Warna did not know, and I neglected to tell her that the keep is forbidden to all. I failed to give her instructions in the matter. You are not to blame."

Ricard relaxed, mumbling his thanks.

Verice gestured, and Warna handed the small lamp to Ricard. "Return that to the kitchen area, and secure that door," he said.

Ricard bowed over the lamp.

Verice gestured again, and the huge main doors slammed shut and bolted themselves. Warna jumped at the violent sound, startled at Verice's action. Everyone else reflected the same surprise.

"If you will join me, the evening meal is ready" Verice inclined his head to Warna. "After you've freshened up."

Warna blushed, noting her tunic and trous were covered with dust and cobwebs. "Yes, m'lord." She fled to her chamber, feeling guilty and ashamed and yet so filled with curiosity. She wanted to know more but...

Her dress was dry now, so Warna washed fast, and changed. She got the cobwebs and dust out of her hair, and braided it, all the while knowing that she'd hurt him.

Why did she feel so guilty?

He'd kidnaped her, after all, used magic on her person, imposed his will on her without so much as a 'please' or 'will you'. He required no protection from her actions, needless to say.

And yet.

She cursed her stupidity, and her thoughtlessness and her idle curiosity, and wondered how she could really make amends. Such a fierce, strong warrior, and she'd wounded him by wandering into the keep. His face—

She dropped her hands into her lap and sighed. She'd no clue how to make amends, beyond the words she'd already said. She felt horrible.

Maybe she could send word that she was ill. Ask to be excused, beg off eating with him. It was true enough. Her stomach was in a knot.

But then she'd be a coward on top of it all. And there'd be the morning to face. It wasn't going to get any easier.

* * * * *

One of the serving lads bowed to Warna and gestured her through the door.

Lord Verice was standing by a chair, waiting to seat her. A fire burned in his hearth, and lanterns glowed in every corner, with one set on the table besides. The other door was shut; she presumed those were his sleeping quarters.

"Good evening, Warna," Verice said.

"Good evening, Lord Verice." She curtsied, and sat as he eased in her chair.

"If you'd be more comfortable, I can have someone sit here in the room with us." Verice offered.

Warna glanced back at the warrior who had escorted her to Verice's chambers. "That's not necessary, m'lord."

Verice dismissed the warrior, with thanks. "I'll leave the door open, nonetheless, lady." He settled in his chair across the plain wooden table from her. There was the sound of running feet and clattering china outside the door. "Shush," someone admonished, and then silence descended. A timid knock on the door frame came next.

Verice's grimness gave way to an odd look of patience. "Enter," he called.

A lad started across to them ever so slowly, carrying a covered dish. He placed it on the table, took a step back and bowed, before dashing off, almost colliding with the next lad, slowly making his way with a covered bowl. That brought an end to any attempt at decorum. The lads all ran in, deposited their burdens, and took off at high speed, leaving the table tottering, but no food spilled.

Warna laughed despite herself.

"They do try," Verice said. He lifted a bottle. "I drink no wine, but for you, m'lady?"

Warna shook her head. "No, m'lord. It's been so long, I would fear to keep my wits."

"The water here is very good, and there's kav for after." Verice placed the bottle to the side. "We'd best eat while it's hot."

"M'lord, I wish to apologize to you again," Warna said. "Except the lamp, I disturbed nothing. I am so very sorry that—"

"Apology accepted." Verice lifted the lid from a serving dish. "Chicken?"

Warna stared at him for a moment, then accepted that the matter was closed. She raised her plate. "Yes, thank you."

They dished out the meal to each other. Baked greens and onions with cheese, chicken roasted with rosemary and onions, and a loaf of bread.

Warna tore off a hunk as Verice cleared his throat. "I'm the one who should offer an apology. I fear that I have been... less than courteous in our dealings. This conflict within the kingdom has destroyed much that was graceful and fair, including my manners."

"You're used to taking command, issuing orders, and seeing them obeyed," Warna said softly. "I suspect that aspect of your leadership has saved more lives than either of us knows."

"I do not deserve your understanding," Verice said. "But I thank you for it. Pernard's roses are lovely, don't you think?"

"Oh yes," Warna smiled. "I do so love flowers."

"Well, I must tell you then, that some of his are cuttings from my gardens," Verice said. "I make a point, when I journey, to see if I can find a new flower or plant to add to my collection. Those roses are from Soccia, if I remember correctly, from a small village—"

* * * * *

Verice lulled her with talk of roses, all the while drinking in the sight of her. How long had it been since he'd talk of things other than war and troop movements? He could not remember.

She sparkled, brown eyes glowing gold as she talked. He felt her warm to him, relaxing and talking about flowers and their care. She shared stories of her mother's garden, her bright brown eyes only occasionally dimming with the memories. She took pleasure in the meal, even though the fare was plain.

So, he kept the talk light as they ate, not wanting to see the shadows in her eyes, although he knew the pain was there, under the surface. Time enough for that.

"So, were you trained in music?" he asked finally.

"No," Warna chuckled. "My family was far too practical for that. My father saw no profit in those skills. No, I was trained to run an estate, with the hopes that my father would arrange a marriage to a minor lord or landed knight, who in turn would aid my brothers to noble wives. My father loved us dearly, and had ambitions for us all."

Verice nodded, understanding. "But you are not wed? Or pledged?"

"My mother sickened shortly before King Everard's death," Warna said. "With the chaos, and her illness, my father delayed a formal betrothal. After she died, the Lord High Baron called every able man to arms. My father, brothers took up arms and…" She trailed off.

"How did you survive?" Verice asked.

"When word came that the Usurper's forces were upon us, Father and Grandfather hid me," her voice was filled with pain. "When the flames started, Father stayed to try to protect his warehouses. Grandfather got me away. He died a short time thereafter. I've been running ever since."

"That explains your song," Verice said quietly.

Warna lifted her head, and he could see the tears gathering in her eyes. "Grandfather always told me, 'Pain's part of the agreement, Warna. Part of the price.'" She blinked away her tears. "I didn't really understand him, because it sounded so cynical, so bitter somehow. I didn't want to think that life was like that."

"Now you know it's just the truth," Verice said. "Your song expresses it well. How did it go again?

Life is fleeting, life is pain
What need then to dance in the rain?
What need then to sleep in the night
Safe in the arms of my lover held tight?"

Warna listened, her amazement clear as he sang, keeping his voice low.

He'd impressed her, and it pleased him that she blinked away tears.

"It sounds so much better when you sing it," she whispered. "Were you trained in music?"

Verice shook his head. "No, not really. There was a time, before I took the Barony of Tassinic, when I thought to become a bard. But after about ten years or so, I realized that it was not truly my gift."

"Ten years?" Warna asked.

"Yes." Verice stood to retrieve the kav pitcher that sat by the fire. He returned, offering some to Warna. "So, I decided to seek my fortunes in the human lands. I offered my sword and my fealty to King Jeverard, and he accepted it. Later, he awarded me Tassinic for my services to the crown."

"King Jeverard was King Everard's grandfather," Warna said slowly, as if trying to absorb what he was saying.

"Oh yes." Verice gave her a wry look. "And I know the answer to your next question."

Warna stared at him blankly. "My next—"

"I'm seven hundred and ten years old," Verice said.

CHAPTER SEVEN

S even hundred and ten?" Warna's breath caught. It was one thing to be told that elves lived long lives. It was quite another to hear one say it so casually.

"Give or take," Verice shrugged, then chuckled. "It always hits you humans oddly. Every time I say it, the humans around me get the strangest look on their faces, as if it couldn't be."

"It's just that your voice is lovely," Warna said. "And ten years studying music seems to me almost a—" she hesitated. "A lifetime."

"For you, perhaps." Verice nodded. "War and magic leave little time to perfect other arts. But I always encouraged others in their endeavors."

"Tassinic is known for its love of music and dance," Warna said.

"It was," Verice agreed. "There is little time for such pleasure now."

There was a tap at the door frame, and at Verice's 'Enter', the serving lads swooped in, removing all the platters, bowls and plates at a rush. Warna managed to save her kav, but the rest was gone in a flurry of clattering crockery.

The door closed behind them, and Warna became conscious of the time. "It's late, m'lord. My thanks for the evenin—"

"What were your plans?" Verice asked. "If I hadn't taken… command?"

"I'd hoped to go back," Warna said. "Try to salvage what I could and rebuild. But no one was sure what was happening, and until the Lord High Baron took control again, it wouldn't be safe to go back. Grandfather had a brother, a wine merchant in the Barony of Wyethe, who would have sheltered us. At least, that was the plan."

Verice studied his cup, then looked her right in the eye. His were so startlingly silver-blue, glittering in the lantern light. "The reports I've had say that Farentell has fallen, and under the control of the Usurper's forces. The Lord High Baron is dead. Farentell is no more."

Warna closed her eyes against the pain welling deep within her.

"The Usurper has crushed any resistance, and seems determined to level every town and village. Slavery is now the law in the areas under his control. There is nothing to return to, Warna."

She tried to hold back a sob, but it escaped her. She covered her mouth as the tears started to flow.

"I've upset you." Verice leaned forward.

"Not you, m'lord," Warna choked out. "But the Usurper has much to answer for."

"In that, we are in agreement," Verice responded. He rose to his feet, and offered his hand. "Tomorrow, I'll take you to see Charrin, a Bard who used to grace my court. He will give an honest assessment of your skills. You will stay with him and some friends of mine, for a time, until you decide what you wish to do."

"M'lord?" Warna rose.

"You are my ward, by virtue of my... taking command." Verice took up the lantern from the table. "But your life is your own, Warna of Farentell, to make of it what you wish. Once you know what that is, I will see you established."

She was having trouble taking it all in, and wanted nothing more than to find her small bed, and crawl within. She reached for the lantern, but Verice shook his head. "I would see you to your chamber, lady."

* * * * *

He allowed Warna to lead the way, careful to hold the light so that she could see. The sorrow was still thick in her eyes. It wasn't the way he'd wished to end the evening, but he owed her the truth.

Not that it was any great distance to her chamber. Up the stairs to the attic of the barracks, down a hall with rooms full of snoring warriors to every side, to the base of a ladder that led to her tiny loft.

"Give me a moment to light a candle," she murmured as she reached for the rungs.

"Take this," Verice handed her the lantern. "There's a mage light within. Far safer than a flame in tight quarters. And see," He flicked the small shutters. "You can control it this way.

I see well enough without it."

"Thank you," She paused, staring at him.

He stood there for a long moment, returning her stare, feeling somehow… disappointed. He took a step back, and bowed. "Good night, Warna." With that he walked off, just far enough that he knew she could not see him.

He paused then, listened to her climb the ladder, and the rustle of her clothing as she prepared for bed. Waited as she crawled under the blankets.

Waited as she whispered a soft prayer for the souls of her family and Farentell.

Closed his eyes as she started crying for her losses, her sobs muffled by her pillow.

Verice cursed the night then, cursed the Lord of Light and Lady of Laughter, cursed his Ancestors, cursed life itself that caused such pain to one so undeserving.

Almost, almost he went back, to climb the ladder and catch her eye, and cast a spell of dreamless, sweet sleep. The urge was strong. But she'd not thank him in the morning, he was certain of that. Let her mourn her dead, let her grieve for what was lost.

He stood guard, bore witness to her pain, listened in the dark as she cried herself to sleep. Once her breathing evened, he turned away, seeking his own bed.

As he climbed within and pulled up the covers, he knew he'd see her off safe in the morning.

It was for the best. This was no place for a human woman. He and his men were prepared for attacks; they were warriors who could defend themselves if need be. There was no comfort to be found here, no safety. She could not stay.

The nightmares claimed him through the night, but the innocents he'd failed to protect all had golden hair, and brown eyes flecked with gold.

CHAPTER EIGHT

Warna woke well before dawn, with a raw throat and scratchy eyes. She rolled to her side, flipped her pillow and burrowed down into its coolness. She'd left the shutters on the small window opened, and moonlight filled the room.

Her heart lay numb and cold, a terrible empty feeling in her chest. It was all gone, and she'd known it before Verice had confirmed her fears. Known it by the dead look in her father's eyes as he'd kissed her mother's coffin. When word had come of the deaths of her brothers. When she'd held her grandfather's hand, and sung him to sleep for the last time.

'Your life is your own, Warna of Farentell, to make of it what you wish.'

All well and good for him to say so, but the thought filled her with dread. It might be freedom in his eyes, but to her it looked like a great, yawning maw of 'unknown'. She'd no skills to speak of, and while Lord Verice thought her songs were special, Warna knew full well they were not.

What did she want? She wanted what she'd had. A home, a future planned for her, a family who loved her and were loved in return. She'd looked forward to building a life with a husband of similar mind, and a family of her own.

Exhausted, drained, she closed her eyes, and fell back asleep with just enough consciousness for a simple prayer. *"Lord of Light, Lady of Laughter, hear my prayer. Grant me grace and strength, Lord. Grant me wisdom and peace, Lady. Show me the way…"*

* * * * *

In the morning, Warna stepped out into a crowd of waiting men and horses. "What's going on?" she asked Constable Ricard quietly.

"It's your escort," Ricard responded just as quietly. He carried the woven lidded basket that held her clothes on his shoulder. "Lord Verice ordered it doubled."

"Looks more like I'm being escorted to my execution," Warna said.

"That's not funny," Verice ground out from behind her.

Warna jumped, startled. "M'lord," she started, then paused when she saw his eyes. "If you'll forgive me, you look like you didn't sleep."

"I'll sleep better when you are safe," Verice growled. "Constable, you will have command."

"Aye, m'lord." Ricard heaved her basket up onto the back of one of the horses, and secured it. He gave Warna a nod. "Be well, miss." He lowered his voice. "The Lord and the Lady go with you."

"With you as well," was all she had time for as Verice took her elbow, and guided her to a horse.

"You can ride?" he asked.

"Yes," she said shortly. She reached for the saddle and mounted quickly, glad she'd chosen tunic and trous for this day.

Verice mounted the horse next to hers. He'd braided his hair, and now wrapped it around his head and put on a helmet. "Narthing, you have point. No ceremony."

"Aye," Narthing called from the front of the group. "Mount up," was the command, and all obeyed. Warna felt dwarfed by the maels around her as they took to their horses.

"Forward," Narthing called, and the group started out, hooves chiming on the stones as they walked toward the great gates. Warna admired the huge doors, which swung open silently, pulled back by the great chains she could hear rattling overhead.

But as her horse's head cleared the gate, some force pushed her hands back, as if she was against a wall. "What is—?" she exclaimed. Her horse continued on, but her body was forced back, pushed back by some kind of barrier. The pressure slammed her knees and chest, and she felt the horse walking out from beneath her—

A strong arm wrapped around her waist, pulling her from the horse before she fell. She gasped, clinging as Verice turned his horse away from the gate, cursing under his breath.

"What happened?" she asked. The warriors milled about her, some stopping her horse. Narthing was calling commands to halt.

"Nothing," Verice growled in her ear. "Let's get you back on your horse."

She became conscious of his arm, holding her up, pressing her body against his. She flushed. "Thank you for the rescue, m'lord."

Verice said nothing, just lowered her to the ground as her horse was brought back.

Warna re-mounted, settled herself in the saddle and grasped the reins tightly.

Verice hovered, whispering something under his breath that she couldn't quite understand.

She urged the horse forward at a walk, and the animal plodded forward patiently, passing through the massive gate without a problem.

Confused, she concentrated on staying in the saddle as they rode forward, at least until she happened to look up. Then the view took her breath away.

She'd caught a glimpse of it when she'd tried to throw herself from the balcony of the keep, but it had only been a glimpse, and she'd been… distracted. But now, the walled city below the castle was spread out before her. The whole thing gleamed white and shining in the sun. The odd thing was, there seemed to be green within the walls.

It didn't take long before they were at the walls, answered the challenge, and through the gates. Warna discovered, to her delight, that there were trees, and even gardens, some with flowers, some with vegetables. The buildings weren't piled on top of one another, like in the towns she'd seen in Farentell. These storefronts and homes seemed crisp, somehow. Everything planned, and in its place. It was lovely, but it felt so different from her home.

The people were the same, going to and fro with tasks and chores. Warna's group didn't draw much attention as they passed down the wide street at a trot.

She glanced over at Verice, who rode straight and tall, his helmet hiding his face.

He met her eye for a moment, then looked away.

They continued on for a while, then Warna grew conscious that the group seemed smaller than when they'd started. When two more warriors pulled away from the group, she knew she was right. She stopped staring around, and focused on where they were going.

Two more warriors stopped at a fountain, announcing that they would water their mounts. That left two riding beside them. Verice continued on, slowing their pace. "It's not far," he offered quietly.

Which was good, because Warna hadn't been in a saddle for some time, and she was starting to feel it.

"Here," Verice stopped in front of a bakery and dismounted. "Best sweet buns in town."

Warna dismounted as well. The warriors with them took the horses, seemingly headed to a smithy down the way. Verice took her lidded basket from one of the horses, and motioned her to a door.

He ushered her in to a small room with a long counter. The three women inside looked up from their work. The oldest one smiled and walked forward.

"Lord Verice," she dusted flour from her hands, and curtsied, even as she darted Warna a glance filled with curiosity. "We were told of your coming, Lord."

"Which door?" Verice asked.

The woman laughed. "You know him, m'lord. Tis through the necessary." She paused, with a twinkle in her eye. "Might be wishing to grab a cloak."

Verice shook his head, which just made the woman chuckle. He shifted her basket to one hand, and headed through a side passage, down to a door. Warna followed.

They passed through a cloak room, and here, Verice gathered up a heavy woolen cloak. "Here," he said. "Put this on."

"But," Warna objected.

Verice ignored her, setting the basket down and sweeping the cloak over her shoulders. "Trust me," he said, clearly amused by her confusion.

Warna huffed out a breath, but left the cloak in place. Verice picked up the basket and led the way.

The door opened into a kitchen garden with a privy beyond. Verice opened the door with its moon carving, and bowed her through.

Warna had brothers; she gave Verice her best 'what-are-you-up-to look'. But he just shook his head in denial of any trick. "Watch the first step," he said as she entered.

She found herself on a high mountain trail, ice and snow glittering in the moonlight, the fierce wind stealing her breath.

CHAPTER NINE

Warna staggered, for she had stepped from bright warm day into crystal cold night. She felt Verice's warm arm wrap around her waist.

"Told you." His breath was warm on her ear as the cold wind swirled tiny snowflakes around them.

The path was clear, but not the peaks. Hard, sheer spikes of stone, decorated with the rims of frost sparkled under the moonlight. What stars could be seen were bright in the midnight sky. It was beautiful and terrifying all at once.

She breathed in. The air seemed thin and insubstantial, as if her breath was not enough to sustain her. And the bitter cold cut right through the cloak. A gust of wind hit them, carrying sparks of icy snow that stung her face.

But Verice stood behind her, warm and strong. She wasn't afraid; although a glance back showed that there was no door behind them. "Where are—"

The rock face farther down the path split open, spilling warmth and light. "Verice! How good to see you," an elderly elf with wisps of white hair poked his head out the door. "And company! Even better. Come in, come in!"

Verice guided her the few steps up and through the door. "Wolfe, it's good to see you."

It was a small room, that smelled of leather, soap, and bread. It was lined with shelves, and cloaks hanging from pegs. Warna watched where she stepped. The floor was cluttered with boots tucked under benches, and parcels and baskets at her feet. Winter woolens spilling from the shelves.

There was a scrabble of nails on wooden floors, and they were surrounded by a pack of large smooth-haired dogs, noses lifted to take in the scents, tails high, barking in their excitement. Warna laughed, trying to scratch as many ears as she could reach.

"Now, now, stop that, settle down," The old elf closed the door, cutting off the cold air. The dogs ignored him as they milled about, knocking into Warna, scattering parcels and tipping over baskets.

"Sit," Verice commanded.

The dogs all sat, tongues lolling out of their mouths, uttering muted whines of excitement and happiness. They were various hues, running from dark brown to soft gray, long noses and all leg.

"They're beautiful," Warna said, as Verice took her cloak. The whole room reminded her of home so much. Her brother's hunting dogs, her father's boots. She blinked away her tears, reaching out to pet the closest. The animal wiggled all over, darting pleading looks at Verice. "Down," Verice said, shaking his head.

The dog yipped as it collapsed onto its side, rolled over and begged Warna to rub its belly. Warna laughed, and obliged.

"Shameless," Verice said gruffly, as he gave the others attention.

"None to blame but yourself," the older elf snorted. "Since they're your dogs."

"They are?" Warna glanced up to find him staring at her, his gaze flicking to her ears. Suddenly self-conscious, she stood.

"They were," Verice straightened. "Wolfe, may I present—"

"No, no, let's wait until Kalynn is with us," Those considering eyes were now twinkling with some inner joke. "Come up, come up," The elf smiled at Warna. "We're on the roof. It's a bitter night, but perfectly clear." He led the way to a door opposite, which opened onto a spiral staircase. "Kalynn will want to hear every word."

Verice gestured, her lidded-basket still on his shoulder. Warna followed the elf up the most cluttered staircase she'd ever seen. The staircase was narrow, the stone steps all worn in the center from years of use. The light was warm, welcoming and steady, but it was as if the very stones glowed, since there were no torches she could see. Even the wooden doors they passed glowed yellow with age.

On each side of every step was a basket, crock, chest, with piles of books and scrolls adding to the clutter. All filled with such a variety of things that Warna's head was spinning before they'd gone a single flight. Baskets of crystals, of rocks, of yarn and cloth. Beads in one, and gold coins in another, none of which she'd ever seen before. Shells, and feathers and dried plants all haphazardly piled in various boxes and containers.

The walls held swords and daggers, shields and lances, all displayed with animal skins spread out between them. At one point she saw two crossed lances, and between them a large rib bone decorated with beads and feather and a strip of bells.

She actually stopped before one beautiful tapestry, showing a warrior-woman on the back of what at first appeared to be a winged horse, carrying a glowing blue sword. But a closer look showed that it was more of a hawk-horse, with fierce eyes and clawed front feet. Still, it took her breath away, the details of the feathered mane, and the light in the woman's eyes.

"Airon," Verice said behind her, re-balancing her basket. "They are called airons. Fierce fighters, and rulers of the skies."

"It's lovely," Warna said, but then she jerked her head at a further thought. "They really exist?" She stared at the skull hanging next to it, covered in etched engravings. "Is that a dragon skull?" she breathed.

"Wyvern." Verice said.

"Are you coming?" Wolfe asked from the stairs above. "Watch your step," the old elf said, as Warna hastened up. "I fear I've fallen behind in my cataloging."

There was a snort from Verice. Warna glanced back to see him shake his head.

The dogs swarmed around them, heading up the stairs, knocking things over as they scrambled past.

"Here now," Wolfe said irritably.

"Don't blame them," Verice said.

"It's my tower, lad," Wolfe retorted. "Age has its privileges."

"Age is not an excuse to avoid cleaning," came a female voice from above.

Warna climbed up the final flight of stairs and found herself emerging onto a rooftop. She stopped dead, and Verice had to urge her up the last few steps.

There were chairs in the center of the roof, clustered around an area rug and a table. Chairs with padding, the kind that Warna had heard of but never seen. But that wasn't what commanded her attention. It was the night sky above them, clear and crisp, with stars scattered over a velvet sky, and the moon low over the mountains that surrounded the tower.

Yet the air was warm. She took a breath, and laughed at the wonder.

"Amazing, isn't it?" a low female voice asked. A woman stood at the table, smiling at them, dressed in embroidered robes of red and gold. Her skin was the color of dark honey, and her white hair was piled on the top of her head. Her eyes were the same silver as Verice's and filled with welcome. Warna couldn't see her ears, but she had the same air as Wolfe, and she looked as what Warna had imagined elves to be, when reading her childhood tales.

"May I present to you Warna of Farentell," Verice said, coming to stand next to Warna. "Warna, these are my friends and mentors, Mage Wolfe, and Seer Kalynn."

Warna would have curtsied, conscious of her tunic and trous, but Kalynn stepped forward and took her hands. "Come, sit. Farentell, eh? That's a barony in Palins, is it not? Next to yours, I believe, Verice."

"It was," Verice said. "Farentell has fallen to the Usurper now. Warna came to Tassinic, fleeing the conflict. She is under my protection, now."

Kalynn drew Warna to one of the stuffed chairs. She sat, trying not to notice the startled looks on the faces of Wolfe and Kalynn. The dogs had followed them up the stairs, and were settling all around them, sprawling on the rugs.

"Protection?" Wolfe asked sharply.

Kalynn silenced him with a glance. "You are most welcome, Warna. It's not often we have visitors."

"As to that—" Verice set his burden down and settled on a chair next to Warna's. "I've come with two requests. I'd ask that you shelter Warna for a time. For her own safety, she cannot continue to stay at the castle."

"Continue?" Kalynn asked sharply.

Wolfe now silenced her with a glance. "She'd be welcome, of course."

"And the second, lad?"

"I'd like Charrin to hear her sing, and evaluate her skills in music," Verice said. "I believe that she has a gift for music that should be nurtured and protected."

Wolfe and Kalynn both stared at Verice. Warna concentrated on the dogs, avoiding the looks of dismay on their faces.

"Verice, are you sure that's wise?" Kalynn asked quietly. "Charrin is still healing, and I am not sure that he would…" Her words trailed off as she glanced at Warna again. "I am not sure this is advisable."

"At the very least, its damned insensitive, lad." Wolfe shook his head. "There are other Bards who could evaluate her abilities."

"Yet you'll shelter her," Verice pointed out.

"Of course," Wolfe said. "And we'd resolve any issues that came up as a result. Might even do him good, to live with a—" He stumbled over a word. "To have other people around. But to ask Charrin's opinion about her talents is just asking for—"

"Whose talents?" A warm, baritone voice floated over to them. Warna turned to see another elf coming up the stairs slowly, with a stick in his hand. She drew in a sharp breath. Unlike Verice and Wolfe, this elf's hair was black, a silky curtain down his back. But his face—

An ugly, raw gash crossed both eyes, empty sockets sightless and staring.

CHAPTER TEN

Warna caught her breath at his scars, then regretted her rudeness. It hadn't been loud, perhaps he'd not heard—

The blind elf turned his head slightly. "Who is that?"

"Charrin," Kalynn rose gracefully from her chair, and moved toward him, her robes swishing against the stones. "Verice has brought a guest who will be staying with us for a while. Her name is Warna and she is of—"

"Why are you speaking the human tongue?" Charrin stood stiff and straight, not advancing further into the room.

"Warna is of Palins, of the Barony of Farentell," Wolfe said firmly. There was a warning note in his voice when he added. "She is a guest in my home."

"She is an innocent, Charrin." Verice said. "She fled her own home in the face of the Usurper's—"

"My Lord Verice, welcome." Charrin's voice was hard. "It has been some time since you graced us with a visit."

"It has," Verice said mildly. One of the dogs at his feet whined softly and pushed its head into his hand to be petted. "Far too long," he added, stroking the dog's ears.

"The demands of your office, I am sure," Charrin said. "Being the High Baron to a savage people."

"Charrin," Wolfe growled.

"Charrin, let me aid you to—" Kalynn reached for his arm.

"No," Charrin bit out the word. "I need no aid." He moved forward, his steps deliberate but confident. The dogs were quick to move out of his way. Charrin sat in one of the chairs, settling himself with an easy grace.

"You seem to be getting around well," Verice commented.

"A spell," Wolfe said. "It occurred to me that it might be possible to allow him to—"

"See?" Warna blurted out.

"No," Charrin said. "It allows me to perceive. To sense the space around me. But it is not sight. There is no color, no depth, no… beauty."

Warna bit her lip at the venom in his tone. "I'm sorry. I—"

"A human," Charrin's voice was flat now.

"I have taken her under my protection," Verice said. "She has a gift of—"

"And we all know how well you protect your own," Charrin snapped.

Verice's head stayed down. His hand paused, then he continued to pet the dogs.

"Charrin," Wolfe growled again, but Kalynn touched Warna on her arm. Warna looked up into her warm smile.

"I think we could all do with hot kav before this conversation continues," Kalynn said. "Would you help me?"

"Of course," Warna stood quickly, more than ready to leave the room.

"I'll brew a fresh pot," Kalynn said to the men. "We'll return when it's done." She paused before descending the stairs. "Try not to destroy the furniture, Wolfe."

Warna followed, down the cluttered stairs. She waited until they were out of sight before speaking. "M'lady, I am sorry that—"

"You are not the cause, Warna." Kalynn glanced over her shoulder with a sympathetic look. "Verice can be insensitive at times, don't you think?"

"Well," Warna said, thinking back. "He expects his word to be law, that's certain."

Kalynn laughed, and led the way down and then through an arched doorway into a bright kitchen with round windows that let sunlight stream in and pool on the stone floor. Day into night; night into day. How marvelous. There was a small fire in the hearth, and a pot of something that smelled wonderful suspended over it, bubbling away.

"This doorway wasn't here before." Warna stopped in the archway, glancing back at the stairs. "And the sun—"

"It's Wolfe's mage tower, dear," Kalynn went to the hearth and pulled over a kettle. "It's what it needs to be."

Warna moved farther into the kitchen, marveling at the idea of a mage tower. On the far side of a wooden table, a cat lay in a patch of sunlight. It had the oddest mottled coat of black, brown, yellow and a kind of green.

Not pretty exactly but—

The cat fixed its watery yellow eyes on her, and rolled onto its back, inviting a belly scratch.

"Oh, you pretty thing," Warna crooned, and reached down—

"Careful," Kalynn said sharply. "She—"

Its fur was warm and soft and Warna gave it a good rubbing, careful not to scratch too hard. The cat started purring, a rough rumble that seemed to echo through the room. Warna enjoyed the moment, then straightened. "My family had cats in the stables and—"

Kalynn was standing there, staring at her unwaveringly. Her light silver eyes seemed unfocused.

"Lady," Warna asked tentatively, worried that she had offended.

Kalynn blinked, then her eyes became sharp. "How long have you known Verice?"

"A few days," Warna said cautiously.

Kalynn nodded, gave her a patient look, then prodded, "And how did you meet?"

"Well, truth be told—" Warna started.

"And it's always best to tell the truth," Kalynn said. Her eyes softened.

"He kidnapped me," Warna blurted out.

"Ah," Kalynn set up the kettle to brew. "To keep you safe, I suspect."

"Well, yes," Warna admitted.

"Still, unsettling, isn't it?" Kalynn had a soft, smile on her face, as if remembering something. "For what it's worth, I do believe he has your best interests at heart." Kalynn gestured at the kettle. "While we are waiting, let's find you a room for your stay."

"If it's no trouble," Warna said.

There was a slight rumble, as if of thunder, coming from overhead. Kalynn shook her head, and took Warna's arm. "No trouble at all, dear. You have much to show me."

Warna tried to puzzle that out, but she must have misheard.

Kalynn lead the way out the archway. "Up, I think," Kalynn suggested. "For a better view."

Warna watched carefully as they went up a few steps, and found a door on what she could have sworn was an exterior wall.

Kalynn clicked on the black iron handle and pushed.

"Oh my," Warna breathed.

It was a lovely room, with a small sitting area, and doors leading off. A fire crackled in a fireplace, but what really caught Warna's eye was the large window in the wall opposite, sparkling with panes of clear glass in a diamond pattern. At the sides were heavy white curtains covered in large pink roses. "Oh, this is marvelous," Warna whispered, and reached out to undo the clasp and open the windows wide. Kalynn stepped to her side.

Under a dark night sky filled with stars, a frozen lake stretched out below, surrounded by snow-covered fields as far as she could see. A breeze caught a flurry of snow and it sparkled as it danced over the windowsill.

On the far shore of the lake, Warna could just make out a crowd of people, dancing slowly and stately in the light of the torches they carried.

Warna took a deep breath. "Oh my." She laughed in amazement as she glanced at Kalynn. "That's all the words I can seem to find!"

But Kalynn's face was somber, not sharing her amusement. "Interesting." Kalynn tucked her hands into her robes. "Have you ever seen the like?"

"No, never." Warna shivered as the cold spilled inside.

Kalynn pulled the windows closed. Warna thought she caught a look of sadness in the woman's eyes, but when Kalynn turned to her, she was smiling. "What do you think of this? There's a bedroom through that door, I suspect."

There was indeed, and Warna took a few moments to explore the empty clothes press, and the privy. But what drew her was the bed. It beckoned her, with bed curtains and a thick comforter with the same flowered material. She glanced at the door, then climbed up onto it, lying flat. Above, the cloth top was embroidered with flowers and all manner of bees, insects and birds.

"Oh my," Warna breathed.

Kalynn chuckled from the doorway. "So, it will suit?"

"It's almost too much, M'Lady." Warna got up, and smoothed her tunic. She felt almost giddy at the idea of living here, sheltered and safe in this lovely room. Yet she wasn't quite sure. Was this what she wanted?

She knew what *Verice* wanted.

"I'll have Verice bring your wicker basket down before he goes." Kalynn opened the empty clothes press and paused before continuing. "We can see about getting you what you need tomorrow." She closed the press, and turned back to the door. "Let's check the kav, shall we?"

Back on the stairs, Warna frowned. "How will I find my way back?"

"It will be there when you want it to," Kalynn said absently. "I think we should find something for the men to eat. It's harder for them to argue if their mouths are full."

The kitchen was bright and warm, and now smelled of brewing kav. Warna settled on one of the benches as Kalynn pulled out a cutting board and a knife. "Here. Slice some of this cheese, and I'll cut fruit."

"M'Lady," Warna hesitated, then blurted out her question. "What happened at the castle? I was in the keep, and I saw the broken window, and dried blood on the floor.

"Dried blood?" Kalynn paused, and shook her head. "Oh, Verice." her voice filled with soft sorrow. She went silent for a moment.

Warna waited.

"Warna, I wasn't there when it happened." Kalynn sighed. "And we can't leave our menfolk alone for an extended time. Wolfe's temper will only hold for so long. But still—" Kalynn took a deeper breath. "You need to know."

CHAPTER ELEVEN

Warna held her breath, waiting for answers.

"During the Festival of Light and Laughter, the castle and keep at Octara were attacked from within by the Usurper's forces. The castle was filled with celbrants at the time. Many were killed, more were left badly injured." Kalynn shook her head. "One of those who died was Summer, Charrin's mate. Charrin was blinded. Summer died in his arms."

"Oh," Warna whispered.

"Verice blames himself, even though he barely survived. Healers have a rule, you see. Save the one you can over the one you can't," Kalynn said. "Verice wasn't conscious when the healers made the decision to treat him instead of Summer. Verice blames himself for all of the deaths, not just Summer's. He commanded the keep be abandoned, and has forbidden any entrance. He maintains a military presence within the castle walls, but that is all."

Warna nodded, thinking it over. "It's all there, untouched, as it was that night?"

"So far as I know," Kalynn said. "And he's gone to extremes to protect everyone and everything he cherishes. His staff and servants scattered among the various towns and villages, kept safely away. A mistake, to my way of thinking. The stars alone know how it will turn out."

"But, you are a Seer?" Warna was confused. "Can't you see the future?"

Kalynn's smile faded, and her eyes grew distant. "If only that were so. What I *see* are possibilities. They swirl about us through the air, like the scent of roses lure one into a garden." She looked at Warna and wrinkled her nose. "Or the scent of muck pulls you to a midden."

"Oh," Warna said softly. She had rather hoped otherwise.

Kalynn's lips curled gently, as if sensing her disappointment. "You are not the first to wish for answers, child. But life does not offer answers. It offers choices. There are endless choices in our lives, Warna. Each choice influences another."

Kalynn's voice was soft and warm, her movements slow and precise in the afternoon sun.

"Every so often, a seer can influence one person. Show them the possibilities. Just a few words can make all the difference in a person's choices. Now, where is that crock of honey?"

Kalynn turned back to the hearth, reaching for a small crock on the mantlepiece, then poured the hot kav into a pitcher. Warna arranged the cups on a tray, and loaded up the cheese and fruit.

"There, all done." Kalynn smiled. "It will be so nice to have you here. Perhaps between the two of us we can organize Wolfe's collections."

"It won't be a problem for me to stay?" Warna asked. "I noticed Verice didn't ask permission before we appeared on your doorstep."

Kalynn laughed. "We've known Verice a long time, dear. Wolfe was his mentor. If it was an imposition, we would have declined, trust me on that. If you decide to stay, we would welcome your company." She gestured to the other tray, and Warna picked it up.

"Decide?" Warna said.

"I'm sure you were a dutiful daughter, Warna of Farentell." Kalynn headed for the stairs. "But now your life is your own. You are free to live as you wish, but that means that you make choices, and live with them." Kalynn turned up the stairs. "Not always easy."

Warna followed, frowning. "Verice told me much the same thing," she said.

"Did he?" Kalynn's voice echoed on the stone walls. "That bodes well, don't you think?"

Warna paused on the step. Honestly, it did. If he was sincere. If he truly allowed her to make her own choices.

"Come," Kalynn's voice echoed down to her again, pulling her from her thoughts. "Let's return before Wolfe decides to express himself with bolts of fire. I rather like those chairs, and he'd melt them to slag without thinking and apologize afterwards."

Warna blinked, then followed.

The air was thick with strain as she and Kalynn emerged onto the roof.

All three men were taut, each face stiff with disapproval.

Warna glanced at Verice as she set the tray down. He didn't look up, so his eyes were hidden from her. His face was carefully blank, concealing his thoughts.

Kalynn ignored the frigid silence. "Verice, I think you take your kav black and sweet, yes? All that honey is going to rot your teeth."

Verice flashed a tight grin, showing his perfect teeth. "Not so far."

"Give it time," Kalynn replied, handing him the mug and the crock.

Warna poured for Wolfe, who thanked her.

"None for me," Charrin said. "Lady Warna, the Lord High Baron Verice has expressed a desire to know the true potential of your musical abilities."

Warna set the pitcher down slowly, almost afraid to breathe. He'd been so angry before she and Kalynn had left the room; she wasn't sure she trusted this turn-about.

Charrin's back didn't touch the chair, his hands still in his lap. But his face seemed composed and professional.

"Lord Bard Charrin," Warna returned formal with formal. "I would be honored, but I would not seek to impose. I would fear to waste your time—"

"Service to one's craft is never wasted," Charrin replied. "But you understand that mine will be an honest assessment? I will tell you the truth."

Warna glanced over her shoulder at Verice. "Lord Bard, you should know that my father had me sing for a human minstrel a few years ago. He—"

"Your pardon," Charrin said, "but a… minstrel's… opinion is nothing to me. Let us begin. Do you have any formal training in music or voice?"

"No, Lord Bard," Warna said. She smoothed down her tunic front, then stilled her hands.

"Very well," Charrin said. "Verice says that you compose."

"I make up lyrics and tunes to go with them." Warna said.

"Then sing for me, Warna of Farentell," Charrin commanded. "And we shall see what you have within you."

CHAPTER TWELVE

W arna froze. She hadn't planned, hadn't practiced. What to sing? Her 'flower' song wasn't done yet, so that wasn't a possibility. The room was so tense, and there was so much grief in them. Nothing sad, then. She drew a slow breath, relaxed her shoulders, and lifted her head.

"The farmer's lass was tall and fair;
her beauty was her fame
Her suitors came from miles around
to try and make their claim."

Warna breathed, trying to pace her voice and her tone, making sure to hit the notes clearly and evenly.

"Daily she'd to market go,
selling cheese and butter.
They'd stand before with hat in hand
their troth to spit and stutter."

Charrin's face was blank, his head down and slightly tilted as he listened. But Wolfe and Kalynn were smiling.

"The lass was also quick and sharp,
her wit like knives a'slicing
She'd toss her hair and lift her chin
and sing out this reprisal."

Warna tossed her own head, tapped her toe three times fast, and broke out into the chorus, giving it her all.

"Hie thee hither and get thee hence,
art not the lad for me.
Hie thee hither and get thee hence,
art not the lad for me.
The lad I'll love is tall and dark
and handsome as can be.
So, hie thee hither and get thee hence,
art not the lad for me."

Kalynn laughed, Wolfe smiled. Verice leaned back in his chair, his face stoic, but with crinkles in the corners of his eyes. Warna felt the fleeting tingle of having pleased her audience, and joy welled up inside. She posed like a saucy maid, and continued:

"Then came the day, a lad rode in
with kind and smiling eyes
Fair, and tall and dark and strong,
he clearly was her prize."

The lad I'll love is tall and dark
so sweetly sang, did she.
So, hie thee hither and get thee here,
thou art the lad for me."

She paused then, waited for their attention, and when she had it, spoke. "And then he sang,"

"Hie thee hither and get thee hence,
art not the lass for me.
Hie thee hither and get thee hence,
art not the lass for me.
The lass I'll love is sweet and kind

and gentle as can be.
So, hie thee hither and get thee hence,
art not the lass for me."

Kalynn and Wolfe laughed and clapped, exclaiming their pleasure. Warna smiled, and curtseyed, risking a glance at Verice.

He was looking at her, his face still set in that bland, neutral look. But there was sparkle in his eye, and the shadows were gone. Warna reached for her mug and sipped her kav, satisfied.

"A sprightly tune," Charrin said. "A peasant's song in nature, certainly not meant for this type of audience. More appropriate to a tavern, I should think. I would have made other word choices, but you carried the story well, and the ending is a pleasant, if obvious, one." Charrin reached for the pitcher, and his mug.

"Come, come," Wolfe said. "Don't leave her waiting. What of her voice?"

Charrin ignored him, pouring the liquid carefully, then returning the pitcher to the table with a slow grace. "Your pardon. I was collecting my thoughts."

He took a slow sip of kav.

Warna settled herself in a chair, her kav in her hand. One of the dogs saw an opportunity and came over, its brown eyes begging. She reached out and scratched its ears.

"Lady Warna, your voice is pleasant, and you have some basic understanding of breath control and pacing," Charrin said. "but you lack the training necessary to develop any further. In comparison to other professional singers, yours is, at best, mediocre. Even if you were to undergo training, I fear you would be unable to advance much past a very basic level."

Warna nodded, hiding her face in her kav. No more than she expected, to be honest, but it still stung.

"Well, I thought it was very good," Wolfe huffed.

Kalynn was about to protest as well, but Warna just shook her head. "Kalynn, that's what the minstrel told me too." She chuckled to ease the shock in Kalynn's face. "But she also told me that the joy of creating is just as important as perfection of the art. Perhaps more so. And that she'd sing with me anytime."

"A human attitude, certainly," Charrin sniffed. "Of course a human would think as much. With no time to achieve perfection, why attempt it? It's amazing that they crawled from their caves and learned to walk, really."

"Charrin, that is uncalled for," Wolfe snapped.

"And rude," Kalynn said.

"It is simply the truth." Charrin made a small dismissive gesture with his hand. "Their lives are as snowflakes, harmless and melting if they fall on your skin individually, but dangerous and deadly as they multiply. They will destroy us all."

"Palins and Valltera have lived in peace," Verice said calmly.

"Because you are the buffer - and what has that created? A barony rife with half-breeds and—"

"Charrin," Wolfe said low and dangerous.

"I'll not be silenced," Charrin cried out. "Why have you come here, Verice? I expected word that you had avenged the attack on your people, but that isn't the case, is it? Why haven't you taken vengeance, Verice?"

"You know why." Verice's voice was flat. "If I gather my forces to attack Edenrich, the Black Hills will rise against me. Rumor has it that the Baroness Elanore has turned to the dark arts to create an army."

"If that is true, then every one of your dead makes her that much stronger." Wolfe grimaced.

"I have no assurances that Summerford or Wyethe would not turn on me as well," Verice said. "And while King Barathiel of Valltera has never threatened, still, he has eyes on my land as well. So, I hold to my own borders and ward them. The time may come when I can strike at the Usurper, but that time is not now."

"Yet the blood spilled cries out for vengeance," Charrin said hotly. The dogs raised their heads, roused by the rage in Charrin's voice. "The Ancestors cry out for it. I cry out for it. You take no action, and that human filth sits on the Throne of Palins and mocks all that is fair and noble. Had I my sight, my sword would be in my hand, and his blood—" Charrin was shaking, his face distorted. He jerked to his feet and threw his mug across the roof where it shattered on the stones.

The dogs sprang up, putting themselves between Verice and Charrin. The one next to Warna shifted slightly, keeping a wary eye on the trembling elf.

"You must have loved her so very much," Warna whispered.

"She was my all," Charrin seemed to collapse in on himself as he sank to his chair. "She was…" He trailed off. "And now here I am, unable to avenge, unable to even breathe."

"I am sorry," Warna said.

"How can one such as you understand?" Charrin turned on her, the rage back in his voice. "How can you even comprehend—"

"It's a deep physical pain, like a part of your soul is gone," Warna struggled to get the words out. "A wound no healing can touch, not that it's healing you want. I've tried to put it into a song, but I can't find the words. My throat closes, my heart breaks, and the tears just come."

"How dare you think you know my pain." Charrin covered his face with his hand. "I have not sung since her death. I do not know if I ever will again."

"You will, Charrin," Kalynn's voice was firm. "Summer would not wish it otherwise."

Charrin turned to Verice. "You could send assassins." His voice held a compelling note of pleading. "As they did. You could open a portal into the castle, and pour your warriors into their midst, as they did."

"Target the innocent, as they did?" Verice's head came up, his anger clear. "Kill the women and elderly, and strike to maim, as they did? Is your honor completely consumed in your hatred?"

"Why should it not be so?" Charrin was on his feet again, his voice a pained cry into the night sky. "Is not my life destroyed?"

Warna feared they'd come to blows. She stood as well, backing away from the two men.

Verice paused, as if her movement had brought him back. He glanced at her, then away. "This was a mistake," he said, shaking his head. "We should not have come. Kalynn, Wolfe, I ask your forgiveness, and thank you for your hospitality. Warna will return with me."

"Flee, then," Charrin spat. "Leave my presence, and carry my rage and despair with you."

Wolfe shook his head. "Charrin, we've tried to help you move past this—"

"Past this? Forgive this?" Charrin cried out again. "Never, not so long as there is life within me."

"A mistake," Verice repeated. "We should go. Come, Warna."

"Is that a command?" Warna asked.

CHAPTER THIRTEEN

W hat?" Verice stopped, taken aback. What had she said?

"Is that a command?" Warna asked him, standing there with an honest question in her eyes. "Do I have a choice?"

Verice stared at her as the dogs milled around his legs. Choice? Did she have a—? He opened his mouth to answer, but the words died in his throat. He'd planned to leave her here. But Charrin's attitude, his rudeness... but now it seemed the safest place for her was at his side. Wasn't it?

Yet, she'd taken his insults in stride, they had to have stung, but she hadn't lashed out at Charrin, hadn't... she hadn't let those harsh words dim her light.

He'd told her that she had a choice, and he'd meant those words, but a strange conflict rose in his heart.

Warna was looking at him, her brown eyes showing her as puzzled as he was. Wolfe watched intently, his eyes flickering between her and Verice. Charrin's lips were pressed in a thin line, his head tilted to the side, frowning. Kalynn had an odd half-smile on her lip.

"Of course you do," Verice said slowly. "But under the circumstances—" he stopped again. "I should make other arrangements. To keep you safe."

"Nonsense," Wolfe said warmly. "You've made it clear that your castle isn't safe. She's more than welcome."

Verice shot him a quick glare. Trust Wolfe to point out the contradictions in his words and actions.

"It would be lovely to have you here, Warna," Kalynn said, that half smile still on her lips. "But it's your choice."

Warna was still staring at Verice, giving him a considering look. He dropped his gaze, frowning, glancing at Charrin. She couldn't stay here; the atmosphere was too poisonous. To say her talent was mediocre; Charrin was lashing out. Verice felt sick. He'd made a mistake bringing her here, a mistake to expose her to—

Warna's voice cut through his thoughts. "Wolfe, Kalynn, I thank you for your kind offer, but I will be returning with Lord Verice."

"Well, in that case, I'll walk you out." Wolfe said. "You can take the dogs with you."

* * * * *

Charrin's stomach roiled with anger as he perceived Verice and his pet human disappear down the stairs, dogs in tow. Wolfe followed behind, insisting that Verice take his animals with him. Charrin's lip curled. All of Verice's animals, to his way of thinking. How dare Verice, one of the Blood, bring a human here. How dare he express concern for one so—

"An interesting turn of events," Kalynn observed.

Charrin frowned at her. She was watching them depart as well, but even in the grayscale of his perception, her expression was… interested.

"What was that I heard?" Charrin demanded, his shoulders tensing. His hands were in his lap, but balled into fists. "I heard something. Something in their voices."

"Yes," Kalynn rose and started to pick up the shards in the pool of kav. "Something starting. Something… fragile. A possibility."

"That can't be," Charrin said.

"I don't think they even know," Kalynn said.

"You think he cares for her?" Charrin spat, his voice an octave higher than he intended. He struggled to calm himself. "That's not possible. She's human. Verice is of a Bearer of the Blood of Tethnar, One of the Founders of the Kingdom of Valltera."

"A kingdom that rejected him," Kalynn said. "and that he rejected in turn. He is of Palins now. By his own choice. Has been for some hundreds of years."

"A passing fancy," Charrin sat back in his chair. "Nothing more." He snorted. "Imagine thinking she'd have a voice worth anything."

"Yes," Kalynn stood. "As to that, Charrin—"

"They're gone," Wolfe bounded up the stairs, rubbing his hands together, looking smug. "Took the dogs with them, thank the Ancestors. Don't know why I ever agreed to care for them." He glanced at the shards in Kalynn's hand. "Let me help you with that."

Ash pan and broom appeared, twirling and hopping up the stairs. Kalynn smiled as they whirled about and the shards themselves danced over to be swept up. "You're in a good mood."

"They took the dogs," Wolfe said with laugh. "And I may be old, but I recognized the look in their eyes."

"Love?" Charrin sat up, his voice sharp.

"Utter confusion," Wolfe chortled. "Both of them. They have no idea what's happening. Pity she decided not to stay. Would have been fun to watch."

"So, you think they love?" Charrin demanded, finding new fuel to his rage.

"How would I know?" Wolfe scowled. "Kalynn's the seer, not me."

"I don't see into men's hearts," Kalynn demurred.

"Ridiculous," Charrin huffed. "Verice knows full well the treachery those vermin are capable of. He'd never—"

Wolfe turned, his face contorted with a rage Charrin had never felt before. Charrin jerked up, suddenly remembering who he had just angered.

Kalynn held up her hand.

Wolfe stopped.

"Charrin," Kalynn's voice was curt. "It would appear that you have forgotten my heritage."

Charrin grimaced, keeping a wary eye on Wolfe. "Seer Kalynn, I—"

Kalynn interrupted. "Wolfe and I offered you sanctuary while you were recovering from the assault. I had also hoped to heal your heart as well, but it would seem that will take you more time."

Charrin went stiff. "It would seem I have offended you. But—"

"You have," Wolfe growled.

"You were rude to Warna," Kalynn shot Wolfe a hard glance, keeping her voice low and firm. "Wolfe and I will not tolerate such a lack of courtesy in our home."

"I ask your forgiveness," Charrin said. "I was taken by surprise at Verice's appearance."

"We accept your apology," Kalynn said.

Wolfe threw his hands up in the air.

"But even so," Kalynn continued. "The time has come for you to take up your life."

There was a long moment of silence. For an instant, Charrin felt stricken, bereft. But he straightened, his pride reasserting itself. Clearly, they did not understand his pain, his anguish. He inclined his head. "I've had many invitations from the Great Houses. The King of Valltera himself has asked for my services."

"It's time to emerge from your isolation, Charrin. A bard needs his audience," Kalynn said. "Wolfe will open a portal to aid your journey, wherever you decide to go. By noon tomorrow, shall we say?"

"I thank you for your care, Lady Kalynn." Charrin rose. "I'll withdraw now, and consider my options."

"On the morrow, then," Kalynn watched as he left, his steps slow but certain. "But Charrin—"

He stopped at the stairs, about to start down.

"The possibilities swirl around you, Charrin," Kalynn said. "'Ware your choices."

Charrin didn't turn back, but headed for the stairs with a slow and steady pace. He'd go, certainly. To where others shared his pain and grief. And would aid him to revenge.

* * * * *

Kalynn settled back into her chair with a sigh. There was a heaviness within her, a feeling building behind her eyes.

Wolfe eyed the stairs, waiting a bit before he spoke. "You handled that well," he said softly. "Better than I would have, that's certain sure."

"Perhaps." Kalynn shook her head, feeling the heaviness settling on her shoulders. "I'd hoped to help him release his hate. But it festers too deep for my skills."

"He lost his love." Wolfe came up behind her, putting his hands on her shoulders. "That's not a hurt that heals easily."

Kalynn sighed and leaned back into his warmth. "Beloved, a *seeing* is upon me."

She felt him tense then, going serious and still. "What do you need?"

he whispered.

"My sketching supplies," she whispered back, and heard his movement as the heaviness grew behind her eyes. It washed over her, dragging her down. She felt Wolfe's hand as he placed parchment and charcoal in her hands before moving the table closer.

Then the power claimed her, and she knew nothing but the dark visions of fire and horror that emerged from the depths of her mind. Her hands moved. She could feel the grit of the paper, and the fine dust on her fingers.

When she returned to herself, Wolfe was kneeling at her side with an anxious look and a cool cloth for her face.

He gave her a moment before he spoke. "What have you seen, flame of my heart?"

"The time is almost upon us. It will be soon," her hand shook as she wiped her face.

"Here," Wolfe took the cloth, and stoked her cheeks. "Rest first,"

"No," Kalynn reached for him and he came into her arms even at that awkward angle. "The time has come and there is that which might be, and that which must be."

"One never really knows all the consequences of one's actions," Wolfe sighed into her neck, his breath warm on her skin. "For good or ill."

Her breath caught in her throat at the weariness in his voice. But then to her surprise, he started to chuckle.

"Ah, but I know you, Seer." He pulled back, and gripped her shoulders, looking at her with quiet mirth. "Is that 'soon' as a mountain understands time? Or an elf? Or as a fruit-fly would define it?"

Kalynn shook her head at his mirth. "I know not," she admitted to his laughter. "But Wolfe, I have *seen*. This must be."

She tapped the parchment, and they both looked at the picture of a man, scarred and horribly burned.

Wolfe grew even more thoughtful. "This is what you've seen?"

"Yes," Kalynn confirmed. Bile rose in her throat, but she knew the truth of her vision. "It must come to be. We must make it come to be. If what was lost is to be restored, this must happen. At our hands if need be."

Wolfe sighed. "I do not doubt you, Seer."

She reached out to cup his cheek.

"When?" Wolfe asked.

"I—" she answered without having to think. "There's time."

"How far?" he rose, studying the sketch.

"Far," she answered, looking off at the horizon. "Perhaps too far for us to be there in time."

"It would help if the visions were a bit more specific," Wolfe said dryly.

"It will come when it needs to be," Kalynn rose.

"The absence of magic means no portals," Wolfe said. "We must gather supplies, get out the riding leathers. We'll get Charrin on his way, and then start preparations. If it can be done, it will be, Kalynn." He reached out his hand to help her rise. "What brought this to you now, I wonder?"

"I am not sure," Kalynn whispered. "But Warna's been touched by its wings."

CHAPTER FOURTEEN

Verice always had to re-orient himself to the right time of day and weather when he returned from a visit to Wolfe's. He blinked in the afternoon light, and tried to ignore Narthing's raised eyebrow when he emerged from the bakery with Warna, her basket and the dogs in tow.

"Back to the castle, m'lord?" Narthing asked, as Brindle reared up, planted his forepaws on Narthing's shoulders and licked his face.

"Yes." Verice handed Warna's basket off to a warrior. The dogs milled about their legs, tongues hanging out. "Warna will return with us."

Narthing raised both eyebrows at that.

"By her own choice," Verice said.

Warna flashed them both a smile as she mounted.

"As you wish, m'lord." Narthing signaled, and the others mounted as well.

Verice settled into his saddle, gathering the reins, gesturing them to start. They'd pick up the rest of the company as they rode, retracing their steps back to the castle. He didn't have to give it much thought; the path and routine was a familiar one. No, his thoughts were free to focus on the woman riding next to him.

What had he been thinking?

If the visit to Wolfe's tower had been a military campaign it would have been a disaster. He'd known that Wolfe and Kalynn would open their arms to her; they offered shelter to any in need, but he should have anticipated Charrin's rage. He'd been a fool to go there blindly, thinking that Charrin would treat any human well.

The horses were walking at a steady beat, their hooves ringing on the road. The dogs ran all around the horses, their tongues lolling out, their nails clicking on the stones. The rhythmic sounds made it easy to stare at his reins and think.

Warna was a distraction from his purpose. Verice shook his head. He'd allowed her brown eyes and lovely voice to come between him and his obligations. The fact that she was a genuinely nice human was also a factor. Still, there was no excuse.

Verice glanced over to see her looking around at the buildings lining the street. Hopefully Charrin's remarks wouldn't cause her to abandon her songs. He'd been too harsh a critic.

He'd find another place for her. Somewhere with more of her own kind. Except that put her in parts of Tassinic that were closer to the borders with Edenrich and Farentell. Too dangerous by far.

There had to be a way to keep her safe. The castle was strictly for military housing. A base of operations and a target for the enemy. It was no place for her.

* * * * *

The sun felt good on Warna's face as she swung into the saddle. After Wolfe's Tower, it was nice to find the weather and time to be what she expected it to be.

"By her own choice," Verice had told Narthing.

Warna flashed them a smile as Verice spoke, hoping they couldn't see how nervous she was. She was grateful that they started out at a walk, her horse content to move at a gentle pace along with the others. It gave her a moment to breathe.

How had she found the nerve to challenge him?

Verice was Lord High Baron, and while she was not of Tassinic, she was certainly under his care and authority at the moment. She'd faced him down, and her stomach was still in knots about it.

She hadn't wanted to stay in the Tower. Wolfe and Kalynn seemed very nice, and the room had been lovely, but isolation wasn't what she wanted. Though she didn't have a clue as to what it was that she wanted, it definitely wasn't that.

She wasn't completely sure of anything right now, other than the warmth of the sun on her face, and the sway of her horse as it walked.

"Your choice, Warna," Kalynn's voice echoed in her mind.

She supposed that she should be glad that she was free, but her heart

ELIZABETH VAUGHAN

still grieved the loss of her family too much to rejoice. Actually, the thought that she could choose was… unsettling. More frightening than anything else. Her father and mother had planned her life, seeing that she had the skills and deportment to marry well. Now that was gone, and the future seemed unknowable and scary.

Warna glanced around at the buildings and streets, trying to distract herself. The city was quiet now, the afternoon lingering on. Folks were closing up their shops and turning toward their homes. Few heads turned to note their passage.

She breathed again, trying to enjoy the warmth and quiet.

Verice was just ahead of her, the sun glinting off his silver hair. The warriors around them seemed relaxed, but Warna saw that they were always looking about, alert to any threat. Hard to believe that was possible on a drowsy, sunny afternoon.

Verice's horse pranced a bit and he settled it down, stroking its neck. He was a fine sight, his armor and sword hilts glittering in the sun.

"*The elven lord went riding, oh,*" new words and a tune danced in her head. Warna repeated the phrase to herself, trying not to lose the notes, watching her source of inspiration. How to capture him in a song? His strength, his sorrow…

What did she want?

Warna frowned as the thought refused to go away. She really had no idea, or maybe she was just overwhelmed by it all. Her life had been planned, organized by her parents. Simple. And she'd been comfortable with those plans. But now it felt like a vast emptiness. Without her family, what did it matter? What did any of it matter?

Warna tried to prevent the tears that threatened to fall. She didn't know what she wanted. She didn't know what to do.

But she did know what needed to be done.

The castle needed cleaning. Restoring. Restocking, even. And if she knew anything, it was how to scrub and polish. How to maintain a manor house as fitting for her future husband. She could bring her skills to bear on the castle of Lord High Baron Verice.

And while she did that, she could think things through. Make some decisions. Plan a future.

She relaxed, the tightness in her shoulders easing, the knot in her stomach letting go.

Oddly, she started to notice more people on the streets, pressed against the various buildings, staring at them. Well, staring at Verice.

The warriors around them were exchanging amused glances and it slowly dawned on her what was happening. She almost burst out laughing. Verice had forgotten his helmet, and Narthing was keeping their pace slow.

She couldn't help smiling. If Lord High Baron Verice had problems with his castle being cleaned and restored, she suspected she'd have the support of his people.

Warna caught the eye of some in the crowd. They returned her smiles, going so far as to wave. She lifted a hand in return, and her approval was enough for the crowd. They started to move closer to the road, and wave kerchiefs of various colors.

Verice was still oblivious, lost in his thoughts. It was only a matter of time before—

"All hail Lord Verice!"

CHAPTER FIFTEEN

"All hail Lord Verice!"

Verice started out of his thoughts to find the streets lined with people, all gazing at him. He lifted his hand to acknowledge the hail out of habit. Delighted smiles flashed over the faces in the crowd, and the cheers began in earnest, growing in volume.

With a sigh, Verice noted his helmet dangling from his saddle. Wryly smiling, he acknowledged the crowd again, and made eye contact with Narthing.

They continued to move forward but in answer to the unspoken command, Narthing slowed his horse, and maneuvered to Verice's side. The crowd thinned a bit, but now they were waving handkerchiefs and ribbons in addition to their greetings.

"You could have reminded me about the helmet," Verice chided his captain quietly.

"You seemed lost in thought, m'lord. I didn't wish to disturb you."

Verice snorted. "You could have picked up the pace as well."

"It's been some time since the people have seen you, m'lord," Narthing's voice held no apology. "Besides, the Lady Warna seemed to be enjoying herself."

She was at that, smiling at the crowds and waving back to them.

"Remind me to reassign you," Verice growled, lifting his hand and nodding his head in acknowledgment of the crowd. "To one of the southernmost bogs, perhaps."

"Certainly, m'lord," Narthing allowed Verice to take point. "I'll make a note."

There was nothing for it. Verice sighed, and picked up the pace just enough that it wouldn't take all day to get to the castle gates.

He cast a glance back at Warna, but there was no reason to worry. She met his gaze fearlessly. There was a twinkling in her eye and enough laughter in her smile that he knew she was enjoying the jest as well.

A woman darted forward then, holding out a roll of parchment, tied with a ribbon. "Pray, oh Lord, hear my petition!"

Verice accepted the roll, and placed it in his helm.

They continued on for a while, people calling out, wishing him well. There were others with petitions. Once his helm was full, he passed back any others to Narthing. They'd all have to be seen to, of course.

They entered the square to find the Lord Mayor and his lady on the balcony of their home, overlooking the fountain in the center.

"Welcome, Lord High Baron," The Mayor seemed a bit out of breath, and his chain of office was slightly askew. The crowd around his house quieted to hear his words. "Had we known of your visit, we'd have prepared a far better welcome."

"An informal visit," Verice called up to the man even as he kept his horse moving. "Impromptu on my part, I fear. I thank thee for thy gracious welcome and ask pardon for the disruption of your peace."

"There is no disruption." The Lord Mayor leaned on his balcony. "And our peace is your doing, m'lord."

"My thanks," Verice said. "You are gracious."

The mayor smiled. "And this lovely lady is…?"

Warna called out in response before Verice could say a word. "Warna of Farentell, your lordship. Octara is lovely!" Her smile was infectious, and the crowd cheered in response.

Verice tensed, and his horse shifted nervously in response. He hadn't wanted to bring any attention to Warna, much less give any information. He brought his horse under control with a firm hand. It was time to leave. "Our thanks, Lord Mayor, but we must be on our way." He gestured to Narthing to continue, but the Lord Mayor pressed up to the railing, looking anxious.

"M'lord, I would inquire…" His words faded as he waited.

"Yes?" Verice asked, trying not to let his impatience show.

"The Festival of Light and Laughter," There was a note of apology in the Lord Mayor's voice. "The date fast approaches, and—" He hesitated. "We've made no plans, waiting on your Lordship—"

The pain in Verice's chest must have been visible on his face, for the man cut off his words abruptly. "Forgive me, Lord High Baron. I—"

"It needed asking," Verice managed. "I'll consider it."

"My thanks, m'lord." The Lord Mayor bowed his head, and raised his voice. "May the Lord of Light and the Lady of Laughter bless thee, our Lord High Baron!"

The crowd cheered at that. Verice bowed his head and waved his thanks, still in shock. Had it been a year? He shook his head to clear it. "Narthing," he called, and let his tone speak for itself.

Narthing took the lead, and set as fast a pace as Verice could wish toward the other end of the square, only to find the path bared by a group of men, bearing banners, and flags. There were jugglers, acrobats, some singing, some playing horns and drums. The activity and the music stopped as they approached, and the leader stepped forward. He wore a cooking pot on his head, and bore a scepter in his hand, adorned with fake gems and false gold. "Stand and deliver, Verice of Tassinic!" the human boomed out in a loud, deep voice.

Verice's horse snorted, too well-behaved to act up, but not happy with the noise, but Verice knew the man well enough. "Master Zester." He gave the man his best forbidding look. "What means this?"

"Lord High Baron Verice, stand and deliver," Master Zester called out. "You owe tribute to our patron, the Lady of Laughter, for your failure to attend our follies and performances."

There were cheers from the crowd. Verice scowled at the man who'd opened a theater a number of years back.

"We have missed your patronage greatly, m'lord, and I would remind your lordship that all must pay the homage due to the Lady of Laughter, or risk her wrath." Zester spotted Warna, and removed his cooking pot to execute a low bow. "But now I see why m'lord does not attend us," he cried out. "He pays homage to another lady, and is lost in her obvious charms."

"Or mayhap your follies and performances aren't very good," Warna called back, startling Verice.

The crowd roared at her comment, and Zester held his pot over his heart, and shook a mocking finger at her even as he grinned. "Oh, ho, now here is one that follows the teachings of the Lady of Laughter well! Bring her to our theater, my lord." Zester donned his pot once again. "We'll restore a smile to your face."

"For now, Master Zester, clear the road," Verice growled.

With a bow, Zester gestured, and the acting company cleared the road.

With a snort, Verice led his men past, making sure that Warna was not harassed. They were through the town gates quickly, and he broke into a swift gallop as they started up the road to the castle. Warna seemed to have no trouble with the gait, her hair coming lose from its braid.

The grim faces of the gate guards gave Verice a clue that there was a problem even before the constable appeared in the courtyard. Ricard's face was grave. "Trouble on the border, m'lord."

CHAPTER SIXTEEN

Verice swung down from the saddle. "Where was the attack?"

"Word's come from Benton's Warren."

"When was the attack?" Verice demanded.

"Not long ago, m'lord." Constable Ricard's response was calm. "Injuries, no deaths reported. The messenger awaits in your chambers." The man's eyes widened as he spotted Warna on her horse. "M'lady, you—?"

"I'm back," Warna said. "If someone will help me with my basket, I'll disappear and leave you to your work."

Verice moved to her side, and held her horse's bridle. Warna dismounted. She grimaced a little as she landed. She shook her head when Verice gave her a concerned look. "No, it's nothing. It's been a while since I've ridden that far, is all."

"I must deal with this," Verice said quietly. "We can talk later."

"Yes," Warna agreed. "Go."

She meant it, to his relief. Verice gave her a grateful nod and headed toward his chambers.

* * * * *

Warna watched him go, hoping that the news wasn't too grim. The constable hovered near her, and caught her eye. "Beg pardon, m'lady, but this is a surprise."

"A sudden change of plans," Warna said, trying not to smile at the man's discomfort. "No way for you to have known."

"Well, but since you were gone, I shifted the men around a bit, and put two in that loft where you were."

"Two?" Warna asked.

"The smaller lads," Constable Ricard explained earnestly, then huffed with frustration. "We need to be in a proper barracks," he said, glancing at the empty buildings along the walls. "I've raised the issue, mind, but, well—" he sighed again.

"I do understand, Constable," she said with a laugh. "Although I wonder how you managed two in that space. How about I wait in the kitchens for a while to give you a chance to sort it all out? This will just be for one night," she added confidently. "There'll be a new plan in the morning."

With a grateful glance, the constable picked up her basket. "Let's see you to the kitchens."

Warna settled on a bench by the hearth, and accepted a mug of hot kav with thanks. Oddly, the cooks were only making kav and setting out the tables. There was no cooking going on. When she asked, one of the men shrugged. "Not enough room to cook here, and M'lord won't let us use the proper kitchens. So, the food's cooked in town and carted up for the meals."

"That's—" Warna stopped, not sure she wanted to say the words out loud.

"Aye," the man gave her a sardonic look. "They cart it up, we warm it here, and then serve it out. Never mind if there's a change in plans, or the number fed, or aught gets spilled or spoiled.

"I see," Warna said slowly. "That means there are no stores of supplies here, either, doesn't it?"

The cook shot her a satisfied look. "You know housekeeping, eh? I think you do understand, m'lady."

The clatter of boots pulled their attention to the door, as Verice walked in. The rest of his men continued on to the courtyard.

The cook hustled back to his duties as Verice strode over.

"The reports are worse than first thought. I need to go now. It can't wait until morning."

"How bad is it?" Warna asked, as memories arose of burning buildings, and fleeing her home.

"Bad enough," Verice said grimly. "I need to see for myself." He hesitated. "The constable told me he'd reassigned that loft room."

"To two men, if you can believe. But it's not his fault, Verice, he couldn't know that—"

"Agreed," Verice held up a hand to stem her flow of words. "I told him to put you in my chambers for the night. He's seeing to fresh bedding, then the room is yours. We'll see to other arrangements when I return, probably after the nooning."

"Safe travels, Verice," Warna said

"My thanks," Verice said, and then he hesitated, staring down at her. He reached out a gloved hand, and stroked her cheek. "Sleep well," he said abruptly, then turned and left the room.

She watched him go with a sigh, and a swift prayer to the Lord and Lady for his safety. Then she took a sip of kav, and turned back to the cook. "Tell me more about the castle kitchens."

It was early when she finally retired to Verice's chamber. She'd eaten with the men, after she'd watched the cooks carrying in large kettles and roasted haunches from carts outside. Then she'd walked around the keep again, noting the buildings along the way, and paying closer attention to their purposes.

She'd kept her distance from the keep.

After all that, she was well and truly ready for sleep, yawning as she mounted the stairs. There was a guard at Verice's door, but he saluted her through, and closed the door behind her.

The outer room was much the same, with maps strewn over the table and weapons on the walls. But what drew her was the large bed, heaped with pillows and blankets. It looked wonderful.

She used the basin and pitcher for a quick wash, and then stripped off her clothes, and pulled on her sleep shirt. She threw back the blankets and crawled in, enjoying the welcoming softness. It was warm enough, she'd only really need one blanket and she curled up, hugging one of the pillows.

Warna let out a slow breath, feeling her body relaxing. She had a plan. Not much of one, but it was her own, and it was her decision, and it felt good. It wasn't all that dramatic, or even very exciting, but she was satisfied. She yawned as she closed her eyes.

Of course, Verice might not agree…

She smiled even as she drifted off to sleep.

CHAPTER SEVENTEEN

G ood riddance," Wolfe muttered as he snapped the portal shut behind Charrin.

Kalynn narrowed her eyes at him. "You practically shoved him through," she scolded.

"After the headaches I had to go through to open a portal in the Royal gardens?" Wolfe snorted. "Permissions for this and authorizations for that and scribes to the Under-assistant of the Herald to the King?" Wolfe flapped his hands in frustration. "Bah. I should have opened the portal during their stupid Ceremony of the Bedchamber. Dumped Charrin on the heaps of blankets and linens and been done with it."

"And be barred from the Elven Royal Court for life, no doubt." Kalynn shook her head.

"Look at me," Wolfe waggled his bushy white eyebrows at her. "So devastated. So heartbroken. Crushed by the very idea."

Kalynn rolled her eyes. "Now that he's gone, we need to consider supplies. Have you checked the flying tack? It's been a while since we used those saddles. Although if we could portal—"

"First, come to the workroom," Wolfe took her hand and pulled her toward the stairs.

"Why?" Kalynn followed, knowing full well there was no use in protesting.

"Still no idea of where we need to go?" Wolfe asked.

"No," Kalynn sighed. "I've tried to focus, but—"

"Hard to do with an unwanted guest," Wolfe continued down the steps.

"Why is it?" Kalynn smiled at the back of his head as she dodged the clutter along the stairs. "Why is it that the stairs are crowded with your books and collections, but your workroom is—"

"Hush," Wolfe opened the door to his workroom, and sure enough the room was empty, without a trace of dust. Mage lights shown above them, glimmering on the stone walls, ceiling, and floor.

"Stand here," He pulled her into the center. "I have an idea."

He closed the door, then stood against it. She watched as he dimmed the mage lights with a slow stoke of his hand through the air. Wolfe had his eyes closed, his fingers spread out, and the hint of a smile on his lips. It warmed her heart to see him so. She loved these moments when he worked the power, his face so intent and serious, yet she could sense the joy within him.

"Watch," Wolfe said, and the floor beneath her feet glowed, and images formed. It was there, their world, all laid out on the floor. Continents, islands, oceans wide and sparkling.

"So many places we have yet to see," Wolfe said softly. "So many places we have yet to go."

"What are you—" she asked, but Wolfe shook his head and the pictures at her feet changed, and grew. Tiny horses raced beneath her feet, through tall grass.

"The Plains," she breathed. And the images around her solidified, of rolling open grasslands. The images tilted slightly, and then grew.

Kalynn sucked in her breath, pressing her hand to her chest. She was standing on the Heart of the Plains.

All around her, the grasses stirred in a breeze she could not feel. They were browning slightly, under the heat of a summer sun she could not feel. Beyond, toward the south, she saw the lake, the waves lapping at the rocky shore. Yet for all the lack of her senses, her heart soared at the sight of home.

"Wolfe," she whispered, not wanting to break the spell. "Have you sent my spirit wandering?"

"No," his voice was soft. "I brought the spirit of the lands to you." Part of her knew that he was standing by the door, but to her it appeared he stood just off the edge of the Heart.

Her tears welled at the sight, with grief and joy and a deep longing. Kalynn tore her gaze away, looking toward Wolfe.

"I know," Wolfe's eyes were warm, his voice was the barest whisper. "But we need answers."

Kalynn nodded, not trusting her voice at that moment.

"Power first," Wolfe said, raising his hand. "Show me," he commanded.

Over the grasslands small bits of light appeared, some dim, some strong, scattered in no particular pattern around the Heart.

"So few," he said. "There's little power left on the Plains, and even less between the Heart and Xy. Not enough to trust to portals. We will take airions."

Kalynn studied the Heart below her feet. No life, no magic pulsed under her feet; the Heart was cold and silent. She'd known that would be the case, but she hadn't been prepared for the reality.

"Flying will be hard on both of us." Wolfe continued. "Been a long time since I have spent much time in the saddle. We could use portals, cut off some travel time, if we—"

Kalynn cut him off, "I'm looking south."

"Well, yes," Wolfe cleared his throat. "But, beloved—"

She ignored the warning tone in his voice, and looked over her shoulder, due north.

"Xy," she said.

There, bright against the mountain at the high end of the valley glowed a blue spark, bright and clear and blue as the morning sky.

"Kalynn," Wolfe warned again. "She will not welcome us."

"She needs to know," Kalynn said firmly. "We need to warn her of what is to come."

"What might come," Wolfe said firmly, his voice pulling her back to look at him. "We can argue the point later. First, we need to find out 'where'. How's about you point out where we must do what must be done."

"Show me the Tribes," Kalynn said.

"It's the Season of War," Wolfe said. "There are scattered thea camps but the armies raid."

The Heart fell away, and shrank. She could see all of the Plains, and the mountains that surrounded them. Below her feet, tiny herds of horses ran, with tiny birds flying overhead.

All around, on the edges, she could see armies attacking, the glow of fire and war. She drew in a breath, let it out slowly, and let her eyes drift close. There was a tug, the faintest of pulls against her heart.

"Where, love?" Wolfe prompted.

"Hush," Kalynn took a step forward, concentrating. "It's like following the faint scent of perfume to find a person in a crowd." She took another step, and moved, slowly following the trace of possibilities through the stream of potentials.

"Here," she said finally. "Here." She swayed as visions came, of an army approaching, raiding and looting. Children taken, foodstuffs seized, and men and women killed. "Oh Wolfe, it's—" She drew in a ragged breath and pressed her hands to her chest. "So much hate, so much destruction. The fire, the death… it's—" Her breath came in harsh gasps.

She felt his warmth as he stepped to her side, his strong hands on her shoulders. "Come back, Kalynn. Come back to me."

Her eyes snapped open, and she returned, back to the room and the map and her love. She sagged, trembling and Wolfe wrapped her in his arms. "Wolfe," she wept. "Will it never change?"

"We'll go," he tightened his arms around her. He looked down at a town on the border with the Plains. "How much time do we have?"

"Weeks," she said. Between their feet a Warlord's army advanced, raiding as they went.

Wolfe nodded, and the map faded away as the mage lights brightened above them. "Best we be about it, then."

"We have to do this," she clung to him, looking for reassurance.

"We'll try." Wolfe promised. "We'll leave as soon as we can."

"We should tell Verice." Kalynn leaned against Wolfe as he helped her to the door. "I want to check on Warna."

"That's fine." Wolfe said, and then she felt the vibration of a chuckle in his chest. She looked up to see his eyebrows dance, his eyes gleaming. "Verice can look after the cat."

CHAPTER EIGHTEEN

Constable Ricard was seeing to inspections when he saw the Lady Warna emerge from the barracks.

The lads were lined up in the courtyard at attention as he marched between the rows, expressing his opinion at their slovenly state at the top of his lungs. Fine way to start the morning, to his way of thinking. A solid breakfast, a strong mug of kav, and a good stint of admonishments, criticism and assigning punishment details for the worst offenders.

Aye, a good morning.

At least until Lady Warna appeared.

She stood in the morning sunlight, blinking at the brightness, her golden hair aglow in the sun. She'd fixed it in a bun, and there was an air of determination about her. Standing there in her tunic and trous, she looked like a woman with a plan for the day.

"Morning, m'lady," he said. "Is there anything you might be needing?"

"Good morning, Constable," She smiled. "That's the healing hall, isn't it? With the red door?" She nodded off to the building next to the barracks.

"Aye, m'lady." Ricard replied.

"I'm going to need buckets, soap, and hot water." With that, she went right to the door of the healing hall, opened the door, and walked in.

The constable blinked.

There was a rustle of amusement from the ranks, and he turned on them with a glare. They all stiffened again, and he opened his mouth to roar when *slam.* The shuttered window on the first floor opened. Lady Warna could be clearly seen, and she gave him a wave, then disappeared.

That brought a few chuckles, and Ricard turned back, putting forth his best bellow. "Seeing as you've so much energy, forward march!"

The men headed off, marching in step, keeping the spacing between them, to make the round about the keep.

Slam. Another window opened. The sergeant glared up, to see the lady now leaning out of a second-floor window. The Healing Hall had been one of those sealed up. Lord Verice had left no orders about this, not to his knowledge. He opened his mouth to call to her, and then closed it.

He'd no orders about this, but then Lady Warna wasn't under his command, now was she? Her and the Lord might have had discussions he'd not been privy too, might'n they? And he'd no reason to think to the contrary, now had he? And this needed doing, now didn't it?

He was still considering that when the top-most window opened, and Lady Warna poked her head out. "There's a tiny room up here, perfect for me," she called down. "Buckets, soap, and plenty of hot water, Constable."

A woman with a plan, it would appear. In an instant, Ricard reviewed all his options, and made the best, safest choice.

"Aye, lady," he called up. "And a few on punishment detail to aid you in the work."

* * * * *

It was a lovely room, to Warna's delight. Not huge, like the one in the mage tower, but a nice bed, with a small table and chair. Even better, a press for clothes and a small cupboard off to the side. A woven rag rug covered the wooden floor. The stone walls were cool, and the air was chill and musty. There was a thick layer of dust and a lace of cobwebs in every corner.

Well, soonest started, soonest done. With the window open there was a bit of a breeze. In a great cloud of dust, Warna stripped the bed. She bundled up the bedding, gathered up the rug, and threw the lot of them down the stairwell.

She clattered down the stairs behind, and started poking in cupboards and storage areas, looking for soap and rags. It seemed this place had been stripped bare of personal items and healing supplies before being closed up, but she found a few rags and some wood polish in one of the cupboards just as the clomp of boots came through the door.

It was two of the constable's men, each with a bucket of warm water and carrying brooms and dust pans, soap, and a basket of rags.

"Excellent." Warna smiled, a feeling of satisfaction rising in her chest. "Let's get to work."

* * * * *

The shadows were long when Verice finally returned with his men, having been gone longer than he had planned. The attack had been more than a raid, of that he was certain. The local commander was a good man, but Verice feared the Usurper was testing the border, looking for a weak spot. And if a weakness was found, no doubt a bolder thrust would follow. He shook his head. He'd need more scouts in that area.

But as he swung out of the saddle, all he really cared for was a meal and sleep. He was short on both. It had been a long two days since he'd taken Warna to Bode's tower.

He'd have to make arrangements for Warna, or find another place to sleep himself. She'd been in the back of his mind the entire time, as he'd tried to determine what was best for her. So far, he'd not made a decision, and that irritated him to no end.

Constable Ricard came toward him and made a quick salute. "All's well, m'lord."

"Thanks be for that." Verice stretched. "All I ask is for a chance at a meal and a bed. Do you know if Warna has eaten?"

"As to that, m'lord, she's not even taken a nooning that I am aware of. She's one for work, make no mistake." There was an odd note of respect in the constable's voice. "Her standards are higher than mine, when it comes to what's proper."

"What's proper?" For his life, Verice couldn't figure out what the man meant. "What has she been doing?" The horses around him shifted as they were led off to the stables, and he caught a glimpse of a bundle of laundry in front of the Healing Hall.

"Cleaning, m'lord," the Constable said matter-of-factly. "Right proper job, too. The lads on punishment detail are none too happy they picked this time to err in their ways, I have to say. Did my heart good to see them poor sods beating out the mattresses."

"Cleaning?" Verice blurted out, staring at the Healing Hall just in time to see a hand emerge from a lower window and shake out a dust cloth.

"What cleaning?"

"Perhaps that's a discussion you might have with M'lady. She's within," Ricard added, nodding toward the building. "Let me see to the meal for these men, and I'll tell the cooks to send yours up to your chambers, once you've convinced her to stop her work, that is." And he was gone.

Verice frowned. He'd given no orders to open the Healing Hall, of that he was certain.

The door was open, and he stepped within. The room was thick with dust, except the stairs and the tracks leading up.

He mounted the steps two at a time, to find a hallway that smelled of soap and water and two of the younger warriors scrubbing the floors with big brushes and resigned expressions. The one lad was tired enough that he looked at Verice without recognizing him for a moment before his eyes went wide.

"M'Lord!" They both sprang to their feet, and stood at attention.

"At ease," Verice said. "Where is Warna?"

"Above, m'lord." One of the lads gestured above.

"My thanks," Verice hesitated on the steps. "Best return to your duties, lads."

They both heaved sighs as he continued up the stairs.

Many doors led off the upper hallway. Verice didn't need to search each one, he could hear her singing toward the back. She sounded so joyful. Charrin's harsh words hadn't spoiled that for her then. That pleased him.

She didn't look up when he entered, so he leaned on the doorjamb watching her polishing the mantel of a small fireplace. A glance told him this room was done, with the smell of drying wood and polish mingling together.

"Warna?"

She turned then, startled, but clearly happy. "M'lord, you're back. Is it mid-afternoon already, then?"

"More like mid-night than mid-morning," Verice said.

Surprised, she glanced behind him to the hallway windows. "Oh, Lord of Light, I lost track of time. And I've kept these poor lads at it all day," Warna shook her head, and moved forward. "I need to set them free. We can finish tomorrow."

Verice moved to block Warna with his body, and she gave him a startled glance, her brown eyes wide and clear. "I gave no order that this building be cleared," he said softly.

The barest blush crossed her cheeks as she lowered her gaze. "M'lord, I thought—"

Her stomach rumbled.

"You owe me an explanation," Verice said firmly. "Over our meal."

"Of course, m'lord." Warna's blonde head was still down, her hands twisting the rag between her fingers.

He held his position for a moment more, until she looked up, her guilt quite clear in her eyes. He moved then, giving her just enough space to slide past him and down the stairs.

CHAPTER NINETEEN

Warna waited nervously in Verice's outer room as he cleaned up in his quarters. The serving boys had already rushed in with plates, kav, and covered dishes. They'd set the table and vanished as quickly as they'd come.

She could hear him in the other room, moving around, water splashing as he washed.

What had seemed like a wonderful idea this morning was feeling not-so-clever now. She'd changed quickly, putting on her only dress for this meal. She smoothed the skirts down as she stood by her chair. The dogs were sprawled all around the room, and seemed to sense her nervousness. The sandy-colored one even came over and leaned against her, looking up with big brown eyes, as if it understood her fears.

Of course, it might have been more a desire to be petted than expression of sympathy; Warna chuckled at the thought, and started scratching its ears.

Verice emerged from the back, in a loose white tunic and his leather trous. His hair fell free, flowing down his back, slightly damp at the temples from his quick wash. He gestured to the table, and Warna sat, bracing herself for his anger.

But Verice just uncovered a bowl of rabbit stew, thick with vegetables, and gestured for her bowl. She handed it to him and reached to unwrap the warm bread, tearing off chunks for both of them.

Verice served her and then himself, and started eating immediately. Warna didn't waste any time starting on her own bowl. The stew smelled wonderful, and she hadn't eaten at the midday meal.

Verice passed a crock of soft cheese, and they ate in silence.

He filled a second bowl for himself. "More?" he asked.

"No, thank you." Warna was still working on her first. "Bread?"

"Yes, thank you." Verice accepted the basket, and tore off another hunk. "Why did you take it upon yourself to clean the Healing Hall?"

Warna stopped eating, and used her napkin. Verice didn't seem upset; his face was set and controlled. There was no hint of emotion there. But there'd been none at Wolfe's either. "It needed doing," she said quietly. "I didn't know the details of the attack, but what would happen if there were wounded that needed tending here? The place was in no state fit for ill or injured warriors, that was certain. And this building is overflowing with the healthy already." Warna raised her chin. "Besides, I needed a place to sleep. The poor sergeant couldn't keep shifting men around to suit my needs."

* * * * *

The worst of it was that she was right.

He should be furious, because even if she wasn't aware, his men knew full well that he'd shut down the castle for security reasons. But—

"In the past, the worst hurt were brought here to my healers. They were the best." Verice admitted, more to himself than to Warna.

"They were Elven?" Warna asked.

Verice snorted. "Elven healers do not concern themselves with human or half-elven anatomy, Warna. They tend to focus on magical healing, and rarely deign to touch a human. No, our healers were half-elven for the most part, from around the barony."

"Where are they now?" Warna asked.

"Most are scattered along the border," Verice said. "Three are housed in the town, in case of need here. They are but a short ride away." He winced a little. That sounded foolish, even to his ears.

"The building sleeps a good many," Warna said.

"Some of the rooms were meant for the ill and injured," Verice said.

"There may be wounded that need tending here at the keep," Warna said. "Best to have the place ready, in case of need. There's a lovely small room at the very top, and I can sleep there."

"I'd thought to send you away, again," Verice said. "Somewhere safe."

Warna dropped her eyes, but he caught the flash of resistance. "Where were the attacks yesterday?" Warna asked.

Verice sighed, and pushed his bowl away. "To the south, along the border with Edenrich. We suspect the Usurper is probing, looking for a weakness." He poured himself some more kav. "We are spread too thin as it is."

* * * * *

Warna nodded as Verice talked in detail of troop placements, and the difficulties of protecting a large border. Most of it went over her head, the names and places unfamiliar to her. But his concerns, his fears for his people came through clearly. He seemed to take comfort in talking, as if it helped him see the situation in his mind's eye.

Finally, he stopped, clearly frustrated, and took a sip of kav. Warna took a breath, and spoke quickly, almost afraid of his response.

"Lord Verice, it strikes me that there is nowhere as safe as here."

His eyes were tired and his pain clear. "It hasn't been, in the past." He stared into his mug. "I think it best that I send you somewhere else. To start your life, Warna."

"That's the problem," Warna said, ignoring her fear. "I don't know what I want yet." She hesitated, surprised she was confiding this to him, but wanting him to understand. "It's all too new, too unsettling. Cleaning though…" she laughed wryly. "Cleaning is something I am all too comfortable with. It keeps my hands busy. Lets me think."

"New songs, perhaps?" Verice said.

"Or finish the ones I've started." Warna smiled, but she let it fade as she grew serious. "I need time, m'lord. Time to think."

Verice stared into his kav, but then he slowly ran his fingers through his hair. "I'm not convinced it's all that safe, but I admit that I don't have an alternative. At least until the Healing Hall is clean."

"I'll see it done," Warna assured him as she reached for more bread. "And I can see it stocked, if you wish. Best there are supplies in place before a need."

* * * * *

He didn't want this.

The kav turned bitter in his mouth, and heavy in his stomach. He knew where this was going. Common sense and simple logic cried out for both castle and keep to be restored.

His heart cried out against it.

He closed his eyes, wanting to hold it all back, stop time and space, make no changes. The lump of pain in his chest grew until he didn't know how his heart had room to beat anymore.

The dogs stirred; Brindle got up and nudged his arm with his nose. Warna was silent, spreading cheese on her bread, her head down, giving him what privacy she could.

In his pain, the mental image of Charrin raging out his grief flashed before his eyes, and Verice felt a flash of sympathy for the elf. How did one ever deal with such anguish?

He opened his mouth, wanting to deny Warna, wanting to order her to stop, order her to lock the Healing Hall back up, order her to leave—

No. He didn't want that.

"Not the keep, Warna." He managed to strangle out the words. "Not the keep."

She lifted her gaze, and her brown eyes were warm, and understanding. "I promise, Verice."

He held her gaze, and knew without knowing quite how, that he could trust her.

A blush rose on her cheeks, and she glanced at the dog beside him, its head just above the table. "M'lord, perhaps you'd introduce us? I still don't know their names."

CHAPTER TWENTY

The next morning Captain Narthing was tightening the girth on his saddle when the Constable Ricard sidled up to him, and muttered something out of the corner of his mouth.

"Eh?" Narthing gave the men around them a glance. They were all preparing to mount. Lord Verice had returned to his normal routine. The day before had been a nice change of pace, but they were back to it this morning.

"My orders have changed," Ricard said again.

Narthing straightened, and gave the man a puzzled look. "Verice changed your orders?"

"Aye," Ricard said.

"Really?" Narthing glanced at his Lord, who was checking his own gear.

"I've said, haven't I?" Ricard replied, his face straight.

Narthing rolled his eyes over to him. "You're enjoying this," he said.

"First change in how many months?" Ricard's mouth quirked.

"And the change?" Narthing demanded.

A stir in the men drew his attention away from Ricard. The Lady Warna was weaving her way through the horses and men. She came right up to both of them, and gave them a warm smile. "Good morning, gentlemen."

"Morning," they both responded. Narthing found himself returning her smile, feeling his spirits lift.

"Ricard, I'm going to finish cleaning the Healing Hall today, and I'll be sleeping there from now on. Would you have someone carry over my basket?" Warna said. "It's in my room, ready to go. You can reassign that space as soon as you wish."

Narthing blinked.

"As you wish, m'lady," Ricard replied. "I've four lads who need to be shown the error of their ways. I'd thought to have them flush the privies, but if you've a need…"

"That would be lovely," Warna said. "Many hands make light work." She gave Narthing a nod. "Travel safe, Captain."

"My thanks," Narthing said, but Warna was already moving, seeking out Verice. The Lord exchanged a few words with her, and then she headed toward the Healing Hall. Verice turned back to his horse, a calm expression on his face.

"Ancestors," Narthing swore. "What's—"

Ricard nudged his elbow. "My orders," he said.

"What?" Narthing asked.

"You asked about my orders," Ricard's smile was a broad one.

"Yes," Narthing narrowed his eyes. "What did Lord Verice say?"

Ricard chuckled. "*Let the Lady Warna have her way.*"

* * * * *

Warna was surprised at the amount of comfort she took from her task.

She'd feared that the mindlessness of the work would force her to think about things that she wasn't ready to confront. But the regular swish of a broom on the wood floor and the slap of a soapy cloth on a dusty surface were sounds she could lose herself in. There was no past, no present; there was simply dust and dirt, and it all had to be dealt with.

It was soothing, to worry about dirt her 'assistants' had missed, or to scan the ceilings and corners for cobwebs. Maybe the peace she found in doing these things was a false one, but it was still a peace.

The Healing Hall was finished by early afternoon. She'd released the lads assigned to her, and they'd escaped quickly. But not before the constable grabbed them, and had them carry her lidded-basket and bedding to the top-most bedroom. As tired as she was, Warna still wanted to make the room as comfortable as she could before she sought her supper.

Not that there was much to arrange. The clothing the supply clerk had provided were all tunics and trous, worn and soft, perfect for cleaning. Warna had to sigh over the state of her skirt and blouse. The hems were all worn, and they were almost grayed out of any color they once had. She'd have turned them both into rags, but they were the only womanly clothes she owned at the present.

She had a comb from the supply clerk as well, along with a bit of soap and towels. Yet there were other things that an army clerk probably couldn't provide. She paused as she put the folded clothes into the press, counting the days. There was time yet, but she couldn't wait too much longer. Although the idea of outright asking the clerk for moon pads made her blush.

She shook out the sheets and blankets and made up the bed quickly, smoothing out the pillow and giving it a pat. This would be better than the barracks, by far.

For an instant as she stood in the clean, small room, however, her heart returned to home. To her old room, scattered about with pillows, the smell of bread baking in the kitchens below, and her brothers' laughter coming through the window as her father called them to task. Grief caught her unaware, and was all the more powerful because of it. Tears welled, threatening to spill, as she stood in that strange, silent, empty room.

"Warna?" Verice called from below, his footsteps echoing as he mounted the stairs, his voice loud and slightly annoyed.

* * * * *

Verice had thought that Warna would be waiting for him, so that they could eat together. He took the steps two at a time as he called out to her. "Warna?"

He stopped, caught by the look on Warna's face. She looked so sad, so… bereft. Standing there, her clothes stained and damp, her hair bound up with strips of rag. Suddenly, all he wanted was to ease her sorrow. Replace that pain with a smile.

He glanced around the room. "Settling in?" he asked.

Warna looked away. He could tell she was wiping her eyes. He hesitated, not sure what comfort to offer, then his gaze fell on the bed.

"You know, if you were the Queen of Valltera, it would take thirty handmaidens and half the morning to make your bed."

Warna turned then, staring at him with reddened eyes. "Really?"

"Oh yes," Verice said. "Each of the twenty has their own task. It's considered a high honor to plump the pillows, place them on the bed, and smooth them to perfection."

Warna sniffled, then laughed weakly. "You're teasing me."

"As I stand before my Ancestors," Verice placed his hand over his heart. "I'll tell you about it over dinner. There's chicken and mushroom pie tonight." He paused. "If you'd join me."

To his relief, Warna's face cleared. "Just let me wash up, and I'll be right there."

CHAPTER TWENTY-ONE

Verice stood by his chair, and patiently waited.

The table was set. The food was still covered, but the smell of hot chicken pie filled the air. The dogs were all settled around him, curled in their normal positions. Brindle sat by Verice's side.

Normally he'd be impatient, waiting like this. But he was feeling something entirely different.

Anticipation.

It struck him that he'd not looked forward to anything in some time. The last few months had all been taken with the care of his lands, the safety of his people...

It felt odd that it felt odd. That he wanted to share the story of the formal rituals of Valltera. That he was going to share a meal with Warna again, someone who wasn't concerned with troop placements, or scouting reports. He'd not done this with anyone else, and certainly not since... the guilt rose from his gut and kicked him hard, remembering those who had died. Who would never share another meal, another laugh, and all his—

Brindle whined and pushed his head into Verice's fingers.

A soft knock, and Warna slipped into the room. Her eyes red-rimmed, she gave him a tentative smile, seeing his expression. "I took too long. Forgive me."

She was hurting; the sorrow was deep in her eyes. Maybe he could help her forget her pain, if only for a moment. It was something they shared, that grief.

"Not at all. They just brought our supper." Verice gestured her to her chair. "No, I was thinking on the Ceremony of the Bedchamber in Valltera." He paused for dramatic effect. "Thinking on it, I think it's more like thirty people required to make the King's bed."

"Now I know you are teasing me," Warna said. "What would they all do?"

"Well, first, the Warder of his Majesty's bedchamber summons the nobles—"

"Nobles?" Warna asked. "To make a bed?"

"A King's bed," Verice pointed out. "And the ritual is the same for the Queen, by the way. At any rate, they are all summoned to the outer room, where they line up in order of precedence." Verice shook his head at the memory. "They gather up the clean sheets, pillows, and blankets. Two carry in the fresh feather mattress—"

"A fresh mattress?" Warna's eyes went wide. "Every day?"

Verice offered her the gravy pitcher for her pie. "So, they file into the room in perfect order. The Four Lords of the Curtains each pull back one of the bed curtains, and hold it away from the bed for the entire ceremony.

"The four Lords of the Bed stand at its sides, their hands upon their sword hilts, as the bed is stripped down to the straw mattress. A nobly born esquire then leaps on to the bed and rolls around, checking that the straw has no weapons concealed therein to the King's harm."

"Lord of Light," Warna exclaimed. "Truly?" She gave a startled laugh as Verice nodded.

"The fresh feather mattress is then laid over the straw one, and fluffed." Verice poured kav for both of them as Warna cut into her pie. "And then begins the placement of the sheets and the blankets, each sheet then being spread out and smoothed, because they dare not leave a single wrinkle to offend the King's body."

Warna shook her head. "They all stand around while this is done?"

"With somber stares, for their presence is an honor, and a right by virtue of their blood," Verice said. "Woe betide any that hold the wrong curtain or fluff the wrong pillow. So, to finish my tale…"

Warna laughed. "There's more?"

"Of course," Verice said. "Once the pillows are in place, the bed curtains are closed and the bed is sprinkled with scented water, and blessed by one in service to the Ancestors, then the entire lot troops back to the outer chamber and are served wine. This happens each and every night, even if the King is not in residence."

Warna shook her head. "What a waste. Their time could be better spent, I think."

"So did I, in my youth." Verice grimaced. "I'm afraid that if I hadn't left the Court of Valltera, I'd have been banished before long."

"You were a trouble-maker?" Warna asked.

"Let's just say I was an impetuous youth, who chafed against every rule, every restriction." Verice said. "If it weren't for my weaponsmaster, I'd have certainly been sent away in disgrace."

Warna tilted her head. "How so?"

"He sat me down after a practice, and told me that being at Court was like fighting a bout. 'Three basic rules, lad. Speak only in response. Answer, but never ask. And never make the first move.'"

Warna shook her head again, mopping up the last of her gravy with bread. "That worked?"

"Yes," Verice said wryly. "After that, I knew well exactly why I was in trouble."

Warna choked on her bread, laughing and sputtering as she reached for ale.

Satisfied, Verice set about finishing his own few bites.

* * * * *

Once she got her throat clear, Warna sat quietly as Verice finished his meal. The silence was a comfortable one. She had so many questions, but each one had the potential to raise the past in a way that might hurt Verice. It made her feel awkward and rude, and suddenly the weaponsmaster's advice made perfect sense.

The efforts of the day were starting to catch up to her, and she was looking forward to crawling into her new bed. She glanced around at the crowded room, the chests lining the walls, and the weapons hanging there. There was a pile of papers that had been cleared off the table, and next to them, the petitions that Verice had taken in town.

Verice caught her glance and grimaced. "I haven't gotten to those yet, and I should.

The petitioners will be expecting a response in a day or so."

"What do people petition for?" Warna asked.

"Various reasons," Verice said. "To complain of an official without drawing his ire or ask pardon for a loved one. Sometimes they wish for money, or aid." Verice pushed his plate back. "I normally have a scribe deal with them, but..."

"What would the scribe do with them?" Warna asked.

"Sort through them and investigate." Verice said.

"You must still have people working in that regard," Warna said hesitantly. "Just not here."

"Yes," Verice said slowly.

"Send them to him, then," Warna said. "Or send for him."

Verice went silent, studying the table in front of him. It went on for so long that Warna thought she had offended, but then he nodded. "I will," he said. "My thanks, Warna."

Warna gave him a smile, that turned into a yawn.

"You're tired." Verice stood, and all the dogs rose with him. "I'll walk you to your new chambers."

CHAPTER TWENTY-TWO

The night air was cool as they walked the few steps to the Healing Hall. The dogs paced beside them quietly.

Warna opened the main door, and stepped within to utter darkness. She paused as Verice came in behind her. "Just a moment, I'll strike a—"

Verice whispered a soft word under his breath and every candle in the room flared to life.

Warna gasped in utter delight. "Lord and Lady," she breathed. "I tend to forget you can do that."

Verice raised his eyebrows. Standing in the center of the rug, he seemed to pull all the light to him, tall and commanding. The dogs had piled in with him, and were sniffing everything in sight.

"My thanks, m'lord," Warna said.

"For lighting your candles?" Verice asked.

"For the meal," Warna answered simply. "For the work, the shelter, the… haven."

"You'll be comfortable here?" Verice peered up the dark stairs. "Alone?"

"I'll be fine," Warna took up one of the small lanterns. The candle within flickered and flamed.

"Wait," Verice moved closer, reaching for the lantern's door.

Warna held it higher, suddenly conscious of Verice's warmth as he leaned down and removed the candle. His scent tickled her nose, his silver hair brushing her arm like silk. Part of her wanted to step back, to seek her own space. Part of her wanted something more. Something exciting, and terrifying at the same—

"Let's make this a bit safer." Verice held out his hand, and started to chant quietly. A small swirl of light started to coalesce in the center of his palm. Sparkling strands of light wrapped themselves in a tiny ball.

Warna caught her breath, afraid to breathe for fear of destroying it.

Verice chuckled. "It's not fragile." He placed it inside the lantern and worked the shutter, dimming and brightening the light. "You see?"

"Will it fade?" Warna asked, admiring the golden glow.

"Eventually," Verice said. "All things do."

Warna glanced at his face then, saw the weariness in his eyes. "You're tired," she murmured. She lowered the lantern, and eased back from his warmth. "Thank you for the escort, m'lord."

Verice frowned slightly. "Sand, Gray," he waited for the dogs to turn their heads, then nodded toward her. "Guard."

"That's not necessary," Warna protested as the dogs heaved themselves up and walked toward her.

"For company, if nothing else," Verice said firmly.

"Thank you." Warna took the lantern, and started up the steps, the dogs following. It felt wrong. She hesitated, glancing back, not really wanting to leave. No, not really wanting to leave… him.

She caught him off guard. For the barest of moments, she saw a flash of heat in his eyes, gone so quickly she must have imagined it.

Verice bowed to her. "Sleep well," and then he was gone, the other dogs with him, the door pulled quietly closed behind him, the latch catching with a click.

* * * * *

His desire caught Verice off guard.

She paused on the stairs, the lantern in one hand, the other on the railing, half-turned in the light to look back at him. The gold of her hair gleamed and her skin glowed.

His body reacted, but he denied it in an instant, stifling the impulse to follow her up the stairs. There must have been something in his face, since her blue eyes went wide, startled but unafraid.

He bowed, hiding his eyes. "Sleep well," and slipped through the door as quickly as he could. He stood there, catching his breath, listening to her fading footsteps. He waited until he heard her above, then he left, cursing himself for a fool.

* * * * *

Warna shifted, restless under her blankets.

The room was cool and dark. Both dogs were sprawled on the rug next to the bed, giving the occasional soft snort.

The little lantern sat at her bedside. She'd left the shutter open slightly, and the dim light was just enough for her to see by.

The bed was comfortable, the blankets warm. She wasn't hungry, frightened, or hiding in a ditch. She just couldn't sleep.

And when she closed her eyes, all she saw was Verice.

She shifted on to her back, and huffed out a breath as she stared at the timbers over her head. She'd imagined it, of course. Verice was a Lord High Baron, so far above her station as to be... not to mention being an elven lord. What was she thinking?

Warna huffed again. Well, pretty clearly, she wasn't thinking, at least not with her brain.

Her mother had warned her that the spirit might be wary and careful, but the body had its own ideas sometimes. "Nothing wrong with looking," she'd said. "just don't act on those thoughts."

"Your life is your own, Warna." Kalynn's voice floated through her mind.

Warna caught her breath.

Then she snorted at her foolishness, shifted on to her side, and thumped her pillow into shape. One of the dogs started and raised its head to look at her. Finding nothing amiss, it yawned and returned to sleep.

Warna hugged her pillow. She was reading too much into a glance. Verice had been kind, had extended his protections to her, given her food and shelter and work. Nothing more than that, and she would not interpret his kindness as some sort of interest. She owed him more than that disrespect.

Lord High Baron Verice was a man caught in his sorrow and grief. The fact that he was reaching out to her; was letting her take actions he himself couldn't bring himself to take, was a matter of trust. Spoken or unspoken, she'd not take advantage of him.

She closed her eyes firmly, and tried to avoid thinking about elven eyes that burned silver-blue. She thought about dust, and soap, and stocking the shelves and cupboards of the healer's house.

But her last conscious thought was how terrible it would be... if the one thing she wanted was the one thing she couldn't have.

CHAPTER TWENTY-THREE

In the morning, Warna delayed going down to breakfast until the dogs were whining at the door, staring at her over their shoulders. "Sorry, boys," she whispered as she opened the latch.

Verice and his men had already departed the castle, which had been her intent. Still, she felt oddly disappointed as she slipped into the dining area and managed to snag a bowl of porridge and a mug of kav. The cooks had scraps waiting for the dogs.

"Aye, he's off," one of the cooks told her. "Said he'd be later this night getting back."

Warna shrugged her agreement, but couldn't help worrying that he might run into fighting on his travels. Still, his absence suited her plans. Warna drained her mug with thanks, and headed for the QuarterMaster's offices. Outside were three carts, filled with casks and duns of ale and beer.

Inside, was complete chaos.

"I tell you, the account is overdue." A rather large man of decidedly more girth than height filled the small area in front of the high counters. He carried with him the scent of yeast and hops. His face was set and he was clearly determined to be heard. "I'll have it paid this day, or know why."

"And I'm telling you, it's been paid." Quartermaster Farnor snapped. "But we can't find the reckoning. If you'll have a bit a patience—"

"That's what ya said the last time and the time afore." The man rumbled. "I've no mind to run a credit until you're—"

Warna slipped in and pulled the door closed behind her.

The big man turned and frowned. "Who's this, then?"

"M'lady," Farnor started, but Warna forestalled him.

"I'm Warna of Farentell." She smiled at the man. "Are you the brewer of that fine ale we've been drinking?"

The man blinked in surprise. "Aye, aye, although I'd naught know'ed the army was taking women into its ranks."

"It's not, Pierson, you daft fool," Farnor snapped. "The lady is here under the Lord's protection."

"The same as what rode through town with him the other day?" Pierson was giving Warna the once over, and she couldn't help but notice his eyes flick to her ears. "Well, then, pleased ta meet ya, lady."

"The same," Warna responded. "I take it there's trouble with the accounts?"

Both men erupted back into their argument, each talking over the other. Warna saw the younger clerk scurrying in the background, searching for something.

She raised a hand, and both men went quiet. "Pay him half," Warna said. "Eh?"

"You're been dealing with each other for years, yes?" Warna raised an eyebrow at both of them. "Neither of you is cheating the other, it's just a matter of resolving the accounts. Pay him half of what he asks, then settle the matter when the books have been located." She waited patiently as they thought that through. "Or waste more time yelling at one another," she added.

Both men looked at each other, then Pierson huffed out an explosive breath. "Aye, that's well. If you think so, Farnor."

"I'll find the accounting by your next delivery," Farnor agreed. There was a swift exchange of coin, and Pierson was on his way.

"My thanks, m'lady," Farnor said with a sigh. "This mess is enough to drive me into my cups. Wasn't this way before."

"Where were your old offices?" Warna asked.

"Second barracks," he said. "Right across the way. A place for everything and room to work," he said. "Not that his Lordship's not within his rights. But…" His voice trailed off.

"But just the same, it causes chaos, doesn't it?" Warna shook her head.

They shared sympathetic looks, then Farnor squinted at her. "So how can I assist you?" he asked.

"I want to order supplies for the Healing Hall," Warna said. "We need to make sure that it's supplied in case of need."

"Well, we never kept that stocked." The clerk frowned. "The Seneschal took care of that aspect. I've lists of the supplies the units carry on the field but that's not what you are looking for."

"Is the Seneschal in town?" Warna asked.

Farnor shook his head sadly. "No, lady. He was slain—" his eyes shifted in the direction of the keep.

"Oh," Warna said. That was right, and it explained quite a bit to her, especially about Verice... Lord Verice's actions. "Well, who else would know?" Warna asked.

"Priest Dominic," Farnor said. "He's the head of the Church, and assigned himself to run the Hall. He's in town now, far as I know."

Warna nodded, thinking. "What about Lord Verice's staff. His clerks—"

"All in town," Farnor said. "The lord shut the castle down, but work of the barony still goes on as best it can."

"So, they are still working with Lord Verice?"

"Oh, aye, Lady. More 'in spite' of than 'with', but aye. The Lord kept them all on, but won't allow them within the walls." He shrugged. "Lord Verice doesn't give the work the proper attention it—" He stopped when he saw her frown. "No disrespect intended, m'lady. Lord Verice is a warrior, and he's seeing to that right well."

"But there are other aspects to ruling," Warna said quietly. "Things that involve paper and ink, and not quite the level of excitement."

Once again, they exchanged understanding looks.

Warna made her decision. "Very well then, I am going to go into town. I will talk to them, and see what needs doing." She hesitated, but then went on. "I also need a few supplies. Would it be possible to get a few coins..." It was her turn to let her voice trail off, trying not to show her embarrassment.

"Oh, aye," Farnor chuckled. "Lord Verice left instructions." He busied himself for a moment, then plunked down a bulging coin purse on the counter.

Warna opened the bag, and gold coins spilled out into her hand. She caught her breath, then shook her head. "No. I am not taking this much,"

"Lady?"

"Silvers and coppers," she said firmly, pushing the bag back. "And not nearly this much."

"But—"

The argument was fairly short, and didn't last long. There was no way she was carrying that much money around with her. She made sure that Farnor counted out the smaller coins, fully intending to account to him for every copper.

Although she might not mention moon pads specifically.

On her way out, she stopped and asked Ricard for a mount and a guide through town. Then she ran up the stairs to change into her skirts. She'd see the healer, talk to the clerk, and then see to her own needs. Maybe a few pieces of older clothing, or cloth and thread, although needles were dear.

She emerged into the courtyard, eager to go—

To find Ricard holding her mount, and an escort of twenty armed and armored men in a semi-circle around him.

CHAPTER TWENTY-FOUR

The twenty warriors were unnaturally still, their armor gleaming in the sunlight. Their horses too, stood without so much as a twitch of their tails.

"What's this?" Warna asked.

"Your escort," Constable Ricard replied. "Ustov knows the town well. He's in command."

Ustov saluted her.

"Did Verice order this?" Warna asked.

"I have no orders as such," Ricard replied.

"Oh, well, then—" Warna started to smile.

"But then I have no orders against it either," Ricard continued.

"Constable," Warna fixed a glare on him. "I'm not—"

"Let's take a moment and consider," Ricard said. "The town watch is under-manned, what with almost all able-bodied maels going to the borders to serve."

"Constable," Warna started.

"And the tide of refugees coming in, means that the town's awash in ruffians and ne'er-do-wells in the streets."

"This is silly," Warna said. "There's no need for—"

"What happens if harm comes to you?"

Warna snapped her mouth shut, and pressed her lips together.

"My Lord Verice would not be pleased, seeing as he entrusted your safety to me."

"But—"

"But more important," Ricard interrupted. "*Far* more important to my way of thinking, is what he's entrusted to you."

"What?" Warna snapped.

Ricard took a step closer to her, and lowered his voice. He stared right at her, his voice calm but emphatic. "For the past ten months, that lad has been afflicted, m'lady. Same routine, same narrow focus every day. You've got him moving. Slow, true enough. But moving. If ought happens to you, what then, eh?"

Warna opened her mouth, then closed it.

"Aye to that," Ricard stepped back and raised his voice. "This is a good start, but I've a mind to add a few more. A foot patrol, perhaps, with some stout crossbows."

"Why not a drum, to keep the beat?" Warna crossed her arms over her chest.

That provoked a twitch from one of the men.

"Not a bad idea, lady. Give me but a moment more—"

"Constable Ricard," Warna could not believe her ears.

"We'll have you fixed up and on your way—"

"Constable, I am not taking a small army to buy moon pads," Warna snapped.

Silence. Utter and complete silence.

Warna blushed furiously. From what she could tell, so did Ricard.

"Stand your men down," she threw her hands up in surrender. "If you can provide messengers…"

"Milo, front and center!" Ricard bellowed. One of the men dismounted and led his horse up to her.

"I've a message for the Priest Dominic, of the Church of the Lord of Light," Warna looked up at the man. "You know it?"

Milo nodded.

"My compliments to the Priest Dominic. I'd like his advice about re-stocking the Healers Hall with supplies. If he could provide a list of all the items required, I'll see it done." Warna said.

"Wait for an answer," Ricard commanded.

Milo nodded and mounted.

Ricard gestured to another man, who trotted his horse over.

Warna looked up. "There's a clerk, one Ersal, who used to aid Lord Verice with petitions. My compliments, and would he call at his convenience and collect some pending petitions that Verice needs assistance with? Tell him to ask for me at the gate."

"Off you go lads," Ricard commanded, and both started off toward the main gate. "The rest of you, return to your normal duties."

The men dismounted, leading their horses back to the stables, removing their helmets.

"As to the other matters, miss," Ricard lowered his voice. "I could talk to my wife, m'lady and..."

"Yes. That would be lovely," Warna figured the day couldn't get much worse than what it already was. "There's no rush," she added quickly, with visions of mounted messengers being sent out across the land.

She turned back toward the Healing Hall. She'd change, return the coins, and find something to clean within an inch of its life.

That thought made her pause at the door then spin on her heels. "Constable?"

"Yes, miss?" Ricard called from across the yard.

"Where is the Second Barracks?"

* * * * *

By mid-day, Warna felt better.

Not surprisingly, her escort of warriors all magically appeared to aid her in cleaning out the barracks. Their motivations were pretty clear, since they'd started discussing the reassignments of quarters before they were even done with the floors.

She, in turn, made it clear that the first ones to move in would be the supply clerks, and sent one lad running over to warn the Quartermaster to start packing for the move. "We need this all done this afternoon," she told the Ricard. "Before Lord Verice returns."

He didn't disagree.

She had to do more supervising than cleaning this time around, firmly explaining that splashing hot water and soap around did not really count as 'cleaning'. But the work got done as the day progressed and at a much faster pace than if she'd done it by herself.

The dogs lounged outside in the sun, occasionally raising their heads to watch the comings and goings. "You're getting fat, you lazy things," she said at one point as she went for more soap.

Brindle yawned, and rolled over to invite a belly scratch.

Warna shook her head, and leaned down to oblige. "We'll have to see about that," she told him.

By mid-day, the entire barracks was clean and done. Still damp from the scrubbing, but the windows were wide open to let it dry.

Warna stood in the clerk's office, looking at the various desks and shelves. She felt hot, tired. Her tunic and trous clung to her skin, damp and stained, and her stomach was telling her it was past time for a meal. But she still had a rush of pleasure in looking at the results of their efforts.

Most of the warriors had trailed out, carrying the last of the buckets and rags. Ricard ducked in the door and came up to her. Warna welcomed him with a grin.

"Can you get them all moved in this afternoon? Before Lord Verice returns?"

"Aye," Ricard seemed confident.

"Before he sees anything more than normal activity? Even the clerks?" Warna continued, giving one of the counters a final wipe. "It would be best if he didn't have a chance to object."

"Yes," Ricard said. "Lady Warna, you've had a response to your messengers."

"Really?" Warna asked, heading for the door. "Lovely, that will give me something to do after—"

"Wait," Ricard said, but she already had the door in mid-swing, stepping out into the sunlit courtyard.

Only to find a crowd of assorted men and women gathered about, staring at her. The dogs were up among the crowd, their tails slowly wagging.

At the very front was a tall elf, with long, straight black hair, a Priest of the Lord of Light.

He raised his head, glaring at her with pure disdain. "You are Warna of Farentell?" he demanded.

At her nod, his mouth twisted. "Just who in the darkest hells do you think you are?"

CHAPTER TWENTY-FIVE

The Constable stiffened. "Here now—" he started, but Warna held up a hand.

"Priest Dominic?" she asked.

The elf lifted his chin to regard her, his robes rustling as he gave her an imperious look.

Warna was sure he'd notice every stain on her trous, but she wasn't about to back down. "How kind of you to come so quickly." Sand and Gray came trotting out of the crowd to greet her. She reached out to stroke their heads, while making sure her expression was warm and welcoming. "And these others are...?"

A tall woman spoke up from the crowd. "We're Lord Verice's staff. We've come to—"

"We have come to learn just who you are and what is happening," Dominic snapped, raking Warna with a withering glance.

Brindle had also appeared, followed by the other dogs. Sand and Gray were leaning against Warna's legs. Brindle just sat, facing Dominic.

"Of course," Warna said. "We've just finished cleaning out this barracks. There's plenty of room within. Perhaps we could go in and talk?" She threw the rags onto the pile just outside the door. "Just give me a moment to clean up, will you?"

Dominic opened his mouth to protest.

"I'll see kav brought, m'lady." The Constable opened the door. "Priest Dominic?" He asked, gesturing for him to enter.

Dominic huffed, but he strode past Warna and into the building. Warna didn't wait for another protest. She just started forward, pushing past the dogs to walk through the crowd. She smiled at everyone, and headed for the Healing Hall.

She didn't let herself hurry until she was through the door and taking the steps three at a time to her room. A quick wash, fresh clothes, and she'd be ready. Her heart was racing and it wasn't just the steps. What if Lord Verice saw this crowd, and they demanded an explanation from him? There was a good chance that Verice would escort them to the gates and she wouldn't chance that.

She was headed down the stairs when the door below opened. The constable and the dogs were all pacing the main room.

"Dominic's the one in charge of the Healing Hall?" she asked breathlessly.

"Aye," The constable was peering out the window. "I've got them all settled and drinking kav. I don't think we want the Lord to see…" he cast a glance at Warna.

"I know," she said. "Who are the others?"

"All part of the Lord's household, before the castle was closed," he said as he followed her out the door and back across the courtyard. "The tall faelle is Janella, the Castle Chamberlain, and Ersal was the Master Clerk," he reached out to put a hand on her arm just as they reached the door of the barracks. "The thick man, with the beard is Roath, the Master Gardener. Warna, what will you tell them?"

She looked up at him and huffed out a nervous breath. "The truth, of course."

* * * * *

Priest Dominic was speaking as she opened the door, and his voice cut her like a knife.

"Why would he listen to her? She's a human woman," he said scathingly. "Who'd want to have anything to do with one of them?"

Warna stood in the doorway, frozen for a long moment, staring right at Dominic in the silence of the room. '*Lady of Laughter, make him regret those words someday,*' she thought, then dismissed it as she faced them all down, stepping forward to let the constable close the door.

"I am Warna of Farentell." She walked through the seated group, then took a chair facing them. "Let me explain how I came to be here."

She kept it short, talking of her 'rescue', and Lord Verice's extension of protection. "I want to work, is what I told him." She looked down at her hands, folded carefully in her lap. "I need to lose myself in a task, and while he's not given me permission, he's not prevented me, either."

The constable had moved behind her, to stand at her shoulder. She felt his quiet support, but so far, he'd remained silent.

"So, what is your intent, Warna?" Ersal spoke first.

"I've cleaned the Healing Hall, and this building," Warna said promptly. "I'll start on the Third Barracks next. By then, I'll find a need to restart the kitchens and the laundry."

"And everything else will flow therefrom," Janella said. "And the keep?"

"No," Warna said. "I made him a promise, that I would not touch it. I must keep my promise."

Janella nodded slowly. "It will work," she said looking at some of the others.

"This is ridiculous," Dominic stood, imposing in his fine robes of white and gold. His long black hair shimmered in the light, a stark contrast to the pale points of his ears.

'Every inch an elf,' Warna thought.

"*If,*" Dominic emphasized the word. "If it's as you say, then all we need do is go to Lord Verice and ask to be allowed to return."

"No," Warna looked up at him. "Do that, and you'll ruin any chance. The castle must come slowly alive around its Lord, and—"

"Lord Verice will come alive with it," Ersal said with a spark in his eye.

"Nonsense," Dominic scoffed. "We've only to ask—"

"We've asked over and over for the last few months," Janella pointed out. "We even had Lord Mayor Penard to ask on our behalf. Much good it's done us."

"Then we ask again," Dominic said. "He's clearly changed his mind. I'll—"

"You'll do no such thing," the constable said, startling all of them by breaking his silence.

"I'll not let you put him at risk," Warna added.

Dominic looked at her with narrowed eyes, then arched an eyebrow. "And for you, Lady? Perhaps you plan to warm his bed?" His lip curled. "Bring him back alive, so to say?"

"Dominic!" Janella gasped.

"Not that it's likely, given your blood," Dominic continued.

The constable growled.

"Constable," Warna said sharply.

He stopped, glaring at Dominic.

Warna kept her voice steady. "Priest Dominic, Lord Verice has offered me shelter and protection. If I can do this for him, it still will not be full recompense for his kindness."

"And if we don't go along with your plans?" Dominic demanded. "What would you do then?"

"I believe you are under orders from Lord Verice to remain within the town," Warna said. "I would ask the constable to enforce his orders."

"Who are you to speak so to us?" Dominic demanded.

"Who are you," Janella interrupted. "to claim to speak for all of us?"

Dominic huffed.

"She's right, and you know it," Ersal said. "We've not set foot within the castle since he ordered us out. This is the first bit of hope we've had since that day."

"Since that night," Janella whispered.

"You were there?" Warna asked. "When it happened?"

"Aye," Ersal rubbed his hand over his face. "We all were."

Warna threw a glance at the constable, but he shook his head. "Not me. I was in town, on leave."

"Would you tell me?" Warna leaned forward, looking at all of them. "What happened that night?"

CHAPTER TWENTY-SIX

Her request was met with bent heads, averted eyes, and a few stifled sobs. "I'm sorry," Warna said, regretting her question. "Kalynn told me the story, but she wasn't there and didn't know the details."

Dominic's head came up, his eyes narrowed. "You met Seer Kalynn? And—" he hesitated. "And Wolfe?"

Warna nodded.

"She needs to know," said one of the women in the back, a round, sweet-faced lady with brown hair laced with gray. "If she's to aid him, she needs to know."

"Aye," Janella said. "But the telling is hard."

There was a shifting in the room as they all exchanged glances, tight-lipped, their eyes full of pain. But there were also nods, and Warna could see the determination spreading. As if by silent agreement, they had made their decision.

Ersal cleared his throat. "It was the Fourth Night of our Festival of Light and Laughter, when we celebrate the Gifts of the Lord of Light and Lady of Laughter. T'is our custom, here in Tassinic, you see?"

Warna nodded in encouragement, afraid she'd stop the flow of words.

"Third Night is the Gift of Music and Dance," he said. His voice trailed off, his gaze fixed on the air behind her.

"Oh lady, it was such a grand night," Janella said softly. "So filled with light and laughter, warmth and music. The whole castle fair glowed."

"We'd prepared for weeks," another voice piped up from the back. "Decorating and cooking."

"Planning the presentations," someone added. "Practicing dance steps."

One rough looking man in the back spoke, his voice a rumble. "The castle and keep were all lit with mage lights. So much magic your skin tingled with it, you know?"

"She doesn't," Dominic said sharply. "Humans rarely have the gift," he continued at Warna's unspoken question. "All those of elven blood can sense it. Not all can manipulate it, but all feel its use."

"Laughter flowed freely that night," Ersal said with fondness in his voice. "Everyone was making merry, dancing, laughing, talking. And in the Great Hall, Lord Verice had broken out the applefire—"

A chuckle from the back. "And wasn't Betnan upset by that?"

The chuckles spread about the room.

"Applefire?" Warna asked.

"A liquor, lady, and highly prized," Ersal smiled at the memory. "There's only one brewer that makes it, and they only put up one pressing a year, and then it's set aside to age. It's said that they've only twelve trees that bear the right kind of apples. There's magic in the making of it, or so they say."

"And Lord Verice orders his stock opened, and a sip for all. And Betnan, who had charge of the buttery says 'Surely, you mean the noble folk alone, m'lord.' And Lord Verice, he says 'For any and all within my halls this night, Betnan.'" Ersal shook his head. "Betnan looked so miserable, opening those bottles," He chuckled but then the laughter faded from his face. "May the Lord and Lady keep his soul."

"Lord Verice opened his cellars in honor of Bard Charrin and his Lady Summer, who had come to hold Festival with the Lord," Janella picked up the tale. "It was such a lovely Festival up to that point. If I could just somehow keep that moment in my mind and preserve it, not remember the screams, not see—" She put her head down into her hands and wept.

Ersal moved over, and put an arm around her shoulder. "Charrin had just finished his last song. The room was stirring, there was applause, and then the Usurper—"

"Regent," Dominic corrected.

Ersal's face darkened. "The bastard sent—"

"The Regent denies it, and we've no proof," Dominic said. "She has asked you for facts, not speculation."

"Fine," Ersal spat. "A messenger, named Daress, stepped forward. He was a human, sent by the Regent of Palins with messages for Lord Verice. He'd arrived that morning with an entourage, and Lord Verice had invited him to the Festival, saying that the business could wait until the morrow. Daress pressed him, but his lordship would have none of it."

"We all knew that most likely he'd brought demands from the Regent, insisting that Verice attend one of the High Baron Councils in Edenrich," Janella explained.

"He is the Lord High Baron Verice's liege," Dominic said.

"The Seneschal announced him, and they stood before the high table, just to the right of Charrin and Summer. Lord Verice acknowledged him, welcomed him," Ersal said. "Daress had this smile on his face," He took a breath. "I remember thinking that he looked like a child with a terrible secret."

Ersal was tense, rigid, his eyes fixed on the wall behind her. Warna listened as he spoke in a flat tone, as if he dare not let any emotion into his story.

"Daress said something," Ersal continued. "I didn't catch the words. Then he gave a crackling shout of laughter. It must have been a signal. Because he turned and attacked Charrin."

Ersal closed his eyes. "The blade glittered as he swung. I suspect he was aiming at Charrin's throat, but he caught his eyes instead." He choked up, unable to continue.

Janella picked up the tale. "Charrin screamed. Summer moved, put herself between Charrin and Daress, so the blade plunged deep within her, not him."

"Lord Verice launched himself over the table at Daress, he'd an eating knife in each hand," Ersal said. "The other four with Daress all pulled out their knives, and they all went for our Lord. But that's when—" he gulped.

"When the screams started from all around us, and from the balconies above." A thick-waisted man in the back spoke up. Warna frowned, trying to remember his name. Roath, that was it.

Roath continued, "Armed warriors appeared within the keep, attacking unarmed celebrants."

"Lord Verice was holding his own, and many of the noble lords sprang to his side. The Seneschal, his aide, they grabbed up whatever they could as weapons," Ersal said. "Betnan grabbed up a bottle and shattered it on the table, wielding the jagged shard…"

"They cut through us like wolves among lambs," he said, rubbing his thigh. "And just as quick. The guards and the mages, they reacted, but it had all been planned by that bastard Daress. They aimed to maim, you see, as much as kill."

"In the end, we took them all down to the last. But not before Lord Verice was fallen, blood spurting from his thigh."

"We got to him in time," Dominic said. "But it was a close thing. We got the bleeding stopped, then littered him out to the courtyard. No further - we feared he'd start to bleed if we took him too far. Captain Narthing ordered the keep evacuated, fearing there were others hiding within."

"What of Charrin?" Warna asked.

"Oh, that was a horror, lady," Janella whispered. "He'd gathered poor Summer in his arms, and he was keening there in the Great Hall. We couldn't get him to move for the longest time, and he wouldn't let us take her body. We had to carry them both out."

"There was nothing you could do?" Warna asked Dominic.

"She was dead when we arrived," Dominic said. "I'd more wounded and dying than healers. Charrin's wounds were not life threatening. Lord Verice was our first concern."

Ricard stirred. "As soon as we heard the alarms, we ran up from the town, through the gates and started dealing with the attackers. Narthing led the search, and I organized the courtyard."

"Narthing came out, grim, his sword still out. They'd combed the keep and brought out the bodies. He was standing on the stairs…"

"Lord Verice regained consciousness," Dominic said.

"He'd lost blood, weak as a kitten until he heard Narthing's report," Ricard said. "But the rage boiled up within him. He staggered to his feet, all the healers trying to stop him, and with a gesture he slammed every door shut, and commanded that no one enter the keep."

"Of course, he then fell back into our arms," Dominic said. "He'd used the last of his energy and his wits."

"And when he woke, he ordered the entire castle emptied," Ersal said. "It was insane, of course. We argued but—"

The gate horns blew, announcing Verice's arrival. Warna started at the sound, they all did. Warna hadn't realized it had gotten so late.

"Lord Verice must not see you," Warna stood. "Ersal, I'd ask you to come with me. Please, the rest of you, wait here until the constable can see you slipped out the gate."

Dominic folded his arms over his chest, glowering, but Warna ignored him. "I'll send a request in the next day or so, for supplies for the Healing Hall. Over a period of time, as I see fit, we will see it staffed during the day, and then the night, and gradually ease into having healers in residence."

She looked around the room, catching their eyes. "I will continue cleaning, and will send for you all gradually. Be patient." She focused back on Dominic. "Or ruin all that has been accomplished so far."

CHAPTER TWENTY-SEVEN

Verice swung down off his horse, sighing with relief to be out of the saddle. He gave his horse a pat on the neck as the stable lads led him off for a well-deserved bucket of grain.

"That, m'lord, was brutal," Narthing said, dismounting from his own horse with a sigh. "I'll confess this has not been a day I wish to see again."

"Agreed," Verice said. "But we got the bastards."

Narthing nodded, his smile reaching his eyes. "Birch Cove on the morrow, then. That's the village on Island Lake."

"On the morrow," Verice said, heading toward his rooms. He peeled his glove off, noting that a seam had given way. He felt as worn as the glove, and wanted nothing more than to peel out of his armor and wash. He could feel the grit on his skin, and the dried sweat itched on his scalp.

He took the stairs two at a time, already attacking the buckles on his armor. It felt good to have tracked down those bastards. Bandits, raiders, whoever they'd been, they would no longer threaten any of his people.

Verice strode into his chambers, and called his aide for water and kav, unbuckling his sword belt, and hanging it from its peg. That was another thing he needed to see to; the edge of his blade. He'd hone it while he and Warna talked this evening, after dinner.

He stripped to the waist, and started washing. There was a tune running through his head, a sprightly one that he didn't recognize. He started humming as he scrubbed his face. It would have been far better to have taken a long soak in the hot springs below the keep, but—

The keep was sealed.

Sealed because—

He stopped, standing with a towel in his hands, water dripping from his face and hair.

A cackle of laughter, a blade flashing through the air, glittering in the mage lights.

The pain washed over him, made worse by the guilt. For the fact that he'd forgotten. Forgotten the deaths, the betrayal, the pain.

All during the day, the chase, fighting, the return, standing here, he'd not once thought of the attack. Bitterness ate at the back of his throat. Ancestors, what kind of man was he to have forgotten—

The clatter of dishes in the outer room brought him back to himself. Verice dried off, and pulled out a clean tunic, feeling oddly numb. He took a deep breath before he opened the door to find Warna standing at the table, waiting by her chair. The table was covered with dishes and plates, all waiting for him.

"M'lord," She bowed her head, with her usual smile. Except there was something different. Verice bowed his head back to her, studying her face. Cheeks flushed, eyes bright, Warna looked as if she'd been up to mischief.

"Warna?" he asked.

"M'lord, I have taken a liberty," she said, her tone and manner very formal. "I saw that the petitions remained untouched," she glanced at Verice's desk where the forlorn pile still sat on a corner. "I'd thought to have one of your clerks come and assist you with them. I sent a message into town, and one Ersal is outside the door awaiting your instructions."

"Ersal?" Verice asked. He hadn't seen Ersal since…

Warna stood there, her hands on the back of her chair, watching him patiently, looking half-embarrassed and pleased with herself at the same time.

"I would have gotten to them," he said.

"I know," she said, suddenly serious. "But it's easier sometimes, with help."

He gave her a wry look. "I never liked dealing with petitions," he admitted. "Would you ask Ersal in?"

Warna stepped to the door.

"M'lord," Ersal put his hand to his chest and bowed.

"Ersal, it's good to see you," Verice said, stepping over to the desk. "As you can tell, once again I've a need for a rescue."

"M'lord, it would be a pleasure." Ersal accepted the bundle of documents. "I can have these sorted out for you quickly." There was the slightest hesitation in his voice, but then he continued on. "When would you wish me to bring them back for your review?"

Verice gave the man a glance. "I'll stop by your offices in the next few days," he said.

"M'lord, you told me that two months ago." Ersal said softly. "Your defense of the barony has consumed the majority of your time. Let me ease some of that burden by bringing the work to you."

"You know me too well, Ersal."

Ersal tilted his head. "This time tomorrow, m'lord? I promise to take no more time than necessary."

"That would be fine," Verice said. "My thanks, Ersal."

"My pleasure, m'lord." Ersal turned. "M'lady," he bowed his head to Warna and left.

Verice returned to the table and gestured to Warna to sit. "You look like someone who's gotten away with mischief," he said mildly.

"You're not upset?" Warna asked, as she started to uncover dishes.

"No," Verice said. "Not about that."

She paused, staring at him with those wide brown eyes, and Verice suddenly remembered the tune he'd been humming.

It was Warna's. She sung it at Wolfe's.

"I think your day was a bad one," she said tentatively, passing him the bread. "What happened?"

Verice shook his head, and started to serve himself. "No. I'd rather hear about your activities. Anything you want to tell me?"

"Well," Warna picked up her fork. Her lips curved in a smile. "I think your dogs are getting fat."

CHAPTER TWENTY-EIGHT

A pounding on the door of the Healers Hall startled Warna awake. Sand and Gray both came to their feet, growling and barking at the stairs.

It took her a moment to orient herself. She'd had dinner the night before with Verice, they'd talked about a variety of things, he'd agreed to let Ersal deal with the petitions...

The pounding came again, more insistent. Now she heard raised voices... what was happening?

She threw on her tunic, went to the small window and leaned out. Three large carts were just below, and a small group clustered at the door.

"Here now," Ricard bellowed. "What's this then? Lady Warna is still sleeping, you rude dogs."

Warna laughed. If she'd slept through the knocking, his voice alone would certainly have woken her.

"She's sleeping here?"

That would be Priest Dominic, his tone implying some nasty things.

"We've supplies for the Hall," Dominic continued. "At her direction, I might add."

Warna darted a glance at the barracks, to see Verice's men gathered for their departure. They hadn't left yet.

Drat that priest. They'd all agreed to help her last night. If this was his idea of cooperation and patience—

"Constable," Warna called, cutting through the argument below her. "I'll be right down."

She pulled back inside, and dressed quickly, braiding up her hair as she ran down the steps.

At least Ricard had stopped bellowing at the top of his lungs. He'd switched to a low menacing growl, one that Warna could feel in her bones even before she opened the door. "—no need for this," he glared at Dominic.

"Every need for it," Dominic glared right back, looking imposing and regal in his white and gold robes. "I've not much time and a responsibility to see this Hall stocked and ready. We'll be done and on our way quickly." The disdain in his face as he gave Warna a glance slid into pure satisfaction. "I've received a summons to the Church at Edenrich, and the portal will open at noon."

"What, among all those humans?" Ricard raised his eyebrows.

"I wouldn't expect you to appreciate the nuances," Dominic's disdain was restored. He was staring down his nose at both of them.

"Constable," Narthing was calling from the midst of the men. Ricard frowned, giving Warna a concerned look.

"Go," she said.

He gave her a nod, and strode off.

Warna swung open the door behind her, and the acolytes started ferrying supplies from the carts into the hall. "I'll be back; I'm going to the kitchens for kav." And to make sure that Verice hadn't noticed this ruckus and interfere. "I'll return shortly."

"No need," Dominic said, taking a basket out of the cart. "We know what needs to be done."

"I want to know what needs to be done," Warna said. "So that in the future—"

"Please," Dominic sailed past her, his robes flapping. "You're little more than a pet, girl."

Warna lashed back. "And yet you are summoned to the human city of Edenrich, elf."

Dominic paused in the doorway. "To the highest offices of the Church I served, where the halls ring with the voices of highborn nobles. Humans, yes, but of the highest blood and breeding. I imagine I'll be most comfortable in their presence. Now, if you will excuse me." He whipped out of sight before Warna could open her mouth.

Flushed with the insult, Warna's hands formed fists, and she took a step to follow and berate the elf. But Verice's men were still milling about, and she desperately wanted kav.

She turned and headed to the kitchens, uttering a small prayer that the cooks had made it strong.

* * * * *

Verice came out of the barracks eager to be on his way, only to run into a bleary-eyed Warna entering the kitchens. Her cheeks were pink, her eyes flashing.

"You're up early," he said.

"I asked for someone to stock the Healing Hall with supplies," she said crossly. "I didn't expect Priest Dominic at the crack of dawn."

"Arrogant bastard, isn't he?" Verice said.

Warna rolled her eyes.

"Skilled though," Verice added, pausing to follow her into the dining area. "I'm surprised he's still in Tassinic. He was angling for assignment to the Church in Edenrich."

"Well, he's apparently received a summons," Warna said as she headed to the hearth, nodding to the men who were eating. "I need kav."

"Ah," Verice said, following her. "I wonder if he realizes what he's getting himself into."

Warna glanced over her shoulder at him as she poured herself a mug. "How so?"

"Let's just say that the Church in Edenrich is more concerned with its power base than its spiritual obligations." Verice shrugged.

Warna took another sip and stared at him over her mug. "Where are you off to this time?"

"Birch Cove," Verice said. "A small town, near a lake, by the Summerford border. We're not expecting trouble."

Warna stared into her mug before she glanced at him. "Take care anyway," she said softly.

Verice looked at her, her golden hair pulled back in a braid, with wisps of gold escaping, crowning her in the morning light. Suddenly, he wanted to sit with her, drink kav and talk about her plans for the day.

Narthing was hovering in the doorway, he had to go.

She gave him a questioning look over her mug, and he suddenly felt foolish. He bowed his head to her and left to join his men.

He mounted, feeling oddly bereft, as if he'd forgotten something, or lost a chance at—

He shook his head, lifted a hand, and started the chant to open the portal.

The glowing circle formed, a doorway of flowing white curtains of gossamer, moving in an unfelt breeze. His men formed up behind him; Narthing moved into position in front. They'd preceded him, so that he could take the portal down behind him as he rode through.

Narthing gave the order, and the horses moved forward at a walk, well used to this mode of travel. Verice waited until the last tail disappeared, then urged his own horse through, concentrating on the closure. There was a moment of white light, of disorientation, and then he was through on the other side.

To find the air filled with smoke and screams, and his men under attack.

CHAPTER TWENTY-NINE

The skirmish won, the enemy in retreat, Verice followed the last of his men through the portal, emerging into the Castle courtyard, filthy and bone weary. With a savage gesture, he snapped it shut behind him, on the ruins of Birch Cove. Nothing left there but burning buildings, smoke-filled air, and the heads of the 'bandits' on pikes along the road.

A fierce bolt of satisfaction went through him at that memory, but the sight of the village dead lined up in the courtyard, covered in shrouds wiped any sense of gratification away. Far too many lost.

It was late, the night was still and quiet, the stars bright above his head. The walls burned with torches and he could see the watch making the rounds.

Constable Ricard appeared at his side, his face reflecting the strain of the day. He cast an eye over Verice with a frown.

"Not my blood," Verice reassured him.

Ricard's relief was in his eyes, but he gave a simple nod of his head. "We'd word you'd be at it till daybreak."

Verice stripped off his gloves. "It didn't take long to hunt them down." He indicated the rows of bodies. "What of—"

"The survivors of Birch Cove have asked to return and bury their dead," Ricard said. "They want to return to their homes as well. I've told them all that must await your decision."

Verice rubbed his face with his bare hand.

"The healers have seen to the wounded, my lord." Ricard gestured over to the other side of the courtyard. "We've housed the villagers as best we can. Some of the men have given up their beds for the night."

"Narthing?" Verice asked softly.

"Not as bad as they first thought," Ricard nodded toward the Healing Hall. "They've got him settled, and they drugged him stupid when he tried to leave his bed to return to your side. Won't be up for much until tomorrow."

"Nor will I," Verice said.

"You look done in," Ricard agreed. "There's naught else you can do tonight. I'll roust some of the lads, we can get you hot water—"

Verice shook his head. "I'll just draw up some water from the well, and wash the worst off." He started to unbuckle his breastplate.

"I'll send out towels then, and something to eat—"

Verice made a face.

"Try to get something down," Ricard said gruffly. "Leave your gear by the well, and I'll have the lads clean it for you," he held up a hand to prevent Verice's protest. "You'd best be to bed, there's more than enough that will need your attention in the morning."

Verice shrugged. No denying that.

His muscles protested as he lowered the bucket, and pulled it back up, brimming with water. It was cold. He stripped to the waist and plunged his hands in with relief. A lad appeared with towels and soap, and he carried off Verice's armor and sword. Verice kept his daggers.

He indulged himself by washing his hair, upending a bucket over his head, letting the cold water wash away the sweat, grime, and blood. The water brought a surge of energy for a time, letting him scrub and towel himself dry.

Ricard approached with a cool bottle of ale, and some cheese between two hard crackers. "Enough to take the edge off," he said.

Verice took a long swig. "You're sure Narthing's well tended?"

"Aye," Ricard said, throwing the towels and soap in one of the buckets. "And they'd not thank you if you tried to wake him or them." He chuckled. "Priest Dominic stayed once the wounded started pouring in; he's bedded down in there as well."

Verice looked over at the Healing Hall and the dark window at the very top. Truth be told, it wasn't Narthing or Dominic he wanted to talk to. He clapped a hand on the constable's shoulder. "Well, then I'd best see to my own bed. Make sure you see to yours."

"Aye," Ricard said. "Dawn comes quick enough." He headed off to the gate, presumably to finish his rounds before bed.

Verice set about eating the crackers and cheese between pulls on the bottle. The weariness of his body had more to do with the magical energies he'd expended rather than the fighting. It was an effort to chew, but he did it, watching the crumbs gather on his trous. The ale was cold, and sweet. It replaced the bitter taste of ash in his mouth.

It was dark and quiet here; the only sounds came from the night watch pacing the walls. A sense of isolation washed over him, an ache of loneliness. The aftereffects of battle, he knew.

He stared up at Warna's window again, trying to will the flaring of a light that showed she was awake. He really wanted to check on her, to see if she was well, maybe talk for a moment. If anything was amiss, he'd have been told. Anything he had to tell her could wait until the morning.

He padded through the barracks bare-footed, silently walking the halls and climbing the stairs. There were soldiers lining the halls, rolled up in bedrolls, asleep. He frowned, thinking about the challenges of relocating the people of Birch Cove. They could rebuild, of course, but he wanted to talk to the village elders before he—

A huge yawn cracked his jaw, and Verice shook his head ruefully as he opened the door to his chambers.

Someone had left a mage-lantern open in his sleeping chamber; its soft glow lit the outer rooms enough to see by.

The dogs were sprawled on the floor around the table, curled in balls. Brindle raised her head and wagged her tail. Verice crooned to her as he crossed the room. Once she saw that he was headed within, she lowered her head, and settled back down.

Verice yawned as he stepped through, just as happy to be seeking his own rest. Tomorrow would be—

Warna was in his bed.

It took a moment for it to sink, for him to understand that the fan of golden hair was hers. She was on her side, facing him, curled around a pillow, covered with one of his blankets. There was a faint frown on her face, as if her sleep was an uneasy one.

Verice hesitated, then leaned against the door frame, taking in the sight. He'd not disturb her. But after a day of death and horror, it felt good to see her so, sleeping safe within his walls.

At least he'd managed that much.

She was lovely, really. Those wide round eyes, and the softness of her face.

She'd probably given up her bed in the Healers Hall for one of the healers or patients. Ancestors, he hoped it wasn't Dominic. A flash of irritation at Ricard was quickly replaced with common sense. He doubted the man even knew she'd ended up here.

There were extra blankets folded and the end of the bed. He'd curl up by the hearth in the kitchens.

He walked over, careful to be quiet, with every intention of taking a blanket and leaving. But he paused for just a moment, listening to her breathing, his eyes on her sweet face as she slept. Something ached in his chest suddenly; a want, a need for her to open her eyes so they could talk. Verice frowned at that, uncertain as to what exactly he was feeling.

Warna sighed, rolled over and opened her eyes, still half-asleep.

Verice suddenly knew exactly what he wanted.

CHAPTER THIRTY

Sleep-filled, Warna's brown eyes focused on him and her lips curved in a warm, drowsy, welcoming smile. She murmured his name, clearly just on the edge of consciousness as she shifted under the blankets.

Verice sucked in a breath, his pulse quickening as pure desire swept through him. The shock of recognizing that fact would have -should have - made him stop, but he was already moving, bracing a knee on the edge of the bed, leaning over Warna. She blinked at him, her confusion clear.

He kissed her, pressing his lips to her softer ones, no more than that. He waited then, conscious of her every breath.

She pulled in a startled gasp against his mouth. His heart stopped for one long, agonizing breath, then leapt as her lips moved under his, clumsily returning the kiss, as if unsure as to what to do.

He groaned, buried one hand in her silken hair and took control.

Warna gave a contented murmur and opened her mouth to him.

Verice took what she offered, crushing her in his arms. She molded against him, warm against his bare chest. She tasted of peace, of home, but she was also Warna and he hungered for her and her alone.

She brought her arms up around his waist, clutching at his waist, returning the kiss.

Something within him broke open even as it sang.

* * * * *

Warna awoke fully, gasping her surprise against Verice's mouth. His lips were warm and dry and he seemed to hesitate just on the brink, waiting for something... waiting for her.

She wasn't sure what to do next, but she pressed up, her lips moving against his.

He pulled her into a tangle of blankets and arms, wrapping his arms around her to lift her up. His tongue teased hers and she opened her mouth to him. For long slow moments, there was nothing but him, his touch, his mouth. She felt so alive, her body on fire. Warna brought her own hands up, threading them into his silver hair.

Verice broke the kiss, and held her close, his face pressed into her neck. The warmth of his breath beneath her ear made her shiver. His arms trembled.

She wrapped her own arms around him, running her hands over his back, breathing in the scent of soap and leather.

He'd kissed her. Her lips still tingled with the lingering heat of his, his taste in her mouth. But he'd broken it off, buried his face in her hair, and now held her like he'd never release her.

"Verice?" she whispered, trying to understand. His kiss had set her on fire, but the desire was fading, leaving her confused. Until she felt his harsh breaths and caught the faint whiff of smoke in his hair.

"Verice," Now there was no question in her voice. She'd seen the wounded coming through the portal, had heard of the destruction of the village. She could only imagine what he'd been through.

Still he held tight, his hair a curtain around them. She tightened her hold, offering what comfort she could.

"Sorry," his voice was harsh and broken in her ear. He released her, his arms dropping away, but the tension was still there in his back. Warna tightened her hug even as he tried to slip from her grasp.

"I've no right," he whispered, trying to pull away.

"Hush," she murmured, and held on until he wrapped his arms around her again.

"You've every right, considering."

His breathing started to slow.

"I didn't expect you to return," she whispered. "They needed every bed in the Healing Hall, so I thought—"

Verice lifted his head, and she could see the exhaustion in his eyes. "I'll go—"

Warna shook her head, still keeping him close. "No," she said. "Don't go." She tugged him down to the bed.

Verice swayed as she pulled, resisting her. "Your reputation," he stuttered out the words.

Warna laughed, shaking her head. "That horse has fled the barn, Verice." She shifted, making room, trying to keep a grip on his shoulders. "Sleep on top of the blankets then. I trust your honor."

"You shouldn't," came his reply, cold and hard. There was a flash of something in his eyes that sent a bolt of heat through her. Warna caught her breath, quickly breaking eye contact.

"Sorry," Verice said. "I'm…" he ran his hand over his face. "I've offended you. I didn't mean to—"

"You are exhausted," Warna said firmly. She tugged again, and Verice obeyed this time, stretching out on the bed beside her. She reached down and covered him with the extra blanket. "Sleep," she whispered, settling back down.

He nodded, closed his eyes - but they opened again and he stared at her, his eyes blurring and unfocused.

She reached out from under her blanket, and took his hand, curling her fingers around his. "Sleep," she commanded.

He tightened his grasp for an instant then sighed, nodded, and closed his eyes. She watched over him as the tension drained and his breathing slowed. Watched as he slipped into sleep.

Finally, when she was sure he would stay asleep, she closed her own eyes. But she left her hand in his.

* * * * *

Verice awoke alone.

Warna wasn't in the outer room, either, although fresh clothes and hot water were waiting for him. He stood staring for a moment, trying to decide if Warna had arranged that. And what it meant if she had.

He ran his hands through his hair, knowing full well that he'd broken faith by kissing her, and trying to remember why he'd thought that would be a good idea. Although he didn't remember thinking so much as feeling… his body tightened as the image of Warna in his bed flashed before him. He remembered that all too well.

He needed to face her.

The thought made him sick. He didn't want to see the betrayal in her eyes, or worse, the scorn. For violating her trust, breaking his promise of—

A knock at the door, and one of the serving lads peeked in, balancing a tray. "M'lord?"

Verice gestured him in, arching an eyebrow at the hot kav and breakfast. "You must have been sitting outside the door."

The lad nodded, intent on his task of delivering the tray to the table. "M'lady's orders. 'Let him sleep, feed him, then tell him Captain Narthing is asking for him.'" The lad set the tray down with a satisfied sigh.

So… he wasn't the only one who wished to avoid the issue. Or at least, avoid him.

Verice sent the lad off. He poured some kav, hot and strong, and tore at some of the bread, leaving the rest of the food untouched.

He washed, changed, stomped into his boots, and belted on his weapons. Best to find her and apologize.

Before he lost his nerve.

CHAPTER THIRTY-ONE

Verice blinked as he stepped into the courtyard, the sunlight hitting his eyes. He'd slept later than he'd thought.

Brindle appeared beside him, followed by the rest of the pack. He whined, shoving his nose into Verice's hand, looking for attention. Verice knelt, and scratched his ears, glad for an excuse to pause for a moment.

The courtyard was quite the contrast from the night before. The dead bodies were gone. The whole place hummed with activity. Wagons rumbled through the main gates, filled with supplies. A few were stopped in front of the Healing Hall, unloading supplies. Other wagons clustered in front of the buttery and ovens. Men were unloading barrels and crates, heaving sides of beef on to their shoulders, calling to one another over the noise. Smoke was rising from chimneys long cold. It felt oddly... normal.

"Hup, hup," Verice said, getting the dogs' attention. He took a moment to concentrate on each of the dogs, checking them over, talking to each one in low tones, even as he glanced around the courtyard. They all gathered around him, vying for his attention. Sand and Gray weren't there, but he knew where they'd be.

He feared to look at the keep itself, but steeled himself enough to take a quick glance. The doors were all closed, the windows dark. He breathed then, feeling the fool. He'd have known if any had entered, after all. But it stood, silent and dark.

Warna had kept her word.

Warna...

He rose then, looking around, and found the constable at his side, waiting.

"All's well?" Verice asked.

"Well enough." Ricard said. "The men have secured Birch Cove, or what's left of it. They report that the remaining bandits have retreated over the border, and they did not pursue." His expression of disapproval told Verice what he thought of that order. "We've managed to get the villagers all fed and seen to. Captain Narthing is awake, and waiting to speak to you. He and Priest Dominic are going at it something fierce." Ricard grinned. "Last I left, Dominic was threatening to tie him to the bed."

"Warna?" Verice asked.

"She's got the women from Birch Cove helping her scrub down the Third barracks." Ricard rumbled, he raised an eyebrow and gestured in that direction. "Walk as we talk, m'lord?"

Verice nodded, and the dogs paced with them.

"M'lady said we need the sleeping space," Ricard said as they made their way past the keep. "She's ordered the buttery, ovens and laundry opened, because the barracks kitchens won't be able to handle much more work than what they've already got." Ricard pointed to the wagons. "We've got food and supplies coming in, but m'lord," and here the man hesitated.

Verice raised an eyebrow, inviting him to continue.

"M'lord, you'll be needing to name a seneschal and fairly quick," Ricard said apologetically. "I can handle it for a while, but you need a man on it to keep it running smooth."

Verice nodded.

"The Birch Cove elders wish to talk with you," Ricard continued. "And the Lord Mayor of Octara and the heads of the Merchants Guild are asking questions about trade. A few others be wanting your attention as well."

"Warna first, then Narthing," Verice said. "We can set up a meeting for the others this afternoon."

Ricard nodded his agreement. "I'll try to hold them off." He indicated a doorway where a cluster of men had gathered. "But they'll not be satisfied just talking to me for long, m'lord."

"They'll have to be," Verice snapped.

Ricard started, but covered it quickly. "Yes, m'lord." He gave a quick bow of his head, and turned toward the group of men headed their way.

Verice grimaced, regretting his sharp words. His irritation lay with himself, not his people. But delaying this conversation with Warna would only make it worse. He quickened his pace, determined to face the consequences of his actions.

There were women gathered before the Third Barracks, with buckets, mops and cleaning cloths, all talking at once. They were wringing out rags, pouring fresh water, surrounded by soap bubbles, wet cobblestones and endless chatter.

Another group was a bit farther along, away from the damp, beating rugs and stuffing mattresses with fresh straw. Children ran in and out of their midst with handfuls of straw, throwing it at each other in a game.

Warna stood at the heart of the activity, her blonde hair caught up in a twist. She was wringing rags with the best of them.

He hesitated, not sure if he should—

She lifted her head, and turned toward him, as if she knew…

Her eyes found his unerringly, like an arrow to the heart.

For one long instant, Verice feared the worst. He caught the red heat on her cheeks, the confusion in her eyes as she dropped her gaze.

Pain sliced through his chest. He was in mid-stride, or else he'd stop where he was, not really wanting to face her.

He caught his breath when she looked up again, her eyes back on his. Was the barest trace of an embarrassed smile on her lips, a light of welcome in her eyes?

He kept walking toward her, half-afraid to hope.

CHAPTER THIRTY-TWO

The crowd of human women silenced as he approached and then all curtseyed, their faces solemn. There wasn't a sense of happiness about them, not exactly. More a sense of contentment. Or satisfaction.

"Ladies." His voice sounded rough even to his ears. "Warna, I'd speak with you, if you've a moment."

Her blush was pink now, but the smallest of smiles was definitely in her gaze. "Of course, m'lord." She stepped out of the shelter of the gathering and walked toward him. The women returned to their work, although Verice could feel their eyes upon him.

Warna approached him, the heat still on her cheeks. He turned slightly away, standing close, hoping to shield her from prying looks. He lowered his voice, "Warna, I—"

She reached out a hand, and touched his arm. He felt the heat of her fingers through the cloth. "For all my training," she said softly, "I've no idea of the deportment required for this situation."

Verice huffed out a breath, feeling his tension ease. "I confess that Elven Court etiquette offers no suggestions either."

Warna chuckled and nodded, her head down. "So, I resolved to apologize for my inappropriate intrusion into your chambers. Except that…"

Her brown eyes darted to his, then she lowered her gaze to stare at the cleaning rags in her hands. Her lashes were dark against her skin.

Verice stepped closer. "Except that?

Her voice was the faintest whisper. "I don't regret the—"

"Excuse me, Lord Verice, but—" One of the merchants was approaching.

Verice lifted his head, throwing the man a long look.

The man blinked and retreated. "Your pardon, m'lord," was all he managed to stutter out.

"M'lord," Warna chided softly. She was standing so close, he could smell her hair.

Verice cleared his throat. "I will confess to you that I was going to ask forgiveness for my unconscionable actions, and beg your pardon," he murmured. "But I will return your honesty with my own. I've no real regrets. Except that…"

"M'lady, do you wish us to start on the next—" One of the women approached from behind. Warna shot her a glare that practically scorched the woman where she stood.

"M'lady," Verice chuffed at Warna as the woman fled.

"Except that?" Warna prompted him, her own eyebrow raised.

"Except that we stopped," he whispered.

She flushed again, but her lips curved upwards, lifting his heart with them.

"M'lord," Ricard said from a distance off.

Verice turned on him, at the same time Warna lifted her head. But the man was impervious to their glares. "There's a need," he said simply.

"We need to discuss this," Verice lowered his head to Warna's ear. "But I fear…"

She leaned in toward him, humming her agreement. "We've duties, m'lord,"

"True enough, m'lady," Verice stood for a moment more, sighed and stepped back. "Dinner, then?"

Warna's eyes were bright, filled with anticipation. "Dinner would be—"

Horns sounded from the walls, calling an alert, warning of assault from above.

Verice snapped his head up, scanning the sky. Two mounted creatures spiraled above. "Warna, get the humans into the—" He paused, frowning, and lifted a hand to shade his eyes as he studied the two figures. "Ancestors, there must be a new man on horn duty. That's—"

The horns sounded again, with an 'All's well'.

"What are they?" Warna asked.

"More like a who," Verice said, frowning. "It's Wolfe and Kalynn."

* * * * *

Warna caught her breath as the creatures from that lovely tapestry spiraled down, beautiful wings spread wide to slow their descent into the courtyard. They gracefully settled to the ground, folding their wings to allow their riders to unbuckle and dismount.

A streak of mottled colors jumped down from the pack on one animal's back and ran for the stables. Warna was fairly sure it was the cat.

Verice started in their direction, but Warna hesitated. Every eye in the courtyard was fixed on the two new arrivals, but there was little welcome there. All work had stopped as Wolfe and Kalynn dismounted and greeted Verice. The bustle of activity had been replaced with an odd stillness, wariness, and fear.

The women behind her had gathered at the door of the barracks, and the children were being hustled inside. The fear in their faces was obvious. As much as Warna would like to see the airons up close, she felt a need to respond to that fear. She walked back, trying to catch their eyes and offer reassurance. "There's nothing to fear. Just friends of the High Baron's come for a visit."

That got her stares of mingling disbelief and exasperation. "Lady," one of the eldest said. "That is the ChaosReaver."

"It's said he tears out the living hearts of his enemies," another whispered.

"No," Warna shook her head, thinking of the cluttered stairs of the Tower and Wolfe's smile. "He's—"

She heard footsteps behind her, and all the woman's eyes went wide. Warna glanced back to find the trio advancing on her.

"What is this?" Kalynn's voice was like a knife as her glare raked over Warna's cloths and the rags in her hand.

"Kalynn," Warna started her greeting, but froze as Kalynn spun on her heel, and confronted Verice.

"You were to care for her, claimed she was under your protection," Kalynn snarled. "And yet what do I find?" Fast as lightning, her hand rose, and she slapped Verice. "Humans are not slaves!"

CHAPTER THIRTY-THREE

Warna gaped at Kalynn, conscious all the while of the gathering audience. She glanced at Verice and Wolfe.

Wolfe snorted and rolled his eyes. "And people think *I* have a temper."

Verice stood there like a stone.

"Caged, dressed in rags, scrubbing out barracks," Kalynn's outraged voice was low and controlled but somehow managed to bounce off every wall and into waiting ears. "I took you at your word." Kalynn's glare was aimed directly at Verice. "You told me you'd offered her protection. I should have known that your own biases would—"

Warna couldn't believe that Verice was just standing there, his face grim and rigid, his cheek red where Kalynn had slapped him. Frustratingly silent, offering no defense as the seer spewed her anger.

"Kalynn." Warna grabbed her arm, and pulled her around. "Kalynn, you're wrong." Warna met her glare for glare. "You know nothing about what's going on here, and you are making something—"

"Really?" Kalynn folded her arms over her chest. "Where did you sleep last night? Beside some hearth?"

Warna flushed and just managed not to look at Verice.

"Ha," Kalynn exclaimed, taking Warna's silence as some sort of affirmation.

Warna straightened, lifting her chin. "Seer Kalynn, you are wrong. All who stand here with me know that. Lord High Baron Verice has offered us shelter, safety and the utmost courtesy. Something which you lack, Seer."

That shut her up. If Warna had slapped her, Kalynn could not have looked more shocked.

"This land is at war," Warna continued. "And *we*," she put emphasis on the word. "are working to restore, preserve and thrive in Tassinic. Did you expect to find me in ruffled silks and fine linens?"

"No," Kalynn shook her head. "Not that. But—"

"There was an attack," Warna pointed out, ignoring Kalynn's protest. "We've people to house and feed, and little daylight left. Your visit is unfortunate, for we cannot offer you hospitality at this time. If you wish to speak to Lord High Baron Verice, please to keep it quick. There's work to be done."

"Warna," Kalynn's tone was apologetic but Warna was in no mood to hear it.

"Offer your apologies to Verice," Warna snapped. "That's where they're owed." She turned on her heel, and stomped back to the third barracks, where the woman huddled, with fear on awe on their faces. "Ladies." She tried to keep the anger out of her voice. "Let's be about it, shall we?" She walked through their midst, and right through the door, her stomach in knots.

It wasn't until she'd set every able body to work, wasn't until she was on her hands and knees, scrubbing a non-existent spot on the floor, that she was willing to face the real reason she still felt sick.

"Warna, get the humans *into the—"*

* * * * *

Verice stood silent, his cheek burning from Kalynn's blow.

"Verice." Kalynn reached out to him, her hand hovering over his cheek. "Verice, I am sorry. I thought that… it looked like…" She sighed, and dropped her hand. "I fear that I overreacted."

"Really?" Wolfe said.

Kalynn glanced at him in irritation. "Verice, I am sorry. I apologize for—"

Verice lifted a hand. "While you may have misread the situation, there is still a truth to your words. A hard truth perhaps, but true nonetheless. Warna is correct, however. We had a village burnt to the ground by the Usurper's forces, and I—" Verice rubbed his cheek. "I have much to do. It would be best to have your say, and depart quickly."

"I'm sorry, lad," Wolfe said. "Kalynn and I will be traveling for a time, and I wanted you to know that we were leaving. Charrin is at Valltera, at the Royal Court, and I've secured the Tower, no worries there. You have the cat." There was a trace of malicious satisfaction in his voice. "It will be some time before we're back in touch."

"It's been years since you've left your home," Verice said. "How long will you be gone?"

"Months," Wolfe shrugged. "Maybe longer."

"That long?" Verice raised an eyebrow.

"I have *seen*," Kalynn said softly. "There's a task needs doing."

"And we must pursue it," Wolfe said. "The places we must go, we can't use any portals."

Verice gave his mentor and friend a long, steady look. "What aren't you telling me?"

Wolfe quirked his mouth. "So much, lad. So very much."

Kalynn looked over her shoulder at the barracks. "I'm going to speak to Warna," she said

and started off in that direction.

"How bad was the attack?" Wolfe asked.

"Bad enough," Verice said wearily. Yet another failure to place at his door.

"Will you retaliate?" Wolfe's voice was soft but his eyes were sharp.

"No," Verice said grimly. "We pursued them to my borders, and then stopped. I can't hope to take on the Usurper's army and win."

Wolfe pursed his lips and nodded.

Verice looked at the wiry old man, "But you could."

CHAPTER THIRTY-FOUR

Wolfe stiffened.

"You could end this," Verice said in a low, urgent voice, not afraid to plead.

Wolfe gave him a quiet steady look. "You think so?"

"I know so," Verice said. "With your powers, you could portal in, kill the Usurper, and portal out."

"Perhaps." Wolfe looked after Kalynn. "After all, I did it once before, did I not? Why shouldn't I do it again? Blaze a bright trail of destruction from your door to his as the Chaosreaver once more stalks the land."

Shame flooded through Verice and he suddenly felt like the apprentice he'd been so many centuries ago. "Master, I—"

"Except that the last time I took such an action, the repercussions were far worse than the evil I thought to end. Innocents paid the price for my arrogance." Wolfe looked at him and the laughter in his bright blue eyes was gone. "Still pay the price, from what little I know."

"Forgive me, Master." Verice lowered his head.

"Answer me this, Apprentice," Wolfe's voice was a lash. "If the Usurper is struck down, who will fill the power void? Who will claim the Throne of Palins?"

"I don't know. One of the High Barons, perhaps."

"You?"

"No, Master." Verice shook his head.

"And if I don't like what actions the new sovereign takes?" Wolfe asked, still standing stiff, radiating anger. "Where does it end, Verice?"

"I do not know, Master," Verice said, his anger cooling.

"I've no time to enter ethical debates with you," Wolfe growled. "Kalynn has *seen*. We are needed elsewhere."

Verice closed his eyes.

"You are under duress," Wolfe took in a deep breath. "Or you would never have asked this of me."

"True enough," Verice said, glancing to where Warna had disappeared into the building.

Wolfe followed his glance and snorted. "But that's not all that has your head and heart in chaos."

Verice stiffened.

"Please," Wolfe rolled his eyes. "I don't have to be a Seer to see, Verice."

"You are not my master in this," Verice said sharply.

"As if I am going to give you advice about women," Wolfe barked out a sharp laugh. "But it's best for all concerned if you face the truth of it now. Before it goes much further."

* * * * *

Kalynn found Warna inside, on her hands and knees, scrubbing at one of the hearths. "Warna," she started, regretting her outburst. "I'm so sorry."

"Did you apologize to Verice?" Warna asked tiredly without looking up from her task.

"I did," Kalynn glanced around, but none of the other women were in earshot.

Warna sat back on her heels, and stared up at her, eyes filled with pain and questions. "Why would you even think that of him?"

Kalynn knelt down to look her in the eye. "I am sorry. I have never had reason to think that Verice holds humans in contempt, or treats them as slaves. I saw you at work, and it brought back—" she cut off her words as sorrow rose up in her chest.

Warna waited.

"Memories," Kalynn forced out. "Of a time long past." She swallowed hard.

"And how does Verice normally treat humans?" Warna asked, her brown eyes intent and serious.

"Like delicate flowers," Kalynn said, forcing a smile. "That bloom and fade, and bloom again, if tended well."

Warna looked at her hands, at the rags and the soap and the floor. She snorted out a weak laugh. "Little he knows," she said.

"He's never been around them enough to know better." Kalynn rose. "I regret this, Warna. We've a journey to make, and I'd only wished to say goodbye. Wolfe and I will be away for some time. I do not wish to be parted from you on this note."

"As if I've never regretted a hasty action or a harsh word." Warna stood, dried her hands on her skirt, and pulled Kalynn into a hug. "Safe travels, Kalynn. May the Lord of Light and the Lady of Laughter both be with you."

Kalynn hugged Warna back. "And the skies be with you, Warna."

* * * * *

Warna watched Kalynn go and returned to her scrubbing. As much as she'd like to see Wolfe and Kalynn take wing on the backs of their airons, she'd no wish to speak to Verice just yet.

She had some thinking to do.

The chatter and clatter of the other women was both familiar and strange. How many months had it been since she'd worked with her mother, talking as they'd sorted silks and spices? The familiarity of it made her heart ache for her family and home. The strangeness reminded her that there was a world outside the walls of the castle. A normal world, filled with regular truths. Where something so extraordinary as an elven Lord High Baron caring for a simple human woman was not to be considered. Not even to be contemplated.

"Warna, get the humans *into the—"*

She paused in her scrubbing, listening to his words in her head. He hadn't said 'get them to safety' or 'get the women to safety'…

"…get the humans…*"*

Warna knelt back on her heels, staring at the stain without seeing it.

Verice had stirred when she'd left the bed, as she'd slipped out from under the blankets. He'd reached out, searching, turning his head toward her. She'd whispered reassurances, and he'd settled back to sleep, never fully waking.

Her lips tingled at the memory of his kiss.

But that was part of the illusion he'd wrought, wasn't it? Verice had isolated the castle from the world, cutting himself off from friend and foe alike in the guise of safety. Cutting her off from what was normal, sane, and true.

The irony being, of course, that she'd set herself the task of pulling him back, of setting the castle to rights. And now it felt like the mundane, the normal routine was returning, only to expose the nature of her folly.

"It's as clean as it's likely to get, to my way of thinking." One of the older women was peering over her shoulder at the stain.

"I'm thinking you're right," Warna sighed.

"They've brought round soup, and kav, and sticky buns for the little ones," the woman said. "The work will wait."

"Thank you." Warna got to her feet. "I'm sorry, I can't remember your name…?"

"Lottie," the woman offered.

"Lottie," Warna dropped her rags in the bucket, tired of thinking. "You're right. Let's see to that kav."

CHAPTER THIRTY-FIVE

The women had gathered round the tables, ladling bowls of soup to the children, who eyed the waiting treats in the baskets of sweet rolls. Warna saved a bowl about to spill from tiny fingers. She smiled at the little girl who stared at her with big eyes.

"What's your name?" Warna asked.

"Lily," the blonde girl whispered.

"Let me help you," Warna whispered back, sitting on a bench and pulling the girl into her lap.

She sat in their midst, and listened to the talk as the children ate. There was no discussion of their plight, not with little ears listening. The women focused on the food, making sure that the soup was actually eaten before handing out the sweets.

Lily managed the entire bowl, and half the bun before she was full. Warna smiled, hugging the child close. "Done?"

The tiny one nodded, her blonde curls falling in her eyes.

"Then outside with you," one of the women said. Warna opened her arms, and Lily slid from her lap to run through the door. Around her, the women were herding the children outside to play.

"We'll have a bit of peace with our own meal," Lottie ladled out another bowl of soup. Warna took it and gave Lottie a grateful nod of thanks.

There was a clatter of heavy boots in the outer hallway. "Is that our men?" Lottie asked, looking toward the door, ladle poised over a bowl.

"It is," An older man stepped in, and greeted her with a kiss. "Is there enough for us?"

"Oh yes," Lottie said. "We've been well provided for."

"That's good," He settled in at the table as others followed him into the room.

"The children are all playing," Lottie said. "No better time for news. What says the Lord High Baron?"

"You're the Lady Warna?" The older man focused on her as he settled on the bench opposite.

Warna nodded. Around them, the other men began talking to their womenfolk, taking up bowls of soup and settling at the tables.

"Well enough," he said. "I am Mayth."

"What news?" Lottie said sharply, placing soup and kav before him.

"Can't I get a bit of food first?" He grumbled, then reached up to stroke Lottie's cheek. "Patience, wife. The Lord High Baron sat with us a good long while, and we talked options. We've decisions to make, true enough, and we'll do that tonight, with all of us gathered."

"Options?" Lottie settled next to him.

"Aye," Mayth sighed. "He'll aid us if we wish to rebuild, but none of us are sure that's wise. He's offered to see us relocated, but that brings its own pain. In the meantime, he's offered shelter here, and time for us to decide."

Lottie let out a breath, and closed her eyes in weariness. "Mayth," her voice was just a whisper of pain.

"I know, sweetling," Mayth leaned over, and put an arm over her shoulder. "Eat something with me, eh? Put the heart back in you."

Lottie nodded against his shoulder, then straightened her back. "Only if you do the same." She nudged his elbow.

Mayth picked up his bowl.

"If Lord Verice made that suggestion he did so with your best interests at heart," Warna said quietly.

Mayth shrugged. "Still bitter on the ear, to hear that you must leave the village and land you were born to."

"Change always is," Warna said with a sigh. "But I'd think he'd only say that if it was true."

Warna excused herself to fetch more bread and kav, and returned, settling herself down to face them both. She placed the bread before them, and poured kav, giving them a moment to eat. "What's it like?" she said casually, taking some of the bread. "Living among the elves?"

Mayth raised an eyebrow at her.

"Warna's of Farentell," Lottie said. "She wouldn't know."

"Ah," Mayth grimaced. "You are one of the few that escaped, then." He took up bread, and reached for butter. "They say you're the Lord High Baron's ward. Under his protection."

Warna nodded, wondering what else had been said. But that wasn't what she wanted to know. "I'm told he treats humans differently."

"I don't know who you've been talking to, but that is not true." Mayth looked her in the eye, serious and intent. "I've lived in Tassinic, in Birch Cove all of my life, as has my father and his father before him. Lord High Baron Verice is equal handed to all, no matter the point of the ear or the slant of an eye. No man can complain of less than fair dealing at his hands."

Warna's shoulders eased, and she let out a slow breath.

"But if she's staying, building a life here," Lottie spoke up softly. "Then there's a truth she needs knowing."

Mayth said nothing for a long moment, concentrating on his food.

"In Tassinic, we have a saying," Lottie said softly. "The ears have it."

Mayth snorted in agreement. "Aye, there's that."

"The ears?" Warna asked.

"Say you're in the market, and there's two stalls of bread side by side, one baker a human, the other of elven blood," Mayth said. "No difference in the bread, mind, or the quality of the baking. But in Tassinic, the honest truth is that the one with the ears will be thought of as better." He shrugged. "It's not deliberate, if you know what I mean. But elves, the pure ones, mind, they're such perfectionists, that everyone just assumes they'll be better. Whether or not they actually are."

"If you have lace woven by an elven blood and lace woven by a human, even if the human one is finer by far, the elven one will always be better," Lottie said. "And they always buy the elven-blood one, every time."

"Didn't I just say that?" Mayth asked.

"But that's not right," Warna said.

"It's wrong, certainly, but it's so common no one even sees what they do as wrong or offensive, you know?" Mayth shrugged. "Even humans will do the same and not think twice."

"How do you cope? Warna asked.

"Well, most have elven in the family, you know, and then there's some that hire elves to sell their wares, or work the booth. Some shrug and carry on." Mayth sighed. "We'd more trade with the human baronies than Tassinic, truth be told. That's one of the reasons rebuilding will be hard. There's no trade with those bandits roaming the lands."

The sound of other voices made them all lift their heads. The constable stood at the door, scanning the room and Warna raised her hand to call him over.

"M'lady," Ricard gave her a nod from the doorway. "A moment, if I may."

"Of course," Warna rose, ignoring the speculation in Lottie and Mayth's eyes. She threaded her way past the tables to walk with him to the door. "Is something wrong?"

CHAPTER THIRTY-SIX

Ricard looked flustered and strained. "Nay, naught beyond concerns for these people." he said. "Will these barracks be ready for them?"

"Yes," Warna said. "There shouldn't be a problem."

"Then they'll need bedding and blankets, and other such things." Ricard looked over the room. "Safe to assume they have nothing and start there."

"Constable," Warna started, but the poor mael cut her off, airing his frustrations.

"The bakery and buttery have started their ovens, and the cooks have started bickering over things I cannot fathom." Ricard was scowling. "Lord Verice is dealing with the scouts and reports from the border, but has left provisioning to me to deal with. Wasn't bad when it was just the lads and I, but now the castle is opened up again and I—"

"Not the keep," Warna gave him a worried glance. "We promised—"

"No, no," Ricard sighed. "Not that. But—"

"I'll see to the cooks and bakers." Warna wrinkled her nose. "And the needs of these people. Is Ersal here?"

"Aye, he's waiting with petitions for Lord Verice," Ricard said.

"The petitions will have to wait," Warna said. "Send him to me and we'll start in."

"My thanks," Ricard's relief was obvious. "Lord Verice said to tell you that he regrets that he may not be available for dinner."

A stab of disappointment went through her. "Understandable," she said.

"He's ordered that you're to sleep in the Healers Hall this night." Ricard frowned at her. "Ordered Priest Dominic to clear out that top bedroom for you. I'm to see to it that your things are moved back."

Warna nodded her thanks, but Ricard's frown deepened as he continued. "I didn't know you were squeezed out."

"My idea," Warna said shortly. "The wounded come first." Suddenly irritable with all of them, she frowned right back at him. "If there's nothing else…?"

Ricard paused, then glanced around the dining hall. "Is there a problem, lady?" he asked carefully. "Did someone say something? Or offer insult?"

"No," Warna said. "Nothing like that," she gave him a frustrated look. "But there's much to be done, Constable."

"Aye to that," he said. "I'll send Ersal to you."

Warna returned to Lottie and Mayth. "Lord Verice wants to see you all settled here as soon as possible."

"It won't take long to finish the cleaning," Lottie said.

"I'm off to see to bedding and whatever else you need," Warna said. "Soap, towels—"

"Swaddling cloths," Lottie said. "Oh, and-" she lowered her voice. "Moonpads."

"Of course," Warna sighed.

* * * * *

Verice sat in his outer chamber, confronting a sea of maps and scouting reports.

The tale they told was incomplete, jumbled, and set his teeth on edge. There was none with Narthing's gift for organizing information, and as such he'd a need to hear all the information directly.

"Is it the vanguard of a larger attack?" He asked the warriors clustered around.

Which brought out new maps, counters and another round of discussion. Because the information they had was uncertain and vague at best. Forces spotted here, camps spotted there, movement of troops in the distance. New scouts sent to re-check what others had seen. Discussions of the scrying that had been done, and the limited information it had produced.

Through it all, through the talk and the maps and the waiting, in the moments between, all he could think of were Wolfe's words about Warna.

"*—face the truth of it now. Before it goes much further.*"

What was he thinking? Wolfe was right. For all that Warna was, well, Warna, she was still human.

It wasn't that he disliked humans. King Everard had been a good man for all that he wasn't of elven blood. Verice had friends that were human, although he didn't go out of his way to cultivate such friendships. Humans came and went with the seasons, never making a lasting impression on him, truth be told.

But Warna had.

Verice frowned at the map in front of him, without seeing it, his mind filled with images of brown eyes and—

"M'lord?" The man who'd placed it before him hesitated.

Verice shook his head to clear his thoughts. "Continue, please."

So, the afternoon wore on. By mid-day, his warriors were positioned, his strategy for the next few days set.

Verice was then free to talk with the people of Birch Cove and listen to their desire to rebuild. Which might indeed be best in the short run, but in the long view the value of that path was doubtful. Their trade with Farentell was gone, and who knew how long it would be before the trade routes with Summerford would be restored. The wiser course could be to rebuild in a new location, farther away from the border, closer to the river that would widen their markets and access to trade routes.

But he could see in their stubborn round faces a determination to argue, and he mentally sighed in frustration. After talking and asking them to consider well the decision, he sent them off for a mid-day meal and gave the constable his orders. Only then did he seek a few quiet moments with his own bowl of soup and bread, alone in his chambers.

It wasn't fair to toy with Warna's heart and life. As short lived as humans were, she deserved more than that. The honorable action would be to pull back gently, so as not to hurt her. Remembering the look in her eyes, the taste of her mouth, a pang of regret arced through his chest, but Verice shook his head at his own stupidity.

Unfair to her, heartbreak for him. It had to be done.

He returned to his tasks, after reassurance from the constable that his message had been delivered. The men of Birch Cove gathered once again and Verice was surprised to find that they seemed more open to the idea of resettling. The maps returned, but this time with a sense of hope in the future.

Then the scouts reported with fresh news and more information and once again his chambers rang with the going and comings of his warriors, all bearing reports. He listened carefully to their words, watching their hands on the maps, pointing out where and what they'd seen.

"So, no massing of troops. A probe perhaps, but one with no real force behind it."

Nods all around.

He stood, satisfied. "Then we've done what we can for now, to see the border secure. Seek your beds, all of you, with my thanks."

They filed out, and he stretched his back, tired. It had gone well enough, given Narthing's absence. He missed having the man at his side. There'd been no word all day as to his injuries, but Verice was inclined to think that no news was good news. But he'd see the man himself before he sought his bed.

Which brought him up short. He'd have to talk to Warna tonight as well. He couldn't let that issue linger any longer. It would be painful enough as it was.

The night sky was clear as he stepped out into the courtyard; it was later than he'd thought. A few steps brought him to the door of the Healers Hall; a quick question told him where Narthing was to be found. But first he went among the wounded, going from bed to bed, taking the time to ask after them and listen to their responses.

Finally, he came to Narthing's door, and after a light tap, he entered the room. "How goes it, my friend?"

Narthing's pale face lit in a smile.

Warna was sitting at his bedside.

CHAPTER THIRTY-SEVEN

Narthing," Verice moved into the room, conscious of Warna's gaze. He took a chair from the far wall and moved it to the bedside. The sharp scents of medicines and mixtures tickled his nose. "How do you fare?"

"Well enough." Narthing's voice was breathy and thin.

"Pain?" Verice frowned.

"Some," Narthing said slowly. "When I take too deep a breath. As long as I move slowly, and don't laugh, it's tolerable."

"They haven't dosed you?" Verice asked.

Narthing shook his head, but Warna answered. "He wouldn't take it," she said quietly. "He put them off, told them he wanted to talk to you."

"Wanted to know," Narthing put his hand over his wound, as if to brace it. "You've reports, Lord?"

"Ah," Verice nodded his understanding. "Then lay there and listen, Captain."

Verice summarized what he knew briefly, but with enough detail that Narthing seemed satisfied.

"So, if it was a probe, it wasn't a serious effort," Narthing breathed out. "That's good. Better than I'd hoped." He let his head sink into the pillow, staring at the ceiling for a moment.

Verice waited, watching his face, letting Narthing mull over the information. "But what of Birch Cove?" Narthing finally asked, his eyes narrowing.

"The town's a loss," Verice said. "I'm sending warriors with the menfolk to see what can be retrieved of personal belongings, and to round up what they can of the livestock."

Narthing gave the slightest shake of his head. "That river ford—" he said and then winced.

"We think alike," Verice said. "I talked to them about building there.

They seem amenable to the idea."

Narthing cast him a doubtful look. "Really? Humans can be stubborn, m'lord." He blinked owlishly at Warna. "No offense," he said.

"I'm fetching that healer," Warna said. "It's past time you slept." She slipped out the door.

"You must have a care," Verice said. "That was a mean slice you took."

"No fear," Narthing said. "Dominic stood here and told me all the complications I risk unless I follow orders. His description of a bowel rupture was graphic enough that I fear to cough, much less anything else."

Warna returned with healers in tow, who gently shooed them both out of the room. "He needs his rest, m'lord." The one said as she closed the door in Verice's face.

Warna was on the stairs, leading up to the room tucked under the eaves. It seemed his orders had been carried out then. She had a place to sleep.

She paused, and turned to look at him, her face closed and warded. "Goodnight, m'lord."

"Warna," he said firmly.

She paused on the stairs, one hand on the railing. There was the slightest trembling in her fingers as they rested on the wood.

"We should talk," Verice said softly. "Walk with me. In the gardens."

* * * * *

The night air was cool on Warna's flushed cheeks, a slight breeze played with her hair as Verice lead her out of the Healing Hall. The dogs gathered around them, tails slowly wagging as they walked.

The courtyard had emptied of all but the watch and a few souls. Light spilled from the buildings around them, which thrummed with life. As tired as she was, as confused as she was about the man next to her, Warna smiled at the visible proof of her labors.

Except for the keep, of course. It lay at the center, dark, still, and daunting.

Much like its Lord High Baron.

"All are settled, it would seem," Verice said quietly, standing next to her.

"Yes," Warna said, just as softly.

"And you've your room back," Verice said.

"Yes, but only for tonight," Warna said. "Dominic was called to Church duties, and he will return tomorrow. I'll need to find another place." Verice scowled, and opened his mouth to speak, but she hurried on. "It's only right that he be with his patients. It's not as if he will sleep on a cot in the dining hall."

"But where will you—" Verice cut off his own words.

Warna glanced away, not willing to look at him.

Verice cleared his throat. "This way," he said softly as the dogs rose to join them.

"I didn't know there were gardens here," Warna said, wincing as it sounded more like an accusation than a question.

"The moat between the inner and outer castle walls was foul and disgusting when I arrived," Verice's face was mostly in shadow, but she could hear the pride in his words. "They were using it for all matter of waste and garbage. The reek was thick. So, I ordered it drained."

"The area between the outer and inner walls?" Warna blinked, frowning as she thought back to the ride through the gates. That area had been big. Really big. "How long did that take?"

"Not long," Verice said absently as he led her around the Healing Hall, to a heavy wooden door set into the wall. "Four, maybe five years."

"Five... years?" Warna said.

"Ten more after that to really get the soil ready, and get the plantings established." Verice chuckled softly. "There was some protest from the warriors, about the need for a moat for protection. But I planted rantha bushes and that put an end to the protests."

"Rantha?" Warna asked.

"Take twenty years to mature," Verice explained. "But well worth it. The flowers are sweet smelling but the vines are thick with thorns that are wicked sharp and as long as a man's hand."

Thirty years? Warna added it up in her head. Thirty years to plan such a thing, and Verice thought nothing of it?

Between the Healing Hall and the next building was a small, heavy wooden door, barred and locked. Verice removed the bar, and began to free the various latches. The dogs milled around their legs, tails wagging.

"This area is more the herbs and medicinal plants," Verice said as the door swung open. Warna peered inside. There was just enough light to see a path, and a garden stretched out beyond. The breeze touched her face, carrying the sweet scents of flowers and herbs.

"After you," Verice gestured.

Warna stepped forward, through the door—

And smacked into an invisible barrier.

CHAPTER THIRTY-EIGHT

Verice froze, not understanding for a heartbeat, then understanding all too well. The warding. He had released it temporarily when they'd left for Wolfe's Tower, but he hadn't taken it down.

Warna stepped back, frowning, staring at the doorway. Before he could move, she reached out, her fingers stopped by the invisible resistance.

Sand and Gray slipped past her and into the gardens, their nails clicking on the stones. Gray returned, coming back to Warna, whining in his throat as if he sensed something was wrong.

"I," Verice's stomach sank. "For your own protection, I—"

"That's what Kalynn was talking about, wasn't it?" Warna's expression was guarded, her eyes shuttered. "When she said 'caged'?"

"Warna—" Verice wasn't even sure what he could say, how he could tell her—

"Lord Verice, perhaps we could discuss this later." Warna took a step back from the door, her gaze cast down, the perfect image of proper deference, but with an edge to her voice. "The day has been a long one, for both of us."

"Warna." He couldn't leave it like this, couldn't let her go without trying to explain. Yet, what really could he say?

"Good night, m'lord." Warna turned away.

"I'm sorry," Verice said. *For so much. For leading you on, for the pain I've caused you.* But he kept those words in his heart.

She paused but didn't look at him. "I'm sure you acted as you saw fit, m'lord."

He watched as she walked away, followed by Sand and Gray.

Brindle whined and pushed his head against his leg. Verice reached down to stroke her ears. He whistled the rest of the pack to his side, and then, with an odd sense of relief, regret, and utter defeat, he swung the door shut and dropped the bar into place.

* * * * *

It's been days since they've shared a meal?" Narthing asked.

Those clustered around his bed all nodded glumly.

Narthing sighed.

They'd all gathered in his room at mid-day, supposedly to share a meal and keep Narthing informed as to events.

Honestly, what he wanted to hear was the gossip.

"They've not eaten together, they've barely spoken," Ersal said, staring at the chicken leg in his hand. "And when they do speak it's of laundry supplies and cooking oil."

"And painful to watch," Janella added, poking at her own plate. "As if each is afraid of pricking the other if they get too close."

"What happened?" Narthing asked. The healers still had him on a soft diet, and he eyed Ersal's chicken leg with longing, then picked up his mug of broth.

"Don't know," Ricard sighed. "They went for a walk the night the Chaosreaver appeared."

Narthing jerked, almost spilling his broth. A jolt of pain went through him at the movement.

"Narthing," Janella scolded.

"She came back alone," Ricard continued. "He followed after a while, looking morose. Well, more morose than normal."

"When was the Chaosreaver here?" Narthing demanded. His stomach clenched

against the tightness in his chest, and he set the broth back down.

That got him surprised looks all around. "The day after you were wounded," Ersal said. "Didn't the Lord mention it?"

"He did not." Narthing closed his eyes and breathed through the pain.

"You're hurting," Ersal said. "Let me fetch Dominic and—"

"He's gone to Edenrich for the day," Narthing said. "He's being considered for a position in the Church."

"Good riddance," the constable muttered.

"He's a skilled healer," Janella said.

"He's an arrogant prick," Ersal replied.

"And I'm to eat something before I can take more for the pain," Narthing said. "How long was he here? The Chaosreaver?"

"Never left the courtyard, and gone just that quickly." Ricard reassured him.

"Thank be to the Lord of Light," Narthing offered up a heartfelt prayer. "But why did he come?"

"Lord Verice didn't say," Ersal said.

Narthing sighed, and picked up his broth again. "There's nothing good at hand when that one roams the world."

"The seer was with him," Janella offered.

"That's no cause for comfort," Narthing managed a sip. The broth was warm and flavorful, but it was still just broth.

"Lord Verice must have done something, said something to her," Ersal said. "You should talk to him."

Janella rolled her eyes. "He didn't listen to any of us for months after the attack. Warna is here for what? A week? Ten days? And she's got things returning back to normal."

"Except for the keep," Ricard pointed out.

"Except for the keep," Janella agreed. "But it's only a matter of time."

"Do you think it was the humans? From the village that was destroyed?" Ersal asked. "Did they say something to upset her?"

"I don't know," Ricard shrugged. "But she seemed odd after she talked to them."

"Now she's humming sad songs under her breath," Janella said. "All the time."

"The Festival's in just a few weeks," Ersal said. "What are we going to do?"

"Nothing," Narthing said firmly.

"Nothing?" Janella stared at him. "But—"

"Lord Verice's relationship with Lady Warna is none of our concern," Narthing said, only to be cut off by Janella's glare.

"I think she'd be good for him," she declared, as others agreed.

"Even so," Narthing said. "That's between the two of them, and I can promise you that our meddling will not aid that process. There's nothing to do but wait and see. Something will give, one way or another. M'lord has enough on his shoulders without us raising this issue. Let them be." Narthing lifted his cup and gave them all a look as he finished his broth.

"Aye," came the chorus of reluctant agreement.

"But to my way of thinking," Ricard said. "We owe a debt to Lady Warna for all that she has done for us. If naught comes of this or them, we'll still see her safe."

The 'ayes' to that statement showed they were all in agreement.

CHAPTER THIRTY-NINE

Thwack, Thwack.

Warna woke in the darkness of her room above the bakery, warm under her blankets, and blinked at the dawn just starting to spill through her window. Verice was back at weapons-practice again.

No. She couldn't call him that anymore. *Lord High Baron* Verice was back to his normal routine, now that matters had settled down. He'd rise early, eat, then take to the pells and practice grounds until the sun rose. He'd fallen back into his old habits, now that they

weren't... doing what they had been doing.

Whatever that was.

He'd done the same before she'd arrived, and likely be the same after she left.

But now she could also hear the workers in the bakery below and smell the faint scent of kav in the air. The castle's Lord may have fallen back into old ways out of frustration, but the castle was returning to its old routine with intent. Warna smiled into her pillow wearily. At least in that aspect she'd done well.

Thwack, Thwack.

She stretched, then curled onto her side, hugged her pillow, and closed her eyes. If she lingered until he was done, he'd be gone before she finished her morning kav.

But the noises continued, and in her mind's eye she could see him, wielding his sword, face so focused and intent... which was not conducive to sleep.

Warmth flooded through her, and she shifted in the bed, trying to still the ache in her chest. Damn the mael. Damn his kiss, for awakening something in her that she put aside as lost to her. Something she didn't want to have to think about. For all that she had tried to avoid Verice - *Lord High*

Baron Verice - it was impossible not to be conscious of his every move, every action. Even if she didn't see him, she heard of him from the people around her.

Thwack, Thwack.

Warna rolled over and buried her head in the pillows. Her emotions churned. Angry, hurt, bewildered, she wasn't sure what she was feeling.

At least, Verice - Warna gritted her teeth - Lord Verice had named a new Seneschal. Ersal was very nervous, but determined to do well. He'd come to her at once, asking questions and she'd aided him in the organizing of the castle's needs. They'd been going over the lists of supplies when Mayth had come to ask if she'd wish to settle with the humans of Birch Cove. Ersal's eyes had gone wide. "But she's not yet done here," he'd blurted out. "The keep... the Festival..."

Before Warna could say a word, Mayth had nodded his agreement. "But after," he said. "Just something to think on. We'd be glad to have you."

Ersal had opened his mouth, then closed it with a snap.

It was all well and good for everyone to look to her to continue, but no one was much help with the 'how'. And now that she and... Lord Verice were no longer... well, whatever they had been, they weren't it now.

Confusingly, that hurt. She flipped her pillow again, and punched it with her fist.

She didn't have any real idea of how she was to open the keep. Return the castle to working order.

Warna reached out and plucked at a bit of fuzz on the hem of the blanket, seeing again the Great Hall, with its shattered window, the stains on the floor, the spilled tables and broken dishes. Verice's face, as he stood within, holding out his hand to her. So much pain.

The silence from outside finally cut through her thoughts. Lord Verice would have started to summon his men, and would be opening the portal soon for his regular patrols.

Warna sighed, threw back the covers, and shivered in the cooler air. She'd promised to aid Ersal with his accounts; she'd best be about her day.

But that ache was still in her chest as she washed. An ache that had settled there as soon as she'd left Lord Verice standing at the garden door. An ache for something she'd lost, or something she was in the process of losing, if that made any sense. A wistful dream, a hope, a desire, slipping away like the mist in the full light of the sun.

Warna huffed at herself as she dried her face. Foolish thoughts.

At least this room at the top floor of the bakery had a few of the niceties. A privy of its own, and a large comfortable bed. Even a dressing table, with a mirror. Clouded with age, but still a mirror. And she'd acquired a few more clothes in the past few days. Dresses and tunics and skirts, underthings, and new shoes. All sturdy and well made. Although there'd been bright colors available, she'd stuck with muted grays, and browns. Both her parents had frowned on full formal mourning, but Warna hadn't the heart to wear the jeweled colors she'd been offered.

She'd combs now too, and hair pins, and a brush. Some cream for her face and hands. Moonpads, and by her reckoning she'd have a need for those soon. Little things, true enough, but it meant so much to have them in her small lidded-basket.

She dug out what she'd wear, and paused when she heard the crinkle of paper within. She couldn't help herself really. She pulled out the note and read it again, as she had done a thousand times since she'd received it.

Warna,
The barrier has been removed. You are free to move about as you will.
Verice

Short, succinct, to the point. But in his own hand. Warna carefully folded the note, and returned it to the trunk.

She settled herself at the dressing table, and started combing her hair, working the tangles out. The noises below were louder now, the scent of kav and bread stronger. She would see to Ersal, then talk with Janella about the keep. Perhaps she would have some ideas. It promised to be a full day, full of things that needed doing.

She started to pin up her hair, humming under her breath.

All it would take to open the keep would be one legitimate reason. Something that was a need, not a want. A meeting that needed a large space, or the visit of a dignitary. Warna frowned, pins in her mouth. Weren't there foodstuffs stored in the keep, in case of siege? Or the mice she'd seen. That might be reason enough. Mice led to rats, and that wasn't healthy. If they could use that to open just one door, Warna was certain the rest would flow naturally. The keep would be open to all, and her work here done.

What will it look like, she wondered, not for the first time. All lit up, with candles and mage lights, those colored windows all aglow, the shattered window restored to its glory. Verice seated in the high seat, herself at his side, a feast before them and friends all around. Laughing and dancing, with his arm around her waist, twirling about—

With a cold, sick feeling, Warna looked at her hair in the mirror and realized she was trying to cover the tops of her ears.

Her hands dropped to her lap, letting the pain wash through her. Tears came unbidden, and for long moments she didn't bother to wipe them from her face.

But after a time, she took a deep breath and removed the pins, letting her hair fall around her shoulders. She'd wear it loose today, tucked behind her ears.

Then she washed her face again, to remove the evidence of her tears.

* * * * *

Narthing."

Narthing looked up from his breakfast tray, startled to see Lord Verice standing there, fully armed and armored, his face grim. The mael had just been out at the pells, Narthing had heard him. What had brought him to the Healing Hall this early? "M'lord?" he asked.

Verice crossed to his bedside. "Look at this."

Narthing took the open scroll, careful to keep it out of his porridge and frowned at the seal. "A message from Valltera?" he asked, working his way through the formal elven wording.

"Worse," Verice growled. "A politely worded summons from the Coeval. And see whose attendance is required?"

"Yourself, of course," Narthing hazarded the safe guess, then sucked in a breath as he read the words. "Lady Warna?"

Verice's face was grim. "I've sent messages out, summoning my most trusted political advisors. If you're up to it, I will see if Dominic will allow us to carry you to my chambers. If not, we will meet here to determine our response. This needs consideration." Verice turned to go.

"And Warna?" Narthing asked. "You'll summon her as well?"

Verice paused, his eyes hooded. "We'll see."

CHAPTER FORTY

By mid-day, Warna was still wrestling with the accounts, determined to slay the beast, but Ersal was far more curious about the activities outside his office window.

"Well, something is certainly happening," Ersal said, gazing out toward the Healing Hall. "Portals opening and closing, and messengers coming and going all morning. What could it be about?"

"Ersal," Warna said, keeping her voice patient and kind. "These accounts will not balance themselves." Her head was down, her eyes focused on the figures on front of her, for all that she wanted to jump up and run to the window.

"Something's happening," Ersal said.

"Yes," Warna said. "Your accounts don't balance for the last three days and they need tending." She continued to compare the tiny numbers.

"But don't you want to know?" Ersal asked, crossing over to plant himself back on his stool.

"Yes, of course." Warna turned the page of the ledger. Of course she wanted to know why Lord Verice hadn't left this morning, and why his advisors were being summoned and escorted to Narthing's room. Lord of Light, the entire castle was abuzz with curiosity. "I am sure we'll be told what we need to know when we need to know it." She strived to sound aloof and above idle curiosity. "Now, is this entry accurate? Did you really order this many candles?"

He examined the lines she was pointing to. "That can't be right," Ersal scowled and started digging through the pile of documents at his side of the table.

"You're going to need help keeping this organized, Ersal." Warna said. "A clerk of your own, maybe two."

Ersal gave her a sharp look as he pulled forth the chandler's statement. "You won't be staying?" he asked. "I'd thought perhaps—"

"Here's the correct figure," Warna interrupted, not wanting to talk about her staying or going. "See?"

Ersal whooshed out a relieved breath. "I knew it couldn't be right—"

A cough had them both looking up, startled.

The constable stood in the doorway. "Lord Verice asks that you both attend him."

* * * * *

Narthing's room was crowded with people and chairs. Warna hesitated in the doorway, recognizing many faces in the crowd as Ersal pushed his way in. Even Dominic had managed to squeeze himself into the room.

From his bed, now moved into the corner, Narthing caught Warna's eye. "Here, Lady Warna," he said loudly, and gestured to a chair placed next to the headboard.

Heads turned to stare at her. Warna felt her cheek grow hot as people stood and shifted to allow her to pass. Warna threaded her way through with soft apologies. "Narthing, what's happening?" she asked urgently as she took her seat.

Narthing opened his mouth, but a sharp knocking silenced the room.

Verice stood in the center of one wall, and commanded everyone's attention. "Now that Seneschal Ersal and Lady Warna have joined us, let's review the situation."

Warna drew a breath. She hadn't been this close to him for some time. His face was set, hard as granite and yet he appeared tired to her eyes. Weary, even. She swallowed hard, and looked away.

"You've all had a chance to read the missive from King Barathiel of Valltera. We can all agree that the wording—"

"Warna has not," Narthing said firmly.

Verice seemed to catch himself, as if forcing himself to slow down.

"It would not be bad, to review what we know," Lord Mayor Pernard said mildly.

Verice nodded. "To summarize then. This morning, when I finished with the pells, a message from King Barathiel awaited me on my desk." He nodded to the parchment on Narthing's lap. "It contains a polite but strongly worded summons to attend upon his Majesty today 'to discuss the welfare of my person and Tassinic'." Verice's blue eyes drilled into hers. "The Lady Warna is also included in the summons."

"What?" Warna couldn't quite take that all in. "Me? But—"

Narthing had pushed the parchment into her lap, and she stared down to where he pointed. She could see her name clear as day in one of the lines of spidery, thin script.

"The document extends me the privilege of opening a portal to the Royal Household this noon, and implies that the visit will be a short one, given that it fails to mention servants or retainers." Verice grimaced. "Our worries stem more from what it doesn't say, than what it does."

"So, the question becomes," Narthing said. "do you accept this invitation?"

"Observations?" Verice said. "We've little time to debate, and no doubt that is by intent as well." He paused, then gave them all a rueful expression. "You've advised me well in the past. Give me the gift of your wisdom now."

Pernard rose from his chair. "M'lord, King Barathiel has not once contacted you since the troubles began within Palins, has he?"

"He has not," Verice confirmed.

Ersal gestured to Warna, and she passed him the invitation to read.

Pernard frowned. "Yet he has brought up troops to our border. Not of a strength that we would fear invasion, but enough to cause concern. I do not know what that portends, but I say do not go. Exchange messages, yes. Use scrying bowls, yes. But do not go."

An older woman rose, someone Warna didn't know. "And I would argue that point. We do not know the intent of this. King Barathiel has not been openly hostile and the borders remain open for trade and travel. They know that if Tassinic falls, they will have to deal with the Usurper, and they don't want that."

There were many nods at that.

"Still, I do not like this," Ersal next rose. "The summons is almost worded as if to a vassal, and you are not a vassal of the Elven King."

"True," Verice nodded. "I was released from my oaths and allegiance to Valltera before I swore fealty to Palins and Tassinic. King Barathiel has no claim on me."

"Yet still, he summons you," Ersal said. "Don't go, m'lord. Send another in your place. Plead illness, plead necessity, plead the coming Festival. Do not place yourself in his hands."

"Any excuse given must be legitimate," Dominic protested. "Lest they discover otherwise and take offense."

Verice raised an eyebrow. "I am not without my own abilities."

"True enough, m'lord," Dominic bowed his head. "But the Royal Court is quick to take offense at any violation of protocol or etiquette. Once there, you must dance to their tune or risk their wrath."

"Well I remember," Verice snorted. "My mother ever feared suffering the consequences of my actions."

That was met with chuckles and nods all around the room.

"It's not just you, m'lord," Narthing shifted in his bed. "All of Tassinic goes with you through that portal. Not to mention Lady Warna."

"Lady Warna is not going," Verice said.

Warna glanced at Verice, then at Narthing.

"M'lord, I hesitate to say this," one of the older maels spoke slowly. "But she is included in the invitation. Her presence will be expected and—"

"No," Verice said. He stood there, considering, his arms crossed over his chest. "Everything you've said to me is true, and I understand your concerns. What we need is information, and its better if it's exchanged face-to-face. King Barathiel can be difficult, but he is honorable. I have no reason to believe this is other than an exchange of information. I will go. Warna will remain here."

"Is that a command?" Warna asked.

"What?" Verice stopped, stunned. "Of course it's a command."

"Why?" Warna asked. "My name is on the invitation. Isn't it my choice?"

The room went silent.

Verice glared. "It's not safe."

"If it's not safe for me, how is it safe for you?" she countered. "And if I do not appear at your side, that could be offensive, correct?"

Heads nodded in agreement around the room, but Verice had a counter. "You've not the wardrobe to visit the Royal Court," he said.

"I'm in mourning," Warna replied. "Plain garments are expected."

"Which excuses her from any formal parities, and those intricate dances,"

Janella piped up from a corner.

"The fact that they've pulled a young woman from her home during a time of mourning will not be viewed favorably," Pernard said with a helpful tone.

"She does not know elven ways, or proper behavior," Verice snapped. "You'll cause more problems than—"

"Speak only in response," Warna threw his weaponsmaster's words back in his face. "Answer, but never ask. And never make the first move."

"That will serve," Narthing chuckled.

Verice shot him a glare. "She doesn't speak elvish." he said.

"Please," Dominic spoke up from his corner. "That's a simple spell for you, one that allows her to speak and understand. And a decision must be made quickly. My patient needs his rest."

"I'm fine," Narthing protested.

"Bowel ruptures," Dominic said.

Narthing sank back onto the pillows with a mutter.

"The decision is yours, of course m'lord," Warna said, standing and brushing off her dress. "And I will abide by your command. But this summons seems to me both threat and promise, to you and your people." Something fiercely protective rose in her chest for him and Tassinic. "If we both go, we may discover their intent easily. If I am not there, you may waste precious time dealing with the consequences."

She lifted her chin, and waited to see if she was pawn, possession, or person in his eyes.

CHAPTER FORTY-ONE

Verice eyed her cooly for a long moment, but the determination in her lovely face just grew. When had he lost control over the situation? Over her?

She'd made her choice, and his heart swelled at the idea that she would put the interests of Tassinic over her own. But that pride also bore a tang of fear. Fear for her stepping into the unknown.

He shook his head in surrender, acknowledging the truth of her words. "Very well. We leave at noon."

Warna gave a sharp nod. "There's not much time then." She started to weave her way towards the door.

"For discussion?" Pernard asked.

"To look presentable," Warna retorted.

"Just be certain to be ready on time," Verice said.

She halted just at the door, and gave Verice a look, raking him from head to toe. "Look to your own self, m'lord."

With a flash of blonde hair, she was gone, running down the stairs, calling for some of the female healers to check and make sure the bath-house was ready.

"You've been given your orders, m'lord," Narthing said with a wan smile.

"It would seem I have," Verice snorted softly as the others started to file from the room.

Dominic stood by the bed, eyeing his patient. "That took more out of you than you'd care to admit," he observed. "You'll sleep now." Narthing nodded weakly, submitting to Dominic's ministrations.

"I needed his advice," Verice said.

"The Royal Court of Valltera places high values on appearances, m'lord," Dominic said. "Appropriate attire and a certain level of grooming would be in your best interests. Think of it as armor for the coming battle, if you must."

"So, Warna is right?" Narthing asked.

"Not that I'd admit to," Dominic said.

Narthing laughed, then groaned, holding his stomach.

* * * * *

The women's bathhouse was ready, thankfully, and Warna plunged in, refusing all offers of oils and unguents, except for the plainest of creams for her face and hands. Black dress, with black shoes, and someone found a black cloak that fit her well. Her hair didn't need washing, and there was no time to dry it anyway, so she braided it tight and wound it up on her head, making certain this time that her ears were exposed. She'd not cover up what she was, not ever again.

There was a tingle of excitement deep in her stomach. Valltera, the palace of the Elven King and Queen. She read so many stories as a child, she couldn't help wondering if it would be like the tales.

It was only when the women were chattering around her and she was putting on the cloak that Lottie entered, hesitating at the door. "M'lady?"

"Lottie." Warna took her hands and drew her into the room filled with faellas. "I'm about to depart with Lord Verice, but is there something you need?"

"I know, we heard, Lady." Lottie had a bundle in her hands. "Mayth managed to pull some things from our home. I thought perhaps—" She lifted her hands, and a black lace veil spilled from the bundle, with a pattern of roses woven within.

"Lottie," Warna breathed as the others ooh'd and ah'd. "You made this?"

"Aye. There's no scent of smoke on it," Lottie assured her. "I thought perhaps… given that you're dressed in mourning…"

"It's perfect. Thank you," Warna took the soft veil from her hands and draped it over her head, winding the ends around her neck. "How do I look?"

Lottie reached out, and adjusted the drape with pride. "Like a perfect lost soul, overcome with grief." She stepped back. "You watch over yourself and our lord now, you hear?"

"I will," Warna said. "I promise."

The women, human and faelle, all curtsied as she turned to leave. Warna flushed and made for the door.

She walked quickly across the courtyard where she could see Ricard standing. He greeted her and gave a nod over her shoulder. "He's just coming now."

She looked behind, and her eyes went wide.

Verice had taken the time to bathe, and his fine white hair was long and flowing outside its normal braid. He was wearing black leathers with a silver chain shirt, belted at the waist with his sword and dagger at his side. He looked like the very picture of an elven prince, down to the black boots and black leather gloves. He wore a black cape, but the chain ran across his chest, and its hem touched the back of his boot.

"I take it I have 'looked to my own self'," he said with a quirk of his lips.

"You'll do," Warna said.

Ricard looked up. "Almost time, m'lord."

"But first there's one thing I must take care of." Verice stripped off one glove. "Warna," he said softly, lifting his hand to her face. "If you would allow?"

Warna tilted her head slightly, feeling Verice ease his fingers under the veil and brush the delicate skin behind her ear. She shivered at his touch.

He whispered something she couldn't quite make out, and a tingle went through her, down to the tips of her toes.

"Lady, can you understand me?" His breath touched her cheek as he whispered strange words.

"Lord, I understand what you are saying," she whispered back, but the sounds were odd on her tongue.

He withdrew his hand, brushing her ear again, looking satisfied as he put his glove back on. "It will not last much more than a day, but it should suffice."

A chime sounded in the air, ringing a perfect tone.

"It's time," Verice said, and a portal opened before them. "Constable, you have the watch, but defer to Narthing in all things."

"Aye, m'lord," Ricard said. "Travel well, and return safe."

"M'lady." Verice extended his arm.

"M'lord." Warna placed her fingers on the back of his wrist and allowed him to lead her through the glowing white curtains of the portal.

* * * * *

Verice grimaced mentally as he and Warna emerged into the sunlight dappled grove in the palace gardens of Valltera.

"Oh my," Warna breathed, and he knew she was taking in the tall spires that rose above the gardens.

How long had it been since he walked these halls? Hundreds of years was his best guess. Yet it looked the same, even down to the vines and flowers. The more the world may change, the more elves remained the same, that was certain.

Verice had no idea how they endured it. It was one of the reasons he'd left these lands.

One of many.

"Verice, Bearer of the Blood of Tethnar, I offer you greetings." A royal herald stood before them in stately robes, holding his staff of office, looking as welcoming as an offended cat. "I am Mathonalar, and I am to escort you to the royal presence."

"Mathonalar, I accept your greetings, and extend my own in return." Verice gave a formal bow. "But I must correct you in your choice of title. I am of Palins now, Lord High Baron of Tassinic."

Mathonalar bowed formally in return, as slow and stately as one could wish. "I offered greetings as I was commanded."

"I see," Verice would have spat the words, if that were permitted. "May I introduce my ward, Lady Warna of Farentell."

Warna curtsied, and Mathonalar bowed, offering his formal greetings yet again. Verice had forgotten the elaborate slowness of ritual welcomes. It made him grit his teeth.

"Once the guard has peace-bonded your weapons, I am instructed to bring you to Their Majesties' presence," Mathonalar continued.

Which was another way of saying 'show up and wait your turn,' Verice thought, but let no hint of it show on his face. He turned to the guard, and they started the ritual of binding each blade in its scabbard with ribbons and wax seals.

This promised to be a very long afternoon.

Mathonalar set a slow pace through the gardens and halls as he escorted them to the King and Queen. Warna was quiet at his side, but a glance told him that her eyes were wide with delight, drinking in the sights.

He could hardly blame her. Elves moved about them, graceful and serene in their bright robes that shimmered as if woven of moonlight and shadow, their ears decorated with the traditional piercings along the edges, glittering with jewels and precious metals. They walked down corridors of glowing white marble, with thick carpets patterned with leaves and birds in patterns that never seemed to repeat.

And the air was sweet with perfume and soft music floated through every window. Perfect, unblemished, unchanged. As it had been for centuries.

"It's lovely," Warna dared whisper.

It's stifling, was Verice's thought.

But at last they turned down a short hall, and at Mathonalar's gesture, the guard drew open the double doors. As they stepped through into the large chamber filled with courtiers, Verice could see King Barathiel on his throne at the other end of the room, with Queen Blesenthala beside him.

Mathonalar led them straight up to the throne at his slow, regal pace to give those present time to study and assess them, Verice was certain of that.

Mathonalar stopped before the throne, and tapped his staff three times upon the floor. "Verice, Bearer of the Blood of Tethnar, and his ward, Warna of Farentell."

Verice narrowed his eyes at the lack of title for Warna, wondering who had instructed that little detail. But the room had gone silent, and King Barathiel was rising to his feet, a smile on his face.

"Welcome, cousin!"

CHAPTER FORTY-TWO

I t was all Warna could do not to let her mouth gape open like a dying fish. Cousin?

Verice took a step forward as the King approached them. The courtiers were all bowing, and moving to the side, creating a path for the King.

"Your Majesty," Verice gave a formal bow. "I offer thee greetings."

"So formal." King Barathiel waited until Verice rose, and then grasped Verice in a hug that seemed to catch him by surprise. Before Verice could react, the King released him, and faced Warna directly. "And this is Warna? Your ward, I believe."

Warna sank down as gracefully as she could and bowed her head.

"So lovely," King Barathiel murmured. "We've heard much of your gifts, Warna."

That brought her head up, to stare into eyes more cruel, rather than kind. A frisson of fear ran down her spine, but Warna remembered herself enough to lower her gaze. "My thanks, your Majesty," she whispered.

"So shy," King Barathiel said. "And so sorrowful. We are saddened to hear of your loss, Warna. The actions of the Usurper of Palins are a threat to us all."

* * * * *

The waters here were deeper than Verice had anticipated, and rapidly rising over his head. "Your Majesty?" he asked, careful to leave his question open-ended. He'd forgotten the layers within layers of the simplest of words spoken in the royal court of Valltera.

"Come, cousin," Barathiel took his arm, and guided him towards the dais. "Charrin has told us much of your ward, and the situation you are facing. We've had many long talks with him."

That came as a shock. Charrin was seated on a stool one step down from the throne. A signal honor. He sat, face turned toward Verice, his harp in his hands.

"We, Your Majesty?" Verice asked.

"Our advisors, the Queen and myself." The King left his side and mounted the steps to his throne. Verice glanced back to see that Warna had followed him, standing one step behind him, a single black rose in a mass of colorful dresses. "We've discussed it for some time, and have reached the only conclusion possible. The Usurper threatens your barony, cousin."

"There is tension within Palins, Your Majesty," Verice agreed cautiously. "But to my knowledge it has yet to reach the borders of Valltera."

"It is only a matter of time." Barathiel settled back on his throne with a confident air. "Tassinic must come under our protection, Verice. And you must be restored to your rightful place in our society."

A political pit yawned wide at Verice's feet. "Your Majesty, I was released from my oaths to yourself and this land many years ago. I have sworn my allegiance to Palins and—"

"To a dead human king, and a lost bloodline," Barathiel said sharply. "That means little now, wouldn't you agree?"

"No." Verice replied and etiquette be damned. He wasn't being pushed into this. "I am bound by those oaths."

"A simple matter, really." Queen Blesenthala's eyes glittered, her voice low and lovely. "In all honor, you will be brought back within the Royal family. Blood binds tighter than any oath. And to that end, we have had a thought to bind you even tighter to us. A marriage."

"Marriage?" Verice gaped at her, as the pit became a chasm. "Your Majesty, I—"

"Too long you have been without companionship, Verice." Barathiel leaned forward. "It's not healthy to live alone without the love of a faella." He paused. "Unless you prefer a mael?"

"No, Your Majesty," Verice said. "But—"

"Then there is no impediment," Barathiel said. "We would see you wed to a faella of a Blood that will bring you all honors."

"Your Majesty—" Verice tried to gather his wits. "My oaths—"

King Barathiel would have none of it. He cut through Verice's protests.

"Tassinic is best brought within the protection of our throne and power."

"Your Majesty—"

"Your blood is of the highest, Verice. It's time for you to stop wasting time with these—" his eyes flicked to Warna and away. "These amusements. Take up the duties and responsibilities imposed on you by virtue of your birth. There's really no reason you cannot be wed, is there?"

Verice's mouth was as dry as his brain. "Your Majesty—"

"Actually, there is," Warna's voice came over his shoulder as she advanced to his side. "He has pledged his troth to me."

* * * * *

Warna watched with a great deal of satisfaction as her words wiped the smug looks off the faces of the King and Queen.

The Queen recovered first, her face serene, her eyes enraged. "We'd no word of this," she said icily, shooting a glance at Charrin.

"Your Majesty." Warna gave her best deep bow, more to give Verice time to find his voice than to honor the Queen. She rose to her feet as slow as grace would allow. "Our vows were only recently exchanged. I'd asked my lord to keep this between the two of us, in hopes that my family might be located and permission given."

Verice seemed to recover, and lifted his wrist, extending it to Warna, who placed her fingers on it gratefully. "I honored my lady's request." He bowed to both the King and Queen. "Please forgive our delay in informing you of our intentions," Verice focused on Warna, and she glowed at the warmth in his eyes. "We'd love to have you for the ceremony."

The silence was icy, but the look in Verice's eyes was enough to protect Warna from the chill.

Verice turned back. "If that was all, Your Majesty, we would return to Tassinic. I offer assurances that I will keep my borders secure, and honor the treaties between Palins and Valltera."

"No." Barathiel stood abruptly. "This warrants private discussions between you and I. But at this time, other petitioners await our attention. Perhaps you wish to show your... *intended*... the gardens? We will summon you to our side shortly."

Verice inclined his head. "Our thanks to your gracious majesties." Before

Warna could start her curtsey, he led her off through tall doors on the other side of the room, and into the gardens.

* * * * *

Verice didn't stop until he was sure they were well out of the range of any listeners. He took Warna's hand and urged her through the rows of hedges and flowers, all perfectly trimmed without a leaf or branch out of place.

Finally, he found a bench surrounded by a field of knee-high lavender, where he had a clear field of vision. He stopped, and checked their surroundings.

Warna sank down onto the bench as if all the energy had drained from her. "Verice, I am so sorry," she started.

"You have nothing to be sorry for." Verice started to pace in the area before her, still keeping watch.

"I've all but trapped you into a marriage," Warna said. "But I didn't see any other way. They both seemed so smug, so sure they'd trapped you—"

"They may have," Verice said. "And please believe my anger is for myself, not you. I should have seen this coming."

"I don't see how," Warna said.

"Barathiel has always resented Palins," Verice said. "And that his father, my uncle, consented to releasing me so that I could swear fealty to King Jeverard."

"So, he *is* your cousin?" Warna asked, her eyes going wide.

"Only when he deems fit to acknowledge that fact," Verice growled. "Now, to find a way out of here without offending their delicate sensibilities."

"You will find a way," Warna said.

"I appreciate your faith in me," Verice paused in his pacing. "Since I have no idea of how I am going to do that." He stared down at her. "But one thing is clear. We are being watched."

Warna's eyes went wide. "But you said—"

"They can't hear us," Verice assured her. "But they can see us. And it would appear that we have been arguing." He shook his head. "So, we need to address this issue," he knelt before her, and reached for her hand, pressing it to his chest. "I will ask forgiveness, as a proud elven warrior should when he has offended his lady."

"And as a gentle human lass, I will forgive." Warna smiled. "This isn't your fault."

"Nor is it yours," he replied.

"I never intended—" Warna started.

"I know," Verice murmured. "We'll discuss this at another time. But in order to hold true to our story, there's another thing we must do."

Warna blinked. "Yes?"

He leaned in, his lips hovering over hers. "With your permission?" he asked.

"Yes," Warna whispered and pressed her lips to his.

CHAPTER FORTY-THREE

Warna melted into his body, bringing her arms up to wrap around his neck. His mouth felt so good on hers. When his tongue danced over her upper lip, she parted them and let him in.

They kissed for long moments, until Verice pulled back slightly. "Not sure we've convinced them," he whispered in her ear.

"I agree," she said solemnly, and captured his mouth again, eager for more.

A clearing of a throat came from behind them. "Forgive me, Verice, Bearer of the Blood of Tethnar, but I've been sent to escort you to the King."

Verice broke the kiss, breathing heavily. "Give us a moment, if you would."

"But of course."

Verice helped Warna with her veil. "They will separate us," he said into her ear as he helped her to rearrange her veil. "Remember the three rules. And if it comes to that, seek out my old weaponsmaster. His name is Arthrano. He would aid you."

"How would he know who I am?"

Verice's chest rumbled in a deep, quiet chuckle. "After our little announcement? I suspect the entire Elven Kingdom knows who you are."

Warna took a deep breath to still her shakiness. "Once we are free of this place, we will discuss this further," she said. "And in more detail."

Verice's face stilled, all humor gone. "You have my word, m'lady." With that he rose to his feet. "We are ready now."

The guard advanced and bowed to Verice. "This way, Bearer of the Blood. There is a small sitting room where your ward can wait. You and the King are to have words."

"We will indeed," Verice said mildly.

Y ou always were the unconventional one," Barathiel said in the privacy of his chambers. "Wine?"

"No, thank you." Verice followed Barathiel into the room. He'd been forced to leave Warna in the care of one of the handmaidens down a distant hall. He chafed at the separation.

"Charrin has told us that you were attracted to the human woman." Barathiel poured himself a glass. "Polluting your blood line even further than it already is."

Verice stiffened.

"Have her if you will," Barathiel continued. "For the time she has left. But no children, Verice."

Verice gave the man a cold look.

"Seal the borders to Palins, and the taint will dissipate from your lands over time. Tassinic can become one with our land. We would honor your boundaries and welcome you into our confidences."

"They aren't chess pieces, Barathiel."

"Take the long view, Verice," Barathiel gestured with his glass. "Sooner or later, there will be war with the Usurper. You and Tassinic will be caught in the middle. Ally with us and we—"

"As in the royal we?" Verice asked. "Is Blesenthala behind this offer?"

Barathiel paused, swirling the liquid in his glass slowly. He finally lifted his gaze to Verice. "She's a lovely thing, your human," he said. "If you like that sort of thing. But at best she's good for what, another fifty years? Your interest will wane, or she will."

"We'll be leaving." Verice stood.

"No," Barathiel said. "You'll stay until this is settled. Attempt to open a portal without permission, and my mage-guards will see to it that small chunks of your flesh rain down on your precious castle."

"I find this hard to believe, cousin," Verice said coldly. "That your sense of hospitality suffers so."

"Nonsense," Barathiel said as he strode to the door, opening it to reveal an escort. "I'd honor you, cousin, by assigning you a role in the afternoon ceremonies. It's rare that one such as yourself is afforded the honor of smoothing the royal pillows."

"What of Warna?" Verice growled.

"Another reason you should consider your position," Barathiel said. "But have no fear, cousin. We will see to her comforts."

* * * * *

A handmaiden escorted Warna into a small room with paintings on the walls, and windows overlooking the gardens. There was no other way out beside the one door, and she was fairly certain there was at least one guard in the hall.

She settled on one of the chairs by the windows, and resigned to wait patiently.

She had to smile in spite of herself. Her picture books of elves and their lands hadn't done justice to the beauty and elegance of these people. And hadn't prepared her for their arrogance either.

The Lady of Laughter alone knew where she'd gotten the courage to claim Verice before the King and Queen. Warna had to admit to herself that part of her motivation was simply anger at their smug faces, certain that they'd caught Verice in their snares.

She hadn't thought of rumors, or that the word of their engagement might travel as swift as flight, but she should have known. Even elves weren't above a good gossip, it would appear. Something none of her childhood story books had mentioned. And wasn't that a disappointment, to find out that elves were human?

Her stomach rumbled a bit, reminding her that it had been some time since her morning meal. Had it only been half a day since she'd awakened to the sound of Verice's sword against the pells? If felt like forever...

With any luck, they'd feed her at some point.

The door opened, and Charrin walked in.

He really hadn't changed since she'd seen him in Bode's tower. Tall, elegant, with that horrible slash over his eyes, puckered and red. He was carrying his harp and wearing formal robes embroidered with flames.

"Warna," he said.

"Bard Charrin." Warna rose and curtsied.

"You needn't bother," he said, moving unerringly to the chair opposite her. "It's not like I can see your courtesies."

"Still I offer them," Warna said. "Out of respect."

"I don't see why," he said. "It's not like I have any respect for you or your kind."

To the hells with the three rules. "Then why are you here?" Warna demanded.

"To tell you that I heard the note of surprise in his voice," Charrin said. "That I know that you are no more betrothed to Verice than I am able to fly." Charrin placed a hand on the back of the chair. "Retract your lies before the court, so that Verice can take his true place in society."

"That which lies between Verice and I is a private matter," Warna said. "And his surprise was in the announcement, not the betrothal."

"He pollutes his bloodline again if he goes forward with this," Charrin spat. "Tassinic needs to be cleansed of its human taint, and brought within the Kingdom."

Again? Warna wasn't going to ask, because a deep chill ran down her spine at his words, his lovely voice filled with hate. Recalling Kalynn's words at the tower, she didn't hold back. "Does your hatred of humans," Warna paused. "Does your hatred of us truly add value to the memories of your Lady Summer?"

Charrin reared back. "How dare you speak her name," he hissed. "What do you know of loss, of pain? You, who have barely seen twenty years, if that? I have underthings older than you."

Warna wrinkled her nose at that, but then answered him honestly. "In the last year, I've lost everything. My family, my home." She looked down at her hands, pale against the black of her skirts. "A degree of belief in the goodness of people, human as well as elven. I am not sure that the number of years matter. We share these things, Charrin. Elf and human alike."

"How dare you," Charrin spat, his face contorted in rage.

"It's easier to hate than to mourn, isn't it?" Warna continued on. "Easier to dwell on the grief than live."

"You miserable, hateful—"

A knock on the door brought Charrin to a stop, trembling as he stood there.

"Forgive the intrusion," it was the handmaiden, peeking in through the open door.

"Enter," Warna said. "Please."

The handmaiden advanced, her flowery skirts rustling on the carpet, and curtsied before Warna. "Please forgive the delay. Queen Blesenthala invites you to take tea with her."

Warna didn't think twice. "I'd be delighted."

* * * * *

Charrin watched the human flee.

How dare she compare her squalid feelings to his. How dare she claim that they shared anything.

Verice had to be made to see his error, his folly, and no amount of song or poetry would convince him, Charrin was certain of that. Only actions would suffice to bring that stubborn Lord around.

Charrin took a deep breath, composing himself. There would be a time and place.

And then he would act.

CHAPTER FORTY-FOUR

Warm sun streamed through the windows as Verice watched the nobles strip the bedding from the King's bed with slow, careful movements.

It was probably for the best that he had been 'invited' to participate in this ceremony. It gave him time - lots of time - to consider his position.

Barathiel had caught him flat-footed and off-guard with his proposal that Verice abandon Palins, and marry to bring Tassinic into Valltera. Thank the Ancestors that Warna had stepped forward with her declaration. Verice's only other course would have been to try to stall, and Barathiel had seemed fully determined to force the issue then and there.

The mattress had been stripped, and turned. They all stood waiting patiently as the fresh bedding was carried into the room.

King Barathiel was an absolute ruler, Verice knew that well enough. But he had a council of Earls who held a great deal of power. Not all of them would be pleased with Barathiel's heavy-handed manner, for what force he brought to bear on Verice could easily be turned on them.

Verice cursed himself for his lapse in not knowing what was happening in Valltera much beyond the borders. He was an idiot, a thrice-times idiot, and he'd pay for that lack now. It would take time to locate the Earls, time to seek out their positions, and in the meantime Barathiel seemed determined to keep him here, a prisoner in the court.

Or Verice could risk the offense, open a portal, and defend himself from whatever happened next. But Tassinic could not stand against the concentrated might of Valltera.

And he couldn't risk Warna.

Barathiel knew that, damn him.

They were spreading the first sheet now. Verice sighed stoically, and girded himself for a long afternoon.

* * * * *

Warna felt like a black stain in a sea of flowery dresses. The hallway that the handmaiden led her down was filled with elven maidens in their finery. But the handmaiden walked serenely on, and Warna followed dutifully as she wove a path through them.

One of the faella leaned forward as Warna passed. "Your veil, so lovely," she whispered.

"Where did you find such quality?"

Warna's merchant soul rose up within her. "Its maker resides in Tassinic," she whispered. "Send word to me there, and I'll pass on her name."

The faella gave her a grateful look, and Warna continued on, following the handmaiden through large double doors. Only to find herself in a large room, as large as any ballroom she'd ever seen in her picture books.

At the far wall was a single throne, capped with a cloth of gold that shimmered under the light of a thousand candles. Before the throne, spread out in a fan pattern, were delicate white chairs, each with a tiny table beside it, each set with a white cup and saucer.

"Private tea?" Warna muttered under her breath.

The handmaiden led the way to the chair facing the throne, almost isolated from its neighbors. "I bid you welcome in Queen Blesenthala's name."

"I thank you," Warna replied, settling carefully in her chair. All she could do was fold her hands in her lap and wait.

The room filled, each faella taking her chair, sitting with perfect posture and composure, looking more like perfect painted dolls than living beings.

The cup and saucer caught Warna's eye, startling in their whiteness, of porcelain so fine she swore she could see through it. She'd love to own such a pretty thing, but right now she had but one thought: *Lord of Light, Lady of Laughter, don't let me drop it.*

The stir behind her finally stopped and a hush fell over the room as the doors were closed. Once all was silent, with each lady facing the throne, the doors opened again, and Queen Blesenthala swept in, and to her throne.

Warna rose with the others, and curtsied, careful not to let her skirts knock over the tiny table.

"Ladies, and Warna of Farentell, you are most welcome," Queen Blesenthala cooed, settling herself on her throne. Her dress was a vivid pink, making her the rose in the garden. "Let us refresh ourselves with tea and conversation.

"Warna, you are a delightful surprise this day, and we extend our greetings to you," the Queen continued. "Verice has been invited by the King to the Ceremonies of the Bedchamber. He is to place the pillows on the King's bed. A singular honor."

"Your Majesties are both so kind," Warna murmured, after it seemed that the Queen was expecting a response.

The Queen tilted her head gracefully to a footman off to the side, and servers flooded into the room, each carrying pots of tea held in towels.

"Verice is held in high regard here," Queen Blesenthala responded. "And we honor his choice of betrothal." She watched as her tea was poured, steaming, into the cup.

"An odd choice, of course," the Queen continued. "Humans are like flowers that bloom only to wither away so quickly. A brief moment in time."

"But, Your Majesty," Warna sent a mental apology toward Verice. "While it blooms, it is cherished all the more for the briefness of its beauty." She watched as the servant poured her cup of tea. "One treasures the time one is given."

Queen Blesenthala had lifted her saucer, her cup poised before her lips. "Well spoken," she said with a lift of her cup. "Shall we drink?"

Everyone else had claimed their cup and saucer. Warna lifted hers as well. She paused as the steam brought a flowery scent to her nostrils. "May I ask, what flavor is this?"

"Hibiscus," Queen Blesenthala hid her smile behind her cup. "My favorite."

No, it wasn't. Warna recognized the scent. It was gwenwyth tea.

'Your pardon, lady,' Aeric had said. "but me mum was full human, and while she liked the taste, it gave her the flux something fierce.'

The cup poised, Warna froze, staring at the Queen as the Queen stared back. The steam rose, the cup warm beneath her fingers, and yes, she could see them through the thin white porcelain.

Warna narrowed her eyes, hoping against hope that her thoughts were reflected in her eyes. *'You think humans are delicate little flowers in your garden, don't you?'* Warna thought. *'Well, guess what, bitch—'*

She drank the entire cup, setting it softly back on its saucer.

'We are not.'

CHAPTER FORTY-FIVE

V erice had the honor of placing the first pillow, and was smoothing the top when there was a flurry of movement and raised voices at the door to the King's Bedchamber.

It would never do to have the ceremony disrupted, so Verice finished his task, and stepped back to allow the next ridiculous step to occur in this foolish ceremony.

Until he heard Warna's name in the talk.

He bowed to the bed, backed from the room, then turned on his heel to face the guards and the clearly agitated handmaiden. "What's this?" he demanded.

"Verice, Bearer of the Blood of Tethnar," the faella was wringing her hands. "Your betrothed has taken ill. Violently ill. She drank her tea, and suddenly—"

"Take me to her," Verice snapped, pushing through the guards. "Now."

The handmaiden turned, and actually ran, telling Verice more than she ever could verbalize. He ran behind her, ignoring shocked looks and quiet protests of outrage as the serenity of the palace was broken.

It wasn't far. Verice charged through the doors, and slid to a stop.

Faellas lined the side of the room, chairs and small tables abandoned. Queen Blesenthala was on her throne, her face pinched and tight. And Warna, his Warna-

—was on the floor, on her hands and knees, heaving violently. Evidence of her illness lay before her, stretching all the way to the tips of the Queen's slippers.

"Warna," Verice breathed.

She turned her head, giving him a miserable blank stare. Then her eyes focused, and she smiled weakly. "Verice." She grimaced as he strode to her side. "No, Verice, don't—"

The retching caught her again, and she turned away as her body was wracked with pain.

"Here, now," Verice knelt down, heedless of the mess. He rubbed her back, offering what comfort he could. "What's happened?"

"Your betrothed has taken ill," Queen Blesenthala spoke, her face pinched. "Healers have been sent for and they will attend her." She glanced at the doorway. "There was no need to send for you."

"There was every need," Verice said mildly, hoped that for her sake, the handmaiden had

disappeared into the crowd. "Warna, let me get you off the floor."

"No," she panted, letting her head hang down. She grabbed his wrist as if to prevent him and tapped the back of his hand three times with her finger.

Verice held his face still, keeping his anger behind a wall. Something then, something the Queen had done. He tapped his finger on Warna's back, so she knew he understood. There were shards of teacups all around them, but no evidence of foodstuffs. The tea? His mind was working even as Warna succumbed to another round of horrible vomiting, her skirts now stained with urine and... his heart stopped.

There was blood seeping through her skirts.

Rage colored his vision red.

Warna spat to clear her mouth, then glanced at him, her eyes tinged red, her face covered in broken blood vessels. Her grip tightened on his wrist. "Verice," she moaned. "Take me home."

That startled him out of his anger.

Running footsteps, and a small cadre of mael and faella healers burst into the room. The foremost ran forward, reaching for Warna.

Warna reared back, seeking shelter in Verice's arms. *"No,"* she warded off the healer's hands. "Do not touch me."

"Our healers are the finest," Queen Blesenthala declared, but the healer only withdrew her hand, and knelt, seeming to take no offense.

"Lady, I am gifted in magical healing. Let me see to—"

"Have you ever healed a human?" Warna demanded, her voice hoarse and thick with pain. She pressed herself closer to Verice, and he tightened his arms around her.

"No, lady, but—"

"My lord and I anticipated our wedding vows," Warna lied as loudly as her throat would let her. "I may bear his heir. Would you risk us both?"

No longer surprised by anything Warna said, Verice moved his hands, making sure the healer caught sight of the blood on Warna's skirts.

The healer's eyes widened, and she lowered her hand. "Your Majesty, it would be for the best if—"

"No," Queen Blesenthala declared.

Verice banked his rage, tamping it down, barely maintaining control.

Another commotion at the door, and King Barathiel arrived. "What is this? What has happened?"

Warna groaned, turned away from Verice and retched.

Barathiel stopped a few feet away, his nose wrinkled in disgust. But then his eyes narrowed. "Blesenthala, what have you done?"

"Nothing," the Queen said quietly, lifting her chin. "Warna has had a bad reaction to the tea, that is all."

"There's a chance she is pregnant," the healer rose to her feet. "It would be best if she is seen to by those who have tended humans and half-elven before."

"Is this true, Verice?' Barathiel demanded.

"Would you take that risk?" Verice demanded in return. "For the sake of any potential child, Barathiel, let me take her home."

Barathiel stood frozen for an instant, then shook his head. "Go. We grant permission—"

"No," Blesenthala rose from her throne.

Verice didn't wait another moment. He stood, and cast the spell, summoning a portal to Tassinic.

"Don't think we are done," Barathiel called out. "We will speak again, and soon."

Verice ignored him. As soon as the oval opened, the white curtains flowing in a non-existent breeze, he swept Warna and her sodden skirts into his arms, and stepped through—

Into a bed-chamber covered in dust from months of dis-use.

His bedchamber. The one at the top of the keep.

Verice stood, paralyzed for a moment, as memories rose up before his eyes. But then Warna moaned in his arms, and he moved to place her on the bed.

"No," she groaned, plucking at his arm. "Privy."

He got her through the door and propped against the hole just as she started to heave again.

"Warna," he rubbed her back, pulling the hair away from her face. "How do you fare?"

She cast her eyes up, giving him a look. "Fine, just fine," she coughed and spat into the hole. "Where are we?"

"Home," Verice stood. "Just give me a moment," he strode out into the bedchamber. Warna muttered something after him, but he was intent on his task. With a word and a gesture, he threw open every window in the room. "Constable," he bellowed, using his powers to amplify his voice so it shook the stones around him.

"M'lord?" came the faint response from somewhere below.

"Warna's ill," Verice shouted, trying not to let his fear echo with his voice. With another gesture he slammed open every outer door to the keep. "Come to her aid."

CHAPTER FORTY-SIX

Everyone came running, healers, warriors, dogs, all thundering through the keep, calling for Verice and Warna. "Here," Verice called from the doorway, and stepped aside to allow the healers through. "She's—"

But the sound of her retching was clear and the healers disappeared into the privy.

"Constable," Verice said to the man huffing and puffing by the door. "Keep them back for now. But have runners ready for whatever the healers might need."

Ricard had a million questions on his face, but all he said was, "Aye, sir."

Verice caught Brindle trying to squeeze through the door. "And try to keep the dogs back as well."

Verice returned to the doorway, watching as Warna, supported by the healers, retched helplessly.

"We'll get you out of these clothes first," Dominic said, his voice holding a rare note of gentleness. "Then we'll see to this."

"There's blood," Verice said sharply. "On her skirts."

"Blood?" Dominic asked sharply. "Warna—"

"Lord and Lady, can this day possibly get worse?" Warna moaned. "It's my monthlies, I think. On top of everything else."

The knot in Verice's chest released, and it felt a bit easier to breath. Not a wound then. Or something worse.

"We'll check you out to be sure," Dominic said, leaning forward to seemingly peer at the vomit. "What brought this on?" he asked. "Was there fever? Pain? Did you eat—"

"Queen Blesenthala said it was hibiscus tea," Verice offered.

Warna muttered a few pithy phrases about the Queen. "It was gwen-wyth," she panted, after her strength ran down.

"Gwenwyth?" Dominic frowned. "That can cause illness in a human, yes, but not this violent a reaction. At least, not usually."

"I drank the entire cup," Warna admitted.

Verice jerked in shock. Dominic sputtered. "An entire cup?"

"Why?" Verice asked. "If you knew—"

"Because she knew," Warna sagged against the wall. "Because she knew I knew she knew." She sighed. "Maybe just to spite her."

"Warna," Verice whispered, half in admiration, half in dismay.

"We're home, aren't we?" Warna closed her eyes, looking sick and weary.

Verice reached out, and gently placed his hand on her head. "We are," he admitted.

Warna swallowed, then grimaced. "But drinking the entire cup," she sighed. "May have been a mistake."

"How long ago?" Dominic asked.

"I don't know," Warna said wearily. "We sat there, staring at one another until… it seemed like forever." She coughed, glaring at the jakes. "It was violent when it hit."

"You vomited on the Queen's slippers," Verice said, thinking on the room.

"I was aiming for her lap." Her disappointment was clear. "No more than an hour, I think."

"Well, now I know what I'm dealing with," Dominic said firmly. "We'll need water," he glanced at Verice. "Fresh clothes, and clean cloths. I'll send one of my apprentices for medicines. There's no sense in moving her—"

Warna heaved, bringing up little more than spit and bile.

"At least until that stops," Dominic added. He raised an eyebrow at Verice. "My lord, give us some time to see to her."

"I—" Verice hesitated. "Warna—"

She gave him a wan smile. "Go," she said. "I'll be fine."

Verice stepped back, reluctantly, then returned to the main doors, to find Ricard waiting with Ersal and a half-dozen of the staff. "Dominic needs water, hot and cold," Verice said.

One of the men in the back darted off.

"Some fresh clothes for Warna, and clean cloths and towels—"

Two more disappeared.

"And I want runners waiting here if he needs anything else," Verice added. "Ersal," he hesitated, glancing back at the bed behind him. Pain rose in his chest, memories of that horrible night—

The sound of Warna being sick again echoed from the privy.

"Ersal, see to it that this room is cleaned and restored." Verice ordered. "Do everything possible for Warna's comfort."

Ersal's face was solemn. "M'lord, I will see it done. It would be easier though, if we could use the hot springs below, and the smaller hearths."

Verice's throat closed. For a moment the pain threatened to overwhelm him. But he didn't let it stop him. "Whatever you need, Ersal. Except the Great Hall. Let no one enter there."

"On my honor," Ersal bowed his head. "It will be done as you command."

"My thanks," Verice said. "Ricard, send word to the commanders along the border with Valltera to watch for trouble." Verice said grimly. "Then join me at Narthing's bedside."

"M'lord," Ricard acknowledged the command. He hesitated for a moment. "You might want to clean up first."

Verice looked down at his stained and fouled leathers. "I will. We'll need to send word to my advisors as well," he started off down the dimly lit and dusty corridor, Ricard at his side. "There is much to discuss."

* * * * *

The stars were out that night by the time Verice returned to the keep. He entered through the main doors, taking the steps two at a time. Painful memories lingered in the shadows, but he ignored them. His thoughts were of Warna. He'd received hourly reports from Dominic, all of which boiled down to 'no change'.

The keep was alive with light and movement as the work of cleaning progressed. Ersal's voice was coming from the Seneschal's office, but Verice didn't pause to inquire. He continued on.

The main corridors were being scrubbed, the carpets removed to be aired and beaten. Verice acknowledge the staff's quiet nods and *'m'lords'* as he strode on, climbing the stairs and walking the halls to his chambers.

He tapped on the door, and one of the apprentices opened it and bowed him in.

This room shone, having been cleaned to a fare-thee-well. The smell of fresh soap and linens filled the air, but there was an underlying scent of medicines and sickness.

Warna was lying in bed, almost dwarfed by the bedding and pillows. She gave him a weak smile. Verice crossed to the bed and took her hand. "You look terrible," he blurted out.

"Trust me," she said wryly. "I'm not feeling much like a delicate flower right now."

Verice sat on the side of the bed, looked over to where Dominic was conferring with the other healers. Dominic caught his look, and motioned for him to wait.

"What's been happening?" Warna rasped. "Anything?"

"Yes," Verice hesitated. "Barathiel has sent messages of concern for your health and assurances of the sanctity of our mutual border."

"What does that mean?" Warna said.

"We're not sure," Verice admitted, enfolding her cold hand in both of his. "There have also been messages from the Regent of Palins, inquiring as to the health of my betrothed and offering assurances of his readiness to defend my borders."

Warna's eyes went wide. "But how would they know? So fast?"

Verice shrugged. "Spies, no doubt. In both courts, probably. Here, even. News flies on the wind."

Warna's fingers tightened weakly around his. "I've made a mess of things, haven't I? I was lying my fool head off to get us out of there, and never thought through the consequences."

"Hush," Verice said. He reached out to push a strand of her hair back off her face. Her skin felt flushed. "Are you cold?"

Warna pulled at the blanket. "Can't seem to get warm."

Dominic and the others approached the bed. "Well, let's see to you," the healer said.

Verice rose, and released Warna's hand slowly, making way for the healers.

"Open," Dominic ordered, and Warna obeyed. "Let this melt under your tongue. That will ease the pain, and let you sleep."

Warna grimaced. "Bitter," she complained.

"Let us help you to the privy before the drug takes effect," Dominic said, and Warna grimaced, but nodded weakly. Dominic pulled Verice away as she was aided out of bed.

"Well?" Verice asked softly.

"She hasn't been able to keep anything down, even water." Dominic said. "I've never seen this violent a reaction to gwenwyth before, but then I've never known any human to drink a full cup of the stuff. We're hoping that a night's rest will settle her stomach. We'll try a bit of broth in the morning, and see what happens. We'll stay with her tonight."

The implication being that Verice was in the way. Verice sighed as Warna walked slowly back to the bed, and was tucked under the covers.

"I'll have warming stones brought—" Dominic started.

"Yes, do that. But for now…" Verice stepped forward. Warna gave him a puzzled glance as he put his hands on the bed. "Allow me," he said softly, then cast a warming spell on the bed.

Warna sighed as the heat enveloped her, some of the lines in her face easing.

"That feels lovely," she whispered.

Verice sat on the side of the bed. "Would that my gifts included healing," he said ruefully. He glanced over his should to see that Dominic and the others were giving them a bit of privacy.

"So sorry," Warna said softly. "Never thought it through." She fumbled her hand out from under the blanket, and reached for Verice. He took hers in his, pleased that her fingers were warmer. "Trapped you in a marriage," she whispered, struggling to keep her eyes open. "Didn't mean to… I'm sorry."

"I am not," Verice whispered, but she was already fast asleep.

CHAPTER FORTY-SEVEN

Well, that explains quite a bit," Verice said, as he studied the map of Tassinic, and the neighboring baronies laid out on the floor of Narthing's room in the Healing Hall. The day had been a blur. Between fears for Warna, and fears for the border, Verice wasn't sure where the hours had flown.

"I can't believe that the Baroness of the Black Hills attacked Wyethe and Athelbryght at the same time." Narthing said. He was seated on the edge of the bed, trying to keep his toes out of Palins. "She had to know that Summerford would rise in response."

"King Barathiel has pulled his troops back from our border," Verice said.

"Not far enough," Ricard growled.

"Far enough to show his intent," Verice said.

"Aye, sit back and wait for a weakness," Ricard grumbled.

"True enough," Verice said. "I've let my sources of information lapse there, Pernard."

"Easily remedied," Pernard replied. "Leave it to me, m'lord."

"And the Usurper," Ricard consulted some notes. "His forces have pulled back as well."

"Thanks to Elanore's mistake. With the Black Hills fighting a war on two borders, he can't count on her support." Verice said with no little satisfaction.

"Warring on two separate borders at once?" Narthing said. "She's mad."

"Well, if she's taken to raising odium then even if she's not now crazed, she soon will be." Verice said grimly.

Pernard shook his head "Has she turned to blood magic?"

"I can't confirm it," Verice said. "And I will not risk scouts to learn if it's true. But what Elanore forgot is that while the High Baron of Summerford and the High Baroness of Wyethe despise each other, they each leap to the other's defense at the slightest hint of a threat. They've joined forces against her, and even if she's using odium, she cannot stand against them."

"Stalemate," Narthing said. "Your enemies afraid to come against you. Exactly as you'd hoped for."

Verice sighed. "True enough," he said. *But at what price*, he asked himself.

Almost as if Pernard had read his thoughts, he cast him a glance. "How is your lady?"

"Not well," Verice sighed. "In fact, if we're done here?" He rose from his chair.

The others rose as well.

"My thanks, Pernard, for coming. Your wisdom is appreciated," Verice said. "Narthing, get some rest. Ersal, continue to draft bland messages of meaningless diplomatic phrases to our 'ally' Valltera." There were chuckles as Ersal nodded. "I'll be with Warna if more news arrives. Gentlemen." He nodded to his advisors, and slipped from the room and headed to her bedchamber.

The keep was quieter now. The work was still going on, and Verice could see that Ersal and others had moved back into their old chambers and offices. But the mood was dampened by the growing awareness that Warna was ill… seriously ill.

Still the work continued on all the rooms and chambers. Except the Great Hall, as he had ordered.

He opened the door slowly, hoping not to disturb Warna if she was sleeping. And she was, curled around a warming stone, buried under the blankets.

The room was lined with cots and pallets; the healers were keeping a constant vigil. He noticed Warna's lidded basket against the one wall. Someone had made sure her things had been brought to the room.

Not that she was in any shape to enjoy them.

He went to the other side of the bed, and sat so that he could see her face. She looked so tired and listless. Her hair had lost its luster, and someone had pulled it back in a loose braid. He doubted she'd had the strength.

Her eyes fluttered open, and after a moment she focused on him and tried to give him a smile. "Verice," she whispered.

"Lady," he said. "How are you?"

"Thirsty," she grimaced. "But when I drink, it starts again. I don't want that," she closed her eyes.

"I should let you—" Verice started to excuse himself.

"No," she complained. "All I do is rest. Tell me the news."

"Barathiel has pulled his forces back," Verice said. "I think he was trying to take Tassinic so fast that no one would have a chance to respond before he had it under his control. But now that word has leaked out, I think he's decided to wait and see what happens." Verice hesitated. "I don't think he knew what Blesenthala was up to," he continued. "I don't think Barathiel would have countenanced it, if he'd have known."

Warna frowned, thinking it through. "But why would she do it?" she asked. "Does she hate humans that much?" She took a shaky breath. "I doubt she was really trying to kill me. More of a cruel prank, don't you think?"

"Blesenthala and I have a bit of a history," Verice said softly.

Warna gave him as much of a glare as she could. "One of these days, you are going to sit down and tell me every day of every year of your life," she whispered.

"What makes you think I remember with that level of detail?" Verice quirked his mouth, and leaned closer.

Warna reached out and captured a lock of his hair between her fingers. "Every detail," she whispered.

"My parents offered marriage for myself and Blesenthala," Verice said. "Many, many years ago. But the offer was refused, and she was given in marriage to Barathiel, next in line for the throne."

"She wanted you," Warna said. "She still wants you." She tugged on his hair. "Charrin said something about a taint in your blood. Was that why—"

"Yes," Verice said softly. "Five generations back, the eldest male of my line married a human woman."

"Five generations?" Warna rasped, licking her lips. "Five elven generations? That's ridiculous."

"That's yet another reason I left," Verice said.

"Thick as posts, those people are," Warna closed her eyes and sighed.

"M'lord?" Dominic approached. "A word?'

Dominic drew him out into the hallway and down a ways from the door. "It would be best if Lady Warna does not hear us, m'lord."

"Dominic?" Verice felt the fear leap in his throat.

"M'lord," Dominic looked him in the eye and there was none of his normal haughtiness in his expression. "Lady Warna is critically ill, and I fear for her life."

"Tell me," Verice said.

"She has kept nothing down these past days," Dominic said simply. "And that includes our herbs and potions. Items that normally end nausea only seem to worsen the problem. She retches up everything we give her. Her urine output is decreased, she complains of thirst, her hair and skin are dry, and her cycle is upon her, which only adds to her misery." He took a deep breath "M'lord, she will die if she cannot drink."

Fear lanced through him, clutching at his heart. This could not be possible, and yet Dominic's face told him otherwise.

"I mean no offense," Verice said, "but perhaps another healer…?"

Dominic gave him a look that managed to combine sympathy and arrogance all at once. "M'lord, I am your foremost healer."

"I—" Verice wasn't sure how to reply to that. True enough, Dominic was skilled but there had to be someone—

Dominic wasn't done. "I met a woman when I was in Edenrich. A mage, but also a priestess with the gift of magical healing." His face was tight, as if with pain. "Evelyn."

Verice frowned. "Lady High Priestess Evelyn?" At Dominic's nod his frown deepened. "She's human, Dominic. And bound to the Church of Palins, which supports the Usurper. I daren't be beholden to—"

"Evelyn is not like that," Dominic said. "She heals all and sundry, even ministering to the poor when she was told to attend only those of the highest rank." Dominic shook his head as if he could hardly believe it. "She'd come, m'lord. And she may be Lady Warna's only hope."

Verice drew a breath, seeing what it cost the proud mael before him to utter those words.

But it was only a breath of hesitation. His heart reflected the fear in Dominic's eyes.

"Contact her," Verice said. "See if she will aid us."

CHAPTER FORTY-EIGHT

L ady High Priestess Evelyn was both mage and priest. After she agreed to come, she offered to open her own portal. But Verice insisted on controlling access. He opened a portal for her right in the bedchamber after excusing all but Dominic.

Dominic stepped within the glowing oval, and returned with a woman wearing the formal hooded cloak and embroidered white and gold robes of a priestess of the Lord of Light. She was short in stature to Verice's surprise, and her smile was serene and kind.

"Lord Verice," she said softly, her attention focused on Warna, who lay in the bed just beyond. "This is Warna?" she asked, moving to her side. "Dominic has told me of the problem." She threw back her hood, and removed her cloak, tossing it aside. "Let me see what I can do for her."

"My thanks, Lady High Priestess. I owe you-" Verice started.

"Nothing," Evelyn interrupted. Verice hesitated, expecting more talk. He blinked in amazement as power started to gather in the priestess's hands. Wasting no time, she leaned over and placed her hands on Warna's breast.

Warna roused, opening dazed eyes, but not seeming to really see. Verice swallowed hard.

Evelyn's eyes were closed. It might have been the effect of her robes and the candlelight, but Verice could have sworn that the woman seemed to glow with divine light as she ran her hands down, moving the bedding aside to get access to Warna's body. Warna shivered for just a moment, then closed her eyes and seemed to relax into Evelyn's touch.

Dominic stood beside Verice, his hands tucked into the sleeves of his robes, and watched Evelyn work. There was a look in his eyes… and Verice was almost sure it was envy, for the power Evelyn wielded. But after another glance, he knew it wasn't jealousy.

It was desire for the human woman.

'*Poor mael*,' was all he had time to think before Evelyn started talking.

"Gwenwyth, correct?" Evelyn said, holding her hands over Warna's stomach.

"Yes," Dominic said. "An elven tea, but humans sometimes cannot tolerate it. I've never seen this severe of a reaction before."

Evelyn nodded, her eyes still closed. "Yes, I can see it, lingering in her stomach and bowels. Poor thing, no wonder she's so weak. She can't rid herself of it with fluids, and it won't dissipate on its own." Evelyn wrinkled her nose. "I'm afraid this is going to be unpleasant."

"Unpleasant?" Verice demanded.

"Once we wake her, we'll get her to drink as much as she can. I'll aid to help cleanse the gwenwyth from her body, but it must come out, and she's already exhausted from vomiting. I'll strengthen her as much as I can before we purge her." Evelyn said calmly, ignoring Verice's reaction. "And we'll carry her into the jakes before we start. Dominic and I can handle the details." She focused calm blue eyes on him. "You might want to leave, m'lord."

"No," Verice started to remove his leather tunic. "I'm staying."

Evelyn raised an eyebrow at that, but she merely glanced at Dominic, who shrugged. "Very well," she said, and leaned over her patient. "Warna? I need you to wake."

Warna blinked at her, rousing with some difficulty. "Are you an Angel of Light?" she asked drowsily.

"No," Evelyn said, putting her hands on Warna's chest. Once again Verice saw her hands glow. "I am Evelyn, a healer. Dominic and I are going to help you."

"Oh no," Warna looked so pitiful. "Evelyn, no more vomiting," she begged.

"Call me Evie," Evelyn gave her a rueful smile. "And no more vomiting. I promise."

* * * * *

Verice resisted when they made him leave at dawn.

"The worst of it is over," Evelyn pointed out as they settled Warna back on the bed. "Dominic and his staff can handle it from here. I must return to the Church for the dawn service, but I would like to return later to make sure that the gwenwyth is out of her body. You can open a portal at—"

"I give you leave to open your own, Lady High Priestess," Verice said wearily. "I will seek my own bed, I swear. I don't know how you will have the strength to perform your duties."

"Long years as a healer." She smiled.

Verice looked down at Warna, who hadn't stirred as they'd covered her with blankets. "Lady High Priestess, you have my heartfelt and undying gratitude. She's—"

"Hush." Evelyn turned him, and pushed him towards the door. "Before you promise me all sorts of impossible things." She opened the door and forced him through. "But Lord Verice?"

He paused just outside the door. "Yes?"

She wrinkled her nose at him impishly, and gestured toward his stained tunic and trous. "You might want to bathe before you take to your bed."

* * * * *

Verice slept longer than he intended, and woke to a mid-day sun streaming through his windows. The dogs weren't about; he couldn't remember when he saw them last. He dressed quickly, threw water on his face, and started for the keep, not pausing for food or drink.

It might have been his imagination, but the sun seemed brighter this day, and the folk that greeted him seemed lighter of heart. A fancy, surely, but Verice took the steps to the keep two at a time, barely nodding at anyone he saw. The door to her bedchamber was closed, and he almost feared to open it when he heard—

Verice stopped, the knot deep in his chest unwinding from around his heart. He leaned against the wall and did something he rarely did. He offered his deep and sincere thanks to his Ancestors.

Warna was singing.

CHAPTER FORTY-NINE

Kalynn stood at the center of the Heart of the Plains and breathed in the air of home.

The sky above was a bowl of blue, darkening to the east as the sun set. The stars were starting to dance along the horizon.

The breeze was soft; the heat of summer fading from the air. She'd toed off her boots, and the Heart was warm beneath her feet. Warm from the sun, but lifeless otherwise.

Wolfe was removing the airion's harnesses, freeing them to hunt. Of course, they had to roll in the grasses as soon as they were free. It made her laugh to see their joy.

Wolfe walked toward her, his wispy white hair floating in the breeze. He carried one of the saddle bags and a blanket. He paused at the rim of the stone.

Kalynn waited.

He shook his head, shrugged, and stepped on to the surface.

Nothing happened.

"Do you remember?" She asked as he walked closer. "When it pulsed with life? When all the Tribes gathered around, and the Heart beat with their energy?"

"Yes, of course," he spread out the blanket, and pulled her down to sit beside him. "Let's see what we have. There's those hard crackers you like, and cheese and—"

"Regrets?" She asked.

Wolfe stilled, and then looked out into the distance. "I regret that they would not listen. I regret that they would not honor your choice. They dragged you from me, screaming your outrage and fear, and I lost my mind in that instant."

Kalynn rose on her knees, and hugged him, pressing his head to her breast.

He continued, his voice muffled. "I regret that I lost all control, tore the magic from the lands in my rage. It fled, from me, from them, from the very Plains around us."

He pulled back, and looked up at her. "But I would do it all again, tear the world asunder to be at your side."

She cupped his face with both hands and kissed him, pouring her love into him.

He broke the kiss, and took a breath. "Now, dried cherries?"

She laughed and settled beside him. The airions took flight, spiraling up into the sky.

"Will they be all right?"

"I'm cloaking them," Wolfe said absently, pulling out wrapped bundles. "I've enough reserves to hide them and us from any wandering eyes."

"Is anyone about?"

"Some thea camps, and one group of Singers, but they are far enough not to be a problem."

"The Ancients?" Kalynn asked.

"Pfft, those little dried turds?" Wolfe popped a cherry in her mouth. "Do not worry. Once the airions have fed, we'll fly north." He grimaced, and she knew it wasn't the taste, it was the destination.

"She may have mellowed," she offered as she bit into the tart fruit, bitter and sweet on her tongue.

Wolfe grunted. "And ehats might fly." He pulled out a loaf of bread. "But you are right. She needs to know."

"Will you have enough power to hide us?" she asked.

"So long as you don't have your mount do any more loop-de-loops." He raised a chiding eyebrow at her.

Kalynn just smiled. "It felt so good to be flying." She reached for the crackers, but then she looked up and off to the west. The tug on her heart came again.

"Seeing?" Wolfe asked softly.

Kalynn nodded absently, lost in the sensation. They needed to be there, at a certain time, a certain place—

"Eat," Wolfe nudged her shoulder with his. "Time enough to do what must be done."

"We did something in the name of our love that reached far beyond us," Kalynn was still lost in the possibilities. "It echos still. This is our chance to make amends."

"Kalynn," Wolfe said, his voice heavy with sorrow. "We can't fix this."

"No," Kalynn whispered as the possibilities faded from around her. She smiled at Wolfe. "But we can set other feet on the path."

CHAPTER FIFTY

I s there any lingering soreness when you move your bowels?"
Warna wrinkled her nose at that. Healers asked the most uncomfortable questions sometimes, and Evelyn was no exception. "No," she answered.

"And your bowel movements are regular? Solid?"

"Yes, and yes," she said patiently.

"And the color?"

"Evie!" Warna sputtered.

Evelyn laughed. "Sorry, it's just that the expression on your face—" she laughed again, looking more mischievous than any priestess Warna had ever met. "Here, let me examine you one last time."

Warna lay flat on the bed, and let Evie have her way. She admired the high ceilings and the sunlight streaming through the windows. Verice's chambers were lovely, but she'd been cooped up in here for days.

"And your cycles?" Evie asked as she moved her hand inches from Warna's stomach.

"Over, thank the Lady," Warna sighed.

That brought another chuckle, but then Evie went silent, her face intent as she invoked her powers. Warna felt a tingle as her hands moved around her mid-section. "That's amazing, you know," she whispered.

"It's a gift of the Lord of Light," Evie said just as softly. "But it has its limits. Dominic can treat an entire village dying of sickness; at best I could treat a limited number before my own life was at risk."

Warna's eyes went wide at that thought, but she stayed quiet, letting Evie do her work.

Finally, Evie breathed a sigh and opened her eyes, pleased. "Gone. Not a trace of gwenwyth that I can find."

Warna sat up, breathless with hope. "Dominic said that if you released me from care, he would lift his restrictions as well."

"Then consider yourself free," Evelyn said. "But bear in mind that it will be a while before your true strength returns. Rest when you are tired," she warned. "Listen to your body."

"I promise," Warna said and on impulse swept the priestess into a hug. "Evie, thank you!"

To her delight, the hug was returned. Warna tightened her arms again, and then released, feeling absurdly happy. "Evie, please, visit as a friend in the future."

Evie smiled back, but then her face dimmed. "I'd like that, Warna, truly. But the times are… difficult."

"I know," Warna sighed. "But if Dominic's assigned to the Church in Palins, perhaps they'd assign you here?"

Evie wrinkled her nose. "As much as I'd like that, it's doubtful. They like to reserve my powers for the nobles at Court." She flashed a grin again. "Not that I let that stop me."

"Dominic's social climbing skills will be most welcome then," Warna snorted.

"He's very skilled, both as a healer and apparently in moving among the ranks of power. Not one of my abilities, I'm afraid," Evie said. "But they won't remove Dominic from his position here until they've found a qualified healer to replace him."

"Use that as an excuse to visit," Warna suggested.

"Lord Verice has said that I might call on him at any time."

"I hope you take him up on that offer," Warna said.

Evelyn gave her an odd look. "I will think on it," she said. Then she smiled, her face once again calm and serene. She stood, reaching for her cloak. "For now, I've promised Dominic I'd look in on one of his patients to see if I can speed his healing. Apparently, the man is such a horrible patient that Dominic wants him healed and on his way before Dominic's own bowels rupture in pure frustration."

"Before you go," Warna took a deep breath. "I wanted to talk to you about—"

"Yes?"

Warna made her decision. "I want to talk about babies. Well, not having babies." She blushed scarlet, trying to find the right words. "Preventing babies."

Evie gave her a direct look. "Warna, I've scanned you. I've heard the rumors, but I know that you have not had relations with a male."

"Yet," Warna said.

* * * * *

I'd like to talk. Please come.
Warna.

Verice stared at the note, and felt an odd flutter in his chest.

"She first asked for hot kav, and a bath," Ricard spoke with satisfaction, having delivered the note himself. "Dominic and Priestess have both given her their blessing. The Priestess even saw to Narthing. Nice of her," he sniffed. "Unlike some healers we know."

"Warna wants to talk," Verice said, and felt that flutter again. It wasn't as if they hadn't talked since her recovery. But there's always been healers or servants in the room, seeing to Warna's care and comfort. There'd been no privacy.

Verice had felt oddly relieved at that when he'd visited. He wasn't certain what to say to her, or how to express so many things. His admiration for her manipulation of the situation. His horror that she would drink gwenwyth and sacrifice herself. His terror at the knowledge that she'd do something so fundamentally stupid as to drink the entire cup without knowing what it would do to her, just to spite her foe.

Ricard interrupted his thoughts. "If the Lady Warna wants to talk," he said, "best be about it."

Verice nodded, and rose from his table. But not before he tucked the note into safe-keeping.

He schooled himself on the walk from the barracks, nodding greetings to all. There were many knowledgeable looks and smiles, so the word must have spread that the healers had released Warna from their care.

He entered the keep from one of the smaller doors, not really ready to trod the main staircase, but the lit hallways and buzz from the various rooms and offices didn't cause any pain. Maybe because he was more intent on seeing Warna, than anything else.

He allowed himself to mount the steps two at a time, and paused at the door just long enough to catch his breath.

He knocked.

"Come in.," Warna's voice was strong.

The room was flooded with morning sunlight. Flowers in vases sat on every open surface. Even though there were chairs by the hearth, Warna sat at the end of the bed, her hair flowing down her back, dressed in one of her light gray dresses. She was smiling, her brown eyes clear and bright.

She was alone.

Verice closed the door. "Good morning," he said.

"Good morning," Warna answered. "Dominic and Evelyn have released me from their care. I'm free."

"That's well, then," Verice stood there, feeling awkward and rather stupid.

"Verice," Warna caught his gaze, her eyes warm and intent, "I know what I want now." She lifted her head, glowing with confidence and strength. "With my life, I mean. At least, for the next month or so."

His mouth went suddenly dry. "What?"

"I'll tell you," she said abruptly. "But right now, I want the sun on my face and the wind in my hair. Let's go walk in the gardens."

CHAPTER FIFTY-ONE

To Warna's delight, Verice extended his hand without hesitation. "As you wish," he said. "But you may not find it as easy as you think to get to the gardens."

"Why so?" she asked.

Her answer came when he opened the door. "Because I will have competition for your attentions," he whispered. The corridor was filled with people cleaning, all turning towards them with smiles on their faces.

"Oh." She hesitated, feeling the heat on her cheeks. "I don't suppose—"

"No." Verice escorted her through the door, and extended his arm again. He lowered his head to her ear. "We can't go another way."

Warna sighed, and returned all the smiles and greetings as they walked along the corridors and down the various staircases.

Out in the courtyard, it wasn't so bad. Most people hung from windows, waving kerchiefs, but those in the yard itself didn't crowd all around them. Warna felt warmed by the greetings, and by the sun on her face. It felt good to be up and about.

The constable crossed the yard to greet her, along with Verice's dogs. "It's good to see your smile, m'lady."

"Thank you. Ricard." Warna smiled back. "I'm going to walk in the gardens for a bit," she explained as the dogs milled about their legs, looking for attention.

"Mind the rantha thorns," Ricard warned. "There's been no gardeners out there, m'lord, and they've probably overrun the paths."

"We'll have a care," Verice said. "I'm not going to let her go far, trust me."

Ricard stepped to the small door in the castle wall, throwing back the locks and releasing the latches.

"You might have Ersal send word to the gardeners," Warna said innocently. "So that they can get to work trimming things back."

"They're already at work in the kitchen gardens." Verice gave her a wry look. "Apparently when I opened the keep, that was interpreted as a general invitation for everyone to return." He gave Ricard a raised eyebrow. "I wonder where my people learned that ploy."

"Hard to say, m'lord," the constable said as he opened the door. The dogs pushed past him, snuffling the air with anticipation.

"Warna," Verice gestured to her to go first.

Warna didn't hesitate as she stepped through the doorway and into the garden beyond.

If this had been a moat, it must have been a wide one, deep and dangerous. The area between the walls was large and spacious and the ramparts towered over her. She could see guards along the outer wall, pacing out their watches.

But the land between the walls was lush and green, and filled with the wildness of over-grown rose bushes, with large pink roses, their blooms as big as cabbages. The plants sagged under their weight, and petals littered the stone walk that angled away from them.

Warna took a deep breath of the flower-scented air, and lifted her face to the sky. She could hear Verice walking up behind her, and the dogs running around through the bushes, stirring up birds in pursuit of a rabbit.

"I should not have neglected it for so long," Verice said. The sorrow was thick in his eyes. On impulse Warna reached for his hand, taking it in hers. Verice squeezed once, and kept hold as he continued. "It didn't take long for this place to turn into a wilderness. Watch out for the rantha vines."

"It's not that bad," Warna said. "I like it better than the palace gardens in Valltera. Those plants were groomed to within an inch of their lives." She tugged once, and they started walking down the paths, Verice reaching to clear the branches out of the way. It wasn't really practical to remain hand in hand. But he didn't release hers, and she wasn't going to pull away.

"Everything perfect, nothing out of its place," Verice said. "Not so much as a fallen petal."

"I never got the chance to ask." Warna laughed. "They told me you'd been invited to make the king's bedchamber for the ceremony. Did you get to smooth the king's pillow?"

Verice snorted. "I was just positioning it on the bed when word came you'd taken ill." He stopped for a moment, lifting his head. "You might want to hold your breath for a moment," he said wryly. At her puzzled glance, he nodded to a bush off to the side. "Gwenwyth."

She wrinkled her nose as she got a faint whiff.

He hurried her past, leading the way. "If I remember correctly, off to the side here…"

He released her hand and thrust aside more branches, revealing a bower under a trellis of large purple flowers, with two stone benches opposite each other. He cleared the leaves and twigs from one. "Here," he gestured. "Sit for a while."

"Tell me about the ceremony." Warna sank onto the bench. The stone was warm from the sun that dappled through the leaves. "And what did Barathiel say to you?"

Verice brushed the other bench clear, then sat opposite her, adjusting his sword as he took his seat. Something flashed through his eyes, but he spoke easily, explaining King Barathiel's position, describing their conversation. There was something he wasn't telling her, but Warna could imagine enough not to need details.

"What of you?" he asked finally. "What happened while I was apart from you?"

So Warna told him about Charrin, and the Queen's invitation to a private tea. "I couldn't think of a way to refuse," she said. "And once I was there, and the tea was poured, she was so superior, so smug—"

"You drank the entire cup," Verice finished.

"I wish I could claim that I thought it all through," she admitted. "That I had this grand plan. But really I just… improvised."

"I find that at once admirable," Verice quirked the corner of his mouth. "And terrifying."

Warna laughed.

"But you need to know what's happened as a result," Verice said. He told her the situation, from the Usurper's notes to the pull-back of

Barathiel's armies.

Warna frowned. "Why would he do that?"

"Warna, elven faella do not conceive easily. Elven children are rare, and as such, are considered precious above all things," Verice said. "Any threat to a child, or an expectant mother, human or faella is unpardonable."

"Oh," Warna thought it through. "So, my lies—"

"I've had several unofficial communications," Verice said. "From elven nobles, from Barathiel, from Blesenthala, even from the Usurper, all delicately inquiring as to the fate of your unborn child."

"Lord and Lady." Warna bit her lip. "It never occurred to me—" She stopped. "But you and I, and my healers know the truth."

"Still, when you don't give birth in the next year, it will be assumed that you miscarried the non-existent child." Verice looked away. "On one hand, you've provided the perfect diplomatic weapon against Barathiel. But on the other, your reputation has suffered, and for that—"

Warna snorted. "Reputation? What reputation? Verice, I'd been fleeing the Usurper's army for months, sleeping in ditches, fields, and sheep lofts before you rescued me. Not to mention sleeping in a barracks full of men once I arrived here. No need to be concerned for what is already broken."

"I fault myself for that," Verice said. "I should have had a chaperone, a handmaiden or—"

"I don't fault you," Warna said. "And I don't regret a moment of it, either." She let her gaze fall to her lap. "I do feel bad that Blesenthala thinks she killed a child," she started, but then in her mind's eye she saw the Queen's expression as she stared over her teacup. "But she knew exactly what she was doing, didn't she? She may not have thought I might be pregnant, but she certainly meant me ill."

"You certainly caught her off guard," Verice said. "What with the vomit on her shoes."

"But not on her lap," Warna admitted with a smile.

Verice looked at her, the laughter in his eyes slowly fading. "So that is where it stands now. Stalemate. Hopefully, a peaceful stalemate. Not that I will relax my guard just yet."

"So that just leaves us," Warna blurted out.

Verice jerked his head in a nod.

Gathering her nerve, Warna sat up straight on the bench. "Verice," she started, her words catching in her throat.

He raised an eyebrow, and waited for her to continue.

"Verice," Warna said. "I know what I want."

CHAPTER FIFTY-TWO

Verice's heart leaped with a sudden, irrational fear that she'd ask to leave. She'd every right to ask to go, but he—

He swallowed, and chose the honorable path, as much as it choked him to do so. "Whatever you want, Warna."

"Hear me out," she chided. She breathed deep, and he took a moment to just look at her, lovely in the scattered sunlight. She seemed to glow against the greenery that sheltered them.

"I want to celebrate the Festival of Light and Laughter with you in the Great Hall." She raised a hand to forestall any protest. "You and I have been dancing around the central issue of the castle and your keep since I've arrived. We've - your staff and I - we've used subterfuge, dissembling, shams and deceit." She gave him a solemn look. "As conspiracies go, it's been a fairly quiet one."

Verice couldn't help but snort, and at Warna's questioning look, he raised an eyebrow of his own. "Isn't that the very nature of conspiracies?" he asked.

That got him a soft smile but it didn't reach Warna's eyes. "And you've let us. Turned a blind eye to our doings; ignored what was happening around you."

Verice said nothing, kept his face as still as stone. But Warna wasn't fooled. She rose, pushed through the dogs, and sat next to him, taking his hand.

He felt the warmth of her skin, took in the soft scent of her hair and the band around his chest tightened.

"That was fine," she assured him. "It worked, in fact. For both you and those around you. But now, going forward, there should be only truth between us. No more lies, no more coy maneuvering. What I want is for us to be honest with each other."

"Very well—" Verice began

"I want to open the Great Hall, bring the business of the keep to its full operations as the heart of your power," Warna said. "We'll honor the dead, I promise you, and then celebrate the full Festival in all its glory."

"Then, after-" she faltered slightly. "After the Festival is concluded, after a week or so, we will quietly break our troth. I'll go to my great-uncle's and rebuild my life."

"This is what you want?" Verice asked, staring at her hand in his.

"Well, there's one more thing," Warna said, and now he felt her fingers tremble in his. She didn't continue, and he glanced at her to see her eyes downcast as well.

"Warna?" he asked in the barest of whispers.

She took a trembling breath, leaned closer, and kissed him.

* * * * *

Her heart was going to beat its way out of her chest. Warna took her failing courage into her hands and kissed Verice.

His lips were smooth and dry against hers, and when he didn't respond she felt all her hope die a long agonizing death. She missed the warmth of his mouth even before she pulled away.

She felt his hand on the back of her neck, and his warmth returned as he kissed her with a power that stole the breath from her body. Warm, wet, inviting, his mouth was all that and more. Somehow, without her even realizing it, she was wrapped in his arms.

She broke the kiss, trying to catch her breath. "I want you," she half-sobbed, half-laughed. "I want this, whatever this is, for as long as I remain." Words failed her now as she plunged along, trying to explain. "I want to explore you, to touch you, to know you, to have you know me. Please, Verice." She was more than willing to plead for this. "I know I won't be more than a flower in your garden, but please—"

He kissed her again, cutting off her words, and she moaned against him, sensations swirling around her like a tempest. Only one real thought remained. She'd be a brief moment of pleasure to him, that was certain.

But she'd love him for a lifetime, and beyond.

It meant separation, it meant having him, and losing him. So be it.

Even those thoughts scattered as his hands stroked her through her dress, and rational thought fled. She was lost in the wonders of his mouth, his touch, and a burning craving that flushed her skin.

He broke the kiss, his voice hoarse in her ear. "Warna, are you certain? Because—"

Warna rested her head against his, and nodded. "I talked to Evie, and asked her to make certain that I can't get pregnant. She's taken care of that with her magic." Warna swallowed hard, leaning back to catch his eye. "Verice," she whispered "Please."

A shadow crossed over him then, but it was gone in an instant, and something else burned there. She caught her breath.

"It would be my honor," Verice said, and the tightness in her chest eased.

"Here?" She trembled with longing, and a touch of fear. "Now?"

"No." Verice closed his eyes. "If you don't think there are more eyes on us now than there ever were at the elven court, you are mistaken." He darted in for a kiss, startling her as his tongue flicked out to lick her mouth. But he rose just as fast, and pulled her to her feet.

"Come," Verice said. "Let's see about getting you what you want."

* * * * *

Narthing stared at the ceiling of his small, clean prison and sighed. "Ersal," he said patiently. "You have many skills. Chess is not one of them."

Ersal sat opposite him, staring at the board and its pieces. "Just give me a moment," he said.

He'd appeared with lunch, bearing the set, and challenged Narthing to a game. Narthing had welcomed the lunch, his first real, solid food, and the company. But after one game it was fairly clear there wasn't going to be much of a challenge involved.

Ersal continued to study the board.

Narthing huffed out a breath. "It's mate in three moves," he pointed out.

"It can't be," Ersal said. "How so?"

Narthing reached over, and showed him.

Ersal shook his head in defeat. "Another," he said, setting up the board.

"Fine. But talk to me," Narthing said, waiting for Ersal's first move. "What's the word on m'lord and m'lady?"

"How can I talk and play at the same time?" Ersal said, reaching out to place a finger on his pawn and hesitated. Then he slid it along the board and sat back in satisfaction.

Narthing folded his arms over his chest.

Ersal rolled his eyes. "Lady Warna has been released by the healers, and I believe she's asked to speak to m'lord."

"Ah," Narthing said. "I wonder what that means."

"Nothing." Dominic breezed in with a tray. "Drink this," he commanded.

Narthing took the cup, eyeing it with trepidation. Dominic's medicines were as sweet as his personality. "Must I?"

"No, of course not," Dominic said. "As an adult, intelligent mael, you're free to ignore all of my treatments and advice and endure the consequences as you see fit. Or take my advice, drink the tea, and perhaps be released from my care as early as tomorrow."

"When you put it that way." Narthing rolled his eyes and drank the cup down in three quick swallows. The bitterness almost closed his throat. "Why do you say 'nothing'?" he forced out.

"Please." Dominic sniffed as he took the cup. "She's too common for a lord high baron. If there's any interest on his part, it's for a fling, surely. Nothing serious—"

Ersal coughed.

Verice and Warna were in the doorway, Ricard standing just behind looking appalled.

To Narthing's horror, there was a slight flush on Warna's cheeks, but Lord Verice's face was set in stone. They must have heard—

"M'lord," Dominic said. "I am pleased to be able to say that Captain Narthing can be released from our care once he's had a successful bowel movement. Possibly as soon as tomorrow morning."

Narthing covered his eyes as Ersal turned slightly purple with what had to be suppressed laughter.

"That's good to know," Verice said.

"Healers." Warna looked a little strained, but she chuckled. "I understand Evie saw to you, Narthing."

"She did," Narthing smiled. "She said she was just supplementing Dominic's fine work but I think it helped."

"I would point out," Dominic was looking down his nose. "That the Lady High Priestess is gifted by the Lord of Light. Any endowment of her power is to be treasured, honored, and respected."

"Oh yes." Narthing managed a straight face. "Especially if it improves bowel function."

Dominic curled his lip.

Lord Verice gave a slight cough. "This is excellent news. Captain Narthing, once you are free of this place, move back into your old chambers. The constable will see to it that my gear is moved back into my old room." Verice paused. "In the keep."

"M'lord." Narthing nodded his head to acknowledge the command.

"Seneschal Ersal," Lord Verice glanced at Warna. "Our troth is fairly common knowledge at this point. I would make it official unto my people. No ceremony, however, so as to honor her period of mourning."

Ersal beamed. "I would be honored to send out word, m'lord."

Verice continued. "Lady Warna is in charge of the planning for the Festival."

Narthing felt his throat close; so many bloody memories.

Lord Verice must have caught his thought. "I trust her to get us through this." He and Warna exchanged a long glance.

Narthing nodded.

"She'll need assistance sending invitations and organizing events. See to it, Ersal."

Ersal rose to his feet and bowed. "Of course, m'lord."

"My thanks." Lord Verice turned and gestured Warna out the door. But just in the doorway, he looked over his shoulder. "Priest Dominic," he said.

"M'lord," Dominic bowed.

"The Church of Palins has informed me that you are to be assigned to Edenrich on a permanent basis. When the summons comes to you, you have our leave to depart without any ceremony." His voice was hard. "They will make full use of your particular skills there, I am certain."

Dominic opened his mouth in surprise, but Lord Verice was already gone.

CHAPTER FIFTY-THREE

"He's right, you know," Warna said.

A scowl passed over Verice's face as they crossed the courtyard side-by-side.

"I am not a noble," Warna continued, taking a deep breath as she tried to match his angry pace. "Father was a spice merchant and Mother was-"

"Dominic is an arrogant bastard," Verice growled. He glanced at her, and then slowed to a walk. "Edenrich and the church are welcome to him."

"As long as they replace him with someone just as competent," Warna said, suddenly realizing that the keep seemed farther away than it had before. She hated to admit it, but she was tiring.

There was a sudden warmth as Verice put his hand on her lower back. She glanced up to find that he was giving her a serious look. "We did too much for your first outing."

"No, no," she protested. Odd. It wasn't that he was pushing, but that warmth at her back seemed to strengthen her steps. "I'm fine," she insisted, afraid that he'd use that as an excuse to put her off. Delay... other things. She didn't want to delay, didn't want to wait one more moment for—

"We'll eat," Verice said firmly as he led her into the keep.

Warna opened her mouth to protest, but then her stomach grumbled. The corner of Verice's mouth quirked and she had to laugh at herself.

"I'll have it brought to our room," Verice said. "Head that way. I'll be right behind you."

His hand lifted from her back, but Warna could still feel its warmth as she started up the stairs, feeling light of heart. Which may or may not have had anything to do with 'our room'.

She managed to slowly climb to the second landing before Verice caught up with her and swept her up into his arms.

"Verice," she protested even as she wrapped her arms around his neck.

"Save your energy for other things," he mock-growled.

Warna laughed, but a soft tendril of warmth wrapped around her that had nothing to do with the heat of his skin, and the strength of the arms that held her.

Nothing at all.

* * * * *

They hadn't been in their chambers for more than a brief moment before there was a knock at the door. Verice noticed that Warna's hands trembled while the servers set out their meal.

He was confident that it was anticipation. Or nervousness. So, he kept the talk light as their food was served, and the servants excused themselves. Nothing too serious; observations about the dogs, and the gardens. The dangers of working around rantha thorns.

Warna responded, and relaxed as they ate and talked.

He owed her a boon for so many things; that much was certain. If she wished to have him as a lover for the duration of the Festival, it was his duty to oblige. That she was inexperienced put an even greater responsibility upon him.

He'd slept with inexperienced women before. Never a human; but from what he understood human women were no different from faella. He wasn't concerned about that. What he wanted more than anything else was to make sure Warna experienced nothing but pleasure at his hands. She deserved nothing less.

He'd teach her all the pleasures he knew. It wouldn't touch him the way it would touch her, but he'd take the utmost care of her body and her heart.

As soon as she'd finished eating, he pushed back his own plate, stood and stretched, enjoying her wide-eyed attraction.

"Food's improved since the kitchens reopened," he observed as he reached for the side buckle on his armor.

"Far easier to cook on-site," Warna said. She stacked their plates, and was frowning at him, watching him as he fumbled with the buckle. "What's wrong?" she asked.

"Stuck," Verice muttered, as he tried to work the strap free. "Not sure what's—"

"Here," Warna huffed a breath. "I'll do it."

She moved closer, bending her head as she reached for the leather strap. Verice held his arm up high, letting her do the work.

"There," she said as she unfastened the buckle. "That wasn't so hard—"

Verice leaned in. "My thanks," he said softly.

She lifted her head, startled.

"Help me with the rest," Verice lowered his arm, brushing her hair back off her face and tucking it behind her round ear. "There's another," he pointed to the next buckle.

Warna blushed, her cheeks pink. "I see," she said, and started to work on the next strap.

Verice turned to give her better access, but he used the movement to his advantage. He lowered his head, so that his breath mingled with hers, and gently stroked the soft skin of her neck.

She shivered, but concentrated on her task. "So many buckles," she said as she tackled the next one.

"It needs to be tight," he explained. He curled his hand around her neck, letting his thumb stroke the soft flesh behind her ear and his fingers sheltered in the warmth of her hair. "Tight enough to keep me safe, flexible enough to let me move."

"You wore elven chain to the court," she said as she freed the last strap.

"True enough," Verice agreed. "But that's hardly for daily usage."

"Ah," she lifted her hands to his collar clasp, but he shook his head.

"The bracers first. Would you mind?" he asked, lifting his arm about her, ensuring that she stayed close. "Just the two clasps."

She turned in his arms, her back against his chest as he presented his forearm to her. She reached for the clasps.

"Careful," he cautioned.

The clasps snapped open. "Oh," she jerked her head slightly at the blade hidden within.

Verice leaned in, and nuzzled her ear. "I never like to be without a blade or two," he whispered. He breathed on her soft skin, and felt her shiver in response.

She tilted her head, giving him a glance over her shoulder as she pulled off the bracer, careful to set it, and the concealed blade, on the table. Verice raised his other arm, letting her work on those clasps. He slowly moved closer, bringing his free hand to her hip, then sliding it over her stomach with a firm pressure.

Her breathing quickened. She removed the other bracer, this time expressing no surprise at the second hidden blade.

She turned back then, in the circle of his arms. The sweet scent of her skin warmed him as she reached for his collar clasp. He lifted his chin, waiting… a soft kiss pressed to his jaw.

He murmured his approval, pulling her close, nuzzling her face until she lifted her mouth to him and he could claim it with a kiss.

Gently, he reminded himself, as much as he wanted to plunge within its depths. She tasted salty and sweet. He went slow, with a gentle firm pressure, as she leaned in closer, and of her own volition opened her mouth to him.

Even then, he just nipped at her lower lip, darting his tongue within to tease, before retreating back. Warna buried her hands in his hair, holding his head, and he returned the favor, one hand buried in her hair, the other at her lower black, pressing her against him.

They broke off when breath became an issue. Still he held her close, unwilling to release her.

She swallowed with a shudder and a sigh. "Verice," she breathed into his ear.

"The clasp?" he whispered.

With a chuckle, she fumbled with the metal, then eased her hands into the opening, pushing the armored tunic open.

Once the leather parted, he rolled his shoulders. Without any further encouragement, she eased the leather back, displaying the linen tunic beneath.

"Careful," he warned again.

She lifted an eyebrow at the blade concealed at the neck. "One or two?"

"Or three," he said, taking the armor from her hands and tossing it on the table.

With a soft stroke, Warna smoothed the linen tunic over his chest. Her hands left a trail of warmth through the cloth as they traced down and around to his waistband. There, she hesitated, and glanced at him.

He waited, keeping his own hands on her hips, and simply lowered his nose into her hair and took in her sweet scent.

There was no need to hurry. Discovery of a new lover, and a first lover, only happened once. They could take their time feeling, touching, tasting, exploring. Slow was preferable.

But he couldn't help a rumble of pleasure when her hands slid along his belt, slipped around his back and started to tug his tunic free.

Followed by a clatter as his throwing knife fell to the floor behind him.

Warna's head jerked back, her eyes wide, then narrowing. "Or four?" she asked.

"Sorry," Verice shrugged. "I was... distracted."

She pulled the shirt up. He cooperated, sliding the cloth over his head and easing his hair free. She laughed as she tugged it off his arms. She caught her breath as her gaze lingered on his chest.

He took the shirt from her hands, and threw it on the floor before drawing her in closer. She rested her hands on his bare chest.

"Are there any other surprises?" she inquired with an impish look as her fingers brushed his belt.

"There might be," he whispered, nuzzling her ear. "Feel free to explore, if you wish."

CHAPTER FIFTY-FOUR

If she wished? She wished for nothing more, and yet…

Warna took a breath, hesitating, letting her fingers rest on the leather of the belt. She dared, but she also didn't dare. She felt like she was trembling on the brink of something amazing and delightful, and terrifying all at the same time.

Verice stood, unmoving, like a rock. His chest rose and fell almost imperceptibly. His skin was dusted with silver hairs that trailed down his chest, narrowing as they reached his waist. She licked her dry lips. Her fingers seemed to take on a life of their own, loosening the belt, untying the laces, slipping her fingers around and back and down to slide the leather over his hips and—

Verice must have helped, because it seemed that he was suddenly, gloriously naked, stepping out of the trous as they fell to the floor with a grace she was certain no human could achieve.

"Do I please you?" he rumbled and she could forgive the lilt of arrogance in his voice. He was certainly entitled. She glanced up to see the glint of humor in his eye, with a touch of something else.

She wanted nothing more than to touch, to explore further, but instead she put her hands up to splay them over his chest, went up on tiptoe, and kissed him. He caught her mouth and returned the kiss.

She didn't resist when he stepped back, following his lead as they kissed. She was slightly shocked when he sat abruptly on the edge of the huge bed, and pulled her down next to him. It was the logical next step of course, but she felt scandalous.

"You're seducing me," she whispered as she tingled with excited realization.

"If so, I'm not very good at it," he chuffed. "I'm the one who's naked."

Warna laughed at that, for it was only the truth. She pushed him down, suddenly greedy to touch every inch of his skin, explore every aspect of his body. He offered no resistance, letting her hands trail down, drinking in the sight of all that he—

What caught her eye was the horrid scar that laced his thigh, running from the outside of his hip inwards at an angle.

"Verice," she whispered, reaching to trace its length.

His leg twitched and he caught her fingers half-way along the scar. He grimaced an apology. "It's still sensitive," he said.

"From the Festival night," she said. "You almost died."

"I healed," he said with a shrug. He kept her hand in his, turning it over palm-up. "It will fade, given time. Fifty years or so."

Fifty years. As if it was nothing. As if it wasn't a lifetime.

He seemed to sense the way her thoughts were tending, because he lifted her hand and kissed her palm, letting his tongue brush the skin. Keeping his eyes on hers, he breathed on the damp patch, sending shivers down her spine. "What matters is that I am here now, and healthy." He took her hand and pressed it against his length. She blushed hotly as she felt him beneath her hand. "And I believe you wanted to explore."

Warna couldn't have made a sound if she'd tried. Her throat closed up, her mouth dry. It was what she wanted, and the thought brought a warmth to her body and loins that swept over her like a fire.

She just wasn't sure where to start.

Verice moved then, keeping his hand over hers, and reached out to cup her neck, pulling her in for a kiss. Her hand tightened, and his body moved in response, and suddenly her reservations were gone.

He was a song, a perfect song, with endless lyrics she'd sing the rest of her life, and a melody she'd never be able to quantify.

And beautiful, so beautiful. Like a marble statue, made even more perfect by the fact that he lived and breathed and had calluses on his hands and scars on his body.

His long silver hair cascaded over her hands as she dared to trace the points of his ears, stroke his neck, place kisses along his collarbone. The silver hairs on his legs were coarse on his calves and thighs, but seemed to turn to silk as she neared his core. He didn't resist, didn't stop her explorations. Just stretched out before her and let her have her way. It was only the trembling of his body, the shortness of his breaths that made her think she'd erred somehow.

"Verice?" she whispered, sprawled next to him.

The intensity of his silver eyes caught her. "I'm roused, that's all," he said tightly. "Do not stop."

"Oh," Warna glanced at him, realizing what she'd done. "I've never done this before. I'm sorry—"

"I'm not," Verice said.

"What can I—" Warna started, but Verice reached for her hand before she said another word.

"Finish what you've started," he growled.

And to her amazement, she did, watching as he threw back his head to expose that long, elegant neck. Watching, as his strong warrior body quivered and succumbed to her touch. Watching as he shattered in her hands.

* * * * *

Verice regained his senses to find Warna curled up in his arms, the fabric of her skirts covering his legs. For a moment he enjoyed the pleasant sensation of being sated and relaxed. But then guilt rose up. He tightened his arms around her. "Warna?"

"Verice," she said against his chest, her breath warm on his skin.

He couldn't see her eyes, and didn't know what she was thinking. He cleared his throat to offer his apology. "Warna, forgive me—"

"For what?" she asked.

He frowned. "I meant to see to your pleasure first. Not take my own before you'd had a chance to experience—"

"It was amazing," she whispered. "That I could do that to you… make you feel that way." She lifted her head, her eyes glowing in satisfaction. "And there's more to it, isn't there?"

"Yes," Verice couldn't keep his amusement out of his voice. "A lot more. But we've no hurry, Warna."

She frowned. "No more waiting."

"Impetuous humans," he teased.

"Staid elves," she sat up and considered her dress. "It was messier than I anticipated."

He laughed, letting it shake his entire body. Warna gave him a delighted look.

"Well, there's a remedy for that," he said, reaching out to trace her collar around her neck. "You are overdressed for the occasion." He hooked his finger on the fabric and gave a tug. "Besides, is it not my turn to explore?"

CHAPTER FIFTY-FIVE

Warna felt the tug of the fabric against her neck, and the heat of his hand through the cloth. As much as she wanted to, as much as she wanted his hands on her skin, she hesitated.

Verice knew it in an instant. "What's wrong?" he asked, releasing her collar.

She looked away, licking dry lips. "It's just… in your lifetime, you've been with thousands of faelles and—"

His snort was explosive. "Thousands?" Verice choked, clearly amused until he saw her face. "Ah, Warna," he said, and sat up enough to reach for the bedding that had piled at the end of the bed. With swift movements he pulled her down beside him, and covered them both in warmth.

Warna didn't resist his tugging. He waited until she'd settled beside him before he spoke. "I admit I am experienced," Verice's voice was warm in her ear. "And in my early days when I was a hundred or so, I was fairly wild. But thousands?"

She shrugged, hiding her face within the covers. "I just don't see how I can compare. Elven women are lovely, and seemingly so perfect."

"The important word being 'seemingly'," Verice said. "Don't be taken in by appearances, Warna."

"But how do human women compare?" She rose, letting the blanket slide off her shoulders.

"I wouldn't know," Verice said. "You are my first."

"Oh," Warna blinked in surprise.

"I have to say," Verice pulled her back down into his arms. "You are amazing."

He turned on his side to face her, pulling her close. "Not that I've seen much, mind, except when you were—" he stopped himself.

"When I was vomiting," Warna said ruefully.

"Well, yes," Verice said, his tone dry and serious. "But even that you did in your own special way."

Warna couldn't help laughing.

Verice reached up, and ran his fingers through her hair, tracing over the tops of her ears.

"Would you like to know what I have learned over all the years? That what really matters isn't the physical attributes or the skills of a lover. The size, the shape, the appearance... that's secondary. It's important to find your lover pleasing, but what really matters is the person you are with, and the depth of the feeling you have for them."

She reached then, to smooth back his hair, and trace the tips of his pointed ears. "Do I please you?"

"Oh yes," Verice whispered. "And I believe it's my turn."

He threw back the blanket, so gloriously naked underneath, and reached for her.

She couldn't have said where her clothing went. But once it was gone, she reveled in the touch of skin on skin from her head to his toes. Her body couldn't contain all of these sensations another moment. She reached for him, looking for an anchor in the wildness. Her hands wandered over him, stroking and gliding over every lovely inch.

And his hands, his wonderful hands, caressed every curve of her breasts, her hips, her thighs, lingering between her folds until she writhed beneath him, begging with soundless pleas for so much more.

He held her close, his hand relentless within her depths, and put his lips to her ear. "It's all right, Warna. Let go. Explore your pleasure for me."

Her entire body seized, every muscle tight with the pleasure of it all. She cried out, and for long, lovely moments, was lost in white heat and light.

* * * * *

Half-asleep, she felt him move, felt him cleaning her with a soft cloth. She murmured in pleasure as he pulled the blankets over their rapidly cooling bodies.

He settled into her arms, pulling her close, entwining their arms and legs deep in the comfort of the bed. "There's more?" she whispered, almost half-afraid of the possibility.

"There is," he chuckled into her hair. "But the delay of pleasure is a pleasure in and of itself."

"Any more, and I'll die," Warna whispered back.

If Verice said anything more, it was lost as she drifted off to sleep.

* * * * *

Verice awoke first, to the hints of dawn coming through the windows, and Warna in his arms.

She radiated warmth, her head on his shoulder and her blonde hair spilling over the pillow. Verice reached and tucked the hair behind her ear, his fingers lingering against the soft skin of her neck. Her pulse was warm and steady under his fingers.

She was beyond anything he'd experienced before. He'd though he was gifting her a boon, but in truth she'd given him far, far more.

Amazing in her passion, in her willingness to let him lead, and then in her eagerness to show what she had learned. There was a playfulness to her loving that he'd never encountered before. Maybe it was the fact that she was human.

Or maybe it was just because she was *Warna*.

He'd not taken her, and he wasn't going to until he was certain that she was ready. This he could gift to her, and he was determined that they'd take their time.

He pulled himself out of her embrace, and left the warmth of their bed. Warna made a small sound of protest, but didn't awaken.

Pulling on trous, he went to the outer chamber. The dogs were all sprawled on the hearth rugs. Brindle sat up from the midst of the pack, yawning and blinking at him.

A servant appeared almost immediately. Verice sent a message to Narthing cancelling his normal routine for the morning. It could wait for a while. He also gave instructions not to be disturbed. They couldn't shut out the world forever; there was too much work to be done. But they could steal a few hours.

As he headed back into the bedchamber, Brindle curled back down with a sigh.

Verice closed the door, and padded back to bed, discarding his trous along the way. He crawled into the warmth of the covers.

Warna was blinking at him sleepily. "All's well?"

"Very well," Verice murmured. He stretched out, pulling her warm, unresisting body to his, and claimed her lips in a gentle kiss.

She smiled against his mouth. "Not time to get up yet, is it?"

"Not in the sense you mean," Verice said, tracing a line of kisses along her neck.

Warna laughed, then matched his every demand with one of her own.

* * * * *

Later, much later, Warna stared down at the account books, her eyes half-closed as she remembered the previous night. And awakening this morning. Remembering Verice's touch, his skin, his mouth—

Ersal coughed.

She brought herself up with a jerk. "Ersal? Did you say something?"

"Well," Ersal was looking at his own accounting, trying to hide his amusement and failing. "I did ask a question a few moments ago. Did Janella include new napkins in the order for the table linens?"

Warna blinked. "Did we place that order yet? I didn't think we had."

"I'll check," Ersal said.

Warna returned to her accounts. But honestly, how was she supposed to be able to work? How was she supposed to focus on anything except how Verice made her feel?

Somehow, she felt like she'd been let in on a huge secret, one that made the entire world feel bigger than she'd ever dreamed. She wanted to sing of it, but she'd never be able to find the words to communicate the experience.

Or that she'd be able to sing in public.

But in private, now. In the privacy of their room, with just she and Verice, she could sing to him, of her feelings, her longings.

She hesitated at that thought.

No, that wasn't fair. She wouldn't burden him with those things. She wouldn't cling. She'd made a bargain and she'd live with the terms. She'd keep her songs to herself, to be sung... later. When the troth was broken. When she'd left this place. After Verice had shared all the physical aspects of lovemaking with her.

Because she did want to know all of it. Verice had awakened her with kisses and touches, and brought her to shuddering pleasure with just his hands. He'd promised more of the same tonight, leaving her sated and gasping in their bed.

He might be determined to move slowly, but Warna had her own feelings on the issue. Her skin tingled at the thought.

She fought to bring her mind back to the task at hand. There were two weeks before the Festival started, and so many decisions had to be made. She needed to be thinking about the work before her, and not about enjoying the time she'd have with Verice.

And wonder what else Verice had to share with her.

"Then there's the matter of the ale to be ordered," Ersal's voice cut through her thoughts. "Given the crowds, I'd thought perhaps two duns, but maybe we should consider three."

Warna sighed. "Three would probably be best."

* * * * *

Narthing was pleased to be back in his regular chambers in the barracks. But he was even more pleased to see Lord Verice looking more relaxed.

Not to the degree that he was laughing or smiling. But his shoulders were looser under his brigandine, and his eyes warmer.

At least until he started talking about the security for the Festival with himself and Constable Ricard.

"I want everyone trained," Verice stood, his arms crossed over his chest. The maps of the barony had been replaced with the schematics of the castle and keep. "I want everyone drilled in responses in case of attack. Everyone, from the clerks to the stable boys. Where to go, what to do." Verice leaned on the table, his eyes now sharp as daggers. "I'll not be caught again. Not ever again."

"Agreed," Narthing said.

Ricard nodded. "Easy enough to do, Lord Verice. We can see to it over the next few weeks."

"The Lady Warna, as well," Verice said. "I'll train her myself."

"If they attack, they'll rue it," Narthing said.

"It's not 'if', Narthing," Verice said grimly. "It's 'when'."

CHAPTER FIFTY-SIX

I t was three days before Warna had a glimmer of a rational thought in her brain.

Yes, she worked with Ersal and the others. Yes, she'd started making decisions about the celebrations. Hopefully, good ones; it wasn't like she could remember them. Yes, she'd some semblance of sanity, but that was all it was. For in truth, it was the nights in Verice's arms that seemed the center of her existence.

It wasn't just the physical aspects, although just the thought of what they'd done, and what they'd do, and what they hadn't done yet was enough to turn her body into a heated lump of pure desire. Verice was still insisting that they move slowly, pox take the mael. Each night she'd argued, he'd touch her and the argument was over, for all intents and purposes.

No, it wasn't just that. It was the closeness. The feel of his leg against hers, or the smell of them in the bedding. Or arguing over whether the dogs would sleep in the bed with them.

She'd won. The dogs slept on the floor.

But as glorious as it was, Warna was suddenly counting the days until the Festival of Light and Laughter started. She began to feel a flutter of panic.

Verice was relying on her to find a way to open the Great Hall of the keep, and for the life of her she hadn't any ideas. She remembered what she'd seen when she'd explored inside, the broken furniture, the dried blood. There had to be a way to honor the dead and yet bring the place back to life, but she wasn't sure quite how to accomplish that.

The Festival lasted seven nights. Back home, most holidays were a few days at best.

In Tassinic, they'd combined the elven and human traditions into a seven-day long party, and while she applauded the idea, it made her task just that much more overwhelming.

Warna frowned. Hadn't Ersal said something about a Priest of the Lady at the church in the city? He might have an idea or two, or at least be someone she could talk to about it without fear of raising old sorrows. She wasn't above asking for help. This was just too important.

Verice entered her sitting room, lifting an eyebrow at the vases spread around the room.

"The gardeners have started on the flowers, trimming some things back," Warna explained. "I didn't want the blooms to be wasted."

"I'll have to check their work," Verice said, coming closer, careful not to let his sword hit any of the vases. "I was wondering if you were free, m'lady?" He leaned on the arms of her chair and kissed her. Warna caught her breath at his touch and taste, and returned the kiss with joy.

Verice was breathing deeply when she finally broke away to take in air. "For lunch?" she asked, licking her lips.

"Or other things," Verice growled.

She reached up, tangled her fingers in his hair and pulled him down for a kiss that left no doubt as to her answer.

Or availability.

Later, when they sprawled on their bed, sated, and breathless, she asked. "When will you show me the rest? Teach me more?"

"Impetuous human," he said softly.

"Staid elf," she whispered back. She curled up, her head on his chest. "Could we make a trip into town? There's someone I need to talk to."

"No," Verice rolled over onto his side, and pulled her close.

"Ersal tells me there is a Priest of the Lady at the church," Warna placed a kiss on Verice's collarbone. His skin tasted salty, and she blew a breath over the moist spot.

"Summon him here," Verice murmured, cupping her breast.

"Verice," she pushed at him back far enough to look into his eyes. "You don't summon a Priest of the Lady. You go the church and you approach them with respect and humility," she started to laugh as he raised an eyebrow. "Well, that's what we poor humans do."

"Unnecessary and far too dangerous," Verice said firmly. "I refuse to authorize any trips into Octara."

They left at dawn.

"Stubborn woman," Verice grumbled under his breath as he mounted. Warna was already up on her horse. Her smile was soft, but he could see the triumphant gleam in her eye.

Once she'd won his concession to this little outing, she'd decided on five other tasks that could only be taken care of in the city.

She'd also sent word to the church, asking when it would be convenient to call upon Priest Dorne, who it seemed, kept early hours.

At least he'd managed to set the size of the escort. With any luck, they'd be done with their errands and out of the city before the crowds developed.

"You have the watch, Constable." he gave a nod to Ricard.

"Aye, m'lord." Ricard responded, and Verice set his heels to his horse, leading the way. They started off with a clatter of hooves on cobblestones.

As they approached the gate, Warna slowed her horse. Verice shot her a glance. She lifted both eyebrows and tilted her head toward the gate.

He snorted.

She laughed, a lovely light sound in the morning air, and urged her horse through the gates.

The ride down was quick. Verice set a fast pace, and with the streets barely awake, he could keep that pace as they made their way to the church.

They were greeted by a faelle acolyte.

"Priest Dorne?" Verice asked as he dismounted, and went to assist Warna.

The acolyte smiled. "He's in the bakery, m'lord," she said with obvious delight.

"Ah," Verice said. "We can wait until—"

"Nay, m'lord." The acolyte's smile grew even wider. "He'll be some time. I'm to take you to him."

To Verice's surprise, Dorne wasn't supervising the bakers.

He was baking.

"Welcome, Lord High Baron, Lady Warna." Dorne was a small, dark human with olive skin and a bit of a paunch. He was dressed in the traditional black robes of a Priest of the Lady, but with an apron over top, and a dusting of flour overall. "May I offer you kav?"

On the table before him was a huge lump of dough. Dorne was shaping loaves, making shallow slices across the tops, basting them with egg, then sliding them in the huge ovens behind him with a large wooden paddle. His hands never stopped as he gestured for them to take seats on a long bench opposite him.

"Please, be seated," Dorne said.

The brick ovens behind him radiated heat, and the room smelled of yeast and bread. Along the length of the room, other bakers were working, taking out the finished loaves. Verice settled on the bench, adjusting his scabbards, trying to keep them out from underfoot.

"Please," Warna said as she settled beside him. She took a deep breath. "It smells wonderful," she said.

"My thanks," Dorne said. "But I can scarce take credit for a bit of flour, water, yeast and heat." He chuckled. "Still, a few warm slices might not go amiss, eh?"

"We already ate," Warna made a token protest.

"What does that have to do with anything?" Dorne asked.

Verice found himself with a warm, buttered slice in one hand, and kav in the other. Warna had the same, a bemused look on her face.

"Eat first," Dorne said. "Then tell me how I can be of assistance."

Warna bit into hers with obvious enjoyment. Verice followed her lead. The bread was good, slightly sweetened with honey. The crust was crisp and chewy but the bread itself seemed to melt in his mouth.

Dorne nodded, seemingly pleased with their enjoyment. He continued his work, preparing the loaves for the oven. "So, you have something you wished to ask me?"

Warna glanced at Verice, drew a breath, and started to explain the situation.

Verice had dreaded this. Dreaded trying to explain to someone how he'd reacted, reliving the pain and grief all over again as they explained the situation. To tell the tale was to relive it, and his stomach had clenched at the thought of talking to anyone about the problem.

But as Warna described the wreckage in the Great Hall, Dorne just kept working, his hands busy constantly as he nodded his understanding. Maybe it was the heat, maybe the warm bread in his belly, maybe the quiet repetition of Dorne's task, or maybe just Dorne's quiet acceptance that made it easier to discuss.

"So, we need to find a way to honor the dead, and yet restore the Hall," Dorne said quietly.

"Yes," Warna said. "I'm not really sure how to do that, and I was hoping that you might know, or have some ideas."

Dorne shook his head ruefully, his hands pausing for just a moment. "I have a few ideas," he said. "Give me a day or two to think on it. I'll come to the keep so we can discuss it in detail."

"Thank you," Warna sighed, giving Verice a questioning smile.

Warmth washed over him that had nothing to do with the heat of the kitchens. She was worried about him, concerned that he'd been upset by the re-telling. "All's well," he murmured, if only to reassure her.

But to his surprise, he found he'd finished his bread and kav. He felt lighter somehow, as if he'd taken off plate armor after a long battle. Something in his shoulders eased as he found it easier to breath.

Warna's relief was clear as her smile widened.

Verice found his voice, "My thanks, Priest Dorne. For the food, and the assistance."

"You are most welcome, m'lord." Dorne turned to shove another loaf in the oven.

"We've other errands," Warna said. "But if there's no hurry," she touched Verice's arm. "I'd like to pay my respects in the Sanctuary. It won't take a moment."

"Of course," Verice said and rose with Warna.

Dorne gestured to one of the cooks. "Show Lady Warna to the Sanctuary," he ordered.

"I'll meet you at the horses," Warna whispered, and was gone.

Verice hesitated then settled back down on the bench. He watched Dorne work for a while, and the other man seemed content with the silence.

"You're different from Dominic," Verice finally said.

"In that I am not a pompous ass?" Dorne paused in the act of slicing a loaf. His dark eyes pierced Verice. "Or that I am human?"

CHAPTER FIFTY-SEVEN

B oth," Verice said, meeting Dorne stare for stare. "It seems odd to me that you are appointed to replace Dominic when the hierarchy of your church is well aware of my preferences."

"No odder than Lady Warna appearing at your side," Dorne said dryly. Verice bristled.

"Peace." Dorne set down the loaf in his hand. "Lord High Baron, I know full well that while you do not follow our faith, you are not ignorant of its tenets."

"True enough," Verice said.

"I cannot *replace* Dominic," Dorne continued. "I have no skill at healing, first off, and second, Priests of the Lady are wanderers. We do not take administrative posts within the church. As you are well aware."

"Yet here you are," Verice growled.

"Yet here I am," Dorne said calmly. "Taking up the loaf and the knife. Word came of a need, and I am here to serve until such time as a permanent replacement can be found. Someone half-elven, as per your requirements." He paused, a flash of sorrow in his eyes. "As it is, I have some experience with planning mourning ceremonies."

"I'd offer thanks again, for your willingness to aid Warna," Verice said.

"But no apology for your obvious hypocrisy?" Dorne asked.

"Watch your tongue," Verice rose to his full height, the bench clattering the floor behind him. His hand went to the hilt of his sword.

"Who else will confront you?" Dorne demanded, standing there, covered in flour and not backing down an inch. "Who else will make you look at your own actions?" The smaller man snorted. "Not to mention the fact that seeing you both together, it seems to me that you fear the pain you are already suffering. Can't you see that—"

"Lord High Baron!" one of his men ran into the kitchen with the cook that had escorted Warna at his side. "M'lord, there's trouble in the courtyard. Lady Warna—"

Verice took off running.

* * * * *

You idiots are going to get yourself killed!" Warna called out as she tried to stay calm.

They had waited until she'd emerged from the church and mounted to swarm into the courtyard, trying to separate her from her escort, banging drums and shouting, demanding tribute for the Lady of Laughter. She'd recognized the company of actors from before. Especially their leader, the one with the kitchen pot on his head and some sort of serving dish as a shield.

Verice's lieutenant had acted quickly. Ustov and his men cut between the mob and her, forcing them back, away from Warna and her horse. The actors re-grouped to the outer gates of the church's courtyard, blocking the exit.

"Stand and deliver," Master Zester shouted as the crowd swirled around behind him. "Tribute is owed to the Lady of Laughter!"

More drums, trumpets, and voices sounded. Warna's horse threw up its head and pranced a bit at the noise, but it seemed more annoyed than frightened. She kept her seat easily enough but one of her guards took the precaution of grabbing the bridle.

"Dismount, Lady," Ustov urged. "In case—"

"Cease that racket," Warna called to Zester. "And Ustov, sheath your weapons. There's no need for bloodshed over something this foolish."

Ustov had his sword out, his men were lined up with their shields and naked swords. In another moment something incredibly stupid was going to happen to someone…

"What is the meaning of this?"

All movement ceased, all heads turned to the speaker. Verice was standing on the steps to the main church doors, looking every inch the warrior. His blade was out, and Warna knew full well that he'd not sheathe it at her request.

He also looked very, very angry.

"M'lord," Master Zester, stepped forward, his pot rattling on his head.

The noise rose in the air as the drums, rattles and horns were brought into play. Zester raised his voice to be heard. "We hold your lady hostage for—"

Verice started toward him. "You threaten my lady?" his voice cut through the air. The noise and the crowd behind Zester melted away as he advanced.

Zester squeaked, but stood his ground. "M'lord, I can explain—"

Verice ignored him as he moved to Warna's side. He paused by her knee. "Are you well?" he asked quietly as his warriors moved up beside them.

"I'm fine," Warna reassured him. "I think they just wanted your attention—"

"They have it," Verice growled, swiveling to stare at Zester.

"M'lord," the actor removed his pot and clutched it to his chest as his men clustered around behind him. "We meant no offense," he said, nervously eyeing Verice's sword. "We'd only meant to ask permission to perform for the castle at the Festival. A tribute is owed to the Lady of Laughter, after all, and we've not been permitted within those walls for almost a year." Zester straightened. "It was a poor joke on the part of our company, m'lord. I beg the Lady Warna's forgiveness and your own."

Verice stared at the man. "Warna?"

"Idiots and fools," Warna scanned the crowd. "It's only by Ustov's good sense that they weren't cut down or trampled. Still no one is hurt," she continued. "One can only hope they are better actors then one might think."

"M'lady," Zester protested.

Verice sheathed his sword. "Very well," he said, and gestured for his horse. The warriors all mounted as well, with Ustov giving the actors a very grim look.

"Lord High Baron," Zester persisted. "About the Festival…"

Verice stiffened in his saddle. Warna glanced over and saw Dorne in the doorway of the church, wiping his hands on his apron. Verice was staring at him, an odd look on his face.

"Very well, Zester," Verice turned in his saddle. "You may set up your stage for one day and night during the Festival. Contact my seneschal for the details."

"My thanks, Lord Verice," Zester said.

"And Master Zester," Verice paused as Ustov lead the others on. "Present a comedy. We've had overmuch tragedy of late."

* * * * *

Verice forbade Warna to dismount in the markets, and for once his stubborn woman listened.

He knew full well that this was a breach of trade custom. One usually walked through a market, leaving horses on the outskirts. But custom could go hang from the battlements. He wanted her up high, where he and his men could scan any that approached her.

And they all approached her. Word must have spread that she was in charge of planning the festivities at the castle. Every merchant with a slice of cheese, mug of wine, pastry, sausage or fruit wanted her attention. And that was just the food merchants. They'd the entire length of the market to go yet. Verice had the men surround Warna, but not close enough to hinder the merchants from drawing near.

Close enough to keep a watchful eye on them, though.

He'd have brushed them aside, or referred them to Ersal, but Warna… she seemed in her element, talking, laughing, eyeing the items and asking prices. No tasting - he'd put stop to that fast enough. Still. She was enjoying herself.

Verice huffed out a breath. It was a pleasure to see, but it was going to take forever.

"M'lord," Ustov moved to his side, scanning the crowd as they walked the horses along. "M'lord, I ask forgiveness. That incident, back in the churchyard, it should never have happened. It was under my command, and I take full responsibility for—"

"Rest easy, Ustov," Verice said. "You did well."

"My thanks, m'lord." Ustov frowned. "They moved fast, m'lord, swarming in and trying to cut her out and away from us. Almost as if they were… more than actors. I am not sure I trust those humans."

And there it was, from the mouth of one of his own men.

"Master Zester has had a troupe here for many years," Verice said. "I've no reason to doubt him. Still, we'll mention this to Captain Narthing. Forewarned is forearmed."

Ustov nodded and drifted back toward the rear, leaving Verice to his own, uncomfortable thoughts.

Dorne's words pricked at his conscience. In the past, he'd striven to be fair to all his people, human, elven, mixed. But now, especially since the attack, he wondered if that was true. How much of his suspicion of the actors was because the majority of the company was human?

He'd been about to deny Zester, until he'd seen Dorne standing there. True, it paid to keep one's friends close, and one's enemies closer, but he'd seen no wisdom in inviting a troupe of humans into the walls. But was that more because they were humans than anything else?

He'd tried to ensure equal justice in his courts for all and sundry, but he hadn't allowed a human within the walls of his castle for many years. Not until he'd carried Warna within the gate in his arms. That was an ugliness within him that he truly did not wish to see, and could not ignore.

They'd passed through the food merchants, and were entering the cloth and leather-workers. People were running into the street with bolts of cloth, and waving lace and ribbons. Warna's horse shied a bit, but she got her under control. "Here, now," Warna called out. "Mind yourselves around the horses."

Verice moved up then, to ride beside her, frowning at the various men and women. They backed off a bit, still trying to get Warna's attention. One in particular had a bolt of velvet, as blue as the sky itself. "A new dress for the dancing, m'lady! I can have it done in a trice!"

Warna just laughed, and shook her head.

Verice frowned as they moved past the man. "You should have new dresses, for the festivities," he was thinking out loud. "Not to mention jewelry. I've some diamonds that you could wear, but you may wish to buy something—"

"No," Warna said.

"But," Verice was startled at the look on her face.

"I'll take nothing from you but what I need," Warna said firmly. "And nothing more than what my lidded basket contains when I leave."

Verice's heart turned to stone.

CHAPTER FIFTY-EIGHT

H er words and her tone struck like a knife, but he kept his face blank. "I meant no offense," he said quietly.

"None taken," Warna had stopped her horse to take up a spool of ribbon, running it through her fingers. She appeared to be inspecting it closely, but Verice saw her glance his way. She smiled at the merchant and handed it back. "Please be sure to approach the seneschal, and tell him that Warna asked to see your wares."

The faelle's face lit with delight. "Bless you, m'lady," she called as she retreated from the crowd.

Warna started her horse forward, giving him another glance. "But when I leave—"

"We can discuss that another time," Verice said, casting a glance around them before he looked at her again.

Warna nodded her understanding.

"As my betrothed, you represent Tassinic when you sit beside me on the high seat," Verice continued, keeping his voice low. "It would be a topic of discussion if you were not suitably clothed."

They continued on in silence, with Warna outwardly admiring the items being shown to her. "I hadn't thought of that," she finally admitted.

"There's jewelry in the vaults," Verice said. "If it is your wish, it can be returned to the vaults after the festivities." He rolled his eyes at her. "And a few dresses will not beggar me or the barony, m'lady."

Warna laughed, then shrugged. "Very well, m'lord."

Verice raised an eyebrow. "That blue cloth was fetching," he coaxed. "I could go back—"

"Velvet?" Warna snorted. "At that price? Think again, m'lord."

"I defer to your wisdom in the matter," Verice said, pleased when Warna laughed again.

But she also gave him a piercing look.

"I'm still not taking anything with me when I leave, Verice."

"A topic for another time," Verice said as pain rose in his chest. This was not a conversation he wished to have in the streets. Seeking to change the subject, he rose in his stirrups, then settled back down in his saddle. "It would appear that the furniture makers' lane is ahead. Perhaps we could pick up the pace after this corner?" Verice raised an eyebrow at Warna. "Before they start coming out carrying chairs and tables?"

* * * * *

Narthing was pleased to find that the stairs to Warna's office didn't wind him. At this rate of healing, he might even be able to dance at the Festival.

Constable Ricard had accompanied him, keeping a weather eye, but even he gave a nod of satisfaction as they approached the door. "I'll leave you to it, then," Ricard paused outside the door. "I'm off to drill some of the young'uns."

"You're just avoiding the desk work," Narthing said.

"Leaving such things to you and the Lady Warna," Ricard said innocently. "Fine, capable hands."

Narthing muttered something rude under his breath as Ricard strode off. Then he squared his shoulders, took a deep breath, and knocked.

"Enter," Warna called.

As he'd expected, the room was filled with a chaos of people and paper. The people were pulling chairs close; the papers were spread over every surface of the room, fighting with the vases of flowers for space.

Warna laughed. "Just move these out of the way," she said, placing a vase on the floor.

Ersal was there, along with two of his assistants. Warna had recruited Farnor, the quartermaster and his clerk. Janella had four people with her, because of the demands on the housekeeping staff. Dominic's replacement, Priest Dorne was already seated at the side of Warna's desk. Even Lord Mayor Pernard had come.

Lady Warna took the chair behind her desk, and seemed in complete command. "Narthing," her face lit up. "We've three days left to get this chaos under control."

"Might as well try to organize mayflies," Janella sighed. "For all the good it will do."

"No plan survives the first encounter with the enemy." Narthing smiled as he took a seat.

"But we need review our plans, none the less," Warna said firmly. "So, let's start with the First Night."

Narthing caught his breath as a sudden stillness filled the room. His own pain caught him off guard, with a sudden swift clutching of his heart. The faces around him all reflected the same. They'd all known it was coming, known that it had to be done. Now it was here, and no easier.

Warna looked stricken by her own words. For a moment, he thought she might start crying, but she took a deep breath and continued. "Priest Dorne and I have talked. We'd like to share our thoughts on how we should proceed." She dropped her eyes to the scroll that was set out before her. "I want you all to aid us in this; to honor the dead, and re-open the Great Hall. So, if you have anything to offer, please do so."

Narthing moved to the chair she gestured him to, glad of a chance to cover his emotions with movement. The others organized themselves around Warna's desk.

"We'll start with a call to prayer," Priest Dorne started. "And then—"

Narthing concentrated, not wanting to miss a word.

Surprisingly, with Dorne's calm demeanor, they managed to review the plan for the entire First Night fairly quickly. Everyone had contributed, and the final plan met with general approval.

Warna handed off the last scroll to one of the assistants for copying, and heaved a huge sigh. Her brown eyes were warm as she surveyed them all. "I think the hardest part is behind us. Let's get some hot kav, and then continue."

The others relaxed as well, and the tension in the room eased.

What a Baroness she'd make, Narthing thought as he took a mug of kav from a servant. She'd the deportment and skills, that was certain. With this Festival, she'd have restored the castle to working order, and restored Lord Verice as well.

Narthing knew, hells, the entire castle knew that she and Verice were sharing a bedchamber. Admittedly, it wasn't proper, but given all that had happened, no one was pointing fingers.

The fact that Warna was human, well, that had raised a few eyebrows. Narthing hadn't heard much talk on that topic, but then he didn't move within the social circles. He glanced at Pernard and wondered. Although from Pernard's expression, he need not have concerns on that aspect. Pernard clearly approved of Warna, and why not? Practical, smart, and lovely as humans go.

Warna caught him staring, and gave him a questioning look. Covering his embarrassment, Narthing gestured to the piles of scrolls on her desk.

It was Warna's turn to be embarrassed. "The morning's delivery. I haven't gotten through it all yet. Mostly responses to our invitations, but I do need to sort them out this morning."

"There's one there with the Valltera royal seal," Narthing noted.

"Probably Verice's, then," Warna said matter-of-factly. "If everyone's been served, let's move on to the Second Day—"

They continued on, covering all seven nights and the days within faster now that the subject matter had lightened in tone.

"You've made arrangements for the actors?" Warna asked Ersal.

"Aye," Ersal said. "They know when and where to place their stage in the courtyard."

Narthing said nothing. He and Lord Verice had already discussed the actors. Nothing seemed out of place, and everyone had vouched for Master Zester. Still, they'd be confined to the courtyard, under the watchful eyes of his men.

"I won't bore you all with the orders for ribbons, banners, flags, and flowers," Warna laughed. "Trust me when I say that the castle will be decorated to a fare-thee-well." She looked at her desk, and then at each of them. "I think we've covered everything. Does anyone have anything to—"

Alarm horns sounded from the battlements.

CHAPTER FIFTY-NINE

Verice stood on the inner wall and scanned the courtyard as the alarm horns were sounding. He watched in satisfaction as everyone turned away from their tasks and responded to the drill. Some ran for designated shelters where warriors already guarded the doors. Others pulled their weapons, and moved to locations where they'd been told to gather. All acted quickly, quietly, and with deadly seriousness.

He knew it was disruptive and difficult. No one complained. His people remembered all too well the betrayal, and the deaths that had resulted. Drills, repetition, knowing what to do, that would make a difference when the next attack occurred.

"Give me time to check the keep," Verice commanded. "Then sound the 'all's well'."

"Aye, m'lord," was the response, but Verice was already headed down the stairs.

Captain Narthing was by the main gates, and he raised a hand to show that his people were in place. Constable Ricard was over by the kitchens and bakery. Verice couldn't see him, but he knew well that he'd be making sure that all was as it should be. He'd receive detailed reports later, but his goal now was the keep, and to make sure that everyone had obeyed their orders.

Ersal was barricaded in his office, with most of his staff and two armed guards. Verice lifted an eyebrow to see Priest Dorne in the room with them, but he didn't stop to talk.

He'd finished checking three floors when he heard the horns calling the 'all's well'. Everything had been in order so far, with everyone barricaded in their rooms, armed with whatever weapons they could bring to bear, knowing what was expected of them. Satisfied, he went to check on the very last occupant of the keep.

Warna's office was empty, as it should be, with a few papers scattered on the floor. He checked the bedchamber, just in case, but it was empty as well.

So, he returned to the outer chamber, locked the outer door, then stepped to the wall, and pressed his hand to the corner. With a soft rumble, the marble wall shifted aside.

Warna was seated within the bolt-hole cross-legged, her lap covered with scrolls and letters.

"You are supposed to leave your tasks," Verice said pointedly. "Stop what you are doing and get to safety."

She looked out at him in exasperation. "This is the fourth drill in three days," she said. "Some of us have work to do," she waved one of the scrolls at him.

Verice folded himself in next to her. She slid over to give him a bit of room.

"If you'd dropped one of those letters or scrolls it could have given your position away," Verice said.

"But I didn't," she pointed out. "I grabbed a handful, waited until the others left, and crawled into the first available of your little cubby-holes, and closed the door behind me." She rolled her eyes at him. "I sat quietly, waiting for you. I didn't leave when I heard the 'all clear'. I waited for you to come."

"And if I hadn't come?" Verice asked.

Warna gestured to the corner. "Then I've food and water for two people to last three days, along with a pallet and a chamber pot." She wrinkled her nose as she recited her instructions. "At the end of three days, I'm to wait until dark, leave the cubby hole, and seek to learn more. Although I have to say that if two people were to hide in here, they had better like each other."

"It was meant for family," Verice said shortly.

"I know," Warna said. She fingered the edges of one of the envelopes. "How did the rest of the castle perform?"

"Well," Verice said. "I've no reports yet, but I am satisfied that everyone knows what to do. Which doesn't mean I won't drill them again, if time allows." He frowned. Warna was staring at the pile of letters in her lap, but she wasn't really seeing them "Warna?"

She lifted her head, blinked at him then bit her lip. "Verice... this letter was addressed to me," She handed him the stiff paper, and he scowled at the royal crest at the top of the page. "It's from Charrin."

Verice took it from her. Warna leaned her head against his shoulder as he read.

Lady Warna,

I have thought on our last conversation and have considered your words carefully. As hard as they were to hear, I have heard them.

I would request that I be permitted to attend your Festival of Light and Laughter, at least on the First Night, to add my voices to the others.

Bard Charrin

Verice let out a long, slow breath he hadn't realized he was holding. "Well," he said. "This is… unexpected."

Warna took his hand in hers, but didn't say anything.

"Charrin has harbored his hate for so long," Verice continued. "I wouldn't expect that mael to change."

"He's harbored his hate as long as you harbored your grief," Warna whispered.

Verice nodded absently, lost in thought, studying the words of the letter. "What do you think?" he asked.

"I wish I could spare you this pain," Warna said. "But we both know that it must be faced. Charrin wants to face his, here with us, in the place that his love died. I do not want to deny him that, but—"

"I don't want him to lash out at you," Verice growled.

"He may," Warna acknowledged. "If we warn Dorne, and Narthing, they can be ready to deal with him gently. With understanding."

Verice snorted as he folded the letter away. "Fair enough." He leaned over and nuzzled her ear. "How goes the planning?"

"Three days left," she said, her voice softening at the touch of his lips. "Really, we are down to tiny details, and sudden crises."

"And is there anything in that pile of paper that can't wait a while?"

"Well…" Warna tilted her head. Her skin shivered under his lips. "There's a lace order for the women of Birch Cove that I want to forward on. From one of the faellas at the Valltera Court."

"That won't take long," Verice said. "I need to check in with Ersal and Narthing to make sure that all went well with the drill, but after that…" he paused, nipping at her neck.

"Why, m'lord," Warna gasped as he dragged his teeth over her skin. "What did you have in mind?"

"More," Verice growled.

Warna jerked her head back, her eyes wide, sparks flying in their brown depths. "I'll meet you back here," she scrambled up and out of the cubbyhole, gathering her letters as she moved.

Verice was right behind her. He took the steps two at a time, trying to rush with some degree of dignity befitting a Lord High Baron.

Ersal, Narthing, and Ricard were waiting for him, all with pleased looks on their faces. "It went well, then?" Verice asked.

There were nods all around. "Although the cooks ask that you time future drills for a moment when they are not spitting carcasses," Ersal said. "But they obeyed orders, m'lord."

"Excellent," Verice said. "I will be conferring with Lady Warna about the details of the Festival this afternoon."

Their well-trained faces were professionally blank, although there was a distinct look of approval in Ricard's eyes.

"Just one thing, m'lord," Ersal spoke up as Verice turned to go. "Lady Warna has written a letter to her great-uncle in the Barony of Summerford. Should I find a special messenger, or send it along the regular trade routes?"

CHAPTER SIXTY

Verice's first thought was to rip the letter from Ersal's hand and tear it to shreds.

"The trade routes are slow and uncertain," Ersal frowned at the letter. "The city of Alsmeda lies along the border with Summerford. We could probably find a messenger there, but there's a cost involved."

Warna had been honest with him. She'd told him what she wanted, and she'd laid out what would happen. Why was he so angry that she was keeping her commitments to him?

Yet, he didn't want that message to go.

"M'lord?" Ersal waited for an answer.

"Special messenger," he managed to croak, but it wasn't what he wanted to say. He wanted the damn thing in the fire, or on the oldest, slowest, fattest pony that ever walked a caravan route.

"As you wish, m'lord," Ersal said.

Not really, Verice thought, but he managed to keep his mouth shut as he left the room. With the door shut, he took a calming breath, and then headed for their chambers.

He was rounding the last flight when he saw her. Warna appeared down the hall, her errands done, heading for their chambers. There was a flush to her cheeks, and a twinkle in her eye as she stopped and stared at him.

His heart started racing.

Warna laughed, and she backed up a few steps, as if daring him to-

With a laugh, a twist of her skirts, and a flash of a lovely ankle, she was gone.

Verice gave chase.

* * * * *

Warna caught her breath at the look of desire in Verice's eyes. She couldn't help laughing in pure delight, and then with an impish leap of her heart, she turned and run down the corridor.

She had spent enough time in the keep to know its twists and turns. She darted up the next staircase, hearing the sound of Verice's footsteps behind her. She flew down the next corridor, avoiding some of the staff scrubbing the floor. With a frantic motion, she shushed them as she ran past. She could hear their stifled laughter as she disappeared around the next corner, and pressed herself against the wall.

Verice ran by, his surprise clear as he sailed past her, sliding to a halt. She fled back the way she'd come, running by the servants who were smiling and giggling. Warna rushed for the stairs, daring a quick glance behind.

Verice was running, gaining on her.

She laughed, picked up her skirts and bolted up the stairs, taking them two at a time. Breathless with excitement, she headed for the farthest door, and dashed through it, onto a balcony of white marble that shone bright in the noon sun.

* * * * *

Verice bolted through the door, and his heart almost stopped in his chest. For an instant, he saw Warna in her tattered clothes, fleeing from him, about to leap out into—

Warna turned, her hair flying free, her laughter ringing out, and the memory was wiped away in the next instant. She launched herself into his arms, and he swept her up, twirling her in a circle that left her even more breathless.

"Verice—" but he cut off her words by claiming her mouth.

She moaned, returning the kiss with passion, wrapping her arms around his waist. It was only when the need for air was overwhelming that he broke away, burying his face in her hair as they both struggled to breathe.

"Bed," Warna whispered in his ear.

He nodded, sweeping her up into his arms. "Bed."

* * * * *

She wanted to preserve every moment in her memory, remember every detail humanly possible. Every touch, every soft sound of pleasure.

Verice's gaze seared her skin. Intent, hungry, focused on her and her alone. It was terrifying, yet she wasn't afraid. There was no fear in her heart as they came together, grasping at clasps and fumbling with buttons and laces. No, the tingles on her skin, the feelings in her chest, those weren't fear.

She reached for him, comfortable now with touching and stroking. She knew the places, the ways to touch him. Verice responded, and reached for her as well.

His kisses were sweet, not just on her mouth, but along her neck and over her shoulders, and her breasts. Warna leaned back, giving him access, confident in the strength of his hands to hold her upright even as she melted against him.

The bed was cold, but the heat of their bodies warmed it quickly. With the bedding thrown back they were free to sprawl together, arms and legs entwined as they kissed and stroked each other.

At first Warna was content to follow Verice's lead, but as her need grew her patience faded. "Verice," she moaned into his mouth, trying to push his fingers deeper within her folds.

"Wait," Verice said.

"Verice," she pleaded, but he stayed her questing hands with his own, pinning her to the bed and distracting her with his mouth.

She arched her body, wanting more. There was no fear, only need when he urged her legs open, rose up over her and slid within. She gasped at the hot, heavy pressure.

More. It was so much more.

Verice released her wrists, bracing himself over her, studying her face intently. He held perfectly still, waiting. "Warna?"

"It's just so-" she shifted and drew a sharp breath at the pleasure that spiked through her.

"Verice, please—" she sobbed, not sure exactly what she was pleading for.

Verice kissed her jaw, just below her ear. He shifted and she cried out as the burning heat crashed over her, carrying her further and further up. Faster, faster, and she moved as well, meeting and matching him as she laughed and cried at the sheer wonder of it all.

Until the heat built white hot and exploded, blocking out all the world, except the sound of Verice reaching his own heights, crying out her name.

The world faded back slowly, sweetly. Warna was cradled against Verice, the cooler air delicious against the heat of her skin.

Verice was stroking her hair, his movements slow. Warna murmured her pleasure, shifting just enough to reach his mouth for a long, slow kiss.

"Warna?" he asked softly. "All's well?"

"Perfect," she whispered.

His chuckle rumbled in his chest. "I'd agree," he said quietly. "Shall we sleep for a bit? Tell me what you wish."

Warna hugged him tighter. *'I wish it could be like this forever,'* She thought silently. *'I wish I could spare you the pain of the Festival. I wish joy wasn't so fleeting.'*

She raised her head to look into his silver eyes, and reached up to rub the very tips of his ears. "More," she said simply, hiding her true desires, taking what was offered.

"As you wish, m'lady," Verice said and pulled her into his arms.

CHAPTER SIXTY-ONE

The airions spotted the entrance to the old eyrie, even thought the trees had grown up in front, blocking it from Kalynn's sight. They back-winged into the tunnel entrance, Wolfe's going in first. The clatter of their claws against the stone was an old and comforting sound. Kalynn had to fight the familiar urge to duck her head as they entered its cool depths. Going from sun to shadow in the stone tunnel brought back a rush of memories.

The solid stone wall at the back did not.

"Are they behind there?" Kalynn asked as she dismounted. Her airion danced toward the wall, clawing at it and clacking its beak.

"They're there," Wolfe said shortly. He started to unsaddle his mount, grunting with the effort as he dragged off the saddle bags. "She locked them safe away, sleeping, awaiting the call to awaken. Awaiting the day."

"A day which comes," Kalynn said. "The trees have grown up." She went to the edge, peering out. "The path has certainly deteriorated."

"Kalynn," Wolfe added her saddle and gear to the pile. "It's been a hundred years, give or take. Trees grow," he added. "Rocks fall."

"Do you suppose the rabbit hutches are still there?" She craned her neck out, looking off to the side. "You can still see a faint trace of the path."

"The hutches are sure to be gone, but the great-great-who-knows-how-many-great grand-offspring are probably still there." Wolfe chirped at the airions. They settled down along the back wall, curling into balls, tucking their wings in tight.

"I guess," Kalynn hugged herself. "I guess I thought it would be the same forever."

Wolfe came up behind her, and wrapped his arms around her. "Everything changes."

She cast a glance back at the airions. "You put them to sleep?"

"You saw the herd below us, probably the descendants of the feeder herds." Wolfe rolled his eyes. "She's not going to be pleased to see us, and even more so if they kill any of those cows."

"True," Kalynn sighed, leaning back against his warmth. "Do you suppose she is there?"

"She's there," Wolfe said confidently. "She'd not stray far from her charges. But let me check," he closed his eyes. "Yes. With two others, both male." He frowned. "They are at the old storage cave, loading a wagon with something. We should wait until she is alone."

Kalynn nodded.

"We should be ready," Wolfe said. "I'm sure her temper has not improved. She might launch a mage attack as soon as she catches sight of us." He snorted. "Well, catches sight of me," he added gruffly.

"She wouldn't," Kalynn insisted, suddenly fearful. She turned in his arms to look at him.

"She might," Wolfe said. His face was calm and resigned. "I have to assume that she will lash out."

"Wolfe," she put her hands on his chest, felt the steady beat of his heart through the leathers.

"Kalynn," Wolfe took her hands in his. His fingers warmed hers. "You're right, we need to talk to her. But we should be prepared for the worst, yes? If she attacks, stay close. I'll shield us, and then portal us out." Wolfe looked down toward the cave. "The men and wagon are leaving. She's alone."

"You are not going to make me walk down that path, are you?"

Wolfe chuckled. "No."

He opened a portal, and they stepped through. Kalynn looked around, recognizing the large boulder that sat by the path, but not much else. The trees had grown up, and the underbrush allowed to thicken. She could hear the cows in the fields beyond. She looked at Wolfe, and he nodded, and gestured for her to proceed.

The cave entrance had been covered by large wooden barn doors, now closed. There was a small door off to the side. The wagon, and its drivers were gone. Kalynn strode up to the smaller door, Wolfe followed. Kalynn took a breath, and knocked.

"Who's there?" came an old, quavering female voice.

ELIZABETH VAUGHAN

"That's not—" Wolfe said, but then the door was thrown open.

An aged, wrinkled woman confronted them, her white hair piled on her head, her back hunched with age. Her eyes went wide, then narrowed.

"Kalisa?" Kalynn couldn't hide her shock. Wizened and bent, this could not be—

"Sister," Kalisa's voice emerged from the woman, stiff and angry. She had to tilt her head to see them, and if possible, her eyes got harder. "Stalking Wolf."

"No more," Wolfe's tone was deceptively mild. "Just 'Wolfe' these days."

"Come in," Kalisa shuffled back. "Before you are seen."

"What happened to you?" Kalynn asked, unable to stop herself from asking as she crossed the threshold. Wolfe followed and closed the door behind them.

"You ask that?" Kalisa gave a harsh laugh. "You and the Chaosreaver, who tore the magic of the elements from the Heart of the Plains and the Kingdom of Xy?"

Wolfe put his hand on Kalynn's shoulder. "I don't regret rescuing my warprize."

"At what cost?" Kalisa snapped. "I lost everything. My love, my position, my flying—"

her voice hitched.

"Yes," Wolfe spoke cooly. "Interesting, what you have done with the place."

Kalynn shot him a warning glance, but finally took a moment to look around. "Is that cheese?"

The cave had once stored flying gear and saddles for the airion wing. Now there were rows and rows of wooden shelves, covered with wheels of cheese.

"Those of my blood, my warrior blood, mind you," Kalisa's words were brittle. "Those of my blood should have claimed the skies by now, riding airions, defending this land. Instead, they make and sell cheese." Her disdain was clear. "None of them dream of battle. None of them feel the call of the sky. Cheese." she looked at the shelves and her lip curled.

"The gift has not passed on?" Wolfe asked, frowning.

"And if it had?" Kalisa snapped. "There is no magic here, Chaosreaver, you saw to that. Airions need magic to survive, as so many things do. I preserved what I could, and used the last to sustain my life. The spell fades, after so long. I fade with it."

Wolfe extended his hand. "I could—"

"Don't touch me," Kalisa hissed.

Kalynn stepped back into Wolfe; the hate was palpable in her sister's eyes and her heart broke to see it. "Kalisa, please," she asked, extending her own hand.

Kalisa looked away. "Why have you come?"

Kalynn let her hand drop. "I have seen," she said. "The day comes, Guardian. Be ready."

"Nothing more helpful than that? No date, no time, no real idea, just a vague warning?" Kalisa snorted.

"Kalynn has seen," Wolfe snarled. "You have a duty, Guardian."

"I will do as I see fit," Kalisa snarled right back. "But do not think I do this for you. I do this for Xy, and for my people, and for my love that no one but I remembers. But do not expect forgiveness, Chaosreaver. Or you, sister, for that matter." Her swollen hands tightened into fists. "I thank you for your warning. Leave."

"Let Wolfe offer you some ease, at the very least," Kalynn took a step forward. "Please, Kalisa—"

"You say 'please'?" Kalisa shook her fist at them. "You, who created this nightmare? You, who deprived me of everything dear?" Her face was reddening, her eyes alight with madness. "If I had the power, I would smite you to the ground, and burn and burn both of you to ash." Her voice dropped into a dark, evil hiss. "You killed my Uppor, and I will never, never forgive. May the very air deny you breath. May the very—"

Wolfe's arm snaked around Kalynn's waist, and she was turned and through the glaring white of a portal in an instant.

They appeared in the tunnel, Wolfe muttering his own curses in her ear. "If you think I was going to let that bitch curse us out the door and up the mountain, think again."

Kalynn shook her head. Everything ached, her body, her heart, her soul. She felt as if all the strength had left her limbs.

"Bitter, withered, dried-up turd." Wolfe stepped to the saddle bags, and started pulling out their bedroll. "We will spend the night here, and leave in the morning."

"She might follow," Kalynn glanced back at the tunnel's edge.

"Without power? In her crippled condition?" Wolfe shook his head as he shook out their blankets. "No. Besides that path is bad enough no one is getting up here this night. Come and get warm."

"I'm not cold," Kalynn said.

"Then why are you shaking?" Wolfe asked as he knelt on the blankets. He opened his arms. "Come."

She went. Let him wrap her in a blanket, and sit beside her. With just a few gestures and words, he had a fire burning and a mug of hot kav in her hands. Then he joined her under the blanket, and wrapped his warmth around her.

"You're wasting your power," she muttered.

"No," he said quite strongly. "I am not."

Kalynn sighed and let her tears come. "She's like Charrin and Verice. They've locked their bitter hate in their hearts, and won't let it out."

"Only she's been at it for years in the making," Wolfe said. "Almost one hundred."

Kalynn choked out a smile. "Give or take," she reminded him as she took his hand.

"Give or take." Wolfe looked at their linked hands. "Here I sit, Stalking Wolf, Mage of the Plains, Chaosreaver, feared and hated and yet I cannot ease your pain."

Kalynn put her head on his shoulder. "No, Wolfe. You are my tent, my winter lodge, my shelter, my home."

"Then shelter in my love," Wolfe said. "Sleep."

Kalynn nodded, and closed her eyes, but sleep eluded her. Instead, her eyes drifted to the solid wall at the end of the tunnel. It seemed to her that shadows moved within, images... and her mind flooded with all the possibilities.

"Wolfe," Kalynn sat straight up.

"Eh?" he asked.

"They are tied to her, aren't they?" Kalynn asked. "She locked them away and—"

Wolfe was already staring at the wall. "Yes," he said distantly.

"I don't trust her," Kalynn said, hardening her heart to face the truth about her sister. "I think she would rather see them locked away forever. And with her health…" she let her voice trail off.

"If she were to die, the airions will be locked away forever." Wolfe shook off the blanket and rose. "If Xyson had only known," he said.

"Not even Seers have hindsight, Beloved." Kalynn rose to stand next to him. "Can you replace the spell?"

"No," Wolfe shook his head, his bushy white eyebrows beetled together. "That requires far more power than I dare use. No," He walked forward, and placed his hand on the wall. "But I can add to it. Bend it a bit."

He started to mutter under his breath, pressing his hand flat to the wall. Kalynn settled down, waiting quietly.

"There." Wolfe took a deep breath, and returned to her side. "I linked it to the crystal Sword and the Royal Signet Ring. Any with the ability to use magic, who wield the sword and the ring can issue the call." Wolfe shrugged at her questioning look. "I thought that any who would wield all three would have the best interests of Xy at heart." He took Kalynn's mug and drank. "Wouldn't old Xyson laugh at that."

"You have enough power left?"

Wolfe nodded. "We'll fly out at dawn."

Kalynn draped the blanket back over both of them. "I still grieve," she said. "She is old and crippled, and it will get worse for her from here." She pressed her hand to Wolfe's heart. "But no regrets."

Wolfe pressed his own warm hand on her cold fingers. "No regrets."

They sat in silence for a moment, then Wolfe turned his head slightly. "So," he said as he waggled his eyebrows. "Perhaps we should balance each other's elements this night?"

Kalynn laughed.

CHAPTER SIXTY-TWO

They gathered at sunset, on the First Night of the Festival of Light and Laughter.

Warna stood next to Verice as the staff, guests and guards clustered at the base of the stairs leading to the main doors of the keep. She breathed a nervous prayer to the Lord and Lady that all would go as planned.

She and Verice were dressed in simple white tunic and trous, as were about a dozen others. The others were all wearing mourning colors, somber, plain clothing. The crowd was thick, made up of people who had been present at the attack, or who had lost loved ones as a result.

Priest Dorne stood at the top of the steps, a small metal bowl in one hand, a wooden striker in the other. He stood, watching the sky as the crowd swelled, greeting each other and talking quietly.

Warna leaned in to Verice, letting her fingers entwine with his. He didn't look down, but squeezed her fingers tightly. She could feel the tension in his body, his back stiff and straight.

Finally, a guard on the far west wall lifted his hand and signaled that the sun was below the horizon.

Dorne lifted the bowl, and struck it once. The bowl rang with a pure sweet tone, calling all who heard it to silence. The tone hovered in the air, throbbing like a heartbeat, then faded away, slow and steady. Warna strained to listen, not sure when the sound stopped, leaving only silence in the courtyard.

"This night is the First Night of the Festival of Light and Laughter. With these seven nights and days we celebrate all the gifts that the Lord and Lady have given us."

Verice tightened his grip on Warna's hand.

"The first gift of the Lord was life, and the first gift of the Lady was death," Dorne said.

"And this night is sacred to the remembrance of all those that have gone from our midst." Dorne's voice rang out in the silence, echoing against the stones of the courtyard and walls. "Let us grieve for our loss, and honor their memories."

He struck the singing bowl again, but this time, the sound was joined by one mael's voice, catching the tune, and extended it into a song of loss.

Charrin stood off to the side, clad in white robes, embroidered with gold and green. His song floated above them, joined with soft sobs and whispered prayers from the crowd. Warna's tears welled, her throat closing, not only for their grief but for her own, for her own family.

The bowl went silent, and Charrin's final note faded in the air.

Verice released his hold on Warna's hand and stepped forward.

She felt his pain and ached for him. Ached for the sorrow etched in every line of his body. But her strong mael mounted the steps slowly as Dorne stepped to one side. He raised his hands and opened the main doors and stepped within the darkness and lit the mage lights to either side.

Warna and the white clad servants followed behind.

The crowd followed as well.

Verice was supposed to advance further into the hall, but he froze in the doorway, seemingly unable to move forward.

They all paused, the others looking at each other uncertainly. Warna understood. "Verice," she whispered as she touched his shoulder. "Wait here." She gestured to the others to follow her, and led them past Verice and into the wreckage beyond.

It hadn't changed. Nothing had been moved, or altered since the night of the attack.

The dying light outside was just enough to light the colored-glass windows, letting their hues spill onto the floor. Spring, Summer, Fall, and Winter stood silent guardians over the tables still set with dishes, some over-turned, with broken glass and pottery shattered on the floor. The high table, was cracked and the area before it covered in a large reddish-brown stain. Old dried blood.

Warna swallowed hard. One glance showed her that Ersal and Janella, as well as the other volunteers that stood with her were just as stricken.

They'd thought they'd known how hard this would be, but the reality was so much harder.

They'd planned this in silence, with Charrin and Dorne outside, chanting a dirge. But suddenly that wasn't enough for the emptiness and the ache she felt within. Warna swallowed hard, and gave voice to her sorrow, one long mournful keen for her pain.

She reached out, picked up a soiled plate, and placed it in her basket.

Her keen was caught by Ersal and the others and amplified as they joined in, lifting their voices in wordless sorrow. Deeper voices joined in, as some of the men added their grief to the rising tide of sound.

Verice stood silent, in the doorway, as still as stone.

The sound of the keening seemed to free them. As they'd planned, the men began to remove the broken furniture and chairs, as the women gathered the shards of glass and pottery. Everything was taken away, the room cleared of everything, all of it carried outside with reverence.

When the men returned, they carried buckets of water, and clean white cloths.

Warna took the first bucket, and one of the cloths, even as she continued the song. She knelt on the floor, at the edge of the dried blood, and started to clean.

The outside light faded as they worked, night having truly fallen. Mage lights appeared around them, and Warna glanced at Verice, sure that he had lit them. But he still stood, unmoving and still. She wanted to go to him, but she knew it was best that this be done and finished as quickly as they could. Only then would she offer him whatever comfort he would accept.

The weeping grew as they worked, the keening broken with the harsh sobs of those that labored. Each took a turn, taking over from another when the pain grew to be too much. Warna eyes stung, and her voice grew hoarse, but she didn't stop. No one stopped, until the floor was clean.

Then the buckets and rags were taken up, and they all started out, weary, their clothing stained and damp. Warna lifted her hand to her hair, drained and exhausted.

A fluttering of wings caught her attention. Her gaze flew up to the huge circular window, as a small bird flew out. She gaped at its shattered opening. The window. Her stomach knotted in a flash of pain.

Lord and Lady above, how had they forgotten the window? She glanced at Ersal, who was staring up at the opening with the same stunned look. There was a sharp intake of breath from behind her, probably Janella. They'd focused on the clearing, and the cleaning. All their plans for the use of the Great Hall during the rest of the Festival—

A warmth at her side, and Verice was beside her. She feared the worst. His face was shuttered as he gazed up into the empty space.

He lifted a hand, and whispered under his breath. She followed his gaze to see the empty space fill with the golden light of a magical barrier.

Warna sighed with relief, and slipped her hand into his. Verice pressed his cheek to her head, and then led the way out and down the stairs.

Outside, Dorne took the lead, with Charrin singing, chanting a hymn to the Lord and Lady, asking for blessings upon the dead. He'd made no protest when Warna had asked him to sing the songs, even though they were of human crafting. His voice was lovely, and Warna was content as she walked at Verice's side and into the gardens between the walls.

A trench had been dug in the garden, and the wreckage of the hall piled within. The contents of the buckets were poured at the feet of the rantha bushes, and the buckets and cleaning cloths added to the pile.

Off to one side a small tent had been set up. Warna and the others went inside, to wash and change. Verice too, Warna insisted.

Once they were all reassembled, Dorne stepped forward, and struck his bowl again, letting the tone wash over them all, bringing them to silent attention.

Dorne handed the bowl to an acolyte, and took up a small pitcher. "With this oil, I ask the Lord of Light and the Lady of Laughter to bless this pyre." He poured the oil into the trough.

Warna watched in silence, standing close to Verice. She knew that the trough had been treated with oil, and given a base that would ensure that it burned through the night.

Dorne took up a torch offered to him by another acolyte. "Let this fire cleanse our hearts and bring us peace." He tossed the torch into the center of the trough. The flame flickered, and caught.

Charrin started to sing, an elven song this time, of loss and sorrow.

Verice stiffened suddenly. Warna glanced up, gasping at the rage and pain she saw in his eyes. She felt a tremor wrack through his body. His whispered words were in her ear. He was casting a-

The pyre flame roared up, blasting them all with the heat, towering over them.

Charrin faltered, his song lost in the clamor of the flames. Everyone stepped back, taken by surprise. Dorne cast a stern look at Verice, but his expression eased as he took in Verice's face.

The tower of fire raged, dancing in the night sky, consuming everything within. Verice's eyes were narrow, filled with malice and hatred.

Warna leaned in to him, not quite daring to break his concentration. Verice glanced over, frowning, and the flame sputtered and collapsed in on itself.

"Lord of Light, Lady of Laughter, we know that our loved ones are at peace." Dorne's voice cut through the crowd's murmurs of surprise. "We ask for the gift of your grace for our grief and pain. Give us strength to bear our sorrow, until the moment we are reunited in your light."

The fire eased down, the pyre already collapsing into coals.

"Let us go, to our homes and our hearths, and remember our dead this night," Dorne said, releasing them all.

The crowd started to disperse, moving off towards the garden door slowly. Dorne bowed to Verice and left with his acolytes. Charrin walked with him.

Verice didn't move, staring at the embers.

Warna waited beside him while the others left. They'd planned to attend the midnight services at the church, but that didn't feel right somehow. She felt so bone weary, so drained. And Verice…

She moved closer then, tucking herself under his arm, wrapping her arm around his waist. Verice put his arm around her shoulders, still staring at the pyre.

"Come," Warna said. She gave a tug, and he turned with her, allowing her to lead him away.

She wasn't certain why, but some instinct guided her to lead him back to the keep, back up those stairs and through the doors.

The Great Hall was silent now, the mage lights dimmed.

But at some point, Verice took control, guiding them to the point on the floor where the high table had been. He wrapped his arms around Warna, buried his face in her hair, and crushed her close.

Warna returned the embrace fiercely, allowing her tears to flow once more.

Verice's body shook. He was weeping, sobs of pure anguish. His knees gave out and he collapsed to the floor. She followed him down, supporting him until they knelt together, wrapped so tight that not even breath separated them

She sheltered her beloved as he finally allowed himself to grieve.

CHAPTER SIXTY-THREE

L ord and Ladies, on this, the Third Night of the Festival, the Night of Music and Dance, I propose a toast," Lord Mayor Pernard held his cup high. "I propose a toast to our gracious Lord High Baron Verice and the Lady Warna!"

"Hear, hear," was the response from those seated in the Great Hall, raising their own glasses in response.

"My thanks," Verice said, glancing at Warna, seated next to him at the high table. "We thank you for your attendance, and offer you welcome. Enjoy the food and wine, my friends, to fortify ourselves for the dancing to come."

The servers piled into the Hall, carrying steaming platters, to noisy appreciation.

"It seems to be going well," Verice whispered to Warna.

"Until one of the servers dumps a platter of sliced beef on the floor," Warna whispered back. But her eyes were grateful as she turned to Charrin, seated at her side. "Bard Charrin, would you let me pick out some choice slices for you?"

Charrin's response was lost in the sounds of the hall, but his tone was snappish. He'd been remarkably pleasant when he'd arrived, agreeing to the details of the mourning ceremony, and to otherwise participate in Warna's plans. But his goodwill hadn't lasted long, and Verice could not blame him. For this night was the actual anniversary of the attack, and Summer's death.

It felt bizarre to be seated here once again, entertaining as if naught had happened. As much as his heart cried against it, the castle and keep were at the heart of Tassinic. Life had to go on, as painful as that was to think on. Warna and the entire staff had put every effort into easing back into the use of the Great Hall.

It still hurt.

Verice glanced at Narthing, seated at his side. His captain caught the look and returned it with a nod. They were both conscious of the hour.

So far, the Festival had been without incident. But if any were to plot against them, this would be the night. They'd taken every precaution, drilled all in attendance, servants, staff and warriors alike. All knew what they had to do.

Even Warna. Verice glanced at her waist, pleased to see that the dagger was still at her side. He'd given her one that he'd sharpened himself, and belted it around her when she'd hesitated. "I've no skill," she'd protested.

"Even so," Verice had said. "I'd have you armed."

She'd huffed at him, but she hadn't removed the blade as she returned to dressing her hair for the night's celebration.

Verice had made a pretense of sharpening his sword as he watched her.

She'd refused all but the plainest of clothes, but he had to admit that she looked lovely in her dress of brown and gold. She'd taken diamond hair pins from his jewel vault for this night, settling them in her hair in such a way that they had seemed to catch all the light in her golden tresses.

Verice drank his wine, and watched Warna, who was trying very hard not to help Charrin with his plate. Even now, those jewels sparkled in the mage light whenever she moved. She was a simple vision of beauty, and he ached to pull those pins from her hair, and let it fall over his naked skin.

Verice shifted in his seat with a sigh, raised his cup and took another sip.

He'd much to be grateful to Warna for. That first night, after he'd broken down, she'd stayed with him, protected him from any prying eyes. Somehow, she'd gotten him back to their bed with no one seeing them. He'd slept deeply, and in the morning, she'd handed him strong kav and urged him up before the dawn ceremonies had begun. Since that consisted of a choir of small, off-key, shrill children gathering in the courtyard to sing to him, he'd been more than thankful.

Warna and Ersal had planned this Festival with the anniversary in mind. They'd kept things subdued, allowing people to ease into the celebration. In years past, Verice could remember trying to plan events ever bigger and brighter, but this felt right. Maybe in the future—

But there was no future. Warna would leave when the Festival was over.

He stared into the depths of his cup. She'd never said a word about what had happened that First Night, never faulted him for breaking down. She'd wept with him, supported him during those dark moments, and then held him as he'd slept.

Verice started as Warna leaned over. "Best eat, m'lord. You'll need your strength for the dancing."

He raised an eyebrow. "You will be dancing as well," he pointed out.

"Only the rustic ones that I know," Warna said. "I'll not risk one of your quadrilles, with those fancy steps and hand gestures."

"They can be complicated," Charrin chimed in. "But you could learn with practice."

Verice glanced at his sightless, scarred eyes, but he could find no hint of sarcasm in the elven bard's tone or expression.

Warna simply laughed, taking the words for what they were worth. "A great deal of practice," she smiled. "Can I offer you more bread, Charrin? Or wine?"

"My appetite is not what it should be, m'lady," Charrin's voice was cool. "But some wine would not go amiss."

Warna poured for both of them. "As soon as the tables have been cleared, we can start. Songs and dances alternating, for so long as you wish to sing," Warna said. "Some of the players have asked to perform for us as well."

Verice stiffened, hiding his surprise.

"But at midnight?" Charrin's voice cracked.

"Priest Dorne will lead us in prayer," Warna said. "And we'll make an early evening of it here in the keep, but the celebration will continue in the rest of the castle."

"Aye," Charrin said, and he slumped in his chair.

Warna glanced at Verice, but he shook his head, and shrugged.

* * * * *

The dancing was marvelous.

Warna clapped with joy as she watched the intricate moves of the dancers. They filled the area before the high seat, interweaving a pattern with swirling skirts and flashing feet. They'd link arms one moment, and then barely touch fingers as they twirled away.

She'd finally convinced Verice to dance, and she enjoyed every move he made. He was dressed in his black leathers, his silver hair braided back, a circlet of gold on his head. He looked every inch the Lord High Baron he was. Part of her felt a bit overawed that a mael like him could desire her.

Part of her just wanted a chance to strip the leathers from his legs and spend a night worshiping the body beneath.

She shifted in her seat, and sighed.

"All's well?" Charrin asked. He'd sung on and off all evening. Warna was grateful that he'd chosen tunes that were appropriate, neither too sorrowful or too raucous.

"Oh, yes," she said. "It's just so lovely, that I don't really want it to—"

Alarm horns split the air.

The room froze, everyone stopping in mid-word, mid-step. The awareness flooded all of them at the same time that this could not be a drill. Then all at once, everyone moved, warriors pulling their weapons, others heading for their assigned places and or duties.

Verice cast Warna a look, but she was already standing, her heart racing but her feet knowing exactly what to do. He gave her an approving look, then ran for the main doors.

"What is happening?" Charrin asked, a note of panic in his voice.

Warna took his wrist. "Come with me."

She led him through one of the rear serving doors, and into a side hall. Charrin didn't resist her, but his voice was anxious. "Warna, please—"

"There's a disturbance," Warna said briefly, as she urged him toward the nearest cubby-hole. "Everyone knows their roles, Charrin. Ours is to hide." She pressed the wall, and glanced around as it slid open. "Kneel down, and crawl in," she covered his head, protecting it as he obeyed. She followed him in, careful to pull back her skirts as the wall slid shut.

"What will happen?" Charrin asked, his hand on her shoulder as if asking for reassurance.

"Verice will deal with anyone who's breached the peace of the Festival," Warna said as calmly as she could. Her heart felt like it would fly out of her chest, and she took a breath to try to slow its pace. "The 'all clear' will sound, and Verice will come to us. We aren't to leave until he opens the door." She laughed weakly. "Our job is to wait."

"Ah," Charrin's voice changed, its tone dark and determined. He wrapped one arm around her waist, tugging her into his lap awkwardly.

With the other, he pulled the dagger at her waist, and set the blade to her throat. Warna gasped, and grabbed his wrist trying to push the blade away, but Charrin had a strength greater than her own.

"Then we'll wait," Charrin murmured in her ear. "And when he comes, he will see you die at my hand."

CHAPTER SIXTY-FOUR

The courtyard was eerily silent when Verice burst from the keep with Narthing at his side. It made Verice pause on the top of the steps, surveying the area.

The torches crackled in their braces, the light spilling all around. His warriors were spread around, their weapons gleaming in the torch light. The men on the walls were still on watch, flags flying in the night. Every doorway had a posted watch, but the windows were filled with Festival-goers, all staring down into the courtyard.

Scattered around were the various low wooden platforms that had been set up for dances and musicians. But Verice's eyes were drawn to the acting troupe's stage, which had been set between the main gates and the keep. His guards were standing over prone men, swords at the ready.

Ustov came forward. "Report," Verice snapped.

"Lord High Baron, the crowd was lively, drifting about a bit, watching the various dances," Ustov said. "We heard a scream, and saw a group of the actors dashing off the stage with drawn swords. The alarm sounded, and the closest warriors responded. There was a quick skirmish, but then the actors flung themselves down, crying mercy." Ustov glared at captives. "Seems they say it was part of the performance."

"Or not," Verice said softly.

"None of our people were hurt," Ustov continued. "But a few of the actors got sliced up." He straightened his shoulders.

"Let's see what there is to see." Verice kept his own blade out as he walked to the prone men.

Humans they all were, he noted as he prowled around them. Their weapons had been piled to one side, and most of them lay face down, spread eagle on the ground. A few were still on stage, clustered together, eyeing

Verice warily.

Master Zester was seated cross-legged, off to one side, breathing like a man who had no experience with pain. He clutched at his arm, where red seeped through the cloth.

Verice sheathed his sword for the moment, accessing the man before him. Zester kept his head down, but he darted a glance up. His eyes had an odd, pleading look.

Verice stared at him, but Zester glanced around at the other captives and then hung his head as if waiting for sentence.

Something wasn't right.

Verice rose, mounted the platform, and pulled down the cloths that had been used to create a 'backstage'. He noted the barrels holding swords and spears, and frowned at a pile of shields and cloaks, more than the number of the company it seemed.

Finally, he moved off, gesturing Narthing to his side.

"The main gates are closed?" he asked softly.

"They would have shut the moment the horns sounded," Narthing said softly. He turned slightly, stretching his neck a bit. "The constable is there, so it's secure."

"I want the grounds searched," Verice murmured. "And a quick check on all the sentries on the inner and outer walls."

"Aye," Narthing said. "I'll see to it." He headed off toward the main gates at a trot.

Verice gestured to Ustov. "Come," he said as he returned to where Zester was seated.

"I thought I instructed you to announce a comedy, Master Zester." Verice knelt close to the man.

"M'lord Verice, I swear we were just having a bit of play-acting," Zester said loudly, but then he winced. "My arm," he pleaded.

"Quality work, there." Verice tilted his head at the pile of weapons. "I'd expected wooden swords, or more pot metal than steel."

"More realistic that way," Zester hissed through his pain. "The crowd likes it better with the ring of true steel."

"You're paying for it now," Verice said as he knelt next to the man. "Let me see that."

He peeled back the sleeve. Zester leaned closer in. "Help us," was his desperate whisper.

Verice didn't react.

Zester winced as Verice exposed the wound. "Prisoners. We've been prisoners in our own-"

"Arrest these men," Verice barked. "Arrest these men."

His warriors closed in. There were a few that resisted, but they were secured quickly.

"Tell me," Verice growled.

"They took us prisoner in our own theater," Zester said shakily. "There's more men, outside the walls, waiting for a signal."

"Do we have them all?" Verice asked. "All those within these walls?"

"Yes," Zester was starting to sag. "We thought maybe, if we did something, we could foil their scheme—"

"Almost cost you your life, Zester," Verice said. "Still, I owe you much for—"

"Bastards," Zester said. "Hiding behind our good name and reputation."

"Narthing," Verice called. "Zester, you need to help us sort them all out."

"They threatened to burn my theater," Zester said. "Lord, the men outside the walls may have fled to the town. They will—"

"No," Verice said. "The City Watch is also on alert. We'll get word to them."

Narthing returned to his side. "The sentries are being checked, and I've a squad to sweep the road to town."

"Let's not mar the Festival," Verice said. "Executions can wait. I want as much information from these prisoners as we can get."

"Aye to that,"

"I'll see to it," Narthing said. "We'll leave the castle gates closed and check any pass through."

"I'll just be a moment," Verice said. "I need to be certain Warna is safe."

* * * * *

Charrin tightened his grip around the human's waist as she shifted. "Be still, or I'll kill you now," he warned.

"I just—" he heard her breath catch, felt her slender fingers tighten on

288   ELIZABETH VAUGHAN

his arm. But she wasn't really struggling against him. He'd pulled her over, half-leaning, half-sitting on his lap. She'd braced herself with her free hand, but the other remained clasped on his wrist, wedged between his arm and her throat. He held the blade angled, just below her ear.

It was awkward and uncomfortable, but she wouldn't feel that way long. Only until Verice opened the door to their hiding place.

The air warmed quickly, with the two of them in this small space. Charrin could see no detail, but he didn't really need to. He'd see enough to know when Verice was before him, and he'd hear the mael's pain. A pity he'd not see his face, but it was enough. It would suffice.

Time seemed to hang in the air, suspended as they waited.

"Why?" Warna broke the silence, her voice hoarse and pained.

Charrin ignored her, still straining to hear footsteps in the hall outside.

"You accepted his bread, his wine," she was trying to get her breathing under control, trying to calm him, distract him. "Where is the honor—"

"Where is his?" Charrin hissed. "He takes no vengeance, and King Barathiel will take no action." He licked his lips, and tightened his grip on her waist, drying his sweaty palm on the fabric of her dress. "He will watch you die, as my beloved Summer died. Let him know my pain."

Warna let out a pained sob, but she said nothing more. He felt her trying to ease herself into a more comfortable position. "Stay still," he snapped.

"You said you were trying to forgive," she whispered.

"You read more into my words than was there," Charrin gloated. "As I intended." He drew a breath, trying to tamp down on his nervousness. He'd planned to kill her at the high table, before all, stabbing deep within her heart and rejoicing as Verice - *Verice* - tried to stem the tide of blood and pain.

But this was surer, better. He just had to be patient, to wait for the right moment. He could do this for his lady. For Summer.

A sob welled up in his chest for his lost lady. What right did love and beauty have to exist in a world she no longer graced? He missed her so, her touch, her laugh—

The human woman squirmed in his arms again, her hand moving on his arm. "Stay still," he growled. "I'm warning you—"

There were running footsteps in the hall, and the door slid open. Charrin could make out a body in front of the opening.

"Warna," Verice said, and then awareness flooded into his voice. "*Warna.*"

Charrin laughed, and pulled the knife back, feeling her flesh part beneath the blade, and warm blood cover his hand. "Here," he pushed her body away, and laughed again as he relished Verice's cry of horror.

CHAPTER SIXTY-FIVE

Warna," Verice's voice was filled with horror.

"Now you know!" Charrin's joy grew as he saw the vague shape of Verice take the body of the woman into his arms. "Now you know what it felt like, Verice. My grief, my pain, my endless sorrow—"

Rough hands grabbed him as the guards pulled him from the hiding place. He let the dagger clatter to the floor. They forced him down face-first, binding his hands. Still Charrin laughed, his heart light for the first time since—

"Ow," said a woman's voice.

"What?" Charrin sputtered, straining his neck up to see. That sounded like—

"Hush, Warna," Verice's voice shook. "I need to put pressure on your palm, to stop the bleeding. The knife went deep—"

"Better my hand than my throat," Warna said.

The world crashed in on Charrin, and he started to howl horrible dry sobs, with eyes that no longer produced tears. He laid his head back down, the marble cold beneath his cheek. He'd failed, he'd failed, and the pain of that failure welled up within him.

Summer. His beautiful Summer.

* * * * *

Warna sat in the shelter of Verice's arms, and winced as he held her hand in both of his, putting pressure on her palm.

He cursed under his breath, his face as pale as she'd ever seen.

She'd not thought much other than to block the blade when she'd slid her hand up as Charrin had pulled the knife over her throat. She shivered, thinking of how close she'd come.

And now the bard lay on the floor, crying.

"Summon healers," Verice commanded. The cloth he'd wrapped around her hand was red with blood. Warna decided it might be best to avert her eyes. She buried her face in Verice's shoulder.

"Already called," said one of the guards. "What should we do with the bard, m'lord?"

"Kill him."

"Verice, no," Warna lifted her head from his shoulder.

Verice's face was cold; his eyes even colder.

"Look at him," she said softly.

"Look at this," Verice said, lifting her hand. "And this," his finger traced a line on her neck and she flinched at the sudden pain. "He almost—" Verice stopped.

"He didn't," Warna said. "Please, Verice. Don't—"

"Why?" Verice growled.

"Because he's helpless, and hurting. Because he's lost it all now. He's failed a king who doesn't forgive errors and betrayed you. He's nothing and no one, and less than naught." Warna shook her head. "Don't spoil the Festival."

There were footsteps behind her then, and she suddenly found herself at the mercies of the healers. Verice gave her up reluctantly, letting them take charge. She struggled to her feet with their support.

Verice stood, looking down at Charrin, implacable and stern.

"Verice," she said, holding her hand to her chest. She took a step in Charrin's direction. Verice frowned, and put his boot on the man's neck as she came closer.

"Listen to me, you treacherous bastard," Warna leaned over the bound mael. "You accepted the hospitality of this house, and you repaid it with perfidy."

The hallway was still, the guards and healers silent. Verice watched her with hooded eyes.

"I will sing of this, false one," Warna kept her voice low and hard. "And know this for a truth, while I may not live as long as you, my song will. Our people will sing of your betrayal for a thousand years, and then some."

She straightened, slowly, her strength starting to wane. "Vengeance is not the answer to your pain."

Warna stepped away then, sagging into the waiting arms of the healers. She paused to look at Verice, who gave her a simple nod.

Contented, she let them lead her where they would.

* * * * *

Charrin lay on the floor, awash in his failure, Warna's words echoing in his mind.

"Take him to a cell," Verice was speaking to one of the guards. "And keep him under guard."

"As you wish, m'lord."

There was a rustle of cloth, and then the vague shape of Verice knelt by Charrin's head. "My Lady Warna would have me spare your life," Verice spoke quietly, without rancor. "She is a merciful woman."

"I pity you," Charrin kept his voice down, but he didn't bother to block his hate. "To see you lose your heart to a human. Are you going to start a kennel, like you do for your dogs? Place another one in your life as soon as this one dies off?"

"Warna is kind," Verice continued calmly. "I am not. I will not spoil the Festival, Charrin, but—" Verice stopped.

"What?" Charrin demanded. "I do not expect to live beyond this last moment. I have failed. Execute me and—"

"No," Verice growled, but there was an odd-undertone to his voice. "I see now, that if not for Warna, I would be locked in the same hate as you."

Charrin snarled.

Verice arose. "Did King Baratheil know of this plan of yours?"

"No," Charrin spat.

"You will be confined. After the Festival, I will open a portal into Valltera, if they will have you." Charrin felt a warm hand on his shoulder, felt magical energies stir around him. Verice's voice was a like a shard of glass in his ear. "Perhaps you will see more clearly someday, old friend."

"I do not want your forgiveness," Charrin shouted, his rage and despair eating at him.

But Verice was already gone.

* * * * *

Verice cradled Warna as she slept, her bandaged hand supported by pillows. The healers weren't certain there'd be any permanent damage. He'd ask the Lady High Priestess to return and check with her gifts.

Ancestors, how had it happened? In that moment after opening the door, in the seconds between Charrin's hate, a spurt of blood, and Warna being pushed into his arms, he'd realized the truth.

From the moment he'd been able to understand, there had been the subtle message of the taint in his blood, brought on by an ancestor and his fit of passion for a human woman. He'd never understood it, and had offered that ancestor insult when it had been thrown in his face, or he'd been denied advancement as a result.

Now, he knew. He understood. His Ancestor's revenge, most likely.

Warna stirred in his arms, and Verice stroked her hair to soothe her back down into sleep. Now he knew, he understood, and he didn't know what to do. The darkness around them held no answers, just the soft sounds of her breathing.

She'd told him what she wanted, and he was obligated to fulfill her desires. It wasn't fair to her to insist she stay. She deserved a man, a human, to love and cherish her, to age with her through all the stages of a normal life.

She wanted to leave and he'd agreed, and he was a fool. For what was between them was more than physical on his part, more than just two bodies together in pleasure. The Ancestors were probably dancing in glee at forcing him to regret that thought.

The idea of wedding a human was foolish, of course. Warna had, at best perhaps fifty or seventy years left to her. Was it fair to him to have her stay and wither away before his eyes?

A jealous pain went through him at the idea that anyone else would share the moments she had left. Jealous that she might share her life, her joys, her sorrow with another.

He breathed in the scent of her hair.

There was time yet. To consider. To find a way to let her go.

But not this night.

* * * * *

ELIZABETH VAUGHAN

No permanent harm done," Lady High Priestess Evelyn said. "Although the knife went deep."

Warna smiled as Evie held her hand, making them tingle with the power of her healing. "Verice shouldn't have asked you to come," Warna said. "Right during the Festival."

"You forget," Evie laughed. "We have no such festivities in Edenrich. I was able to slip away with no one the wiser. You've disturbed nothing," she continued. "Although I do wish to speak to Lord Verice when he has a moment."

"He'll be here shortly," Warna sighed. "He won't be content unless he hears your report from you directly."

"I've heard of the Festival," Evie said as she worked. "But I've never seen it."

"It's amazing," Warna said. She described the seven nights and days. "This is the Last Night," she explained. "The Last Day and Night celebrate the gifts of magic. I wish you could stay," she added. "They say the displays of power are amazing."

"I wish I could," Evie said, as she gently pulled away from Warna's hand. "But my duties require me to be at the church this evening."

"Our loss, Lady High Priestess," Verice said as he came through the door.

"Lord High Baron." Evie rose, and bowed her head.

Verice settled next to Warna. "How does the Lady Warna?" he asked, taking up Warna's hand. Warna shivered at his touch. Verice glanced at her, a gleam in his eyes. But he turned back to Evie with all due attention.

"She's fine," Evie said, standing before them, suddenly looking serious. "There's no lasting damage, and the scarring will fade with time." Evie took a breath. "Lord High Baron, you have said that you are in my debt, and I wish to exercise that at this time."

"How so?" Verice's pose didn't change, but Warna could feel the sudden tension in his body. "What boon would you ask, Evelyn?"

"Only this, Lord High Baron," Evelyn licked her lips, clearly nervous. "I do not ask you to grant my request. I only ask that you hear me out in all the particulars and that you speak to no one of what I am about to tell you."

Verice frowned. "I do not understand."

"But you will listen?" Evelyn pressed. "And you will hold this secret, both of you?"

"Of course," Warna said. "Evie, sit and tell us."

"Say on, Lady High Priestess," Verice said. "Because I am certainly intrigued."

Evelyn remained standing, shaking her head at the offer of a seat. She drew in a deep breath, and let it out slowly. "It concerns a prophecy…"

Verice listened as he'd promised. Evelyn wove an incredible tale of a dagger-star birthmark, and a child born as the Chosen, who would claim the throne from the Usurper and return justice to Palins and its people.

"You've found such a child?" Verice asked.

"I have," Evelyn said with just enough hesitation that he knew there was more she wasn't saying. "I have her well hidden, but if you desire proof, I can bring—"

"I do not doubt your word, Lady High Priestess," Verice said.

"Just my sanity," Evelyn said with a faint smile.

"No." Verice shook his head. "Not even that." He paused, then spoke deliberately. "Evelyn, I've lived long enough to see prophecies both fulfilled and failed. Usually by the actions of the people caught up in them." Verice leaned forward. "Tell me, what have you besides a child and a birthmark?"

CHAPTER SIXTY-SIX

W hat do you mean?" Evelyn frowned.

"It will take more than a birthmark to rend the Usurper from Palin's throne." Verice stood, starting to pace. "It will take men, money, support, arms, and a great deal of planning. You've none of that, have you?"

"No," Evelyn sank down into a chair, looking resigned.

"Verice," Warna said as she rose and stepped the Evelyn's side. "If there's any hope that we could—"

"It's just what he's doing to the people of Palins," Evelyn said. "What he does every day to innocent—"

"No," Verice said, folding his arms over his chest and shaking his head. He felt a pang for the sorrow in their eyes but on this he would not be budged. "I've just won a stalemate on my borders, and I must protect what is mine. My lands and my people. I cannot afford to support your cause, Lady High Priestess."

"I acknowledge the difficulties," Evelyn rose, her normal calm returning. "And if I should return, one day, with men, and money, and support?"

"Then I would pledge to listen and consider," Verice said.

"I will return." Evelyn lifted her chin, a spark of determination in her blue eyes.

"Of that, I have no doubt, Lady High Priestess."

* * * * *

On the Last Night of the Festival, they gathered on the keep balcony, bringing out chairs and pillows to watch the final magical displays in the night sky.

Warna had been rather surprised to find that Verice would not be displaying his skills. Yet his reasoning was not displeasing. "No, I won't spend my power that way," he'd leaned closer and whispered in her ear. "I'll save my energies for the magic we make between us."

She'd blushed, and shivered at his breath on her skin. Even now, the memory made her tingle.

The night sky was darkening, and the guests had all gathered. Priest Dorne gave her a nod as he chose a chair close to Narthing. No formal seating this night, the Last Night of the Festival.

They'd seen smaller magics all day. They'd strolled through the courtyard filled with people showing off their prowess. Tiny creatures that played with her fingers, butterflies of vibrant colors that settled in her hair, and one enterprising young faelle that had juggled balls of fire. Warna had especially liked the dancing teapot and cups. The young mage with that idea had tried too many cups, and they'd falter as he lost his concentration, but he'd laughed with the rest at his failure.

Now there were teams of mages working together to display their arts. Apparently, the Mage's Guild acted to coordinate all of it, otherwise it would have been chaos.

Warna relaxed in her chair, glad to know that it was in other hands. With the final feast done, she could relax and enjoy, without worrying about the details. The Festival had been a delight, but it had also been hard work. She glanced at Ersal, sitting with Janella, both looking just as relieved.

She settled back as a single bright red light soared into the sky, and exploded in a million sparks. Followed in quick succession by all the other colors of the rainbow. Warna flinched at the blasts, startled by the sounds. A glance at Verice showed there was nothing to fear.

Roses bloomed on intertwining vines, filled with buzzing bees and dragonflies that danced around the flowers. The roses faded, leaving the dragonflies to dance in the night, their jewel-colored wings glowing against the dark sky.

Warna clapped when one of the huge creatures floated down to hover over the balcony, then dissolved in a shower of gold and red sparks. She raised her hand to catch one. It faded even as it touched her skin.

The sky seemed to roll, and suddenly streams of horses galloped over wide plains of grass, their manes and tails flowing behind them. Warna caught her breath at the beauty of it all. Without thinking, she reached out her hand to Verice.

He took it in his, his hand warm under her fingers.

She looked at him, tears in her eyes. "Thank you," she whispered.

He tilted his head, raised one of those lovely arched eyebrows.

"For all this," she said, knowing he probably wouldn't understand what she really meant. "For the Festival. For everything."

A shadow crossed his face for just a moment, then he leaned over, still holding her hand. "You might not thank me when we have to start cleaning up after it all."

Warna's laughter bubbled out

* * * * *

Verice ignored the crowd around them as he claimed Warna's lips in a kiss that left them both breathless.

Warna blushed, settling back to watch the sky, still keeping his hand in hers.

She'd sounded so definite, thanking him, as if their time together had ended. Verice settled back as well, but he kept stealing glances at Warna. She was entranced by the display, and her face reflected her pure pleasure at the sights and sounds.

It was too soon. She should enjoy the results of all her efforts. Besides it would take weeks before the regular routines were restored, and the castle and keep set right after all this celebrating.

"What are those?" Warna breathed. "Dragons?"

The sky above was filled was filled with aerial combat, with airons diving and swooping down on their foes.

"No, those aren't dragons," Verice explained. "They're wyverns."

The scene flickered and changed, with tiny boats with white sails and a giant sea monster, tentacles flying and smashing into the sea, just barely missing the valiant boats.

The spectacle continued on, to the pleasure of the entire company, until at last the bells of the church began to peal midnight.

With that, the display once again erupted in explosions of light and magic, sending tiny shards of diamond bright lights floating down to the ground as the Festival counted down to its end.

Verice rose as the last of the colors faded, keeping a tight hold on Warna's hand. They bid farewell to their guests. Warna glanced at him, smiling a smile that was for him alone.

She knew well his intent.

He tried to remain the gracious host as he saw his company out. Courtesy was, of course, important. Still, he tried to make sure his guests kept moving.

The night was not yet over. He and Warna still had their own magic to make.

* * * * *

Just how much cooking oil did the kitchens use?" Warna asked.

Ersal unrolled the accounting and placed it before her. "See for yourself, Lady."

"Ersal, I don't doubt your figures," Warna sighed. "But one would think the entire staff bathed in it, given those amounts." She pulled over the list of the supplies they were restocking. "Can the merchants provide so much to us?"

"We'll order extra each week," Ersal said. "Over time, we'll have enough."

"Well, next year, start ordering more earlier, before the Festival," Warna said. "It's not good to have our supplies so low, even if we can see to the daily needs."

"Yes, m'lady," Ersal said.

There was a knock at the door, and Ricard poked his head in. "Seneschal, there's a delivery of hams and the butcher is waving his cleaver at the carter. Will you come?"

"Lord and Lady, now what?" Ersal said, as he hurried off.

Warna chuckled, and turned to the next list of supplies. The festivities had been lovely, but they'd drained the castles supplies down to bare shelves in some cases. Of course, they hadn't had much on hand, but she wasn't pleased with the situation. She'd underestimated the food and drink necessary, that was certain. They'd not run out of anything, really, but larger reserves were needed. She'd leave notes for Ersal for next year-

Because she wouldn't be here.

Warna looked up with a sigh, not really seeing the room or the documents before her. The task of cleaning and restocking after all the celebrations was absorbing, and over-seeing the rebuilding of the window in the Great Hall, and the memorial in the gardens had taken a great deal of time.

They'd restored the practice of dining in the Great Hall every other night. Verice had seated her at the high table beside him. The staff certainly appreciated a return to the normal routine, and it was good to see the tables filled with laughter and talk, no matter how subdued.

The other nights, she and Verice dined privately. They'd talk of their day, the work being done, of the security at the borders, and the news of Edenrich and Valltera. And then-

Warna flushed.

She'd raised the issue of her departure, but Verice so far hadn't been inclined to discuss it. He'd ask how work was going with the restocking, or tell her a new bit of gossip he'd heard, or he'd lean over and kiss the breath from her body.

Warna frowned, thinking. How many days had it been since the Festival? She added them up in her head, and her eyes widened. So long?

Warna closed her eyes in pain as she realized the truth.

Verice wouldn't do it.

For whatever reason, Verice was stalling. Delaying the inevitable. She huffed out a breath. Drat the mael. Putting off what had to be done, leaving it up to her to do it, no doubt. Typical.

Warna closed her eyes. She didn't want to be the one to do it, either. To say the words, to break the arrangement between them, as they had agreed to do.

To leave his bed.

Her sob caught her off guard, welling up in her chest. Verice deserved so much. As much love as she could give him for the rest of her days. But he also didn't deserve the pain she'd cause him, growing old, dying before his eyes.

She sank down into a chair, staring at the roses. Even freshly picked, one or two petals had fallen to the table.

She hadn't heard from her great-uncle yet, and that was a real reason to delay. Except that she could live in Octara, but she shied away from the thought. Of living in town, seeing him from a distance, just another face in the crowd, waving to her Lord High Baron.

Or worse, seeing him with a faella beside him, riding through the streets.

Warna clutched at the rose in her hand, and felt the thorn prick her fingers. No. That wasn't even to be thought of.

Unbidden, a verse of her song leaped to mind.

Life is bitter, life is grim
What need then to be with friends?
What need then to laugh with glee
when you smile so sweet at me?
What need to kiss, to touch, to take,
or my oath to ne'er foresake?

Warna closed her eyes against bitter tears.
It was time.

CHAPTER SIXTY-SEVEN

Verice was seated at the high table, talking to Narthing, just starting to wonder why Warna was late when she appeared. She didn't smile, didn't head for her seat, just approached and stood before him.

In her eyes, he saw a look he both admired and feared. The determined, focused drink-the-entire-cup intention.

"Warna." Verice placed his hands on the table as the room went quiet.

"Lord High Baron." Warna wasn't really looking at him; her red-rimmed eyes were focused slightly above his head. "I wish to thank you for the shelter and protection you have extended to me. As painful as it is, as much as we might wish it otherwise, it is time to make public what we both have come to know."

'Ancestors,' Verice throat closed, his mouth as dry as the sun.

Warna's face was stark as she turned away, facing the confused and dismayed gathering. "Lord High Baron Verice and I, by mutual agreement, have decided to sunder our betrothal, for reasons that are our own." Warna's back was straight and stiff, her voice clear. "I will depart for Summerford as soon as I may, to join with my great-uncle and his family. I thank you all." Warna's voice wavered, but she kept on. "I thank you all for the care and kindness I have received at your hands."

With that, she walked out, the silence so deep Verice could hear her footsteps as she went through the main doors, heard her breaking into a run down the stairs and out into the courtyard.

"You're an idiot," Pernard said, not looking up from his plate.

The room was buzzing now, with angry glances being thrown his way.

Verice was aware of them as he stared out the doors, still stunned at Warna's action.

"That's a bit harsh," Narthing said calmly. "But accurate."

"In truth, the Lady Warna is a fine choice of a wife," Ersal didn't look up from his plate. "It strikes me that Lady Warna was a fine helpmate, skilled in running a household as large as this castle and keep."

"It's unlikely that you'd need to make a treaty or alliance marriage outside of Palins, given the current political situation," Pernard added. "And certainly not with the Elven Kingdom. You should feel no hesitation to marry as you would wish. Besides," and here the old mael cocked his head at Verice and gave him a sympathetic look. "There are few that would put up with your personality. Or be willing to overlook certain character flaws. Unless, of course, you've made her unhappy?"

Now his advisors were all glaring at him.

"No, that's not—" Verice shook his head. "She's—" he swallowed hard. "I'm—"

"I suspect that this is a misunderstanding. A private matter," Narthing said. "Something that needs to be discussed between the two of you." He raised an eyebrow as if waiting.

Constable Ricard leaned forward. "Go after her, you fool!"

Verice did just that. Striding from the Great Hall, down the stairs into the darkening courtyard. The dogs ran to greet him, milling around his feet.

The courtyard was empty. Verice looked to the walls, but there was no sign that the guards had noticed anything out of the ordinary. The castle gates were closed, so she was still—

The garden door was open.

"Hup, hup," he commanded. Brindle and the entire pack focused on him. "Warna," he commanded. "Find Warna."

Tails wagging, heads high, the dogs set off for the garden door, barking with joy at the game.

Verice followed.

* * * * *

Warna ran, picking up her skirts, blinded with tears, and found herself in the gardens.

She kept running, kept moving, afraid that her sorrow would catch up with her if she stopped. She hadn't wanted to do it, to say it, and Verice's face had been so shocked.

She ran until she couldn't breathe, and her face was a mess, and the path was narrowing because the gardeners hadn't come this far yet. She slowed, wiping her face with her hands, and finally gave up and used her skirts to wipe her eyes and blow her nose. It didn't matter, nothing mattered, not anymore.

And she kept walking, brushing aside leaves and branches, still crying, because she knew full well that she still had to face Verice, still had to talk to him, damn it, and it all hurt so very much.

A sound, the slightest stirring under a bush and she jumped away, her heart in her throat. It was the cat, walking up to her, rubbing against her skirts, its tail in the air. Warna stumbled slightly, trying not to step on the silly thing. She staggered to the side of the path.

Something caught at her skirt, and she turned quickly. Too quickly, for the rantha thorns caught the fabric and with her twist it wrapped itsself around her legs.

The cat ran off into the garden, its tail high, the tip flicking back and forth.

Warna cursed

Dogs barked in the distance. Warna jerked her head up, cursed again, and reached down to try to pull the thorns free.

Sand and Gray ran up, their tails wagging, barking at their joy of finding her. The rest of the pack wasn't far behind, and they all pushed into her hands, so pleased with themselves. "Careful," Warna said, trying to push them away from the vines, their lean bodies moving all around her. But the dogs were smarter than she was, seemingly able to avoid getting snagged.

"Warna."

Verice stood there, in the fading light. Her tears started fresh.

"I'm sorry," she said. "So very sorry, but it had to be done, Verice, and it was better that I do it, and you wouldn't—"

"Impetuous human," he said.

"It had to be done," Warna huffed at him. "And sometime in my lifetime."

He took a step forward, and she flinched back, the vine tightening around her. Her skirts started to tear and she froze at the sound.

"Warna, stand still." Verice knelt on one knee, shoving the dogs aside.

She obeyed, wiping at her tears again, without much success. She felt his hands on touching her skirts as he examined the tangle.

"The thorns are buried deep," he said softly. "I'm not sure I can free you. Not without tearing it. Hurting it." He looked up at her, his eyes so silver, so kind. "You're crying."

"Sorry," she said. "I can't seem to stop. I'm trying to be reasonable, and logical, and—"

"Marry me," Verice said.

Warna stared at him, in shock. "I just broke our engagement in front of your entire court."

"I know," Verice quirked his lips. "They are rather upset with me at the moment." He continued to look at her, his face calm and composed. "Marry me."

"No, no, you don't mean that," Warna sputtered. "Not for forever. Not for a lifetime. Verice, please. Just let me go."

"Is that a command?" Verice asked.

Warna snorted out a sob, trying to catch her breath. Her face was hot, and her nose stuffed up. "I can't, I won't— I'll hurt you."

"Hurt me?" Verice raised an eyebrow. "Warna, I am a Bearer of the Blood of Tethnar, a Lord High Baron of Palins, a skilled warrior—"

"And just as vulnerable as the rest of us," Warna said. She let her fingers ghost over his cheek, his skin warm under her cold fingers.

"Far too late to worry about that," Verice said. His hands moved in the fabric, trying to work the thorns free. "My heart is already pierced through, my rose."

Warna jerked back.

"Struggling against it won't help." Verice placed a firm hand on her hip.

"I'm so sorry," Warna whispered.

"I'm not," Verice stood, and wrapped his arms around her waist. "You are essential to my home, my hearth, and my heart. Whatever comes, for the rest of our lives and beyond, you are my love, Warna of Farentell."

Warna buried her face in his chest, wrapping her arms around him even as she felt the tug of the vines around her legs. Verice leaned in for a kiss, but she pushed back, wiping her face. "I'm a mess."

"You haven't answered my question," Verice said. "Marry me?"

Warna stilled then, shaking her head in disagreement. "Verice, the day will come when you will regret this choice."

"No," he said firmly. "Never. Every moment of our lives together will be worth any grief that might follow. We don't know what comes, do we? I could be the one to fall, to a sword or crossbow bolt."

Warna grasped his shoulders with a jolt of fear.

"I want 'us' for as long as we last," Verice said. "I want to have that with you. I want to build memories with you. I know there's pain to come but it would come regardless at this point, if I let you go, if I beg you to stay." Verice drew a deep breath, and backed up a step. "Please. Be my love and life and lady. Marry me."

Warna trembled, suddenly cold without his touch. "But what if tomorrow—"

"What if?" Verice sighed. "I don't know what tomorrow holds. Do you?"

"No," she admitted.

Verice held out his hand. Warna held her breath when she saw those long, elegant fingers shaking. "Please, Warna. Shall we find out? Together?"

For one breath out, she thought to deny him. But then she breathed in, and joy swelled within her heart. "Yes," she took a step, and then another. The thorns shredded her skirts as she threw herself into Verice's arms. "Lord and Lady, a thousand times, yes."

Verice wrapped his arms around her, and met her kiss with equal passion.

It was the cheering from the walls and the balcony above that broke them apart.

"Shall we go announce our betrothal?" Verice said into her ear.

"I'm not sure that's necessary," Warna smiled. "And only after I've changed my dress."

Verice laughed, and tugged her along, and they both raced back toward the keep, laughing, the dogs running along beside them barking all the way.

The End

EPILOGUE

They were a quiet, still bit of peace in a world of utter madness.

Wolfe sheltered Kalynn in his cloak, holding her tight against him. They stood upon the walls of a besieged town, amidst fire and flame. The name of the place mattered not; what mattered was that war raged at the gates as waves of attackers rode forward, firing arrows and hurling deadly lances, only to ride away to circle round and come back again.

The defenders were outside the gates, trying to hold a precious bit of ground, striving in a hopeless cause.

Here on the walls, men struggled desperately to work the ballista under a rain of deadly arrows. "Bring up the naptha," one shouted. "We'll show these Firelanders!"

It would not save them, Wolfe knew full well. The town was lost; this was but the death throes. He tightened his grip on Kalynn's waist and concentrated on keeping them both cloaked, both wrapped in magical cushions of quiet and shelter.

The journey had been long and difficult, harder than he'd imagined. It hurt to see a beloved land stripped of magic, torn and sundered. Less than what it had been and worse; it had been by his hand.

Traveling without magic to aid them. He and Kalynn were worn to the bone.

But he'd enough reserves to do this task, what they had journeyed so far to accomplish.

Whether he had the will or not was another question.

Amid the frantic movements of the protectors, he waited for the right moment to move. The air was filled with grunts of pain and fear.

Wolfe moved then, urging Kalynn forward. He guided her through the frantic men and maels struggling to load sacks onto the throwing arm of the war machine. The air was filled with grunts of pain and fear. And over all the acrid smell of pitch.

He got Kalynn close to the wall, covering her with his body. He'd wanted desperately to spare her this, to leave her with the airons, but that wasn't possible. She trembled against him, but although there was fear in her eyes, there was also determination. He swallowed back tears at her pain. Best to be about this and done.

"Do you see him?" he whispered as the chaos raged around them.

She nodded, the hood of her cloak moving against his hair.

"Show me," he said, and the world tilted slightly as her vision became his.

The attackers had ridden forward now, and dismounted for the final battle before the gates. One man, small in build, but powerful, led his men over the ground, savagely striking down any that stood in his path. Fierce, and unstoppable.

"Him," Kalynn breathed.

"Light the sacks," came the call behind them, and Wolfe pulled up his reserves, readying himself. There was but one thing—

"Kalynn. Close your eyes."

She looked up at him, his precious love, with a frown. He pressed his fingers to her cheek. "You have seen," he whispered. "But you need not see this."

Behind them came the crackle of flames, and black, burning smoke. "Release!" came the command.

A man hit the pin with a mallet, and the ballista jumped, throwing its deadly load.

Kalynn closed her eyes, and pressed her face to Wolfe's shoulder.

For long moments, the naptha arced overhead, the small burning sacks spreading out, hovering over the battlefield. Wolfe followed one with his eyes, caught it with his power, and changed the arc of its path ever so slightly.

The man, his target, turned his head at the last moment. His ear was woven with a pattern of wire and beads that sparkled in the light.

Bonded. He'd destroy two lives, then. Not just one.

The naptha hit. The man exploded into fire, pain and burning flesh. He fell, sprawled out, screaming.

'I'd offer regrets,' Wolfe thought. *'But I do what must be done.'* He leaned

down, pressing his head to Kalynn's, taking in the gentle scent of her hair. "It's done," Wolfe whispered into her ear. "We can go."

She nodded silently as he started to wrap his power around them.

Below, from out of nowhere, a muscular, dark-haired warrior appeared, dropping two swords as he flung himself down beside the man on fire. His face torn in anguish, the warrior screamed out a name as he started to beat out the flames with his own hands. The sound came faintly to Wolfe's ears as the magic took them away.

"Marcus!"

ACKNOWLEDGMENTS

Every ending is a beginning and
every beginning is an end.

This book brings to a close the Chronicles of the Warlands and the Epic of Palins. What an adventure it has been, both for my characters and myself as a writer. Friendships forged, lessons learned, and challenges overcome. The list of people who I have met, befriended, loved and lost during these years would fill another book.

I'm not sure how I can thank everyone involved in my journey. So I will take this moment to acknowledge every one of you, and that includes you, dear reader. Please know that you all have my gratitude and my thanks. You bring me joy.

Please also know that while this book ends the series, have no fear.

For I have more stories to tell.

Beth

ABOUT THE AUTHOR

Elizabeth Vaughan is the *USA Today* Bestselling author of *Warprize*, the first volume of The Chronicles of the Warlands. She's always loved fantasy and science fiction, and has been a fantasy role-player since 1981. By day, Beth's secret identity is that of a lawyer, practicing in the area of bankruptcy, a role she has maintained since 1985. More information can be found at her website, WriteandRepeat.com.

Beth is owned by incredibly spoiled cats, and lives in the Northwest Territory, on the outskirts of the Black Swamp, along Mad Anthony's Trail on the banks of the Maumee River.